Crush

Svetlana Chmakova

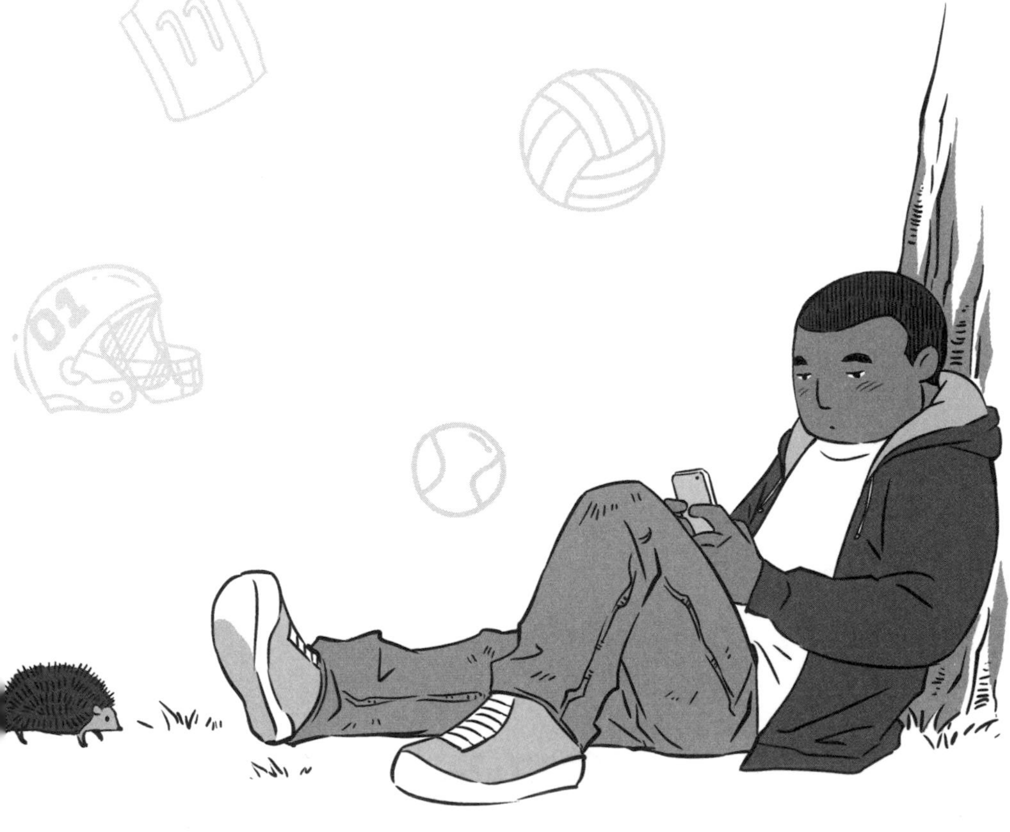

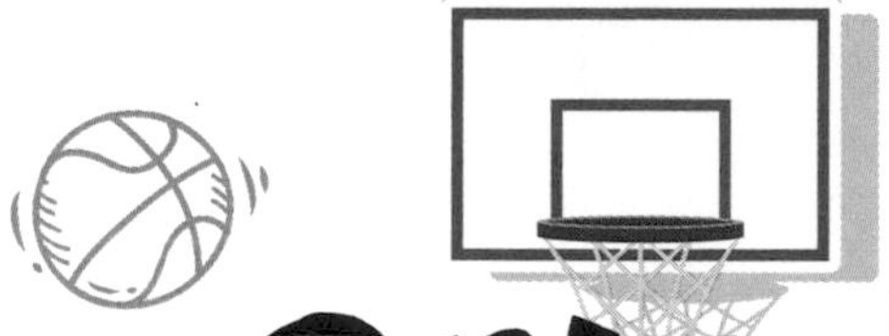

Crush

SVETLANA CHMAKOVA

Coloring assistants: Melissa McCommon, BonHyung Jeong
Inking assistants: NaRae Lee, BonHyung Jeong
Lettering: JuYoun Lee

JY
1290 Avenue of the Americas
New York, NY 10104

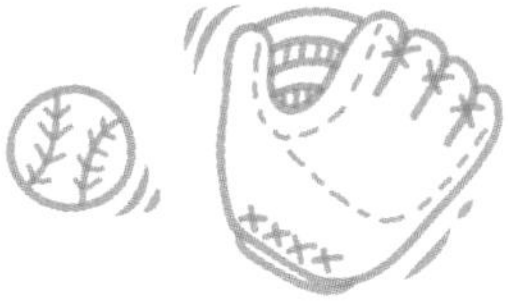

Visit us at jyforkids.com
facebook.com/jyforkids
twitter.com/jyforkids
jyforkids.tumblr.com
instagram.com/jyforkids

First JY Edition: October 2018

JY is an imprint of Yen Press, LLC.
The JY name and logo are trademarks of Yen Press, LLC.

The publisher is not responsible for websites (or their content) that are not owned by the publisher.

Library of Congress Control Number: 2018948318

Hardcover ISBN: 978-0-316-36323-5
Paperback ISBN: 978-0-316-36324-2

10 9 8 7 6 5 4 3

LSC-C

Printed in the United States of America

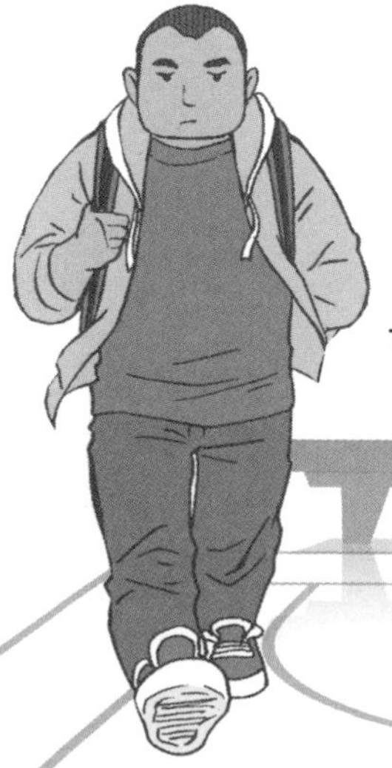

Table of Contents

CHAPTER 1

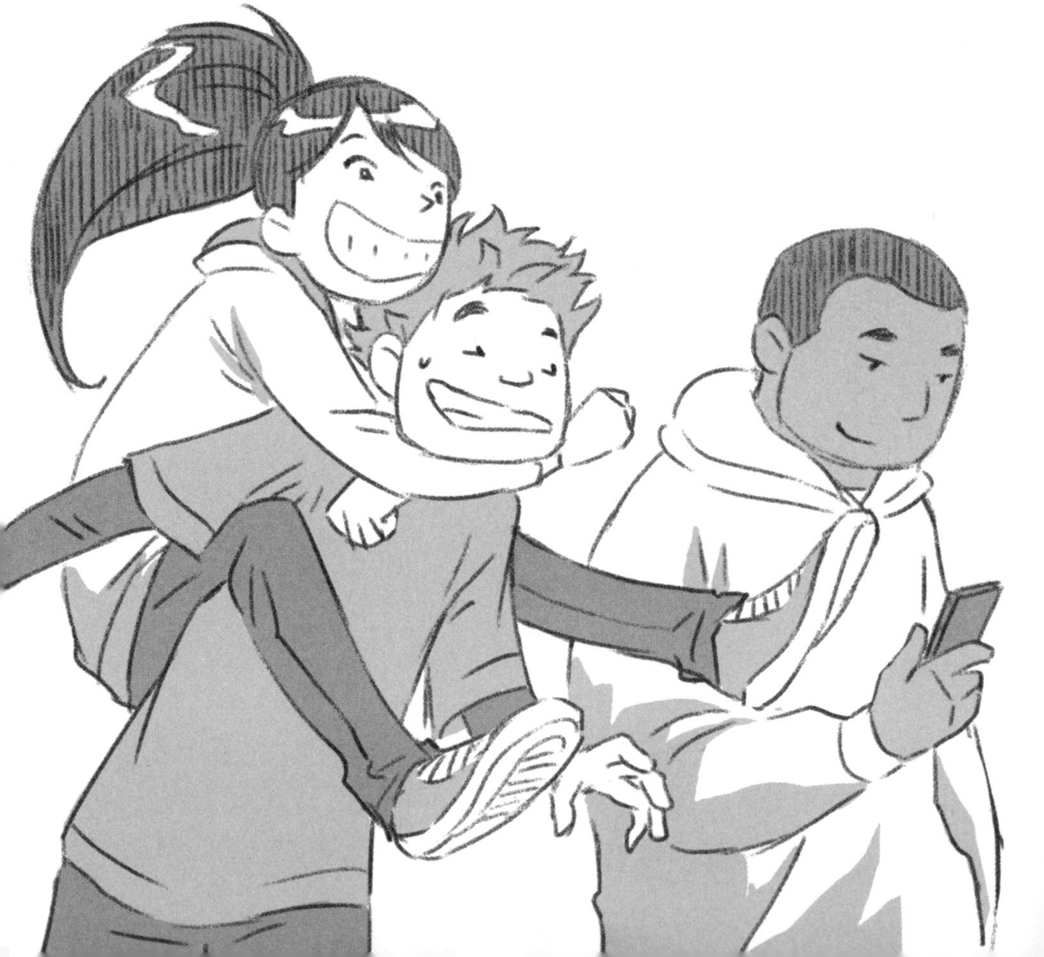

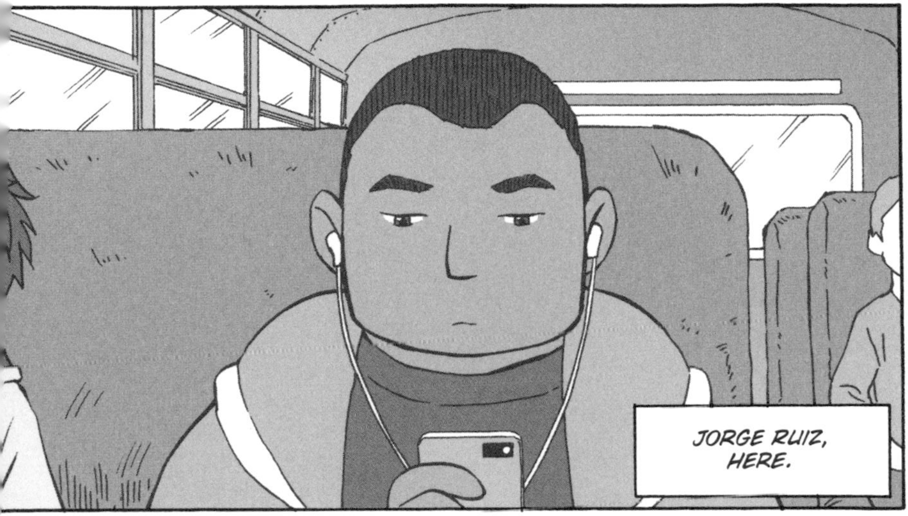
JORGE RUIZ, HERE.

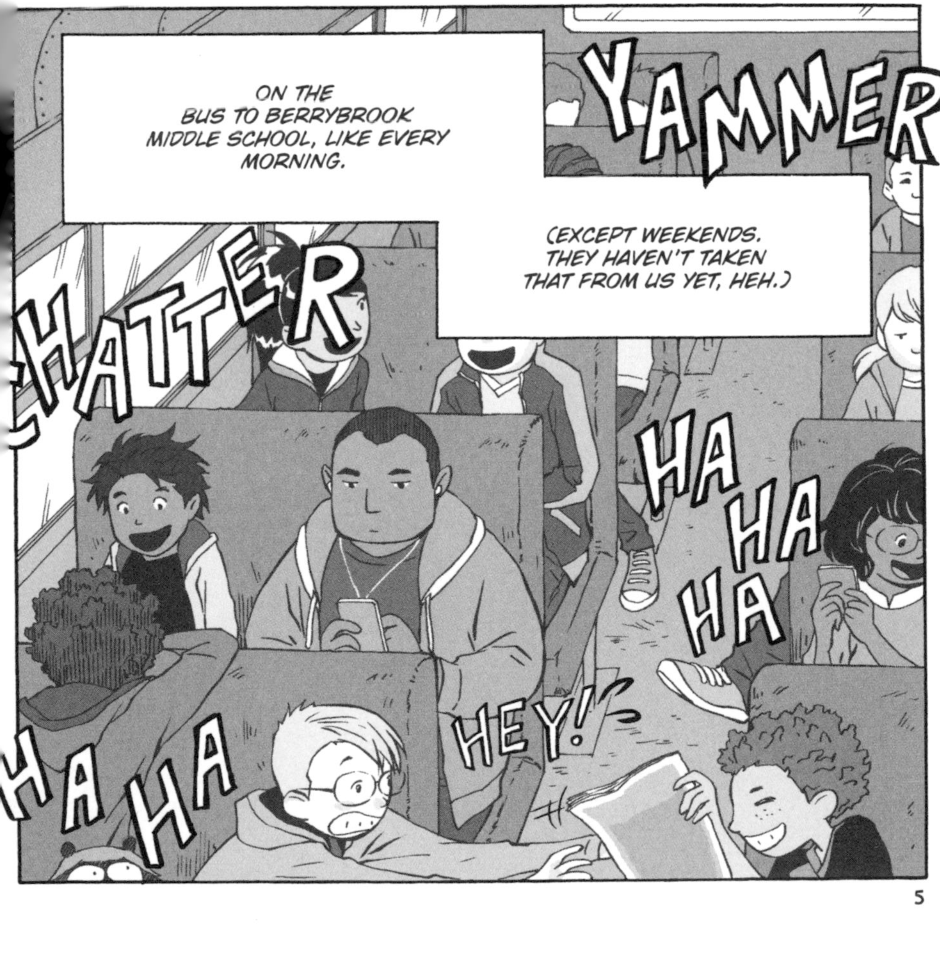
ON THE BUS TO BERRYBROOK MIDDLE SCHOOL, LIKE EVERY MORNING.
YAMMER
(EXCEPT WEEKENDS. THEY HAVEN'T TAKEN THAT FROM US YET, HEH.)
CHATTER
HA HA HA
HA HA
HEY!

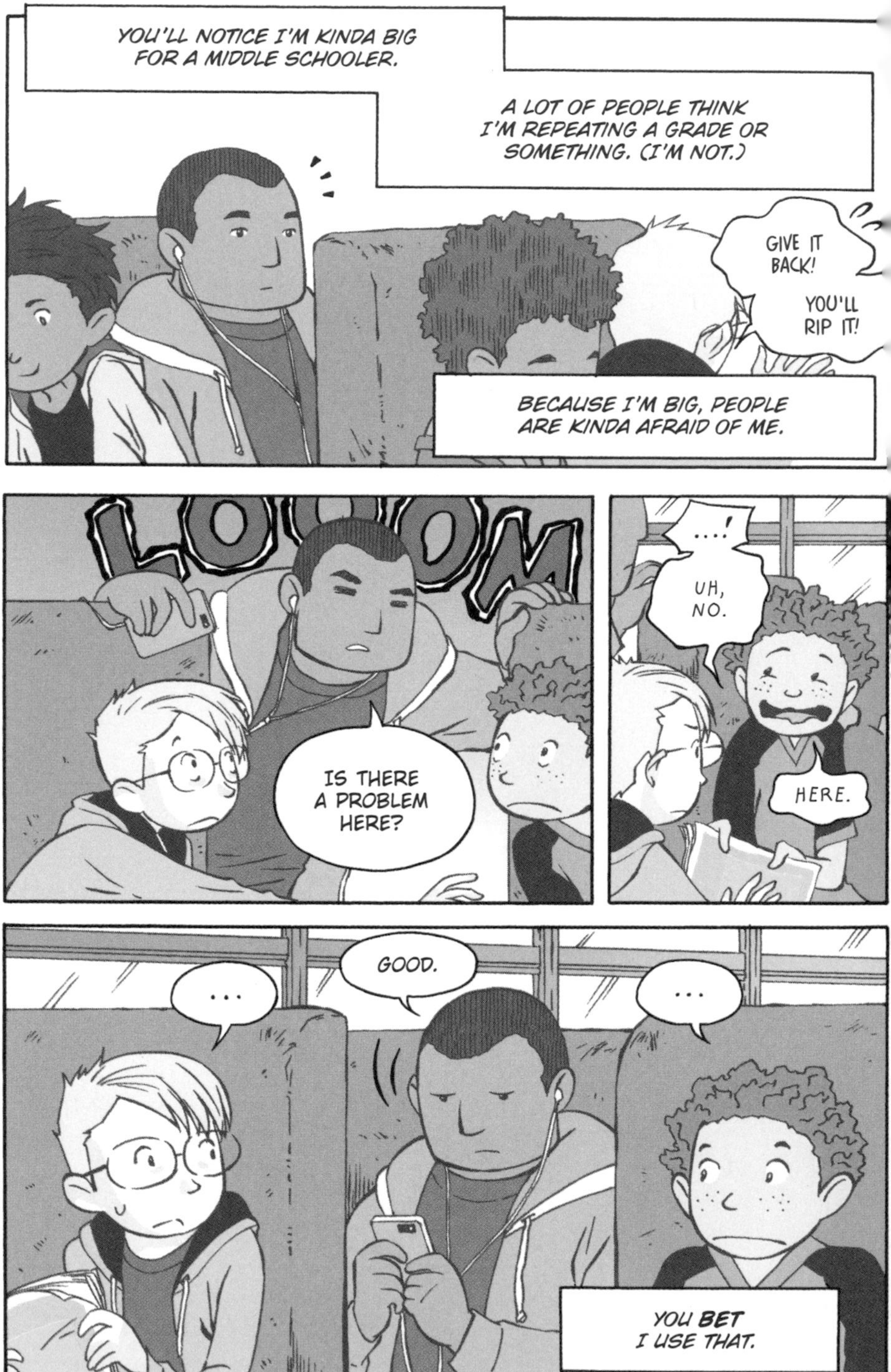
YOU'LL NOTICE I'M KINDA BIG FOR A MIDDLE SCHOOLER.
A LOT OF PEOPLE THINK I'M REPEATING A GRADE OR SOMETHING. (I'M NOT.)
GIVE IT BACK!
YOU'LL RIP IT!
BECAUSE I'M BIG, PEOPLE ARE KINDA AFRAID OF ME.
LOOOM
IS THERE A PROBLEM HERE?
...!
UH, NO.
HERE.
...
GOOD.
...
YOU BET I USE THAT.

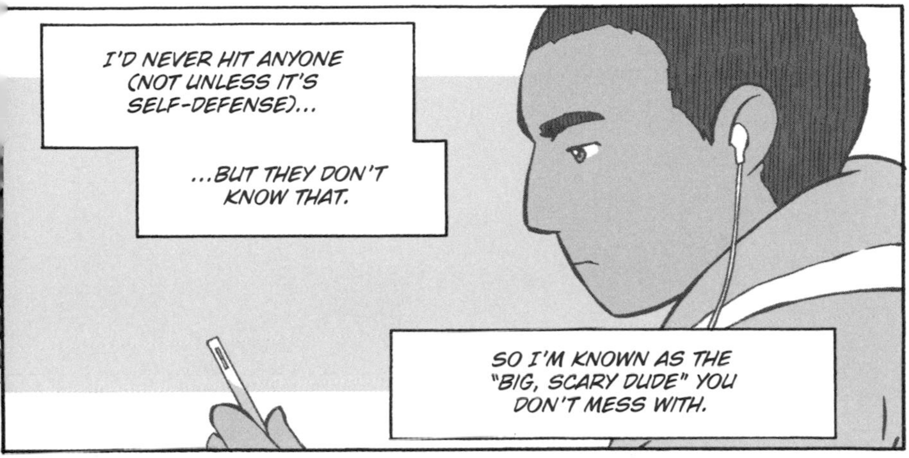
I'D NEVER HIT ANYONE (NOT UNLESS IT'S SELF-DEFENSE)...
...BUT THEY DON'T KNOW THAT.
SO I'M KNOWN AS THE "BIG, SCARY DUDE" YOU DON'T MESS WITH.

KINDA MAKES IT HARD TO MAKE FRIENDS, I GUESS...?

THE **REAL** KIND, PEOPLE YOU CAN JUST BE YOURSELF WITH.

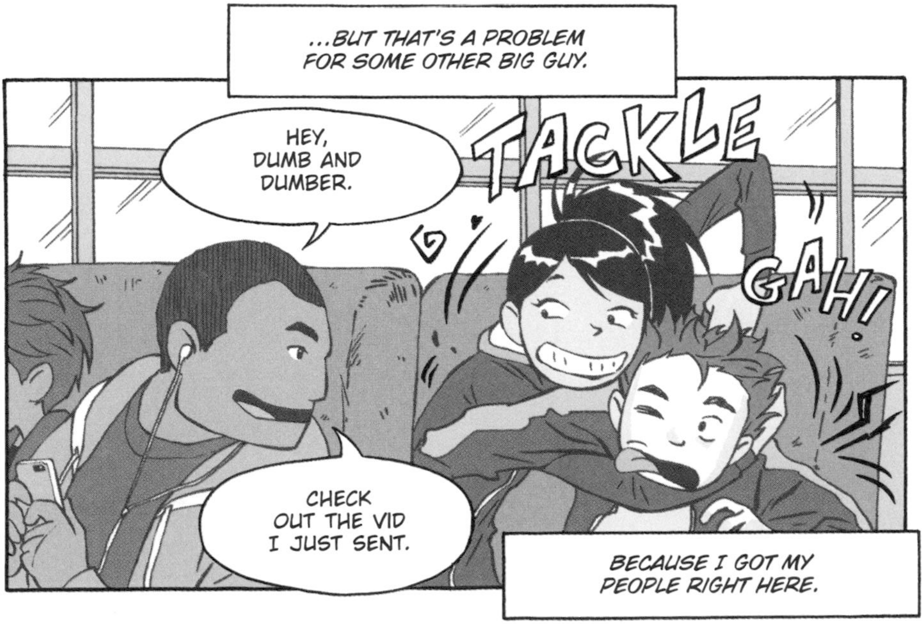
...BUT THAT'S A PROBLEM FOR SOME OTHER BIG GUY.
HEY, DUMB AND DUMBER.
TACKLE
GAH!
CHECK OUT THE VID I JUST SENT.
BECAUSE I GOT MY PEOPLE RIGHT HERE.

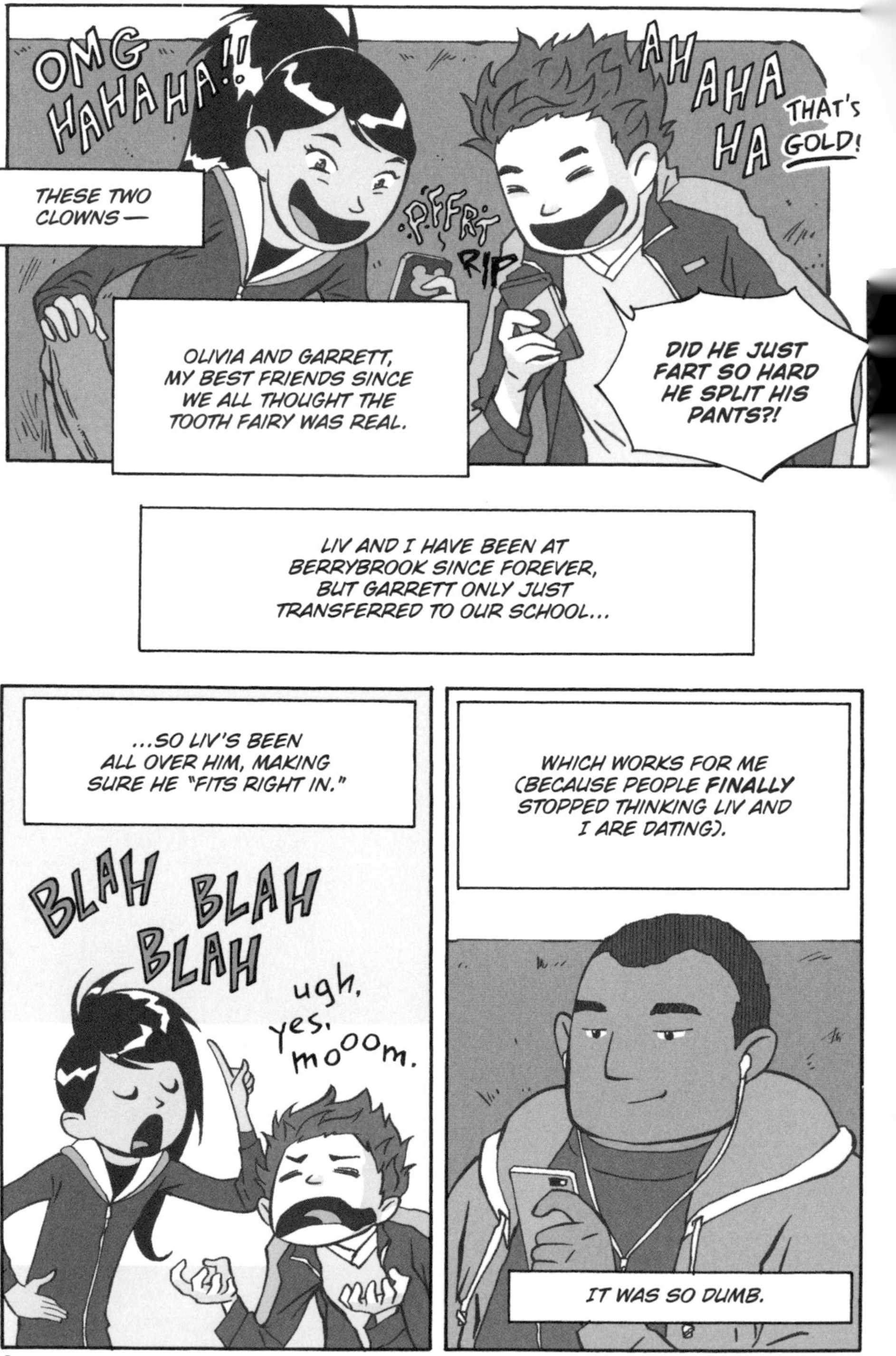
OMG HAHAHA!!
AHAHAHA
THAT'S GOLD!
THESE TWO CLOWNS—
PFFRT
RIP
OLIVIA AND GARRETT, MY BEST FRIENDS SINCE WE ALL THOUGHT THE TOOTH FAIRY WAS REAL.
DID HE JUST FART SO HARD HE SPLIT HIS PANTS?!
LIV AND I HAVE BEEN AT BERRYBROOK SINCE FOREVER, BUT GARRETT ONLY JUST TRANSFERRED TO OUR SCHOOL...
...SO LIV'S BEEN ALL OVER HIM, MAKING SURE HE "FITS RIGHT IN."
BLAH BLAH BLAH
ugh, yes, mooom.
WHICH WORKS FOR ME (BECAUSE PEOPLE FINALLY STOPPED THINKING LIV AND I ARE DATING).
IT WAS SO DUMB.

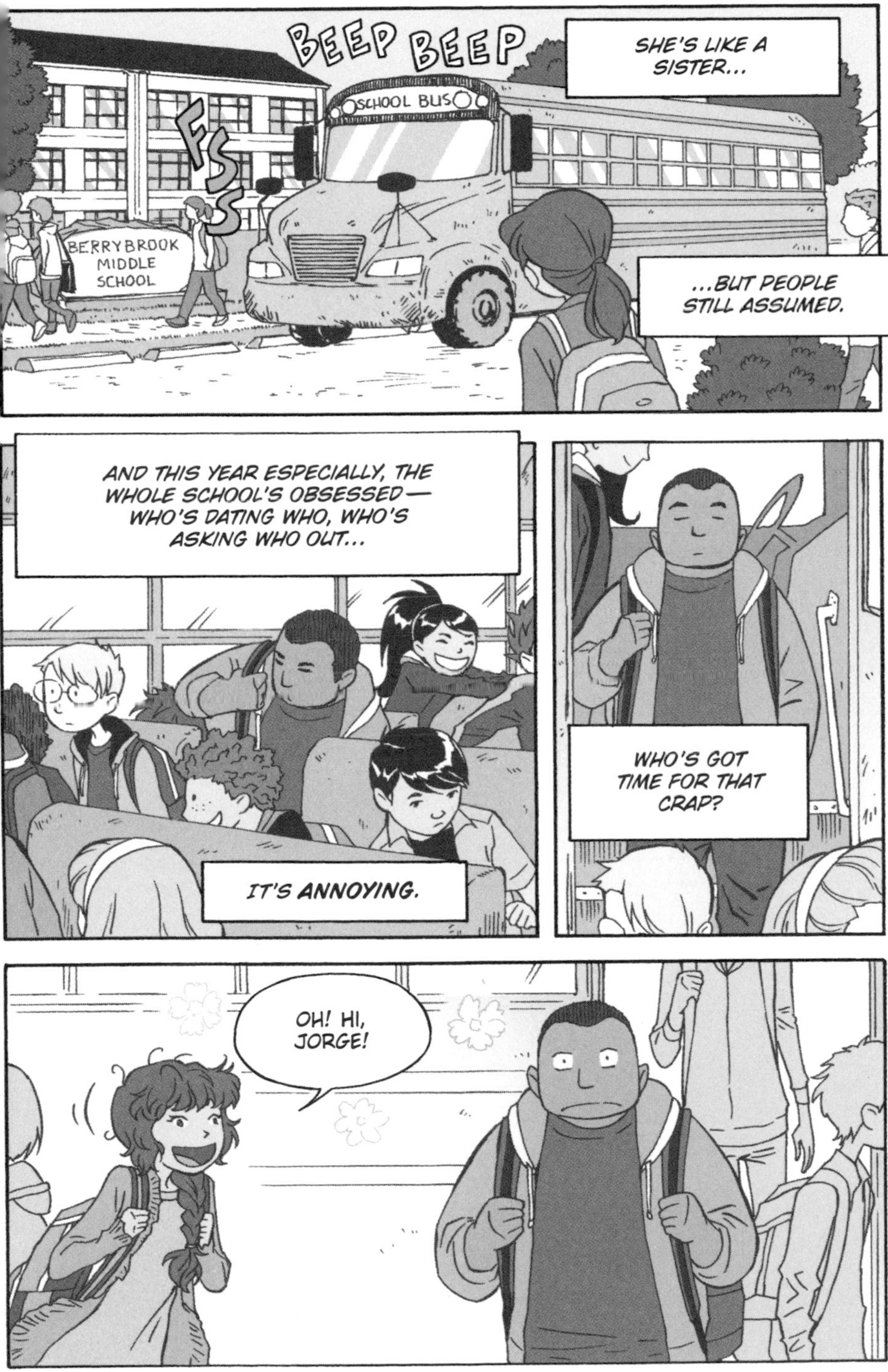
BEEP BEEP
SHE'S LIKE A SISTER...
SCHOOL BUS
FSS
BERRYBROOK MIDDLE SCHOOL
...BUT PEOPLE STILL ASSUMED.
AND THIS YEAR ESPECIALLY, THE WHOLE SCHOOL'S OBSESSED— WHO'S DATING WHO, WHO'S ASKING WHO OUT...
IT'S ANNOYING.
WHO'S GOT TIME FOR THAT CRAP?
OH! HI, JORGE!

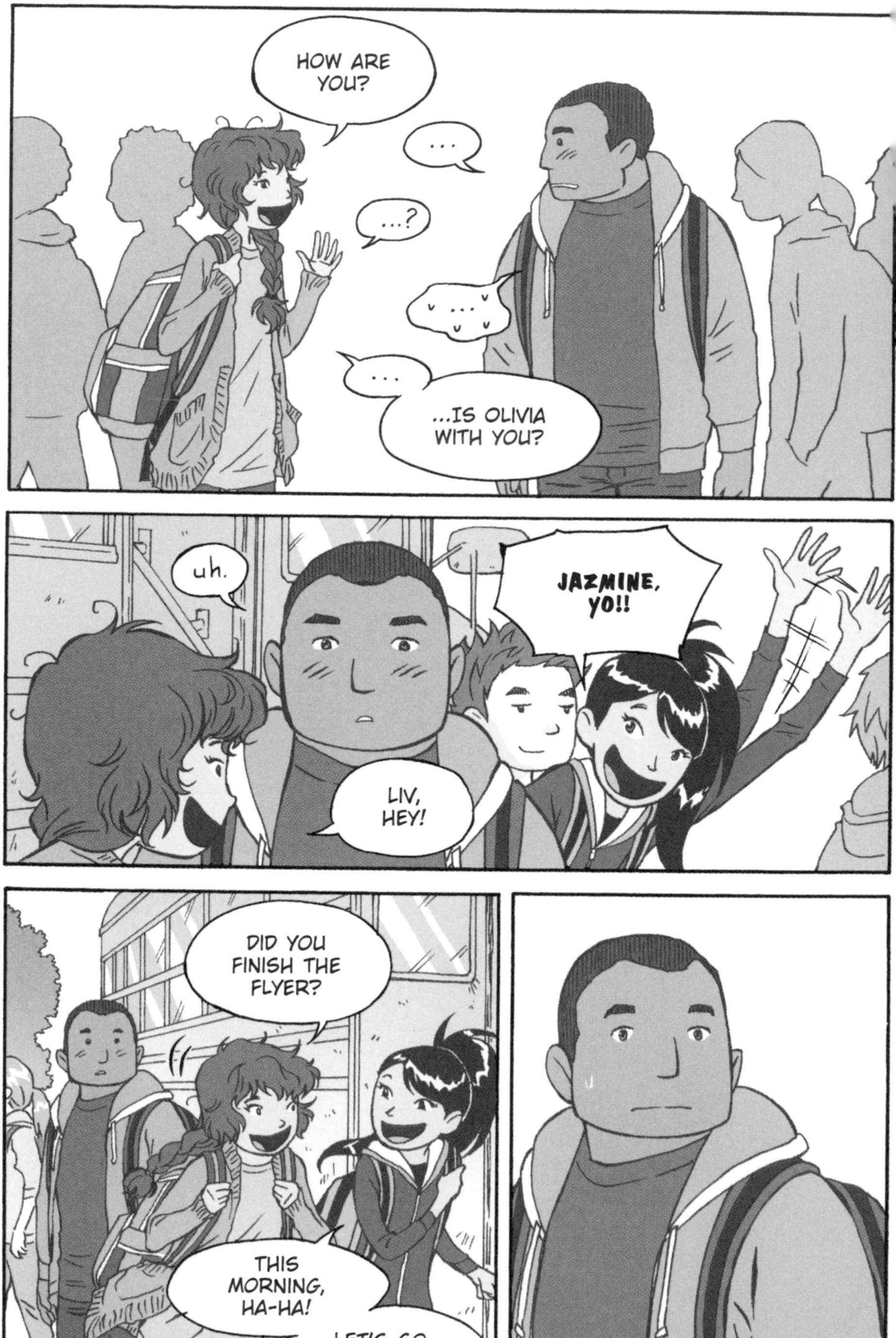
HOW ARE YOU?
...
...?
...
...
...IS OLIVIA WITH YOU?
uh.
JAZMINE, YO!!
LIV, HEY!
DID YOU FINISH THE FLYER?
THIS MORNING, HA-HA!
LET'S GO PRINT IT!

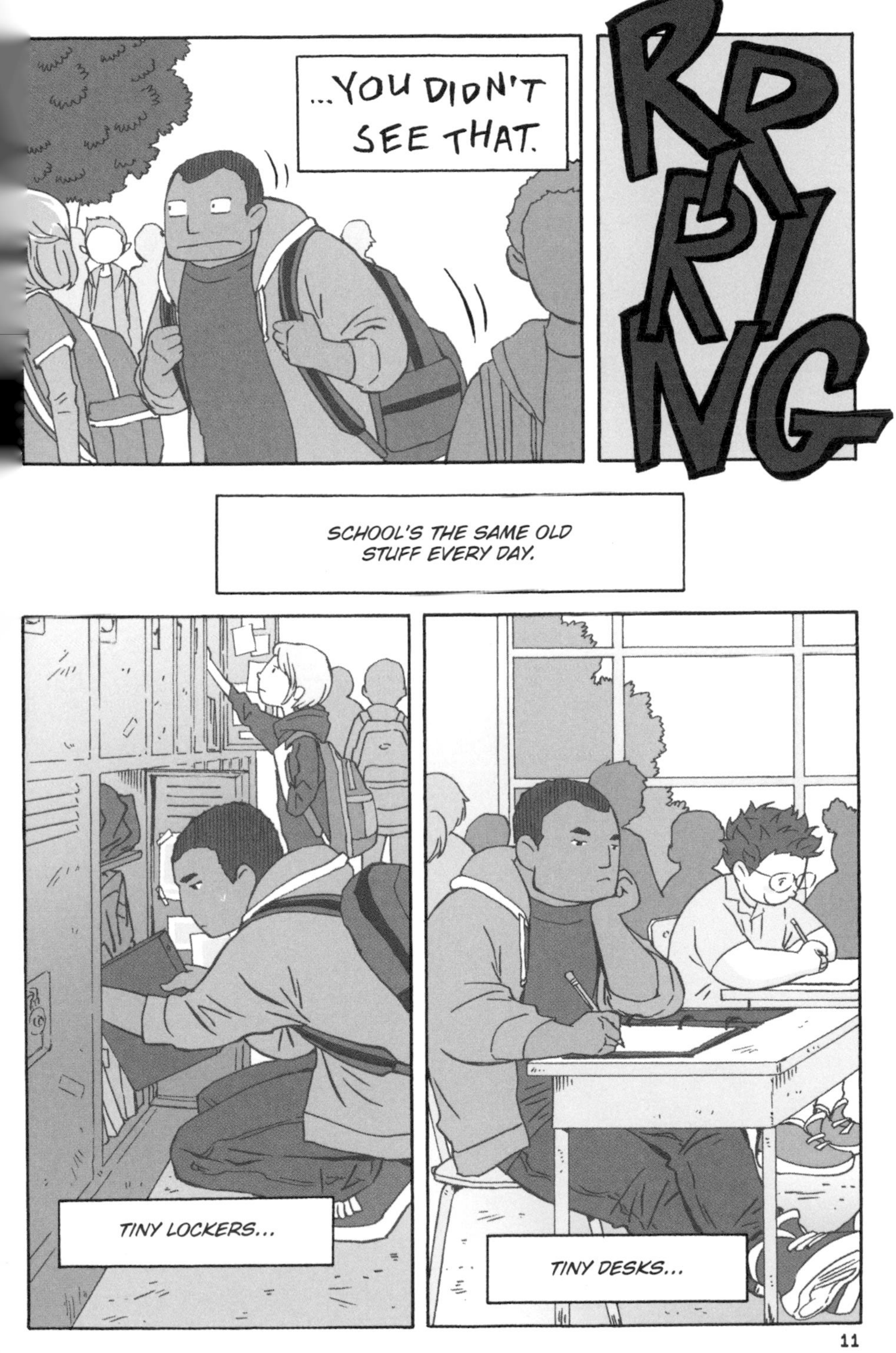
...YOU DIDN'T SEE THAT.
RRRING
SCHOOL'S THE SAME OLD STUFF EVERY DAY.
TINY LOCKERS...
TINY DESKS...

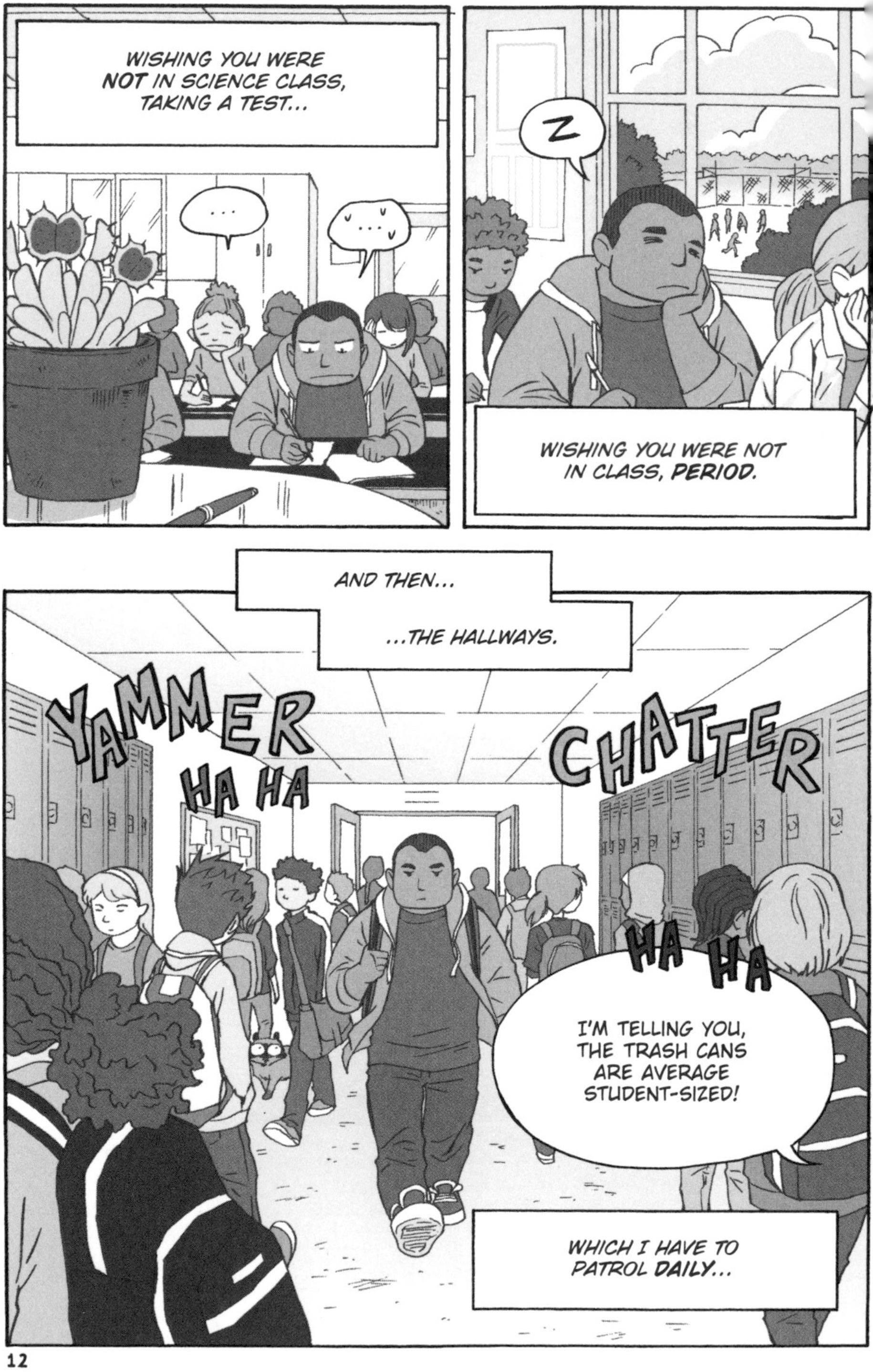
WISHING YOU WERE NOT IN SCIENCE CLASS, TAKING A TEST...
...
...
Z
WISHING YOU WERE NOT IN CLASS, PERIOD.
AND THEN...
...THE HALLWAYS.
YAMMER
HA HA
CHATTER
HA HA
I'M TELLING YOU, THE TRASH CANS ARE AVERAGE STUDENT-SIZED!
WHICH I HAVE TO PATROL DAILY...

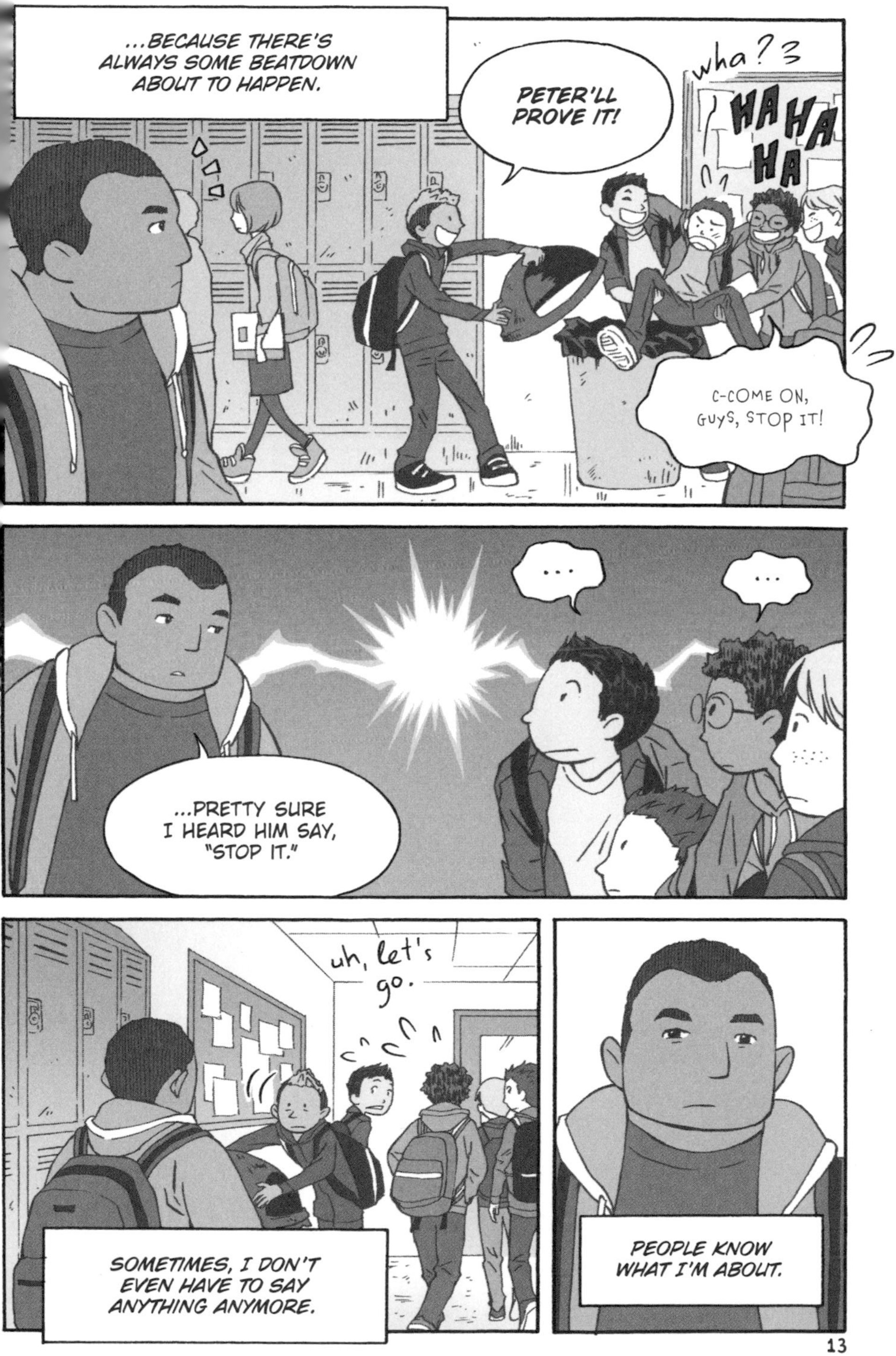
...BECAUSE THERE'S ALWAYS SOME BEATDOWN ABOUT TO HAPPEN.
PETER'LL PROVE IT!
wha?
HA HA HA HA
C-COME ON, GUYS, STOP IT!
...
...
...PRETTY SURE I HEARD HIM SAY, "STOP IT."
uh, let's go.
SOMETIMES, I DON'T EVEN HAVE TO SAY ANYTHING ANYMORE.
PEOPLE KNOW WHAT I'M ABOUT.

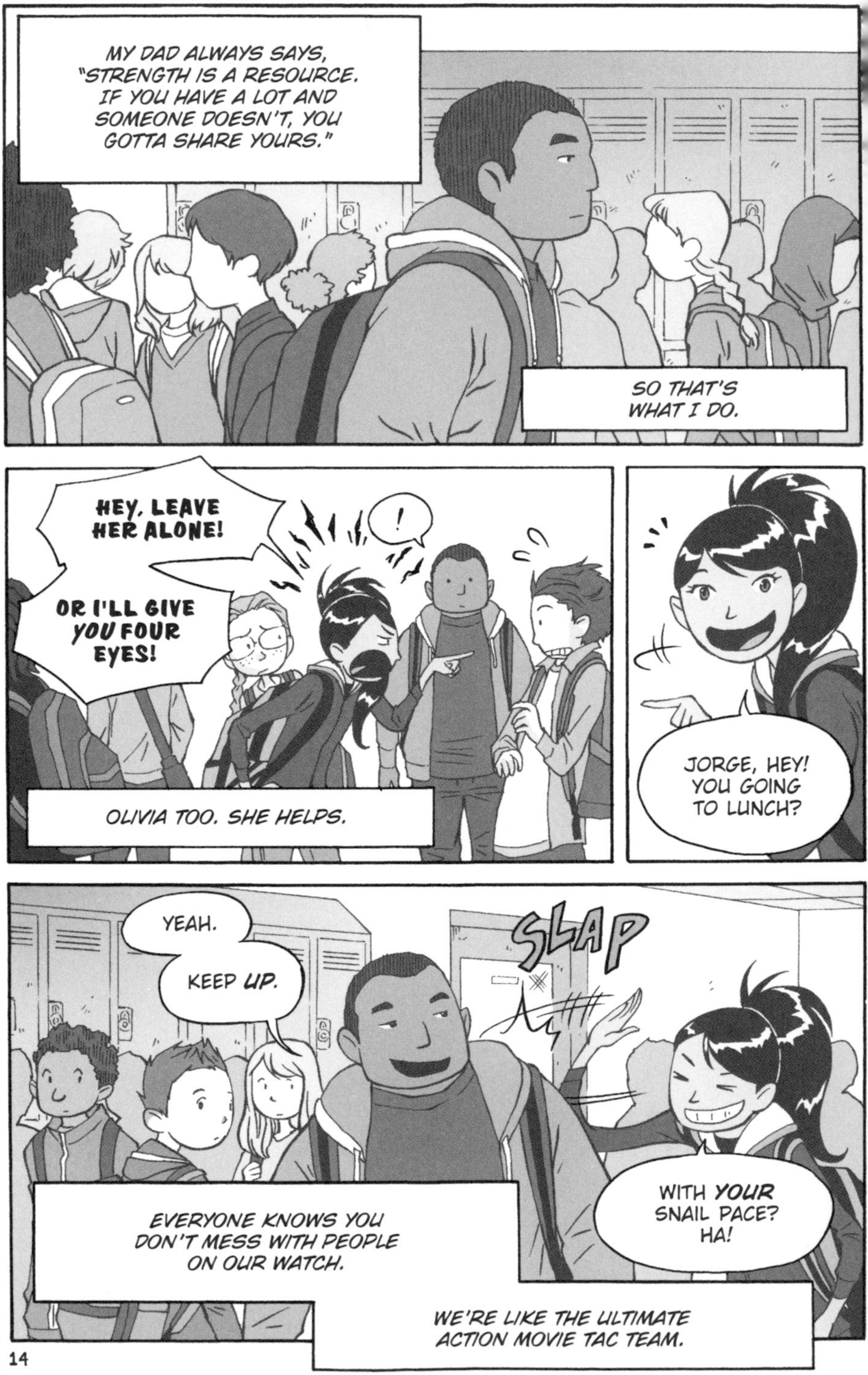
MY DAD ALWAYS SAYS, "STRENGTH IS A RESOURCE. IF YOU HAVE A LOT AND SOMEONE DOESN'T, YOU GOTTA SHARE YOURS."
SO THAT'S WHAT I DO.
HEY, LEAVE HER ALONE!
OR I'LL GIVE YOU FOUR EYES!
!
OLIVIA TOO. SHE HELPS.
JORGE, HEY! YOU GOING TO LUNCH?
YEAH.
KEEP UP.
SLAP
WITH YOUR SNAIL PACE? HA!
EVERYONE KNOWS YOU DON'T MESS WITH PEOPLE ON OUR WATCH.
WE'RE LIKE THE ULTIMATE ACTION MOVIE TAC TEAM.

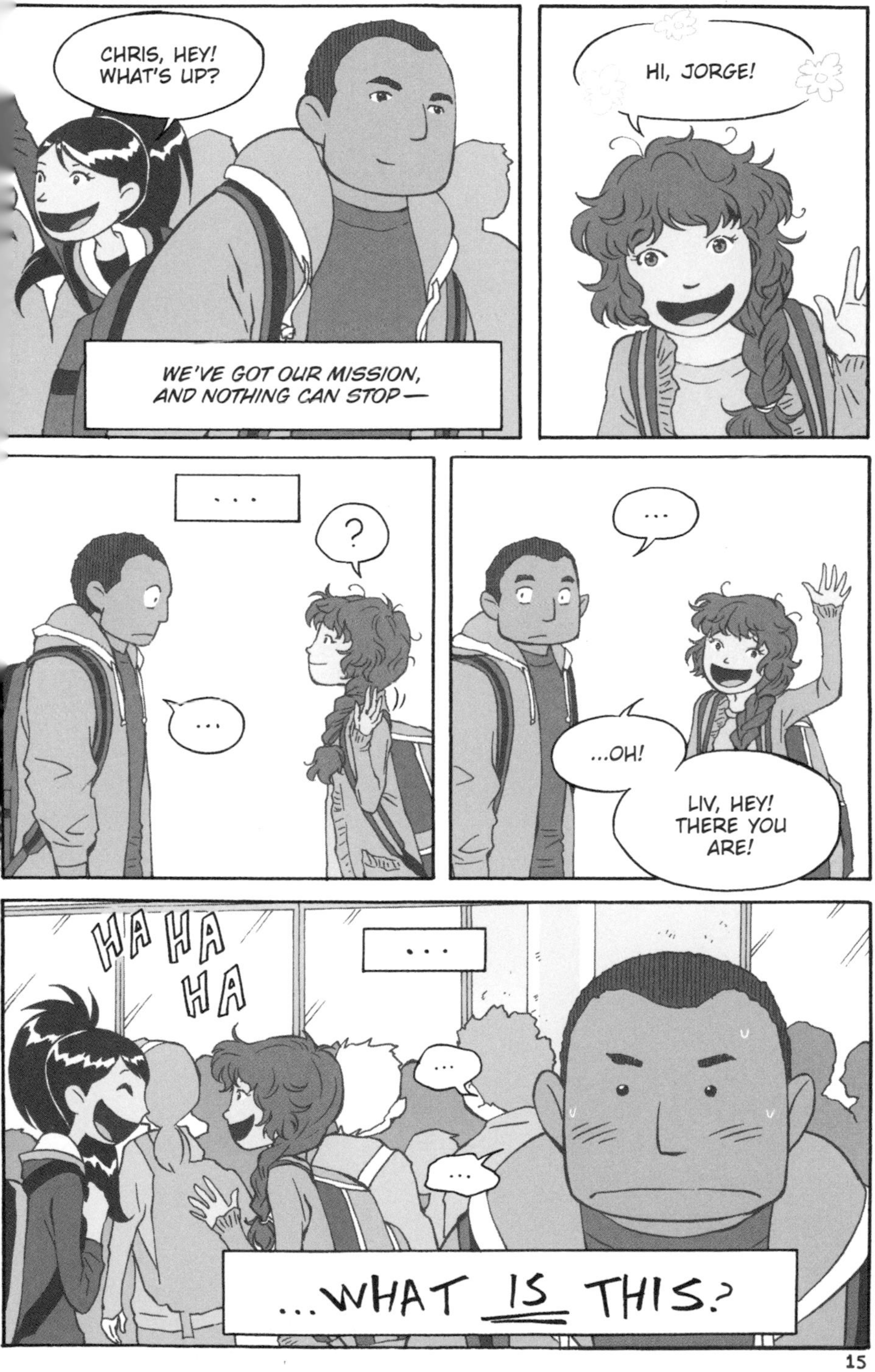
CHRIS, HEY! WHAT'S UP?
WE'VE GOT OUR MISSION, AND NOTHING CAN STOP—
HI, JORGE!
. . .
?
...
...
...OH!
LIV, HEY! THERE YOU ARE!
HA HA HA HA
. . .
...
...
...WHAT IS THIS?

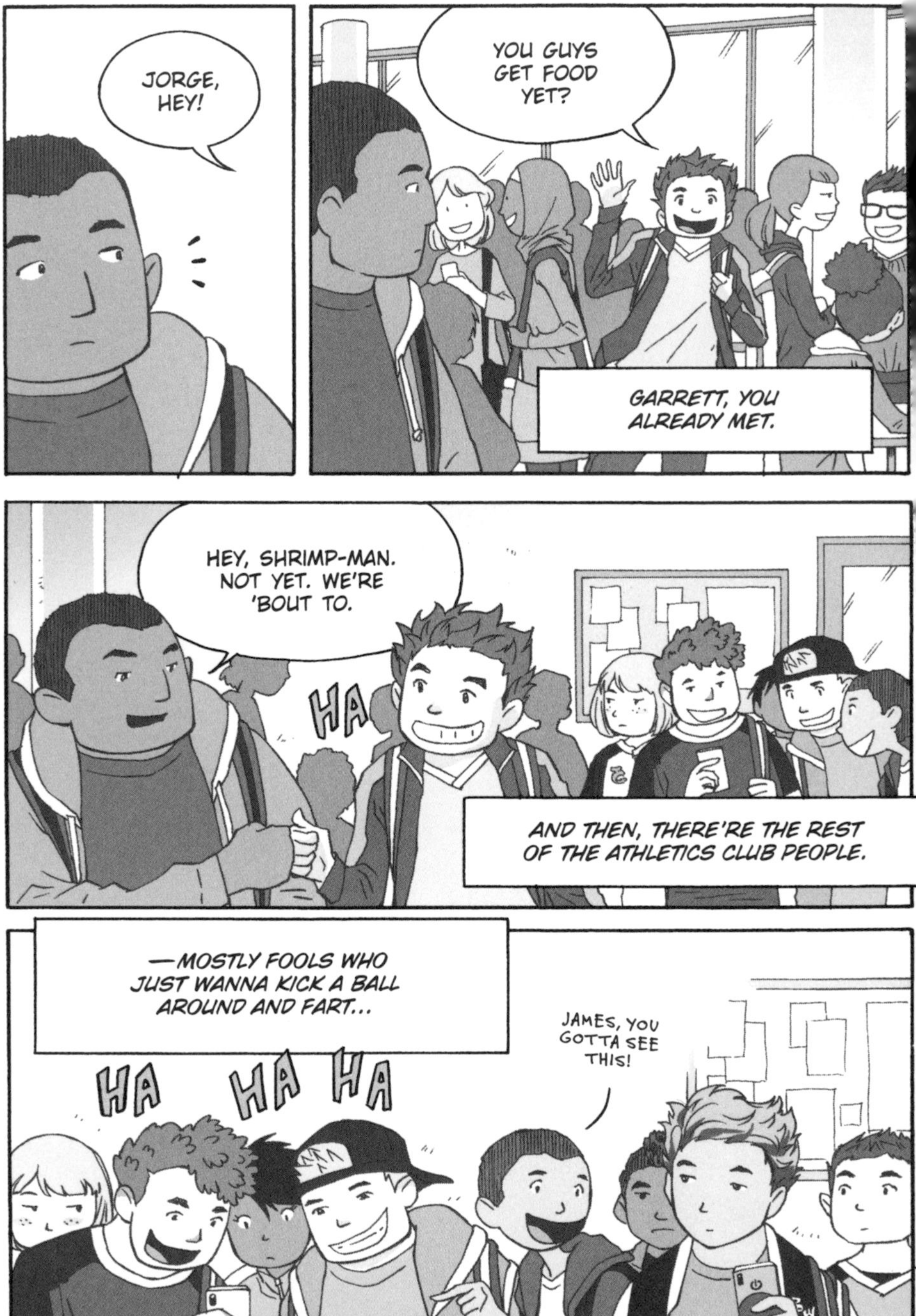
JORGE, HEY!
YOU GUYS GET FOOD YET?
GARRETT, YOU ALREADY MET.
HEY, SHRIMP-MAN. NOT YET. WE'RE 'BOUT TO.
HA
AND THEN, THERE'RE THE REST OF THE ATHLETICS CLUB PEOPLE.
—MOSTLY FOOLS WHO JUST WANNA KICK A BALL AROUND AND FART…
HA HA HA
JAMES, YOU GOTTA SEE THIS!
…EXCEPT FOR JAMES.

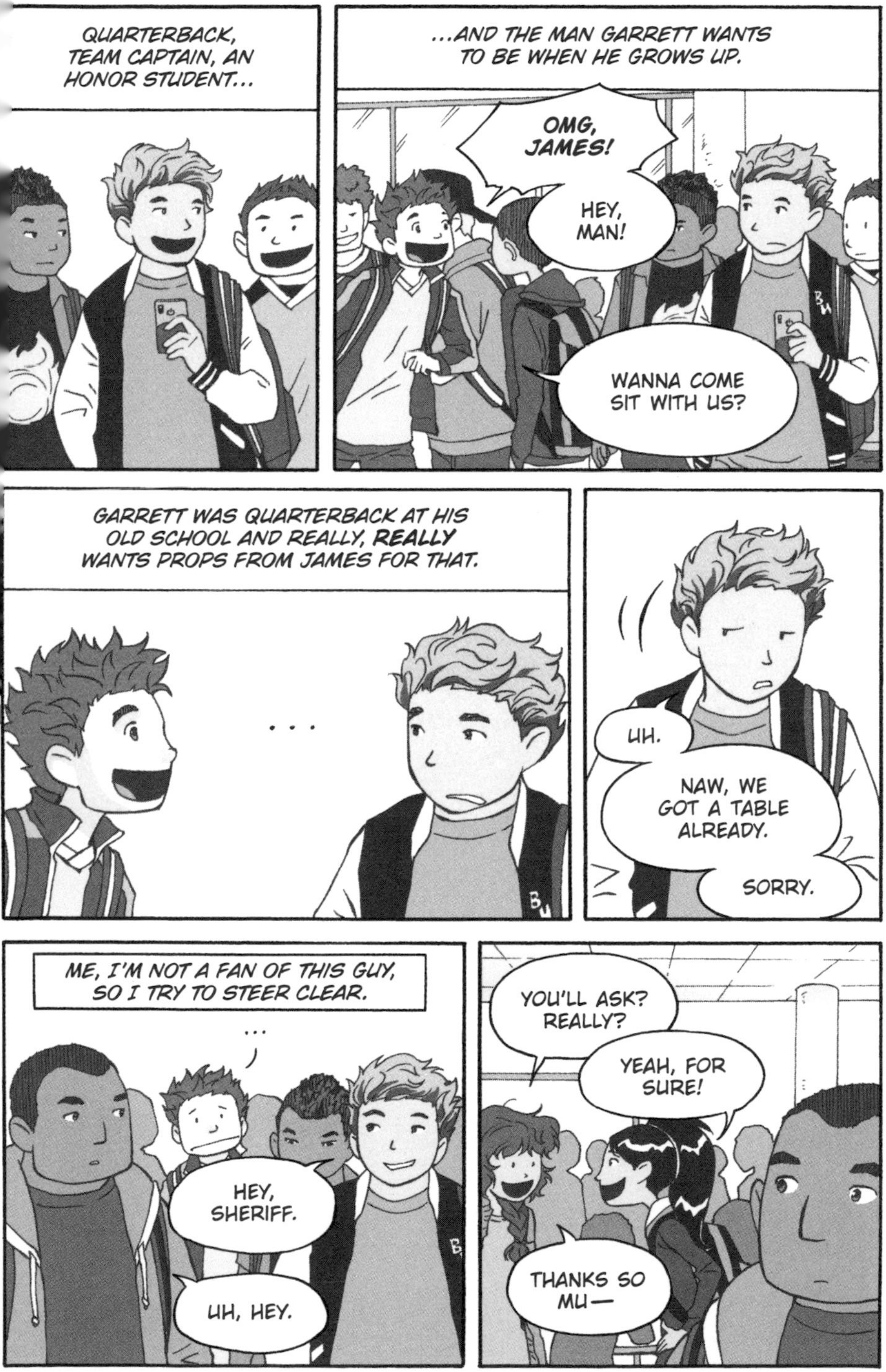
QUARTERBACK, TEAM CAPTAIN, AN HONOR STUDENT...
...AND THE MAN GARRETT WANTS TO BE WHEN HE GROWS UP.
OMG, JAMES!
HEY, MAN!
WANNA COME SIT WITH US?
GARRETT WAS QUARTERBACK AT HIS OLD SCHOOL AND REALLY, REALLY WANTS PROPS FROM JAMES FOR THAT.
. . .
UH.
NAW, WE GOT A TABLE ALREADY.
SORRY.
ME, I'M NOT A FAN OF THIS GUY, SO I TRY TO STEER CLEAR.
...
HEY, SHERIFF.
UH, HEY.
YOU'LL ASK? REALLY?
YEAH, FOR SURE!
THANKS SO MU—

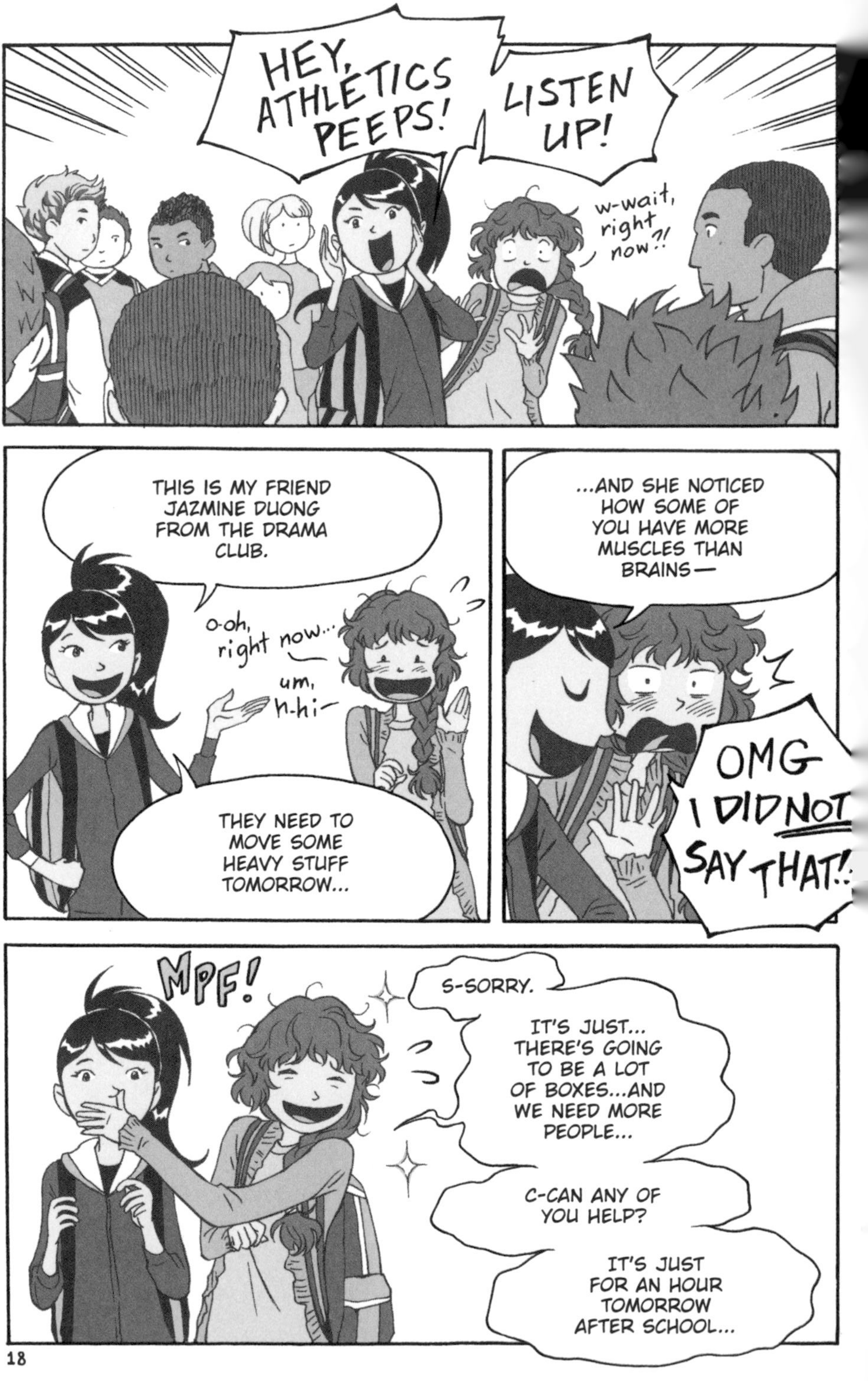
HEY, ATHLETICS PEEPS!
LISTEN UP!
w-wait, right now?!
THIS IS MY FRIEND JAZMINE DUONG FROM THE DRAMA CLUB.
o-oh, right now...
um, h-hi-
THEY NEED TO MOVE SOME HEAVY STUFF TOMORROW...
...AND SHE NOTICED HOW SOME OF YOU HAVE MORE MUSCLES THAN BRAINS—
OMG I DID NOT SAY THAT!!
MPF!
S-SORRY.
IT'S JUST... THERE'S GOING TO BE A LOT OF BOXES...AND WE NEED MORE PEOPLE...
C-CAN ANY OF YOU HELP?
IT'S JUST FOR AN HOUR TOMORROW AFTER SCHOOL...

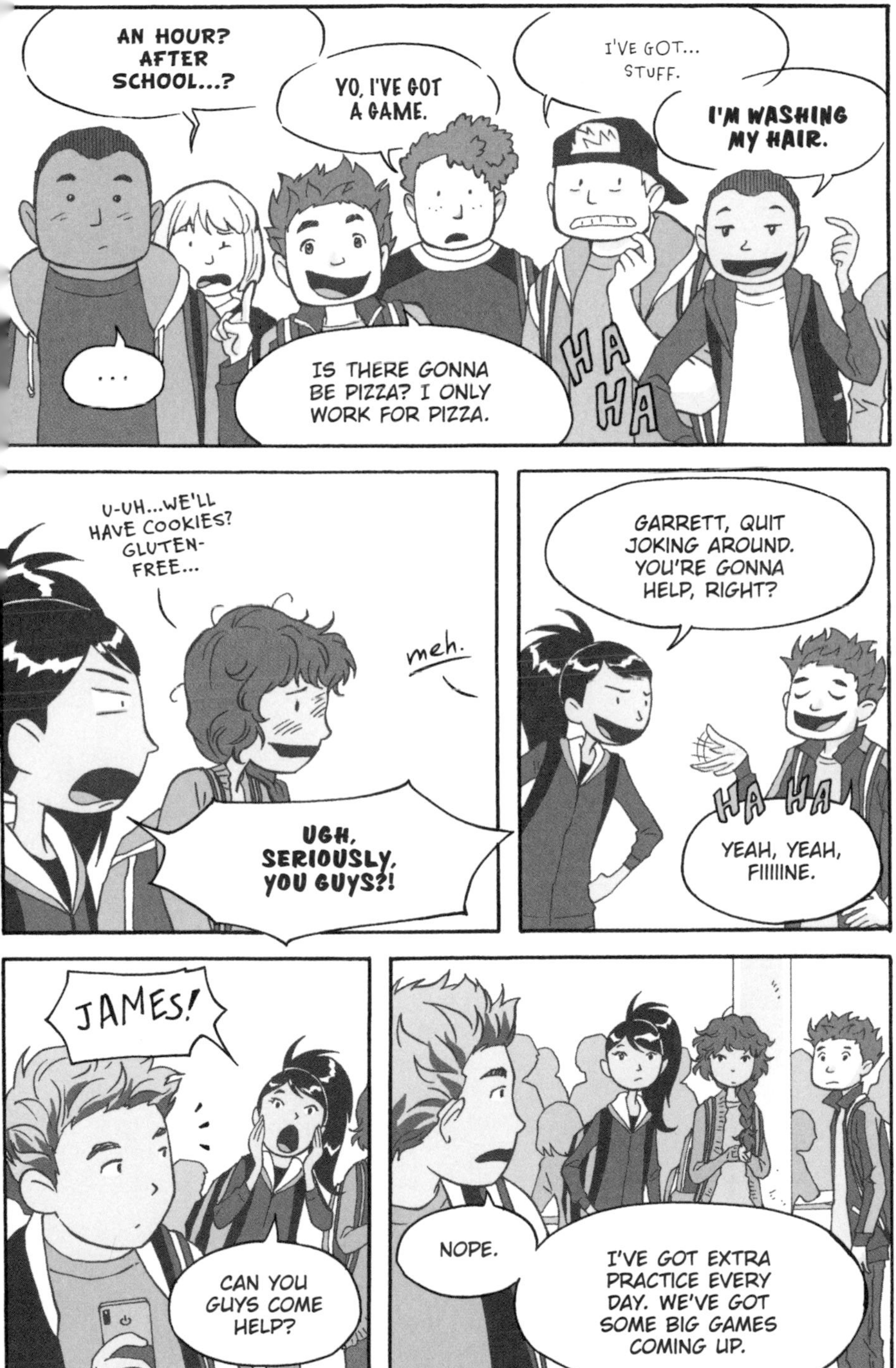
AN HOUR? AFTER SCHOOL...?
YO, I'VE GOT A GAME.
I'VE GOT... STUFF.
I'M WASHING MY HAIR.
...
IS THERE GONNA BE PIZZA? I ONLY WORK FOR PIZZA.
HA HA
U-UH...WE'LL HAVE COOKIES? GLUTEN-FREE...
meh.
UGH, SERIOUSLY, YOU GUYS?!
GARRETT, QUIT JOKING AROUND. YOU'RE GONNA HELP, RIGHT?
HA HA
YEAH, YEAH, FIIIIINE.
JAMES!
CAN YOU GUYS COME HELP?
NOPE.
I'VE GOT EXTRA PRACTICE EVERY DAY. WE'VE GOT SOME BIG GAMES COMING UP.

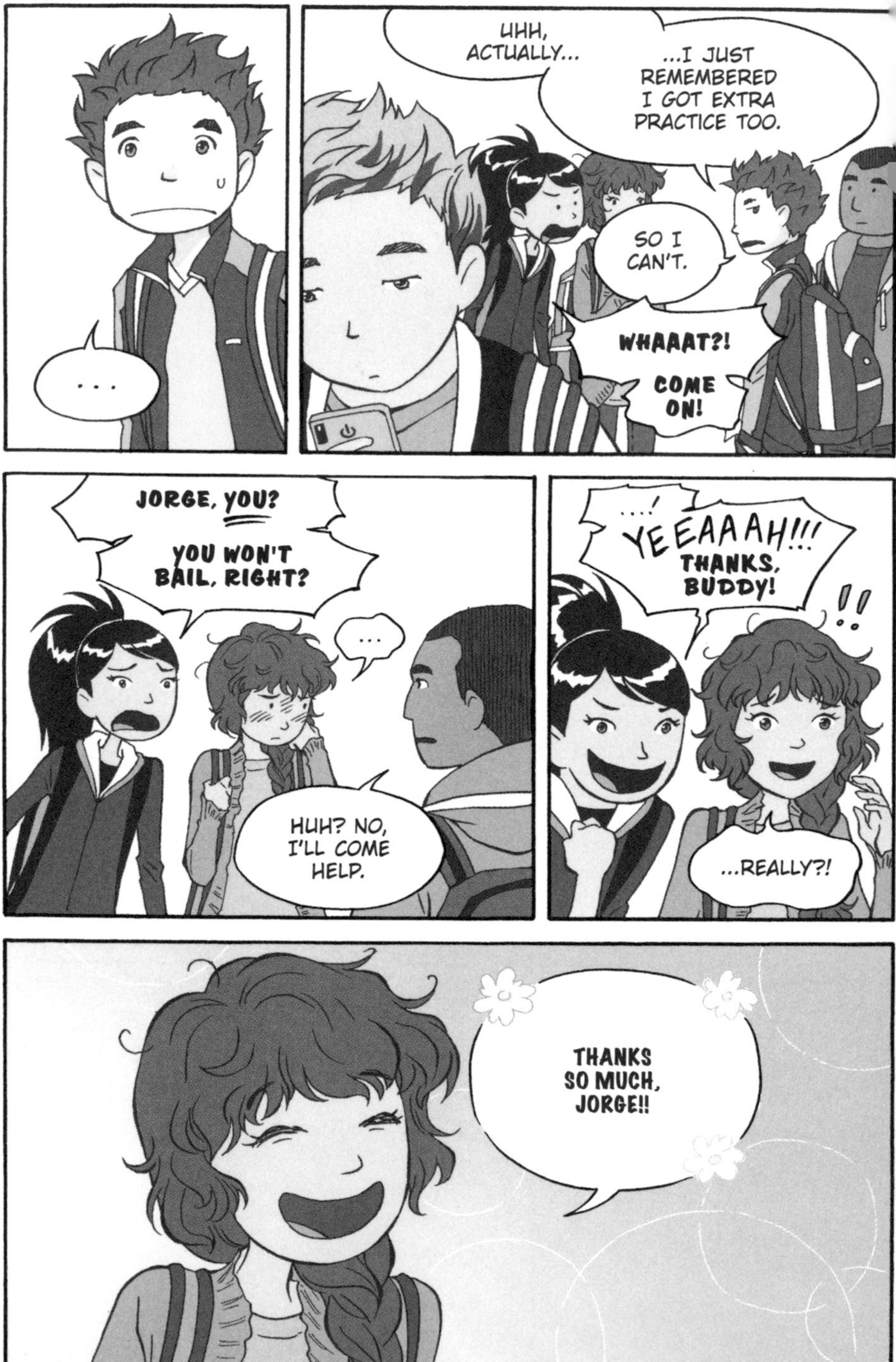
...
UHH, ACTUALLY...
...I JUST REMEMBERED I GOT EXTRA PRACTICE TOO.
SO I CAN'T.
WHAAAT?! COME ON!
JORGE, YOU? YOU WON'T BAIL, RIGHT?
...
HUH? NO, I'LL COME HELP.
...!
YEEAAAH!!! THANKS, BUDDY!
!!
...REALLY?!
THANKS SO MUCH, JORGE!!

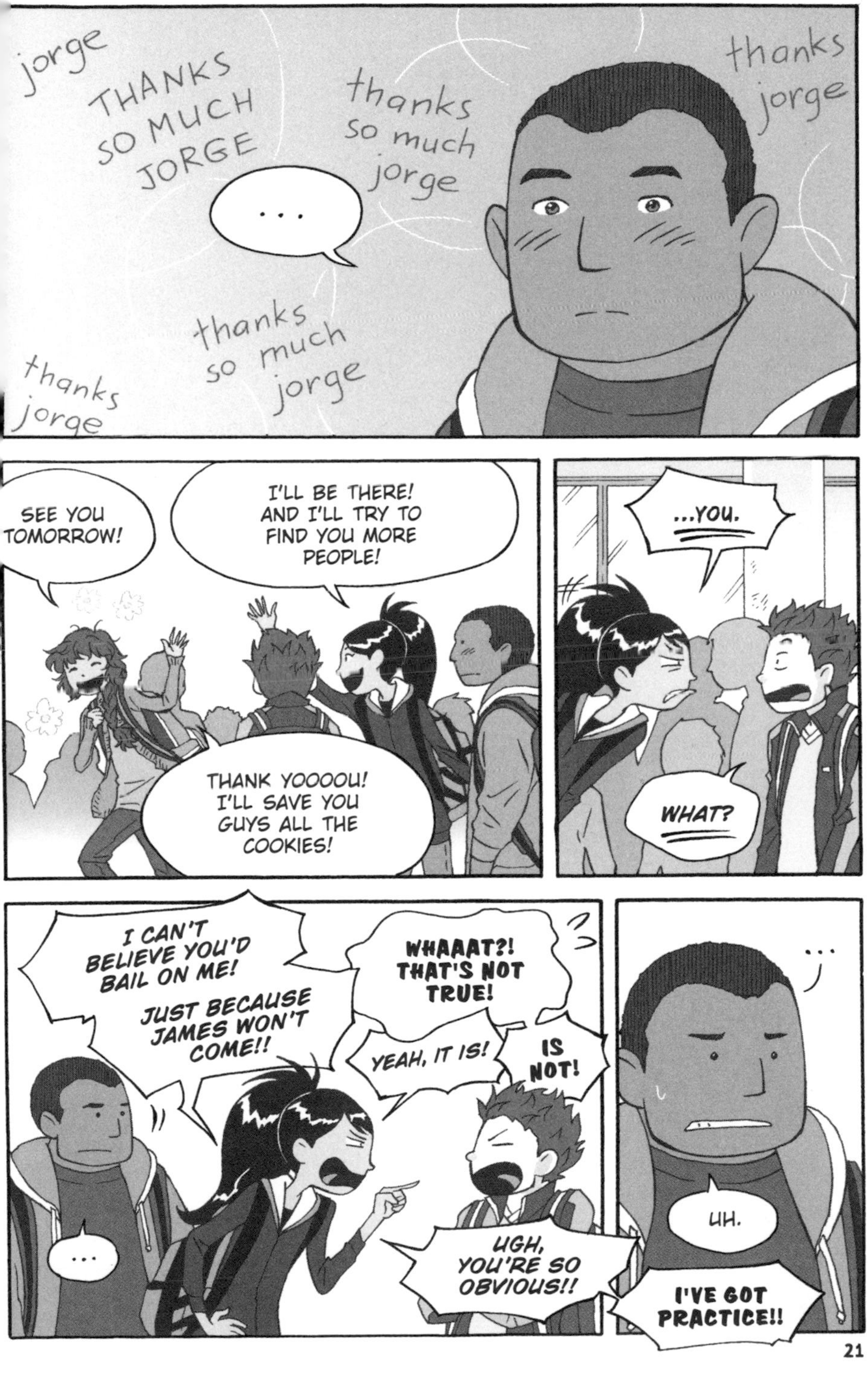
jorge
THANKS SO MUCH JORGE
thanks so much jorge
thanks jorge
...
thanks so much jorge
thanks jorge
SEE YOU TOMORROW!
I'LL BE THERE! AND I'LL TRY TO FIND YOU MORE PEOPLE!
THANK YOOOOU! I'LL SAVE YOU GUYS ALL THE COOKIES!
...YOU.
WHAT?
I CAN'T BELIEVE YOU'D BAIL ON ME!
JUST BECAUSE JAMES WON'T COME!!
WHAAAT?! THAT'S NOT TRUE!
YEAH, IT IS!
IS NOT!
...
UGH, YOU'RE SO OBVIOUS!!
...
UH.
I'VE GOT PRACTICE!!

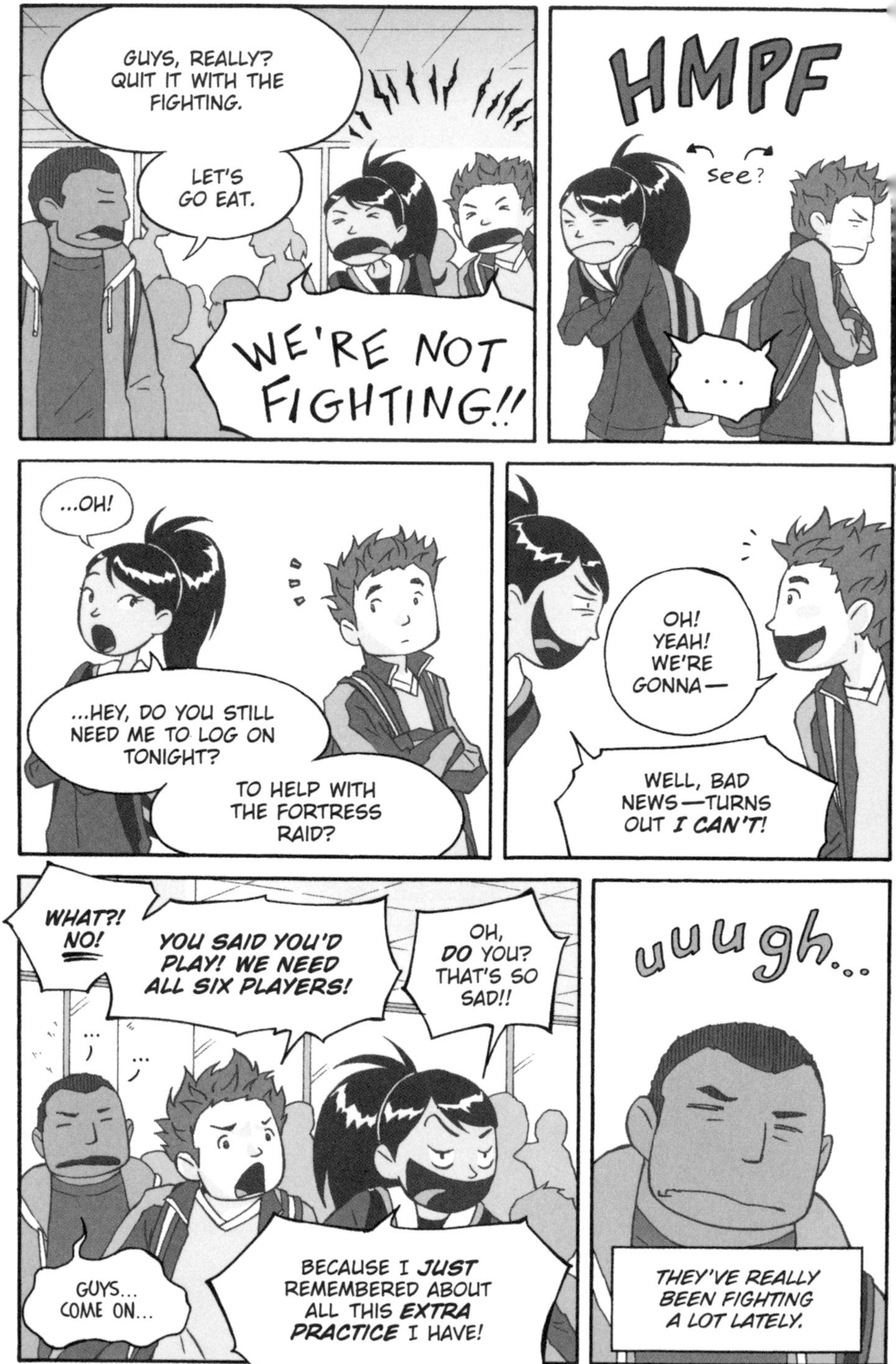
GUYS, REALLY? QUIT IT WITH THE FIGHTING.
LET'S GO EAT.
WE'RE NOT FIGHTING!!
HMPF
see?
...
...OH!
...HEY, DO YOU STILL NEED ME TO LOG ON TONIGHT?
TO HELP WITH THE FORTRESS RAID?
OH! YEAH! WE'RE GONNA—
WELL, BAD NEWS—TURNS OUT I CAN'T!
WHAT?! NO!
YOU SAID YOU'D PLAY! WE NEED ALL SIX PLAYERS!
OH, DO YOU? THAT'S SO SAD!!
GUYS... COME ON...
BECAUSE I JUST REMEMBERED ABOUT ALL THIS EXTRA PRACTICE I HAVE!
uuugh...
THEY'VE REALLY BEEN FIGHTING A LOT LATELY.

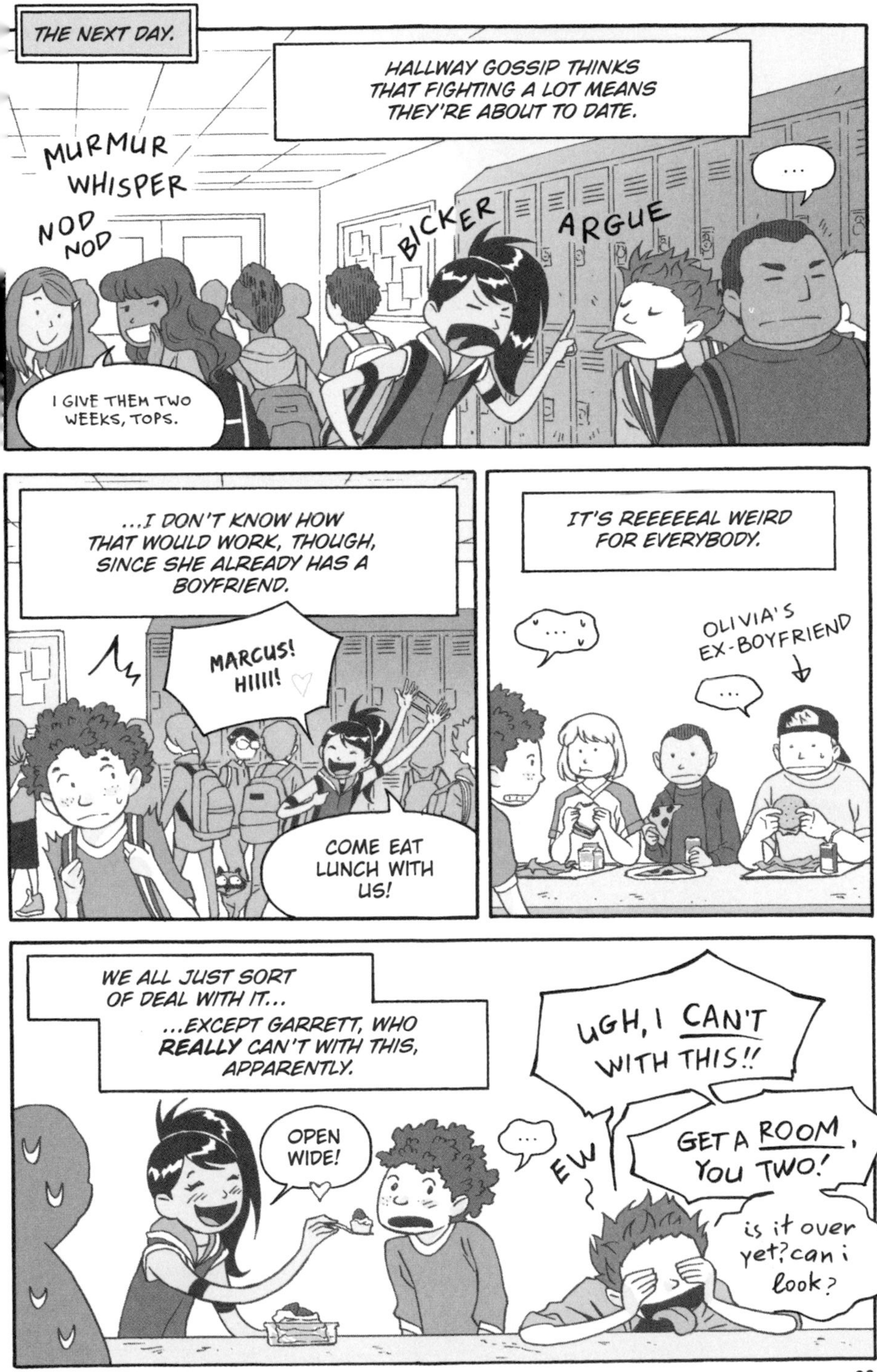
THE NEXT DAY.
HALLWAY GOSSIP THINKS THAT FIGHTING A LOT MEANS THEY'RE ABOUT TO DATE.
MURMUR
WHISPER
NOD NOD
BICKER
ARGUE
...
I GIVE THEM TWO WEEKS, TOPS.
...I DON'T KNOW HOW THAT WOULD WORK, THOUGH, SINCE SHE ALREADY HAS A BOYFRIEND.
MARCUS! HIIII!
COME EAT LUNCH WITH US!
IT'S REEEEEAL WEIRD FOR EVERYBODY.
...
OLIVIA'S EX-BOYFRIEND
...
WE ALL JUST SORT OF DEAL WITH IT...
...EXCEPT GARRETT, WHO REALLY CAN'T WITH THIS, APPARENTLY.
UGH, I CAN'T WITH THIS!!
OPEN WIDE!
...
EW
GET A ROOM, YOU TWO!
is it over yet? can i look?

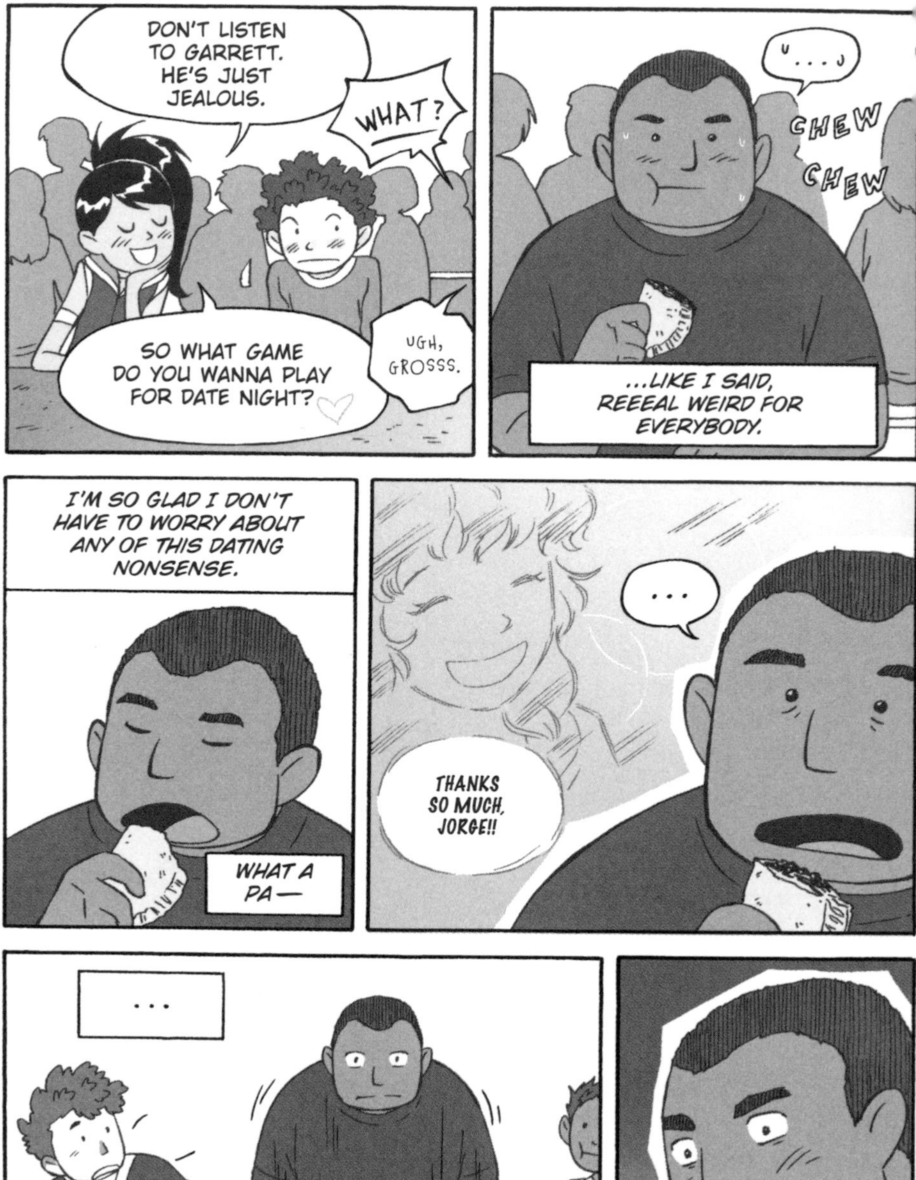

DON'T LISTEN TO GARRETT. HE'S JUST JEALOUS.
WHAT?
SO WHAT GAME DO YOU WANNA PLAY FOR DATE NIGHT?
UGH, GROSSS.
CHEW
CHEW
...LIKE I SAID, REEEAL WEIRD FOR EVERYBODY.
I'M SO GLAD I DON'T HAVE TO WORRY ABOUT ANY OF THIS DATING NONSENSE.
WHAT A PA—
...
THANKS SO MUCH, JORGE!!
...
NO.
WHAT. IS. THIS?

CHAPTER 2

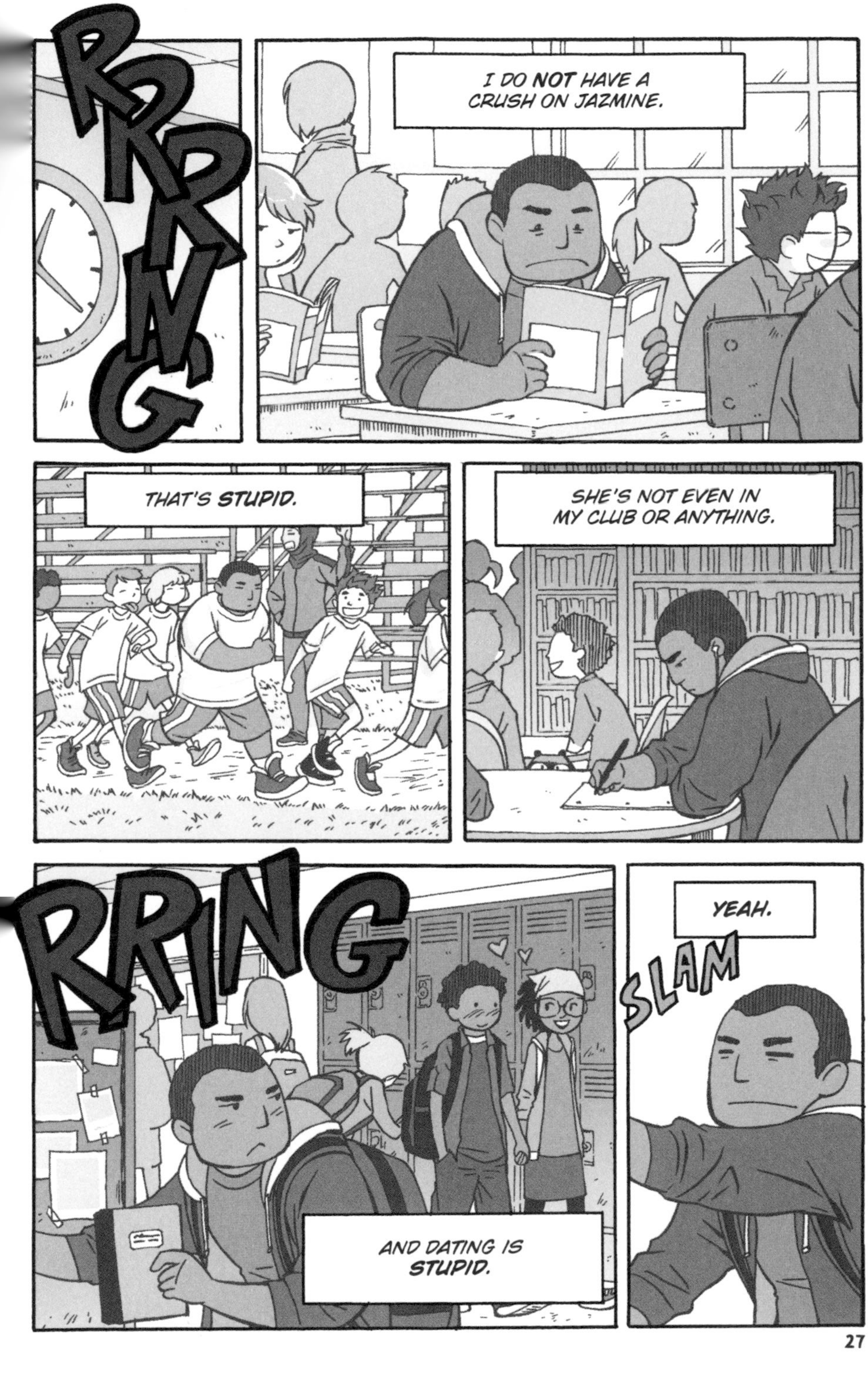
RRRRING
I DO NOT HAVE A CRUSH ON JAZMINE.
THAT'S STUPID.
SHE'S NOT EVEN IN MY CLUB OR ANYTHING.
RRING
AND DATING IS STUPID.
YEAH.
SLAM

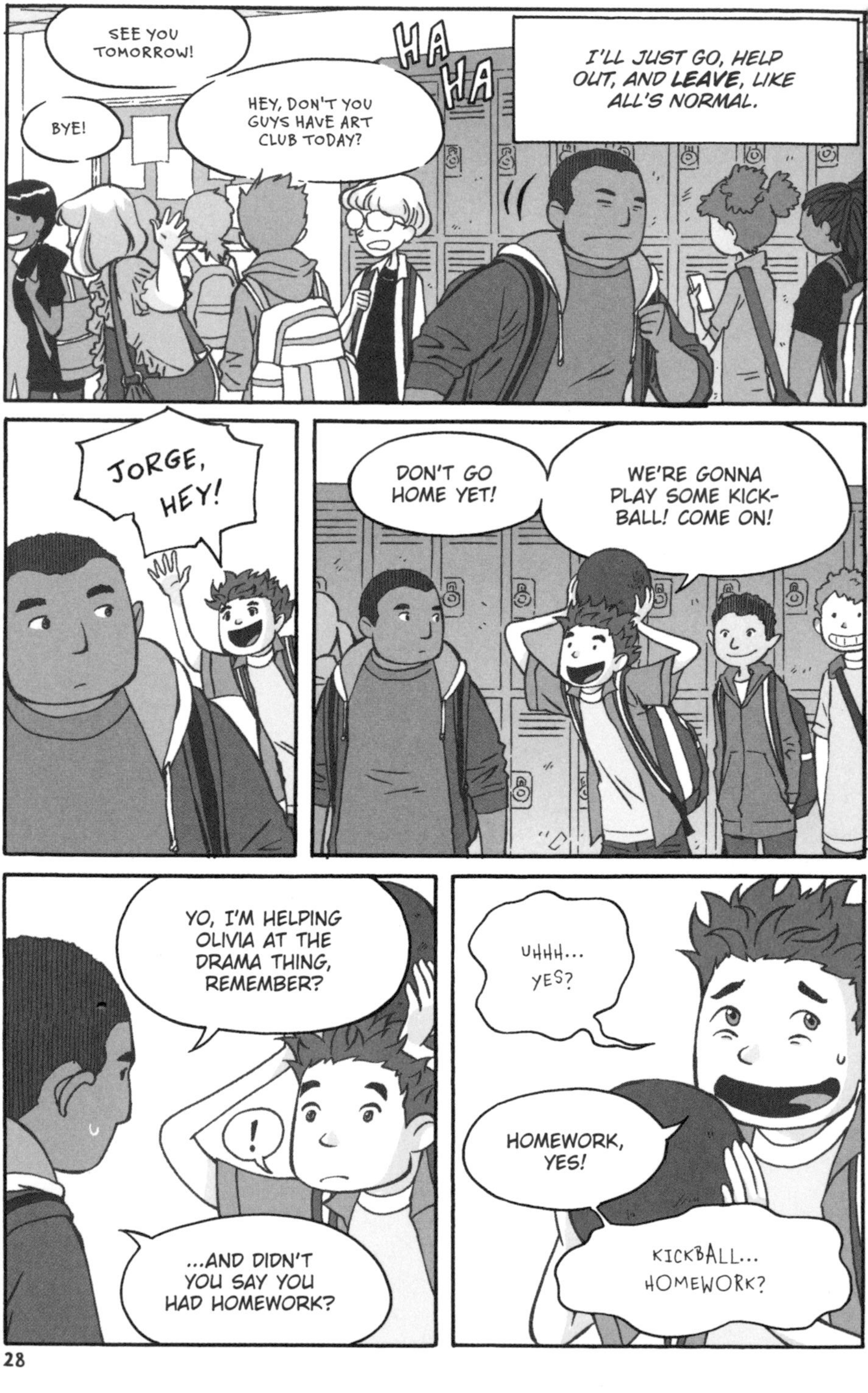
SEE YOU TOMORROW!
BYE!
HEY, DON'T YOU GUYS HAVE ART CLUB TODAY?
HA HA
I'LL JUST GO, HELP OUT, AND LEAVE, LIKE ALL'S NORMAL.
JORGE, HEY!
DON'T GO HOME YET!
WE'RE GONNA PLAY SOME KICK-BALL! COME ON!
YO, I'M HELPING OLIVIA AT THE DRAMA THING, REMEMBER?
!
...AND DIDN'T YOU SAY YOU HAD HOMEWORK?
UHHH... YES?
HOMEWORK, YES!
KICKBALL... HOMEWORK?

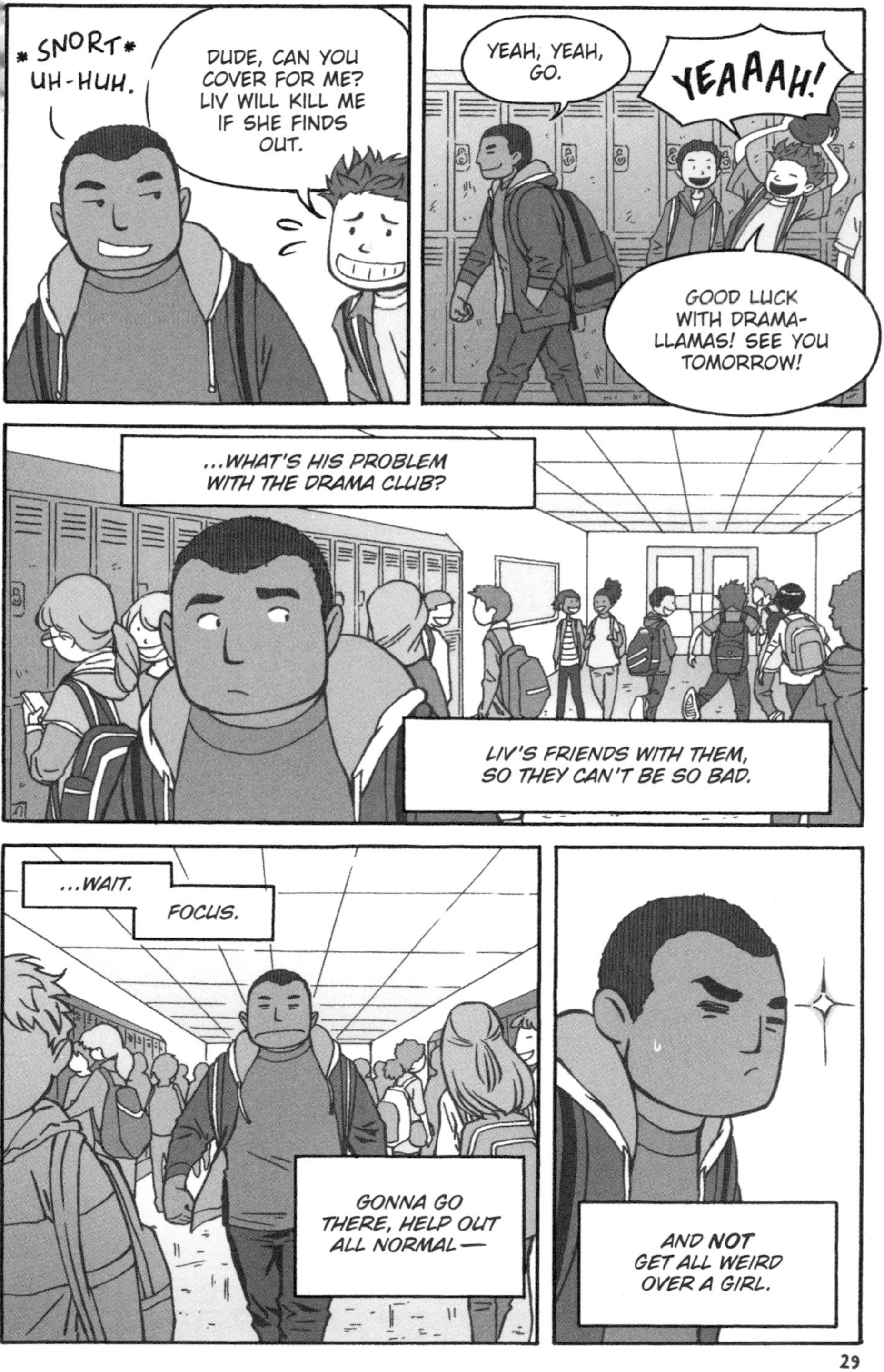
SNORT
UH-HUH.
DUDE, CAN YOU COVER FOR ME? LIV WILL KILL ME IF SHE FINDS OUT.
YEAH, YEAH, GO.
YEAAAH!
GOOD LUCK WITH DRAMA-LLAMAS! SEE YOU TOMORROW!
...WHAT'S HIS PROBLEM WITH THE DRAMA CLUB?
LIV'S FRIENDS WITH THEM, SO THEY CAN'T BE SO BAD.
...WAIT.
FOCUS.
GONNA GO THERE, HELP OUT ALL NORMAL—
AND NOT GET ALL WEIRD OVER A GIRL.

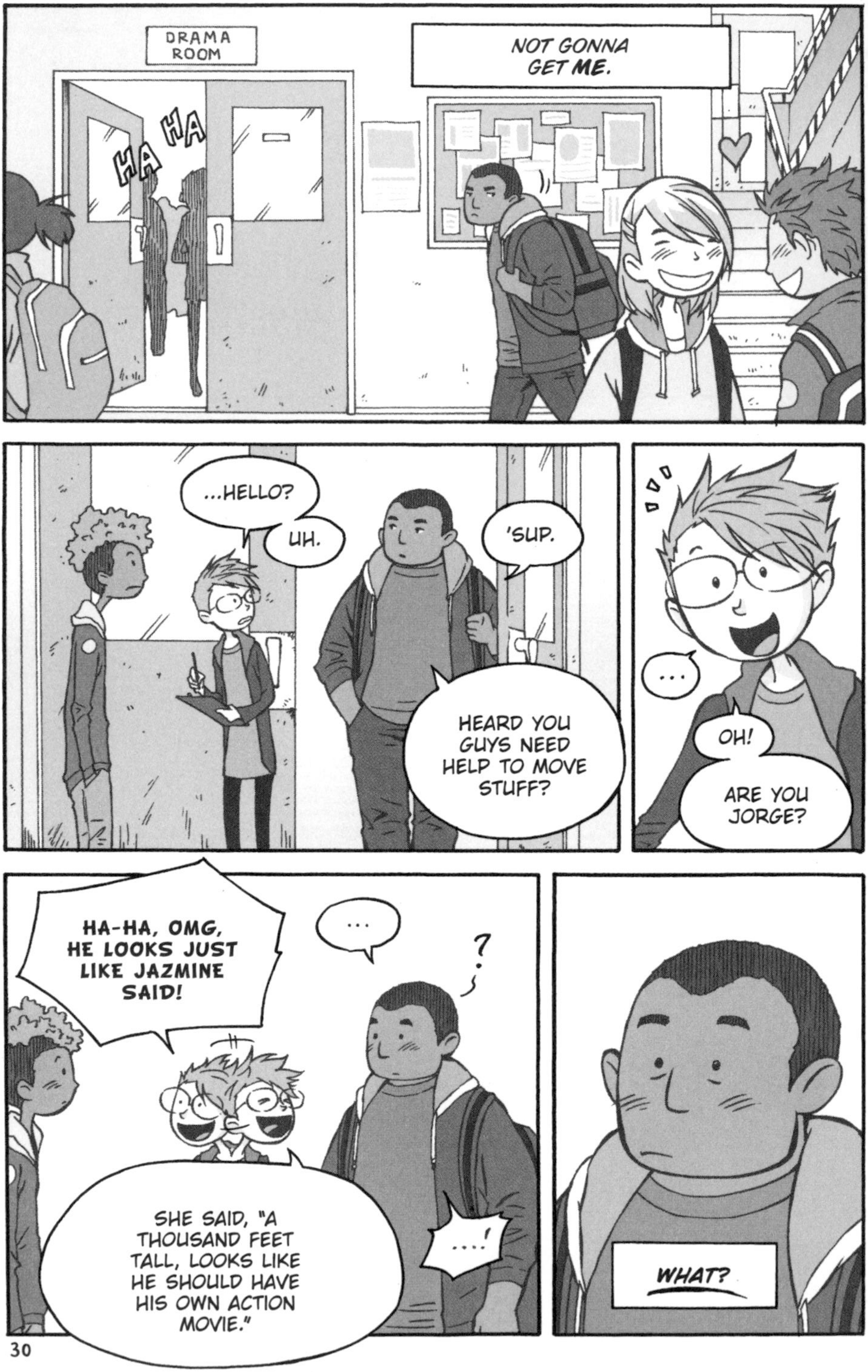
DRAMA ROOM
HA HA
NOT GONNA GET ME.
...HELLO?
UH.
'SUP.
HEARD YOU GUYS NEED HELP TO MOVE STUFF?
...
OH!
ARE YOU JORGE?
HA-HA, OMG, HE LOOKS JUST LIKE JAZMINE SAID!
...
?
SHE SAID, "A THOUSAND FEET TALL, LOOKS LIKE HE SHOULD HAVE HIS OWN ACTION MOVIE."
....!
WHAT?

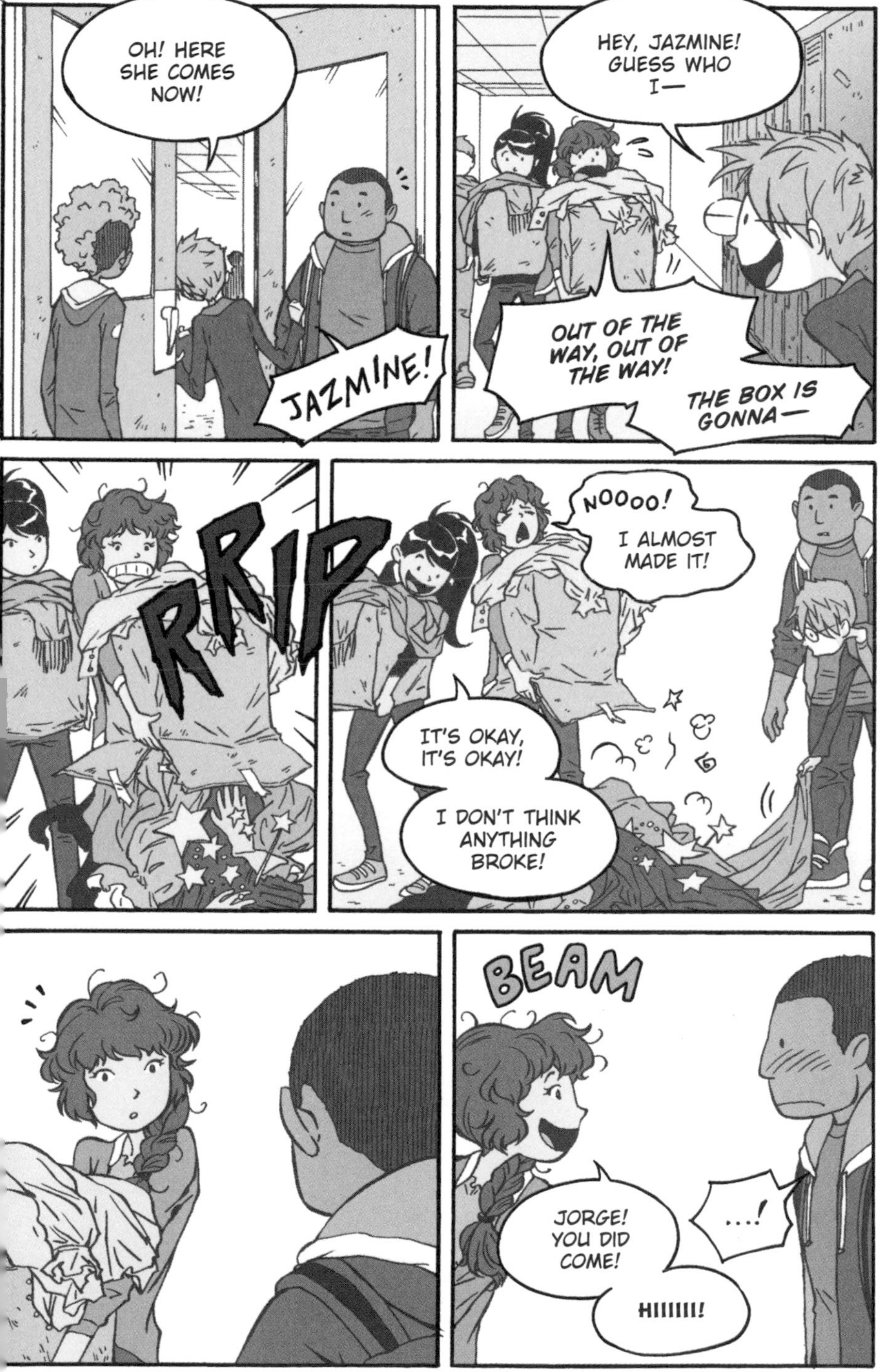
OH! HERE SHE COMES NOW!
JAZMINE!
HEY, JAZMINE! GUESS WHO I—
OUT OF THE WAY, OUT OF THE WAY!
THE BOX IS GONNA—
RRIP
NOOOO!
I ALMOST MADE IT!
IT'S OKAY, IT'S OKAY!
I DON'T THINK ANYTHING BROKE!
BEAM
JORGE! YOU DID COME!
HIIIIII!
...!

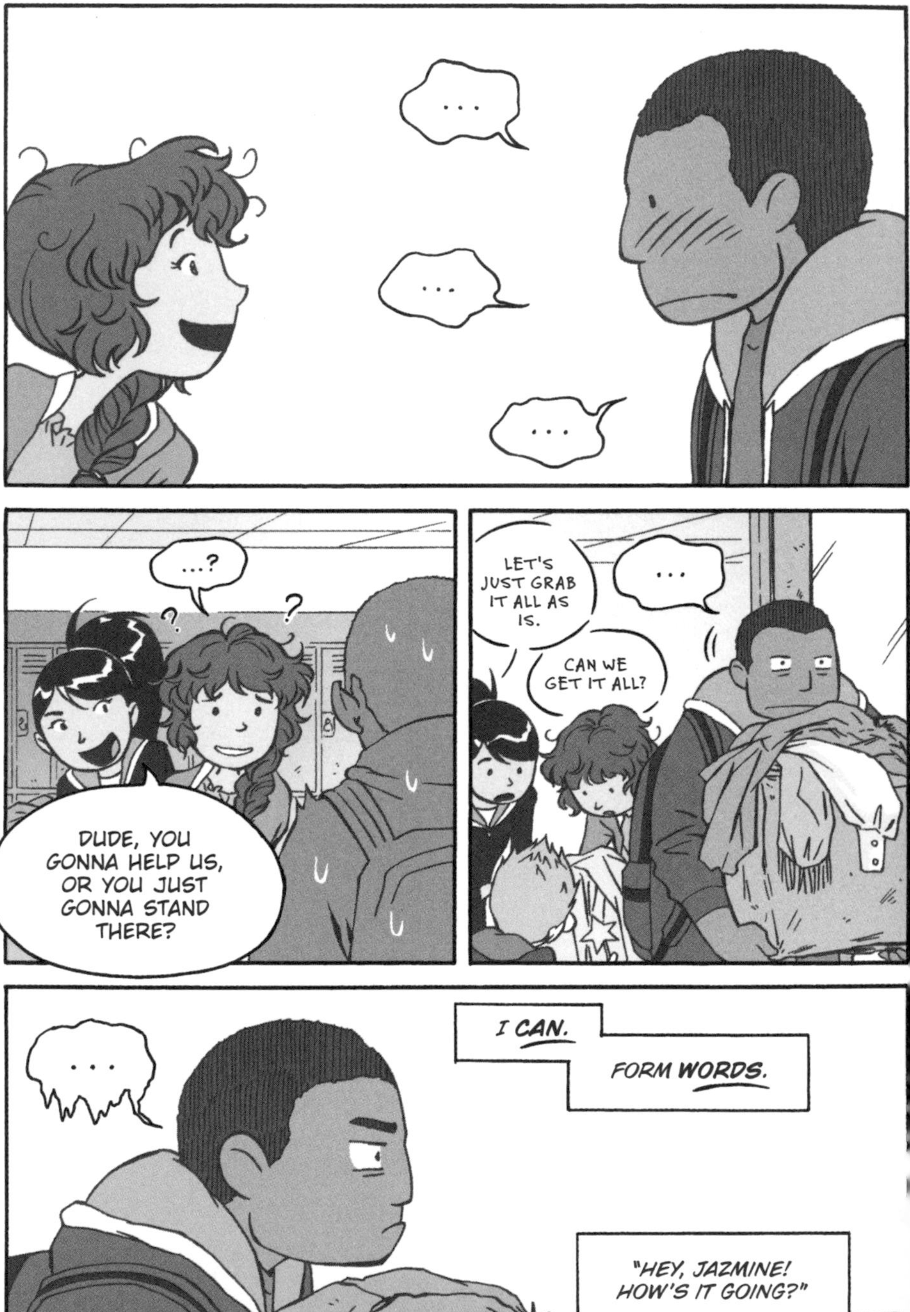
...
...
...
...?
DUDE, YOU GONNA HELP US, OR YOU JUST GONNA STAND THERE?
LET'S JUST GRAB IT ALL AS IS.
CAN WE GET IT ALL?
...
...
I CAN.
FORM WORDS.
"HEY, JAZMINE! HOW'S IT GOING?"
JUST LIKE THAT (ONLY OUT LOUD).

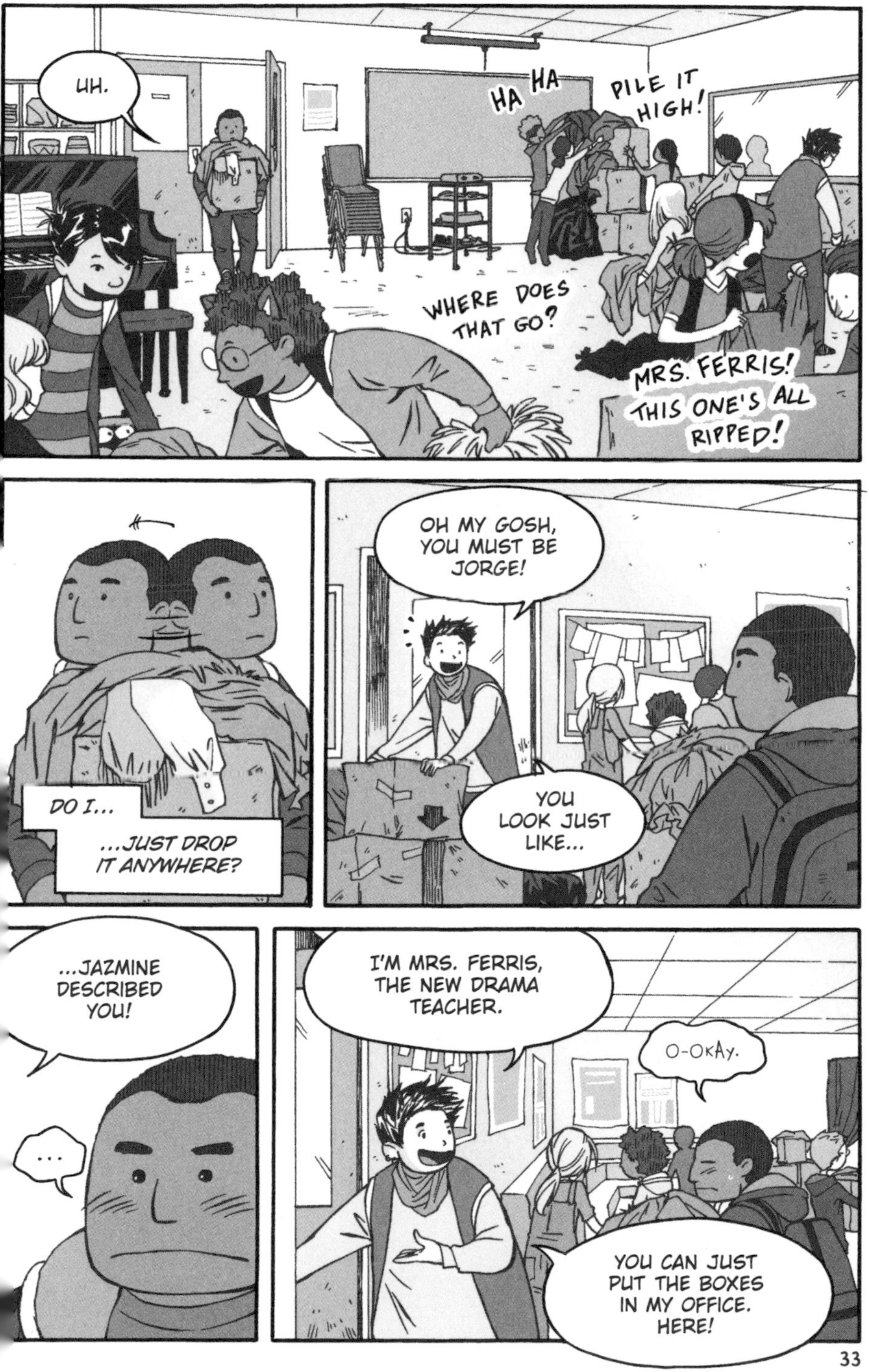
UH.
HA HA
PILE IT HIGH!
WHERE DOES THAT GO?
MRS. FERRIS! THIS ONE'S ALL RIPPED!
DO I...
...JUST DROP IT ANYWHERE?
OH MY GOSH, YOU MUST BE JORGE!
YOU LOOK JUST LIKE...
...JAZMINE DESCRIBED YOU!
...
I'M MRS. FERRIS, THE NEW DRAMA TEACHER.
O-OKAY.
YOU CAN JUST PUT THE BOXES IN MY OFFICE. HERE!

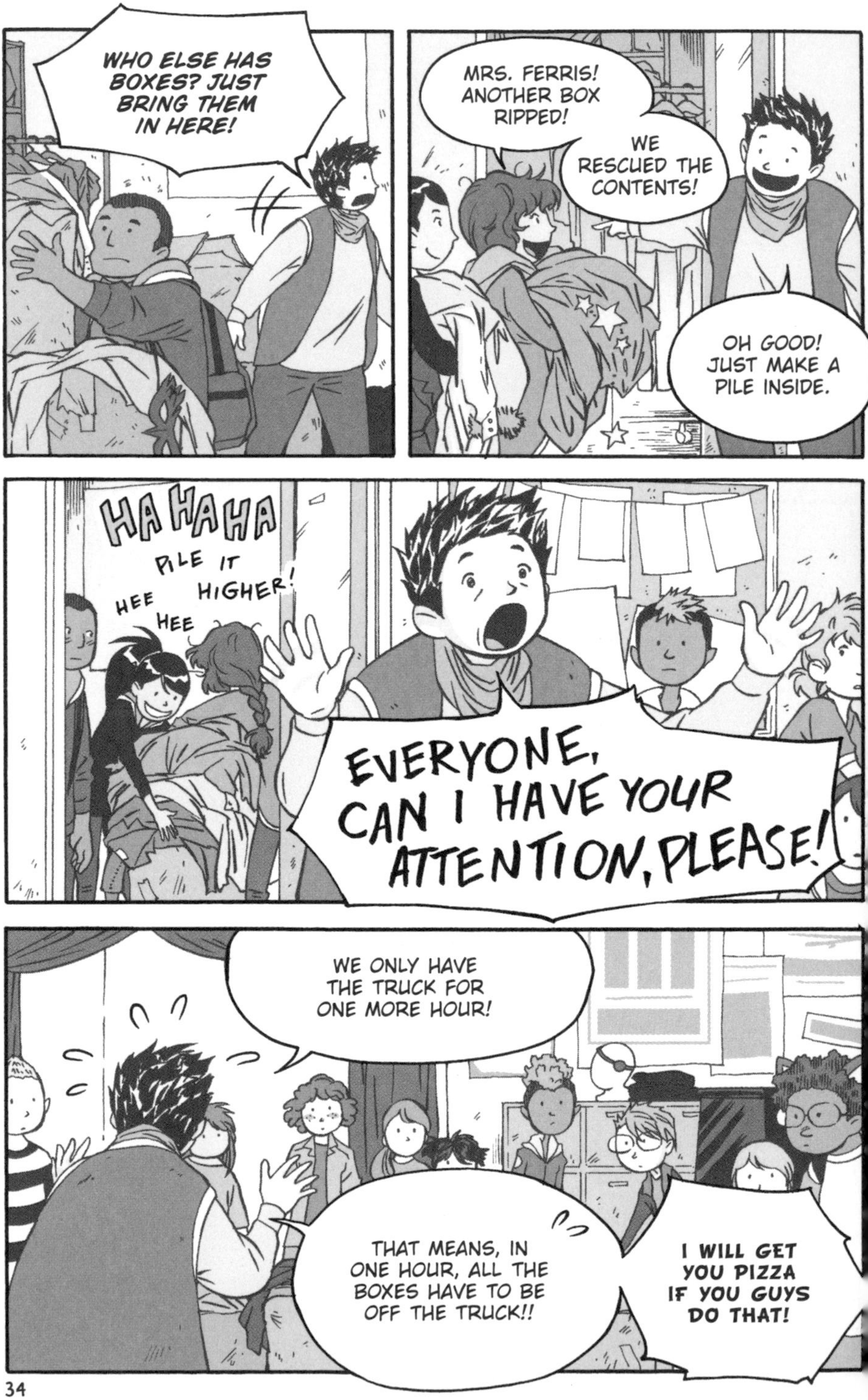
WHO ELSE HAS BOXES? JUST BRING THEM IN HERE!
MRS. FERRIS! ANOTHER BOX RIPPED!
WE RESCUED THE CONTENTS!
OH GOOD! JUST MAKE A PILE INSIDE.
HAHAHA
PILE IT HIGHER!
HEE HEE
EVERYONE, CAN I HAVE YOUR ATTENTION, PLEASE!
WE ONLY HAVE THE TRUCK FOR ONE MORE HOUR!
THAT MEANS, IN ONE HOUR, ALL THE BOXES HAVE TO BE OFF THE TRUCK!!
I WILL GET YOU PIZZA IF YOU GUYS DO THAT!

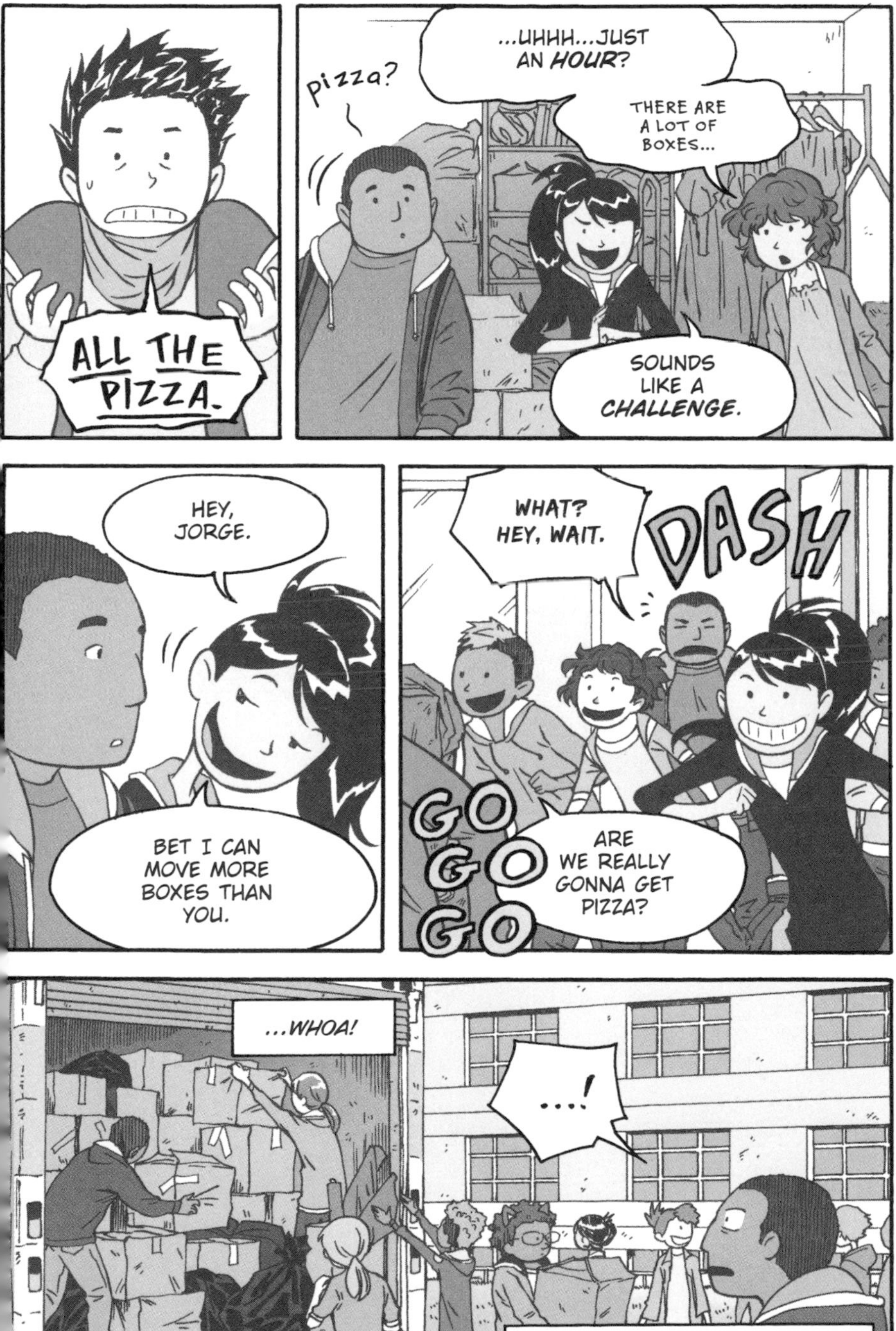
ALL THE PIZZA.
pizza?
...UHHH...JUST AN HOUR?
THERE ARE A LOT OF BOXES...
SOUNDS LIKE A CHALLENGE.
HEY, JORGE.
BET I CAN MOVE MORE BOXES THAN YOU.
WHAT? HEY, WAIT.
DASH
GO GO GO
ARE WE REALLY GONNA GET PIZZA?
...WHOA!
...!
...SHE WASN'T KIDDING ABOUT THE BOXES!

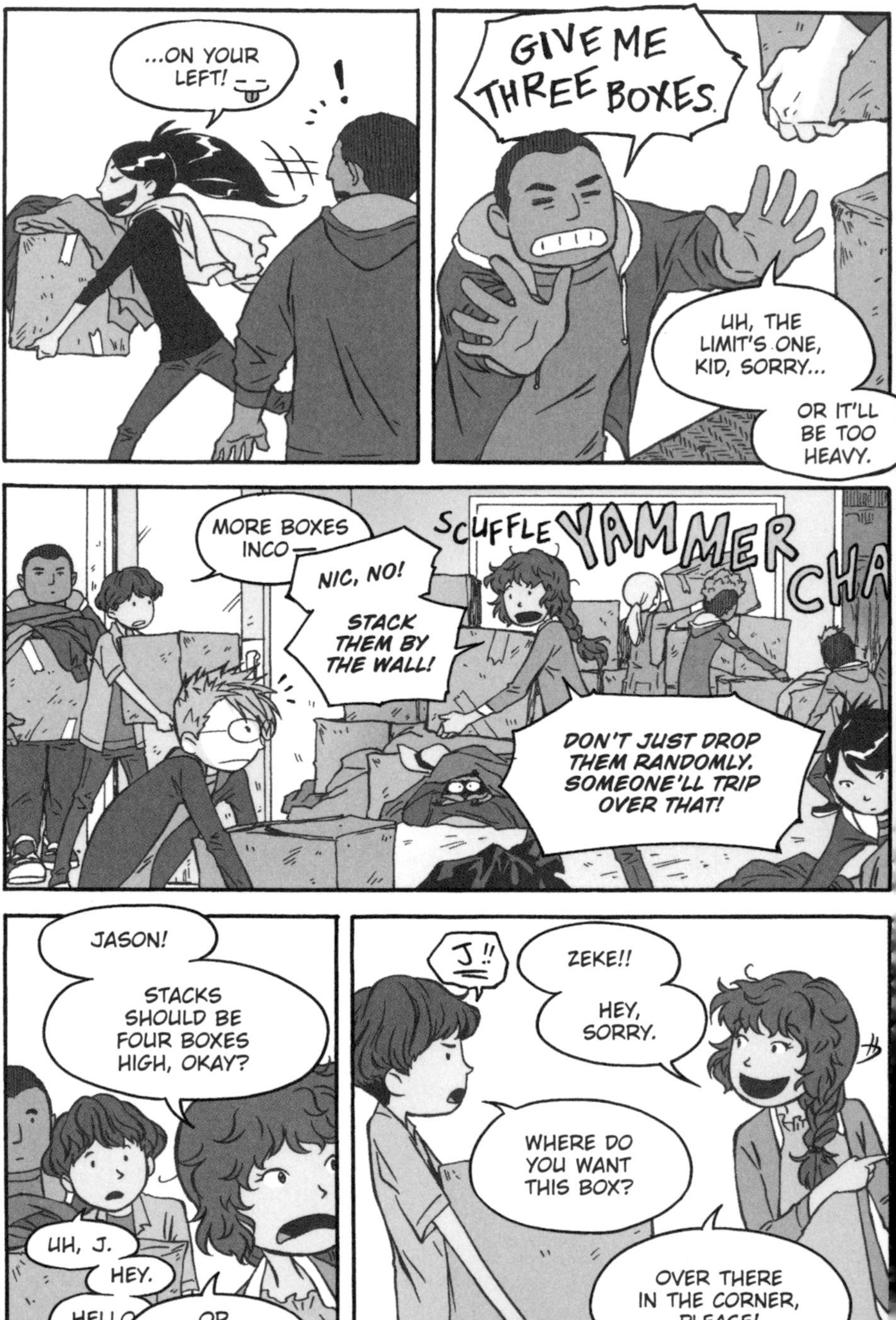
...ON YOUR LEFT!
!
GIVE ME THREE BOXES.
UH, THE LIMIT'S ONE, KID, SORRY...
OR IT'LL BE TOO HEAVY.
MORE BOXES INCO—
NIC, NO!
STACK THEM BY THE WALL!
SCUFFLE
YAMMER
CHA
DON'T JUST DROP THEM RANDOMLY. SOMEONE'LL TRIP OVER THAT!
JASON!
STACKS SHOULD BE FOUR BOXES HIGH, OKAY?
UH, J.
HEY.
HELLO
OR THEY'LL TOPPLE!
J!!
ZEKE!!
HEY, SORRY.
WHERE DO YOU WANT THIS BOX?
OVER THERE IN THE CORNER, PLEASE!

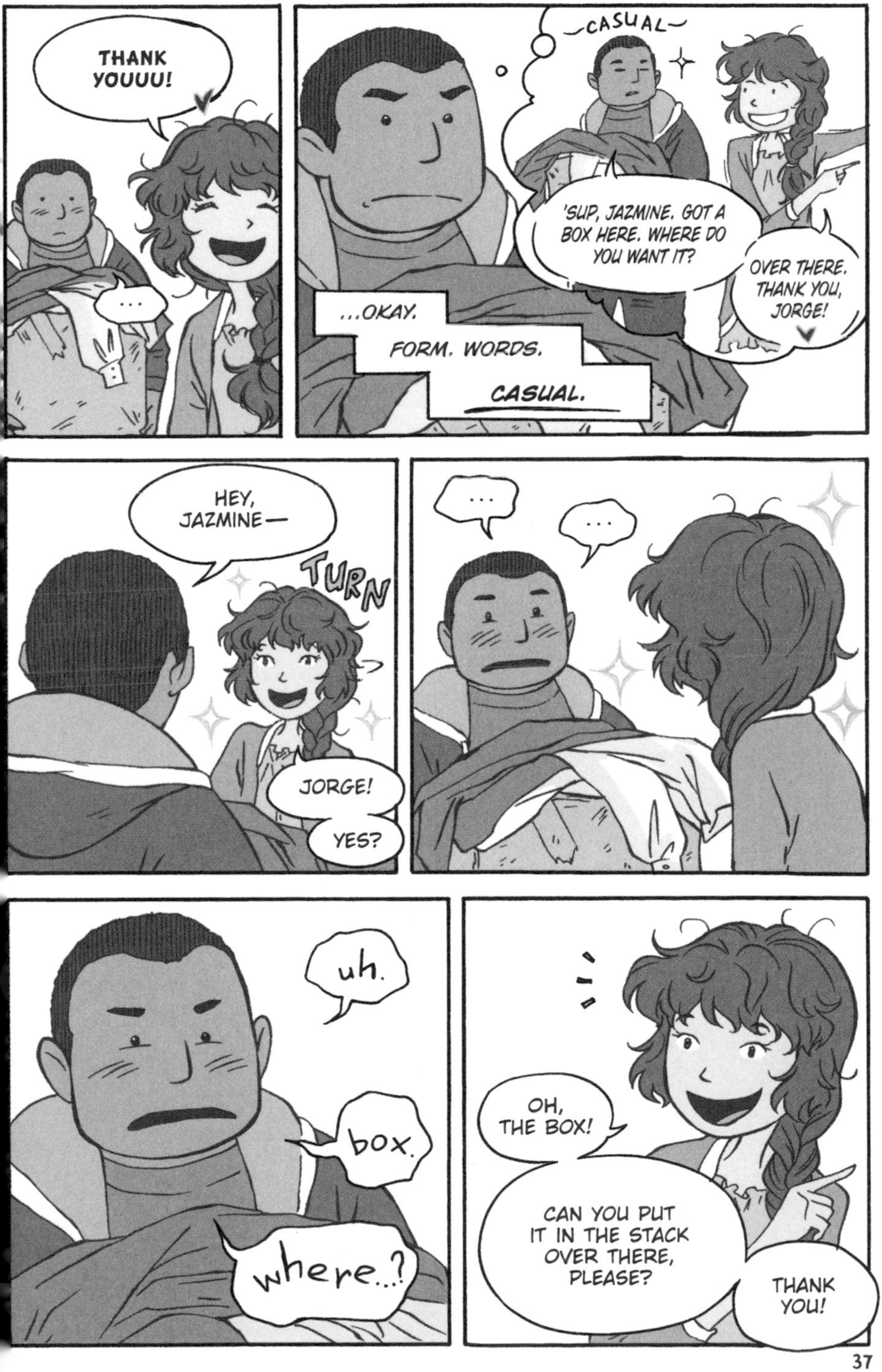
THANK YOUUU!
...
—CASUAL—
'SUP, JAZMINE. GOT A BOX HERE. WHERE DO YOU WANT IT?
OVER THERE. THANK YOU, JORGE!
...OKAY.
FORM. WORDS.
CASUAL.
HEY, JAZMINE—
TURN
JORGE!
YES?
...
...
uh.
box.
where..?
OH, THE BOX!
CAN YOU PUT IT IN THE STACK OVER THERE, PLEASE?
THANK YOU!

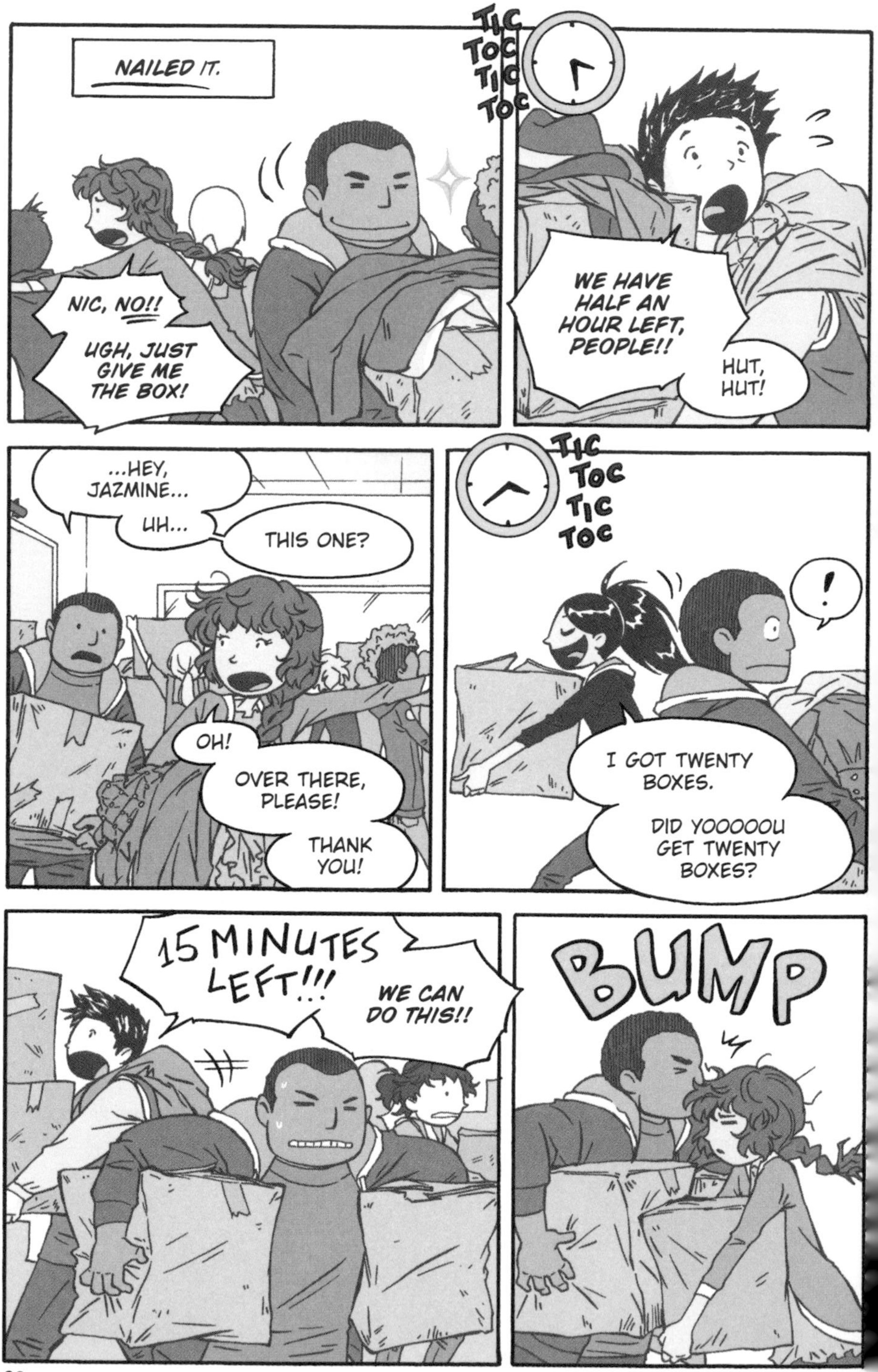
NAILED IT.
NIC, NO!!
UGH, JUST GIVE ME THE BOX!
TIC TOC TIC TOC
WE HAVE HALF AN HOUR LEFT, PEOPLE!!
HUT, HUT!
...HEY, JAZMINE...
UH...
THIS ONE?
OH!
OVER THERE, PLEASE!
THANK YOU!
TIC TOC TIC TOC
!
I GOT TWENTY BOXES.
DID YOOOOOU GET TWENTY BOXES?
15 MINUTES LEFT!!!
WE CAN DO THIS!!
BUMP

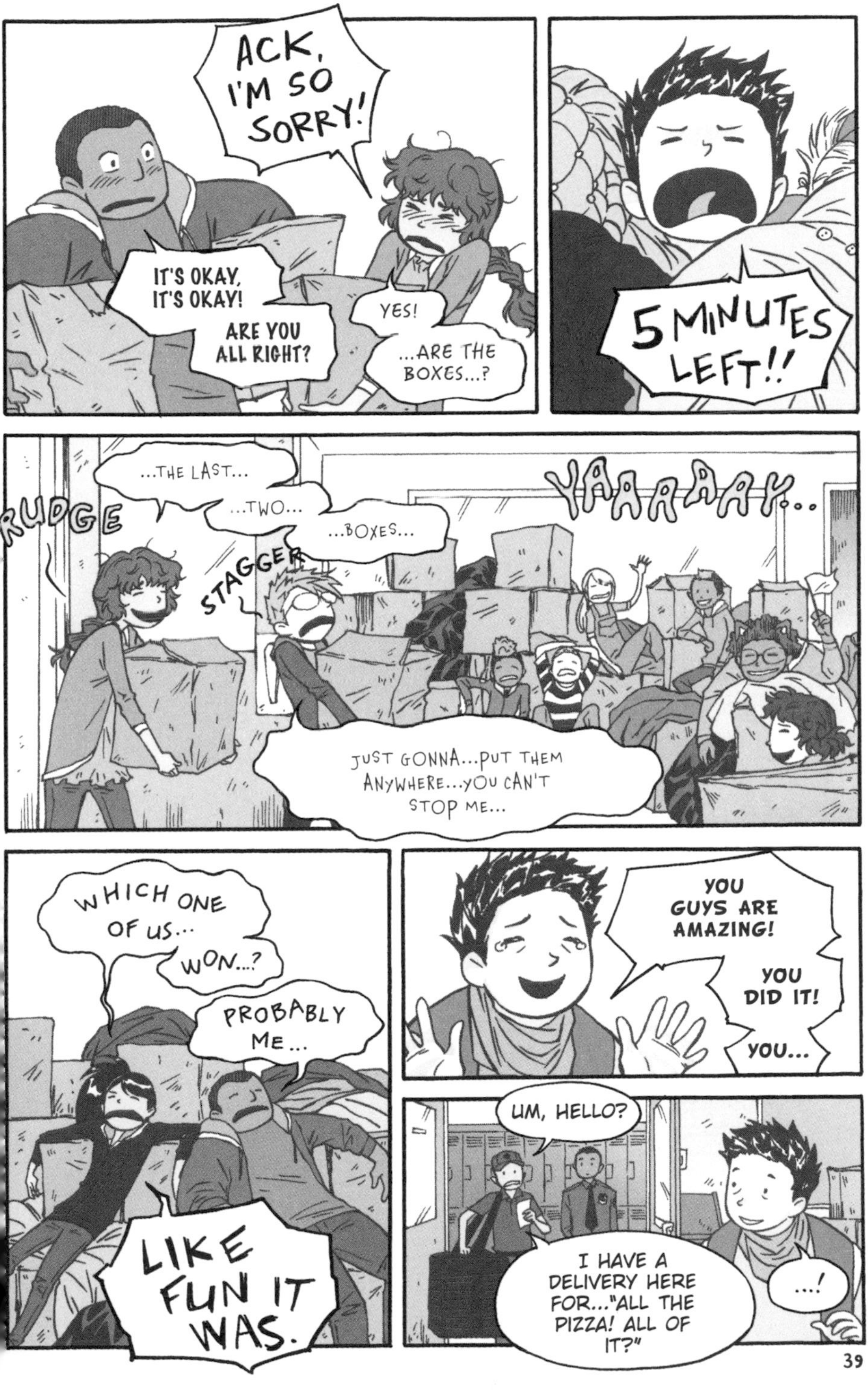
ACK, I'M SO SORRY!
IT'S OKAY, IT'S OKAY!
ARE YOU ALL RIGHT?
YES!
...ARE THE BOXES...?
5 MINUTES LEFT!!
...THE LAST...
...TWO...
...BOXES...
RUDGE
STAGGER
YAAAAAY...
JUST GONNA...PUT THEM ANYWHERE...YOU CAN'T STOP ME...
WHICH ONE OF US...
WON...?
PROBABLY ME...
LIKE FUN IT WAS.
YOU GUYS ARE AMAZING!
YOU DID IT!
YOU...
UM, HELLO?
I HAVE A DELIVERY HERE FOR..."ALL THE PIZZA! ALL OF IT?"
...!

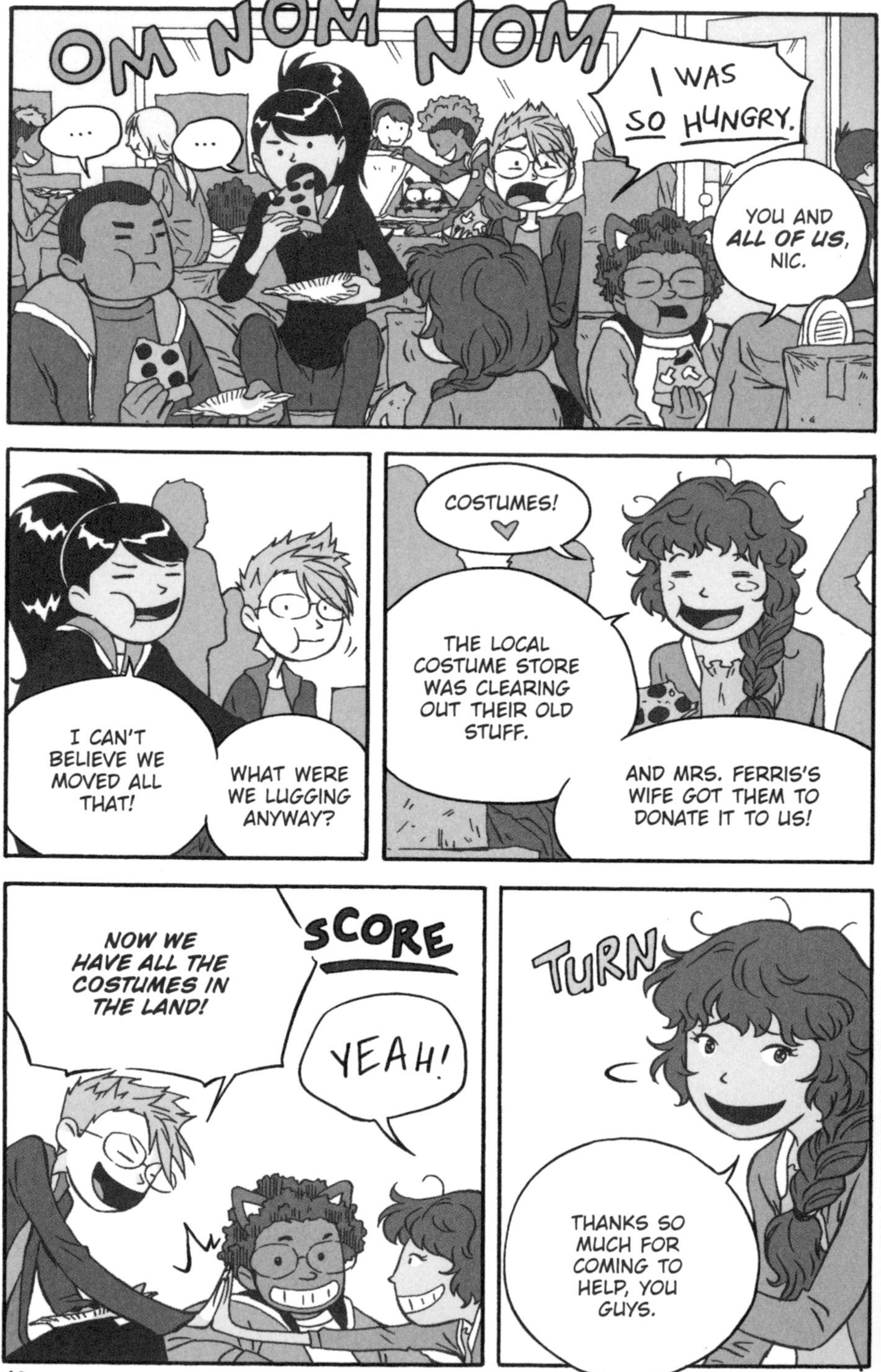

OM NOM NOM
...
...
I WAS SO HUNGRY.
YOU AND ALL OF US, NIC.
I CAN'T BELIEVE WE MOVED ALL THAT!
WHAT WERE WE LUGGING ANYWAY?
COSTUMES!
THE LOCAL COSTUME STORE WAS CLEARING OUT THEIR OLD STUFF.
AND MRS. FERRIS'S WIFE GOT THEM TO DONATE IT TO US!
NOW WE HAVE ALL THE COSTUMES IN THE LAND!
SCORE
YEAH!
TURN
THANKS SO MUCH FOR COMING TO HELP, YOU GUYS.

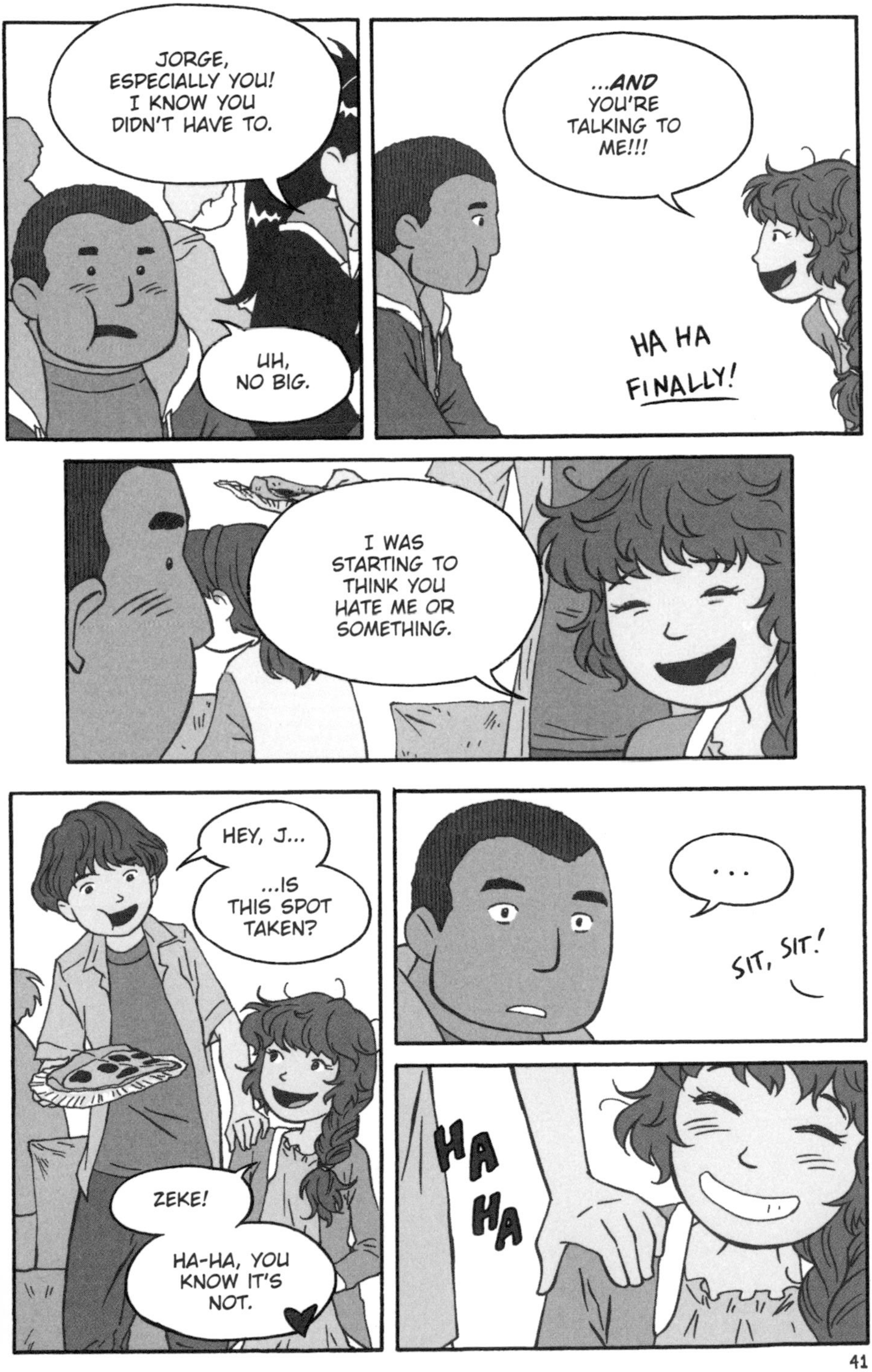
JORGE, ESPECIALLY YOU! I KNOW YOU DIDN'T HAVE TO.
UH, NO BIG.
...AND YOU'RE TALKING TO ME!!!
HA HA FINALLY!
I WAS STARTING TO THINK YOU HATE ME OR SOMETHING.
HEY, J...
...IS THIS SPOT TAKEN?
ZEKE!
HA-HA, YOU KNOW IT'S NOT.
...
SIT, SIT!
HA HA

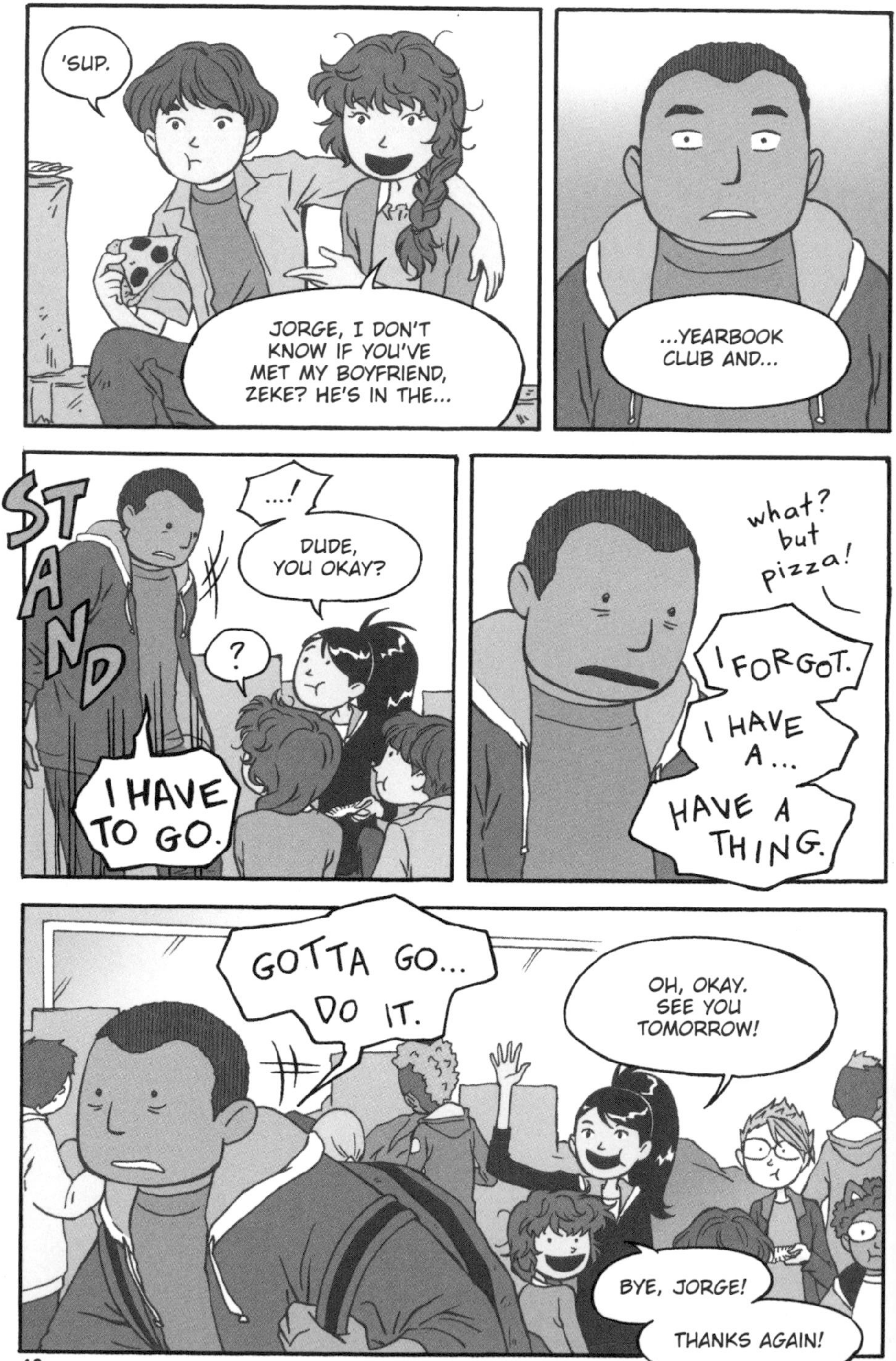
'SUP.
JORGE, I DON'T KNOW IF YOU'VE MET MY BOYFRIEND, ZEKE? HE'S IN THE...
...YEARBOOK CLUB AND...
STAND
...!
DUDE, YOU OKAY?
?
I HAVE TO GO.
what? but pizza!
I FORGOT.
I HAVE A...
HAVE A THING.
GOTTA GO... DO IT.
OH, OKAY. SEE YOU TOMORROW!
BYE, JORGE!
THANKS AGAIN!

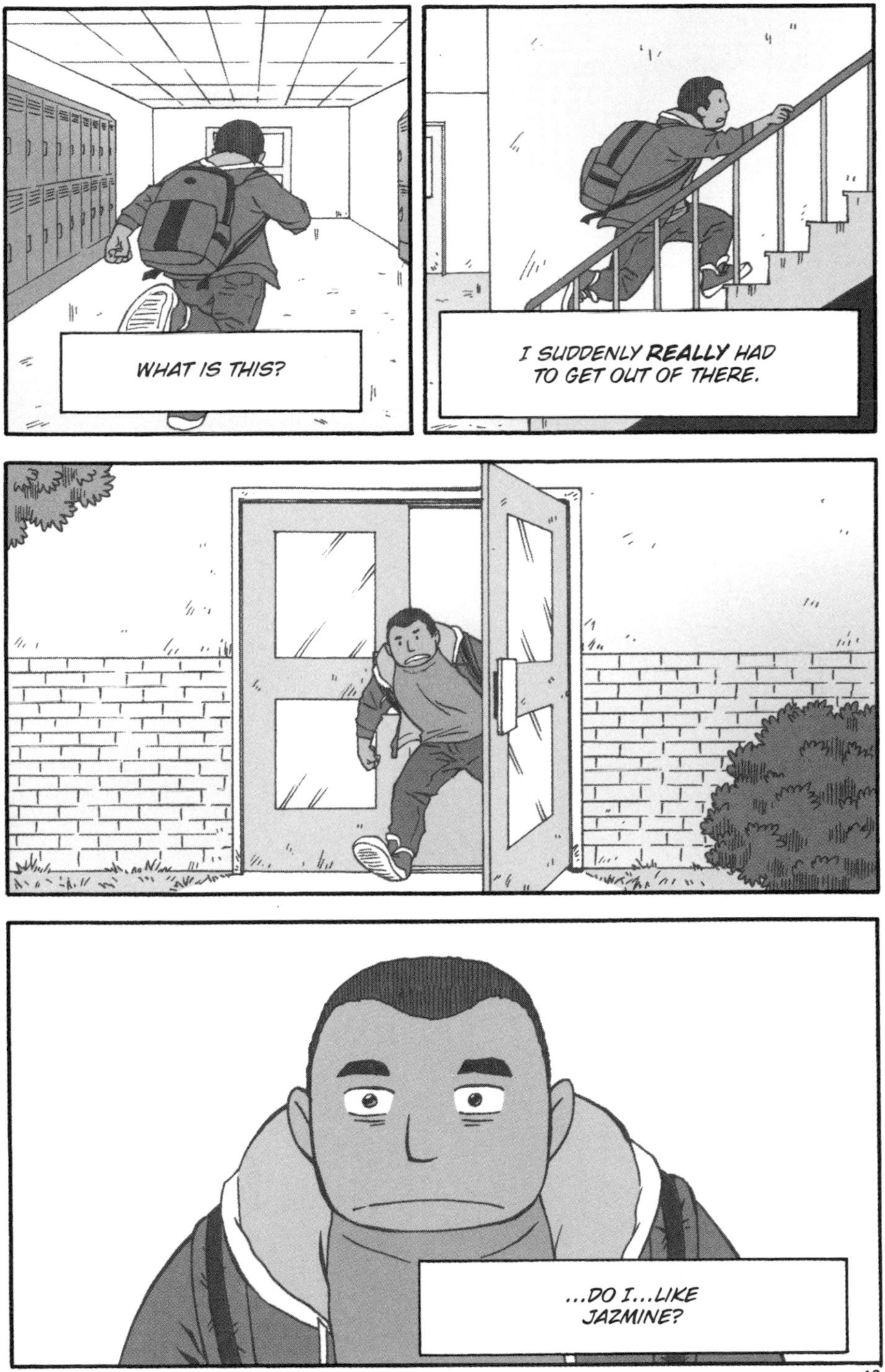
WHAT IS THIS?
I SUDDENLY REALLY HAD TO GET OUT OF THERE.
...DO I...LIKE JAZMINE?

CHAPTER 3

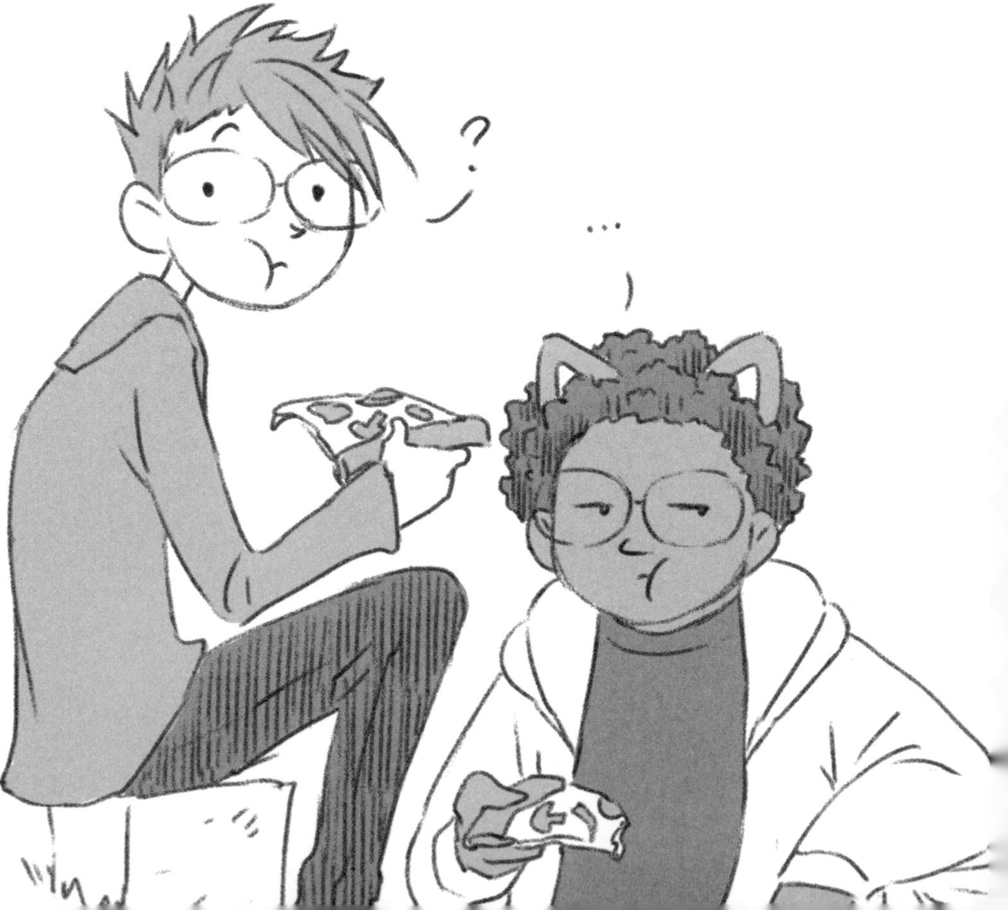
?
...

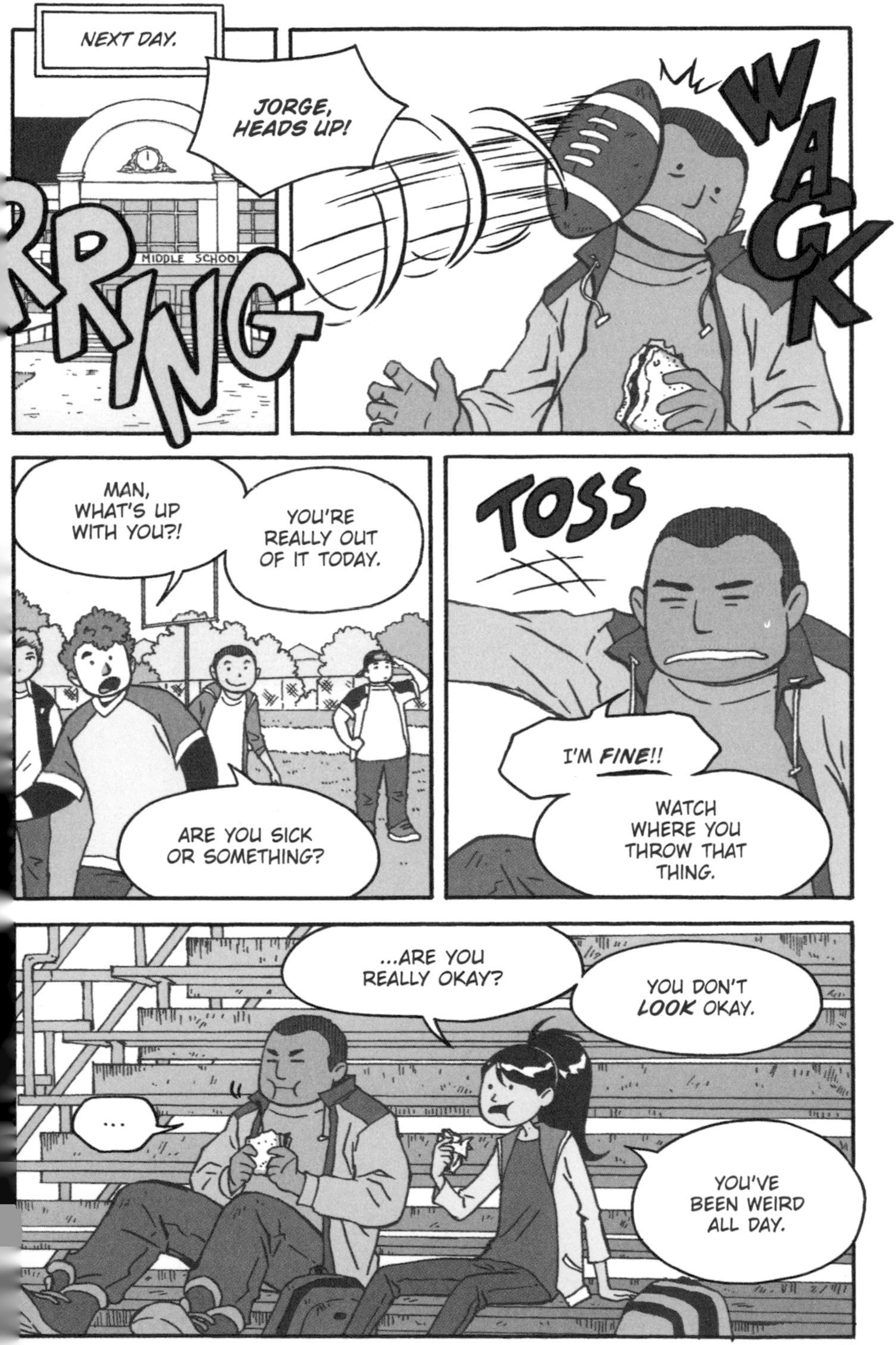
NEXT DAY.
RRRING
JORGE, HEADS UP!
WACK
MIDDLE SCHOOL
MAN, WHAT'S UP WITH YOU?!
YOU'RE REALLY OUT OF IT TODAY.
ARE YOU SICK OR SOMETHING?
TOSS
I'M FINE!!
WATCH WHERE YOU THROW THAT THING.
...ARE YOU REALLY OKAY?
YOU DON'T LOOK OKAY.
...
YOU'VE BEEN WEIRD ALL DAY.

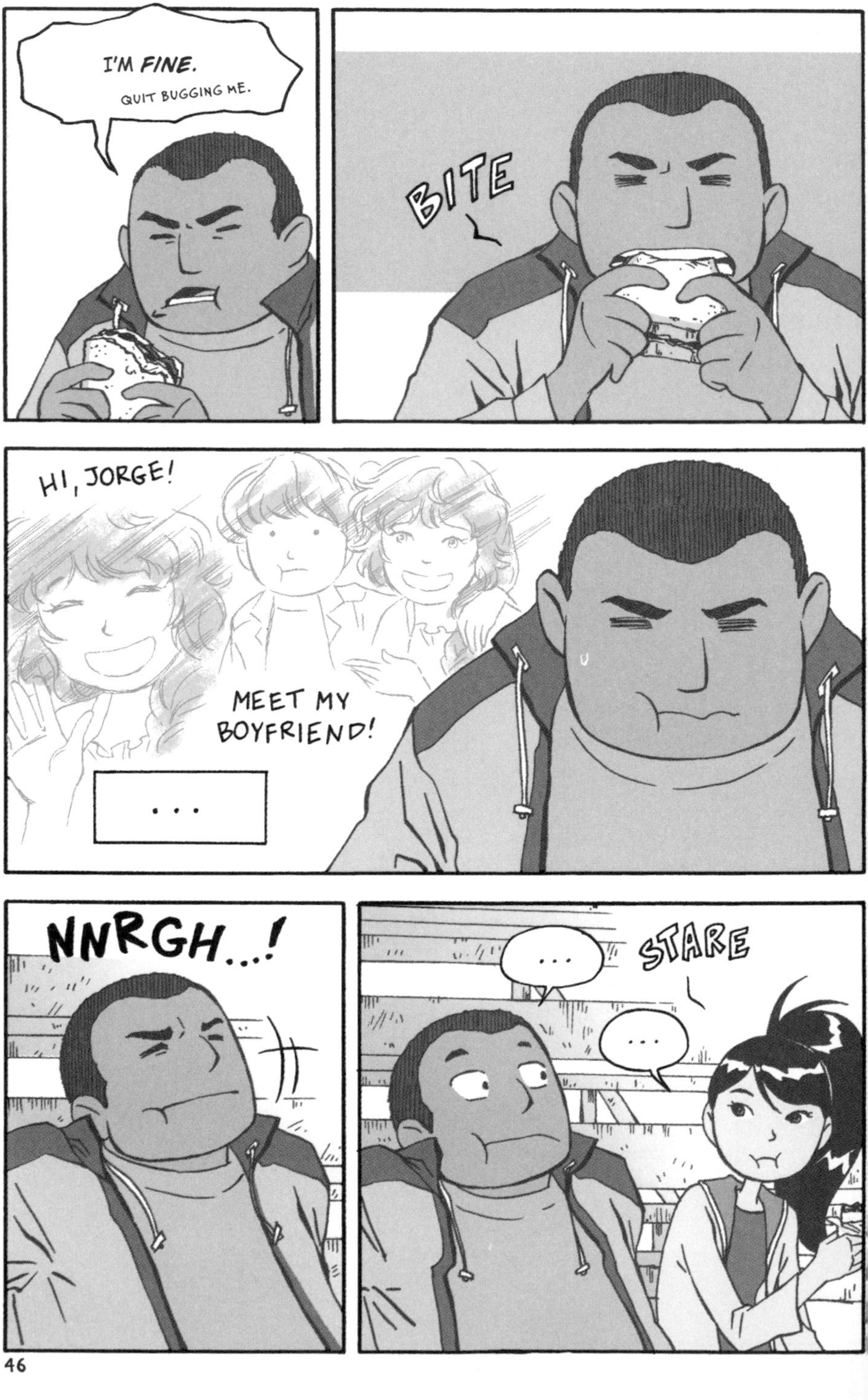
I'M FINE.
QUIT BUGGING ME.
BITE
HI, JORGE!
MEET MY BOYFRIEND!
. . .
NNRGH...!
. . .
STARE
. . .

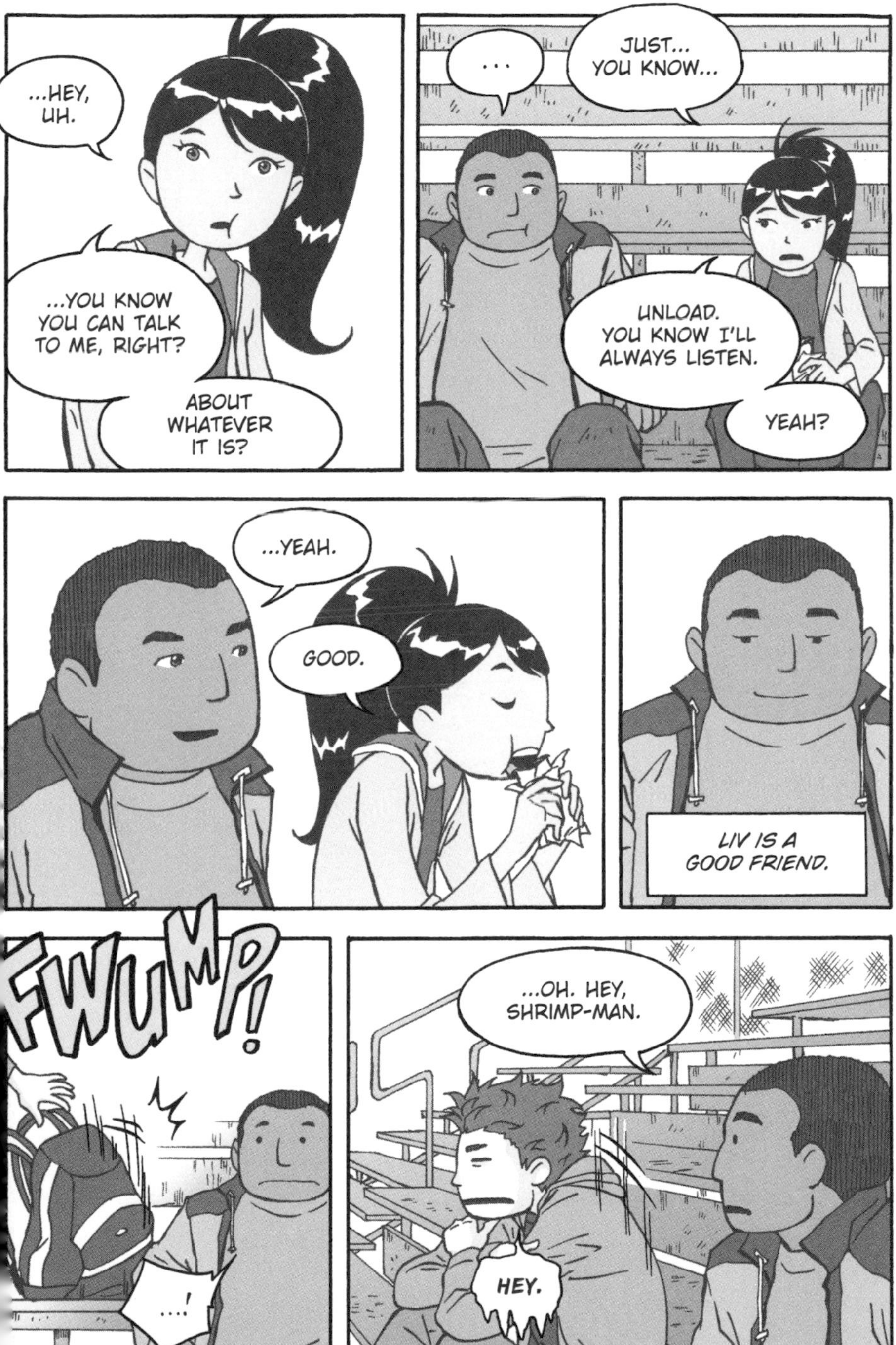
...HEY, UH.
...YOU KNOW YOU CAN TALK TO ME, RIGHT?
ABOUT WHATEVER IT IS?
...
JUST... YOU KNOW...
UNLOAD. YOU KNOW I'LL ALWAYS LISTEN.
YEAH?
...YEAH.
GOOD.
LIV IS A GOOD FRIEND.
FWUMP!
...!
...OH. HEY, SHRIMP-MAN.
HEY.

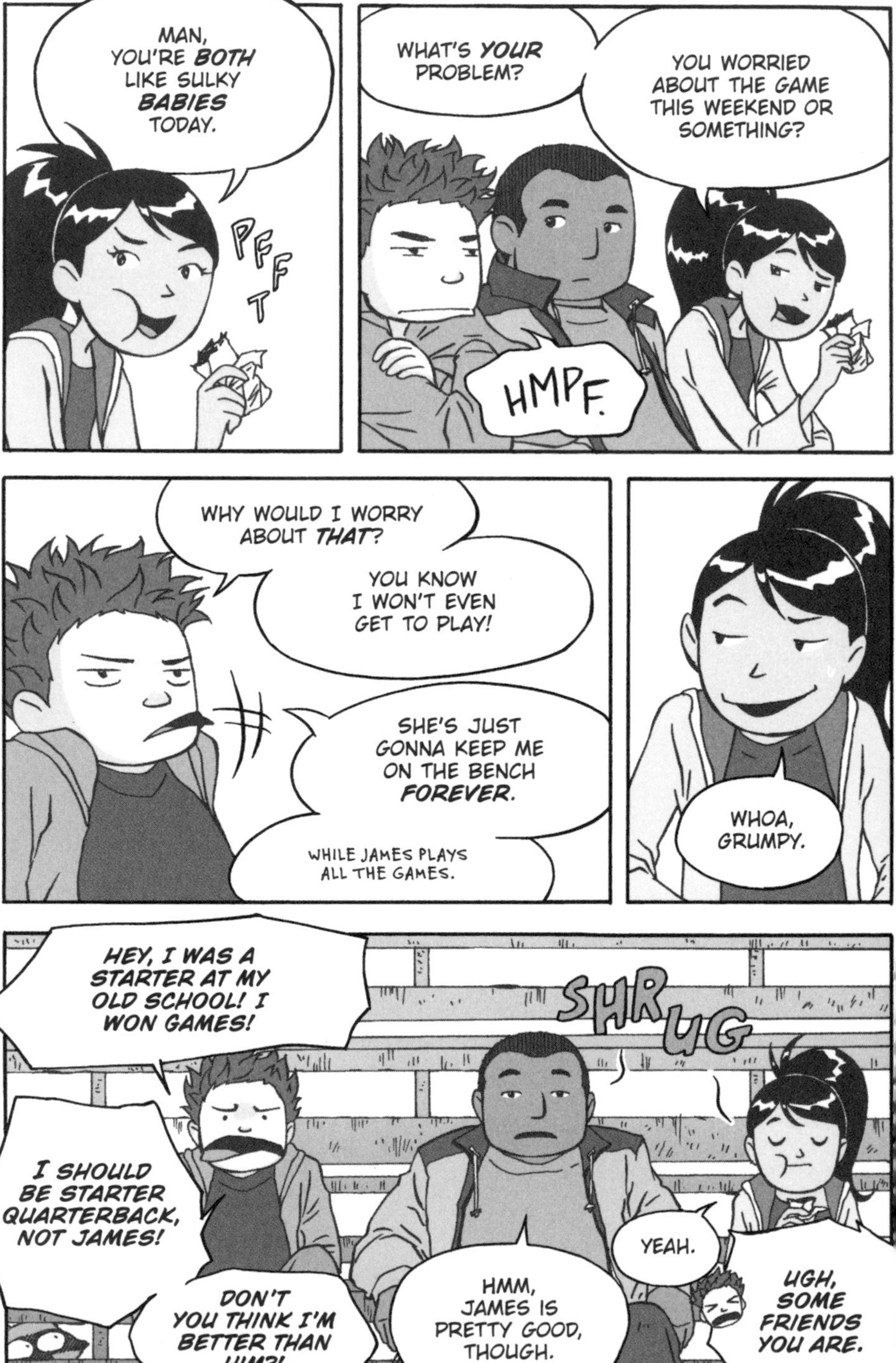
MAN, YOU'RE BOTH LIKE SULKY BABIES TODAY.
PFFFT
WHAT'S YOUR PROBLEM?
YOU WORRIED ABOUT THE GAME THIS WEEKEND OR SOMETHING?
HMPF.
WHY WOULD I WORRY ABOUT THAT?
YOU KNOW I WON'T EVEN GET TO PLAY!
SHE'S JUST GONNA KEEP ME ON THE BENCH FOREVER.
WHILE JAMES PLAYS ALL THE GAMES.
WHOA, GRUMPY.
HEY, I WAS A STARTER AT MY OLD SCHOOL! I WON GAMES!
SHRUG
I SHOULD BE STARTER QUARTERBACK, NOT JAMES!
DON'T YOU THINK I'M BETTER THAN HIM?!
HMM, JAMES IS PRETTY GOOD, THOUGH.
YEAH.
UGH, SOME FRIENDS YOU ARE.

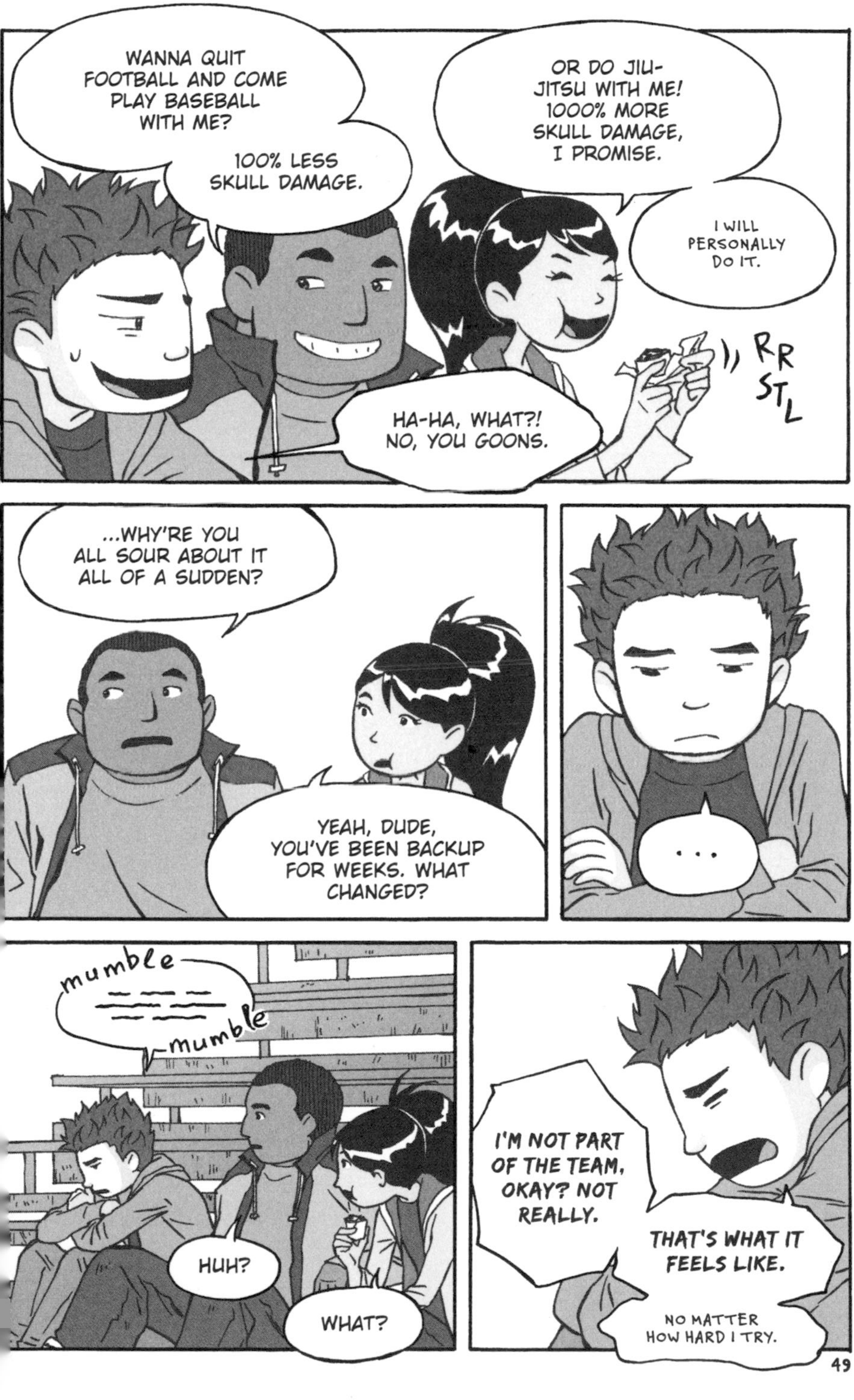
WANNA QUIT FOOTBALL AND COME PLAY BASEBALL WITH ME?
100% LESS SKULL DAMAGE.
OR DO JIU-JITSU WITH ME! 1000% MORE SKULL DAMAGE, I PROMISE.
I WILL PERSONALLY DO IT.
RRSTL
HA-HA, WHAT?! NO, YOU GOONS.
...WHY'RE YOU ALL SOUR ABOUT IT ALL OF A SUDDEN?
YEAH, DUDE, YOU'VE BEEN BACKUP FOR WEEKS. WHAT CHANGED?
...
mumble mumble
HUH?
WHAT?
I'M NOT PART OF THE TEAM, OKAY? NOT REALLY.
THAT'S WHAT IT FEELS LIKE.
NO MATTER HOW HARD I TRY.

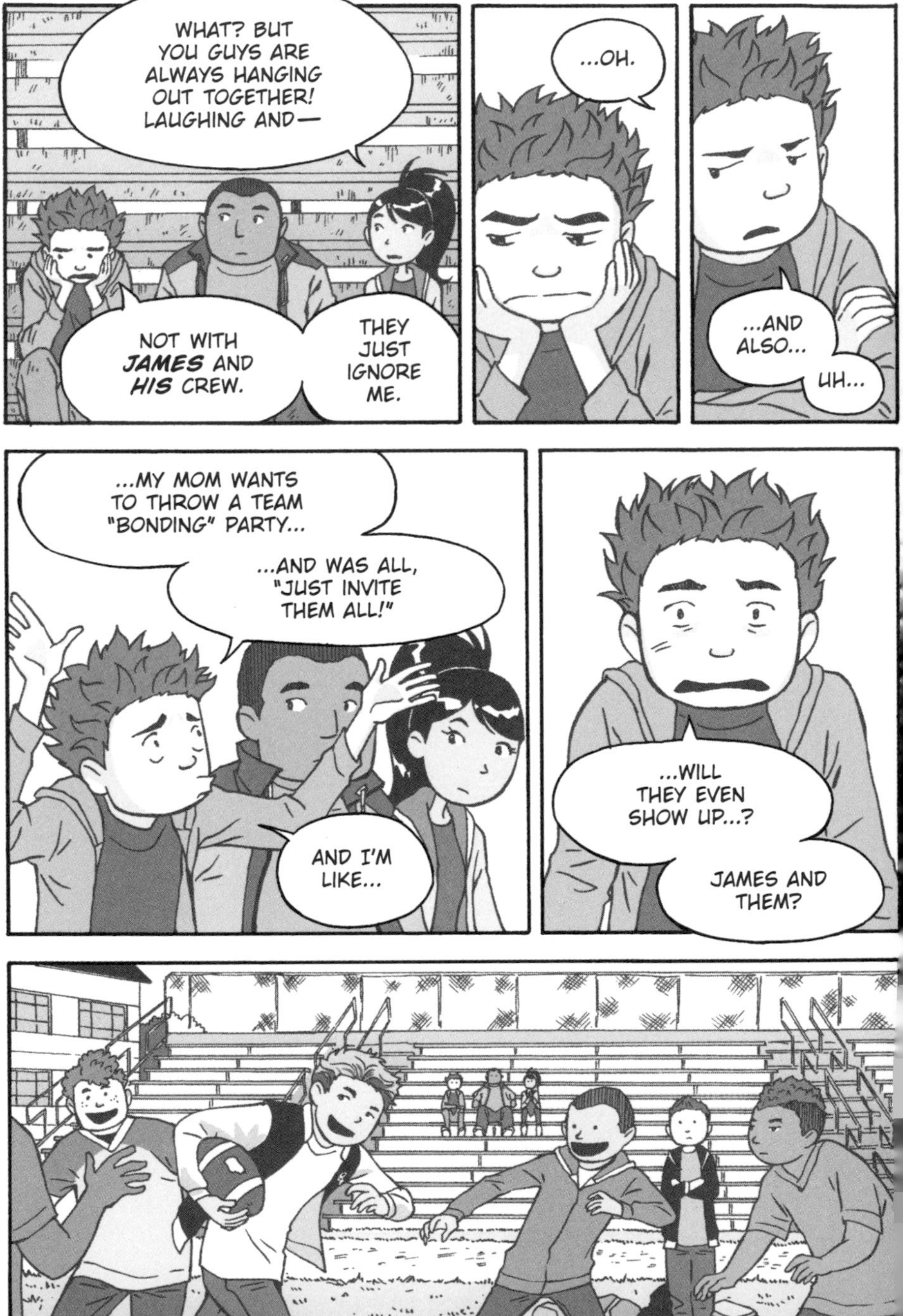
WHAT? BUT YOU GUYS ARE ALWAYS HANGING OUT TOGETHER! LAUGHING AND—
NOT WITH *JAMES* AND *HIS* CREW.
THEY JUST IGNORE ME.
...OH.
...AND ALSO...
UH...
...MY MOM WANTS TO THROW A TEAM "BONDING" PARTY...
...AND WAS ALL, "JUST INVITE THEM ALL!"
AND I'M LIKE...
...WILL THEY EVEN SHOW UP...?
JAMES AND THEM?

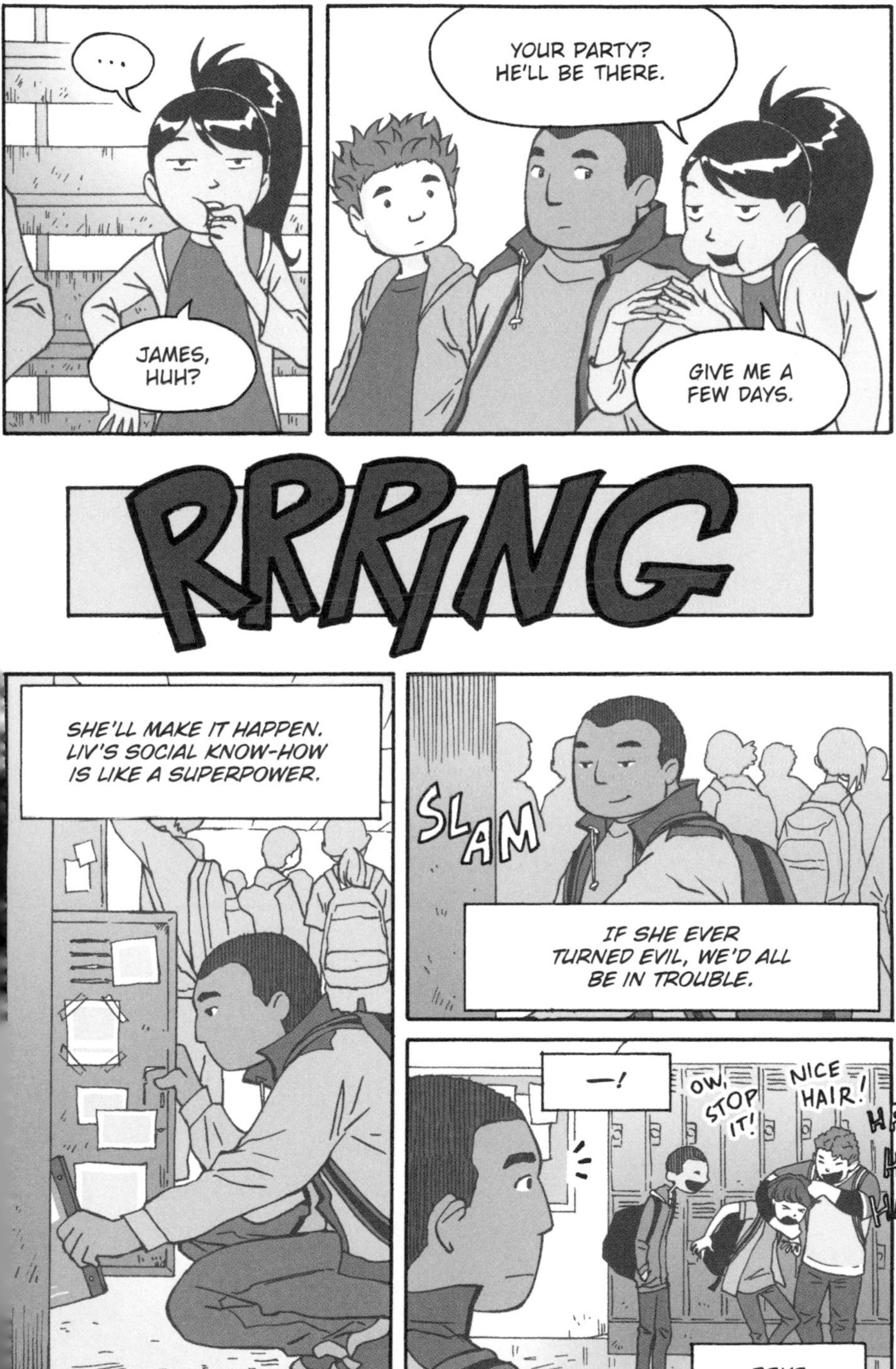
...
JAMES, HUH?
YOUR PARTY? HE'LL BE THERE.
GIVE ME A FEW DAYS.
RRRING
SHE'LL MAKE IT HAPPEN. LIV'S SOCIAL KNOW-HOW IS LIKE A SUPERPOWER.
SLAM
IF SHE EVER TURNED EVIL, WE'D ALL BE IN TROUBLE.
—!
OW, STOP IT!
NICE HAIR!
HA HA HA
ZEKE.

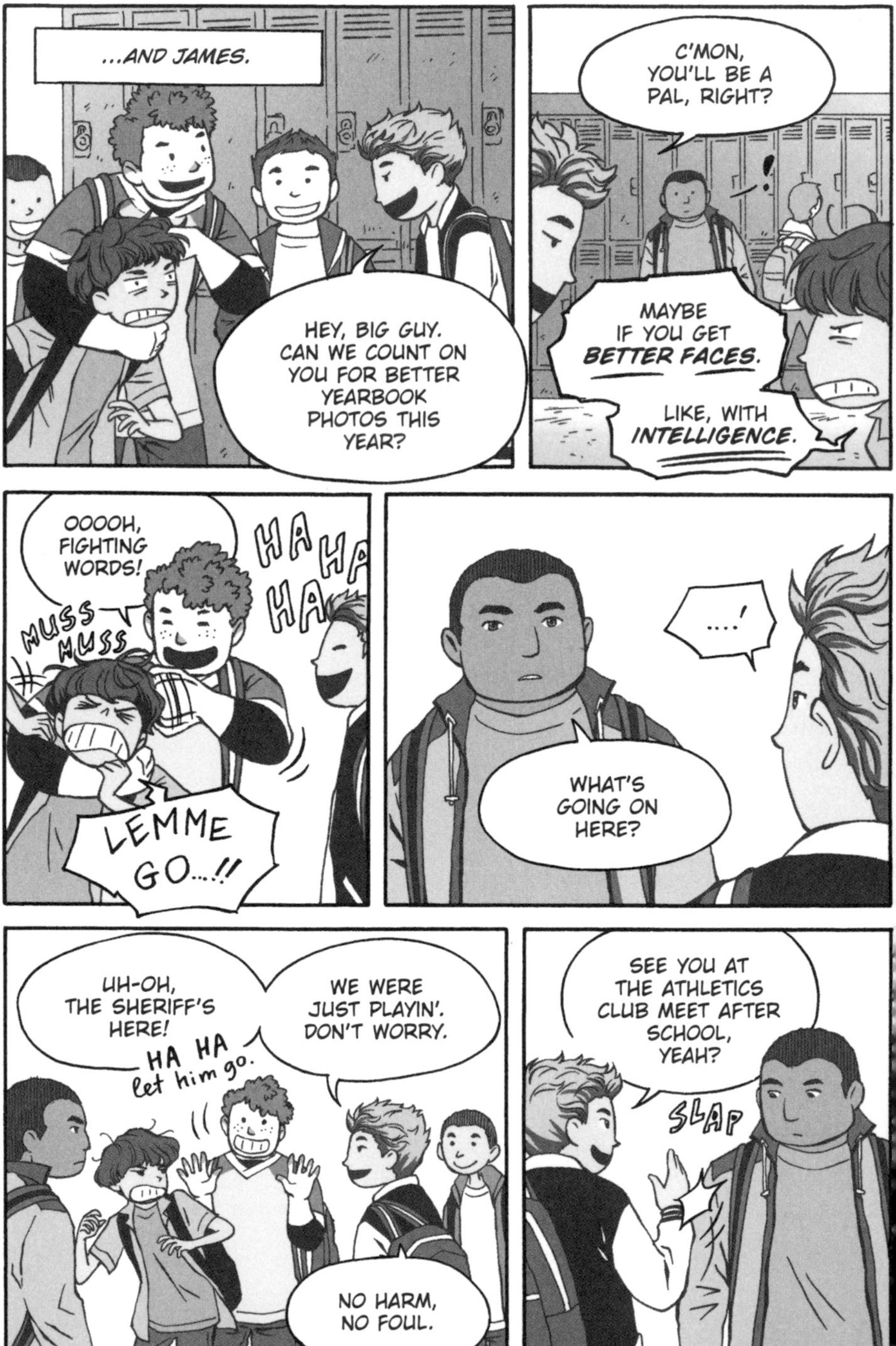
...AND JAMES.
HEY, BIG GUY. CAN WE COUNT ON YOU FOR BETTER YEARBOOK PHOTOS THIS YEAR?
C'MON, YOU'LL BE A PAL, RIGHT?
!
MAYBE IF YOU GET BETTER FACES.
LIKE, WITH INTELLIGENCE.
OOOOH, FIGHTING WORDS!
HA HA HA
MUSS MUSS
LEMME GO...!!
...!
WHAT'S GOING ON HERE?
UH-OH, THE SHERIFF'S HERE!
HA HA
let him go.
WE WERE JUST PLAYIN'. DON'T WORRY.
NO HARM, NO FOUL.
SEE YOU AT THE ATHLETICS CLUB MEET AFTER SCHOOL, YEAH?
SLAP

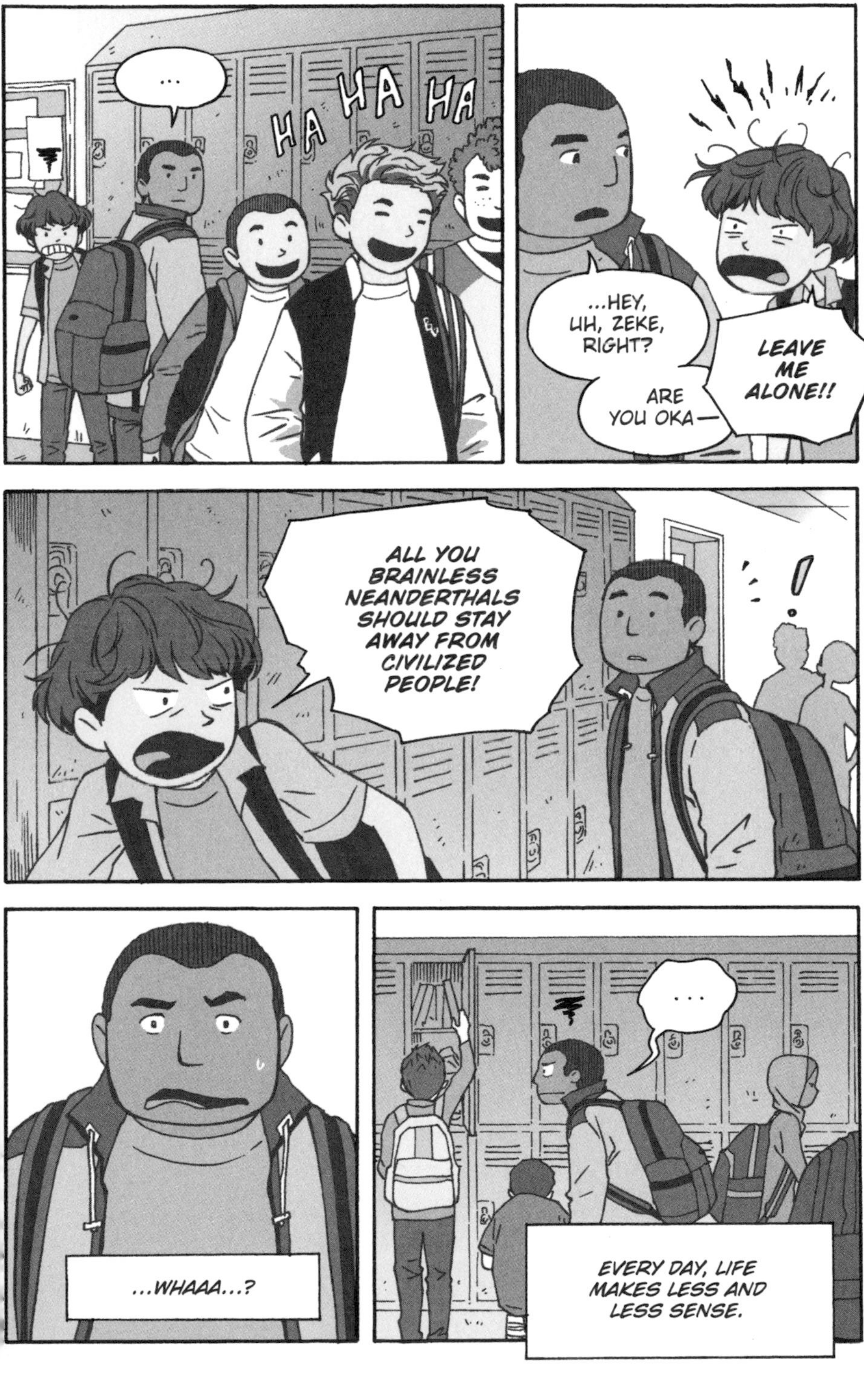
...
HA HA HA HA
...HEY, UH, ZEKE, RIGHT?
ARE YOU OKA—
LEAVE ME ALONE!!
ALL YOU BRAINLESS NEANDERTHALS SHOULD STAY AWAY FROM CIVILIZED PEOPLE!
!
...WHAAA...?
...
EVERY DAY, LIFE MAKES LESS AND LESS SENSE.

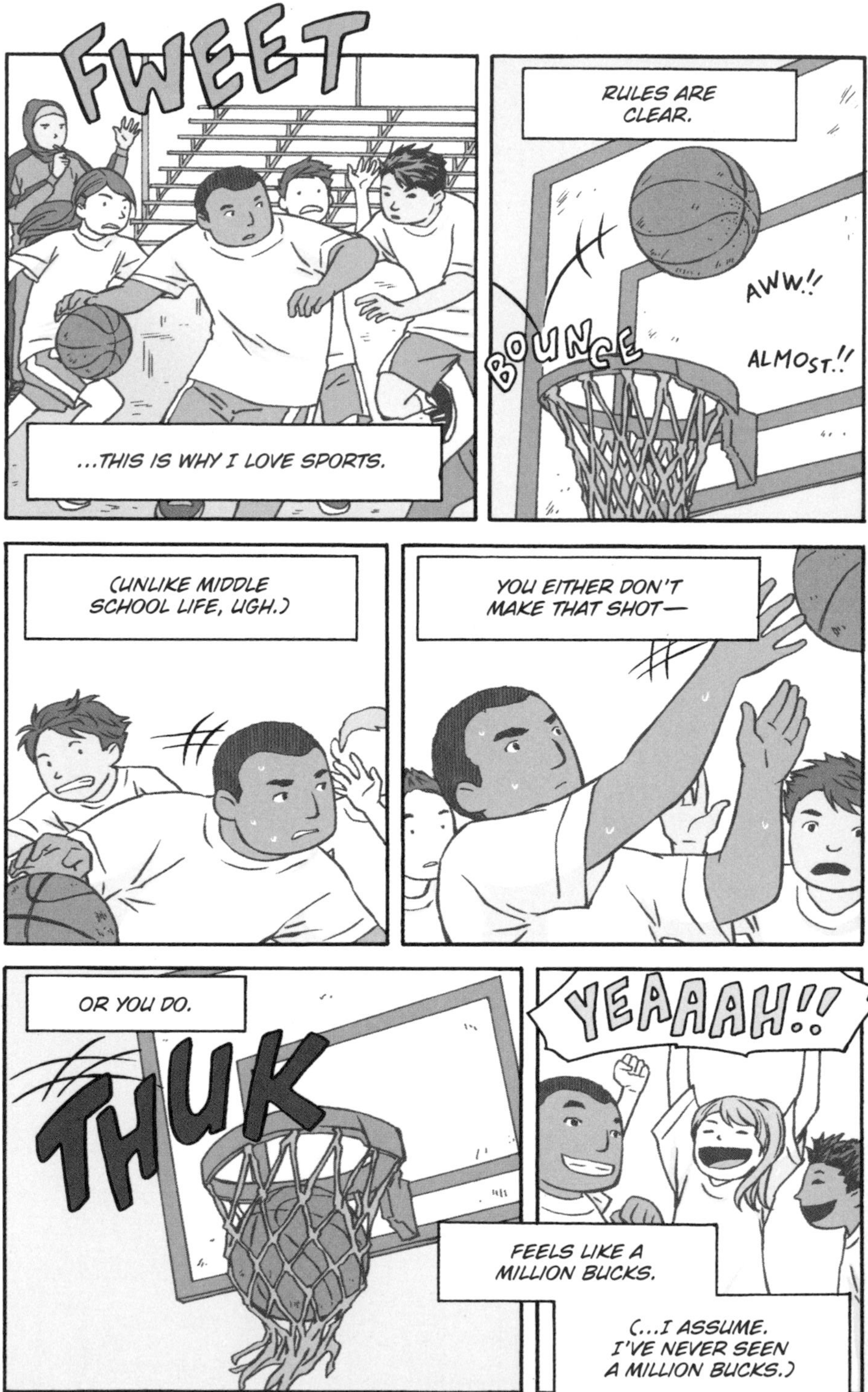
FWEET
...THIS IS WHY I LOVE SPORTS.
RULES ARE CLEAR.
BOUNCE
AWW!!
ALMOST!!
(UNLIKE MIDDLE SCHOOL LIFE, UGH.)
YOU EITHER DON'T MAKE THAT SHOT—
OR YOU DO.
THUK
YEAAAH!!
FEELS LIKE A MILLION BUCKS.
(...I ASSUME. I'VE NEVER SEEN A MILLION BUCKS.)

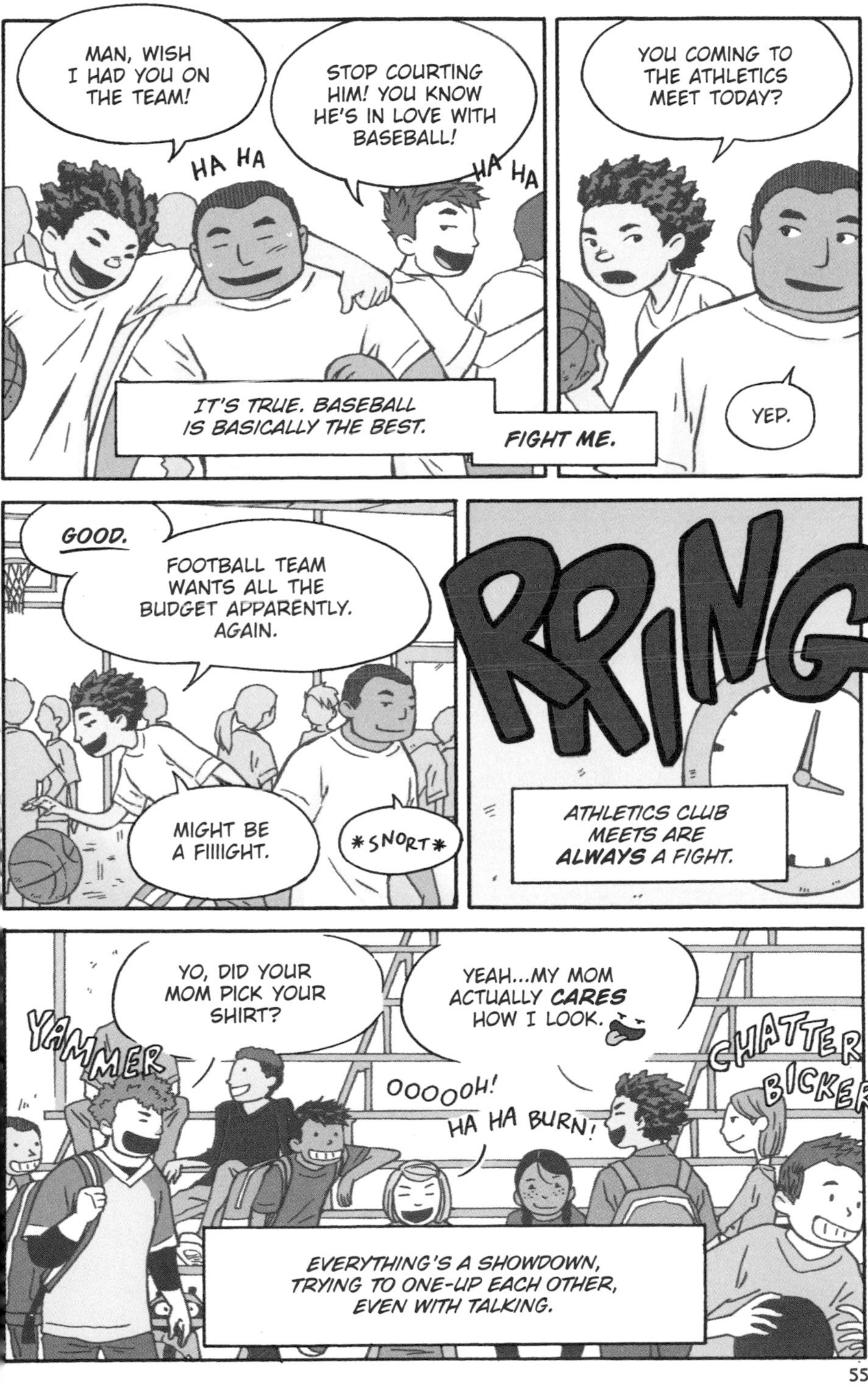
MAN, WISH I HAD YOU ON THE TEAM!
HA HA
STOP COURTING HIM! YOU KNOW HE'S IN LOVE WITH BASEBALL!
HA HA
IT'S TRUE. BASEBALL IS BASICALLY THE BEST.
FIGHT ME.
YOU COMING TO THE ATHLETICS MEET TODAY?
YEP.
GOOD.
FOOTBALL TEAM WANTS ALL THE BUDGET APPARENTLY. AGAIN.
MIGHT BE A FIIIIGHT.
SNORT
RRING
ATHLETICS CLUB MEETS ARE ALWAYS A FIGHT.
YO, DID YOUR MOM PICK YOUR SHIRT?
YEAH...MY MOM ACTUALLY CARES HOW I LOOK.
YAMMER
OOOOOOH!
HA HA BURN!
CHATTER
BICKER
EVERYTHING'S A SHOWDOWN, TRYING TO ONE-UP EACH OTHER, EVEN WITH TALKING.

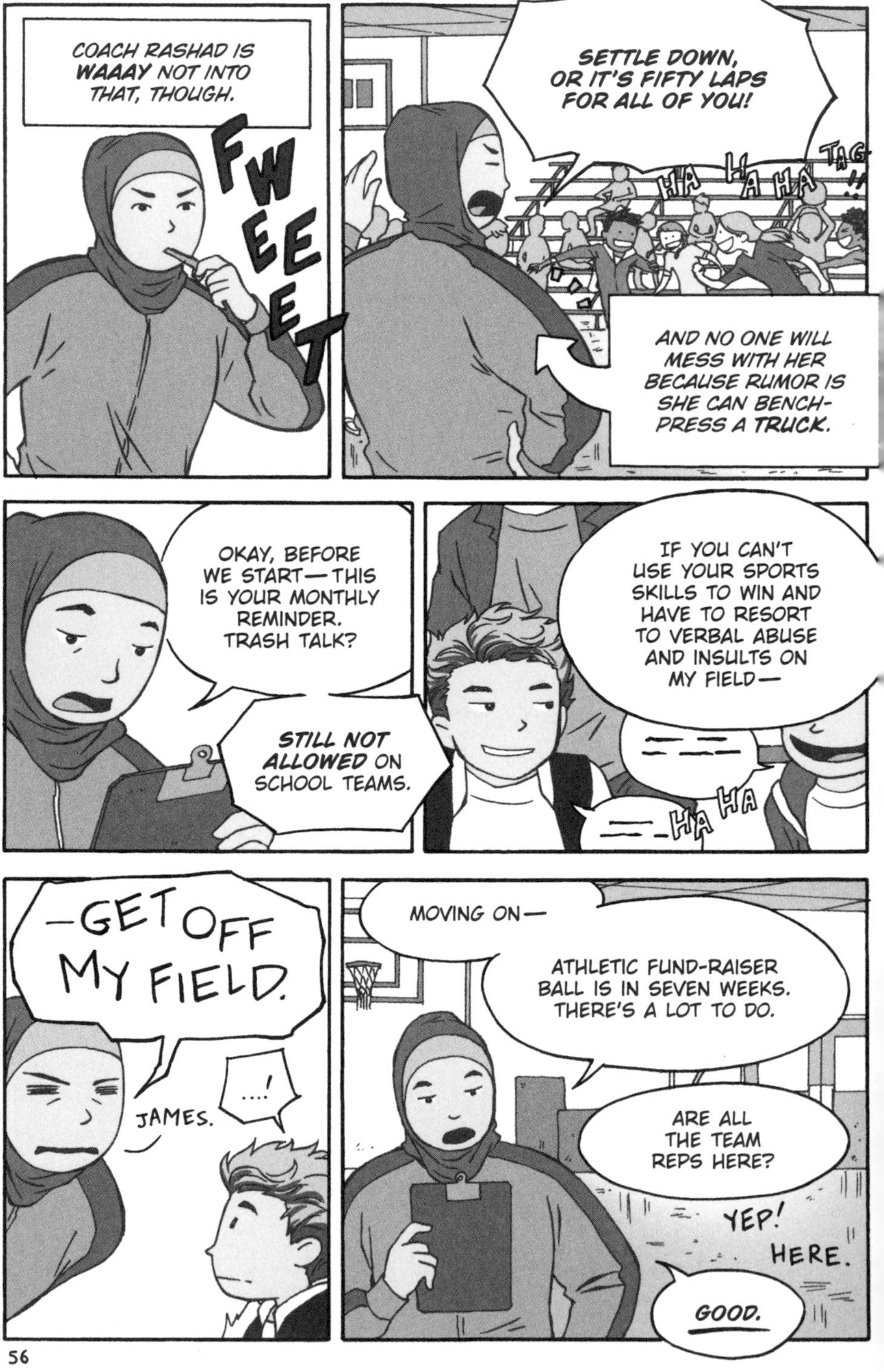
COACH RASHAD IS WAAAY NOT INTO THAT, THOUGH.
FWEEET
SETTLE DOWN, OR IT'S FIFTY LAPS FOR ALL OF YOU!
HA HA HA HA
TAG!!
AND NO ONE WILL MESS WITH HER BECAUSE RUMOR IS SHE CAN BENCH-PRESS A TRUCK.
OKAY, BEFORE WE START—THIS IS YOUR MONTHLY REMINDER. TRASH TALK?
STILL NOT ALLOWED ON SCHOOL TEAMS.
IF YOU CAN'T USE YOUR SPORTS SKILLS TO WIN AND HAVE TO RESORT TO VERBAL ABUSE AND INSULTS ON MY FIELD—
HA HA
—GET OFF MY FIELD.
JAMES.
....!
MOVING ON—
ATHLETIC FUND-RAISER BALL IS IN SEVEN WEEKS. THERE'S A LOT TO DO.
ARE ALL THE TEAM REPS HERE?
YEP!
HERE.
GOOD.

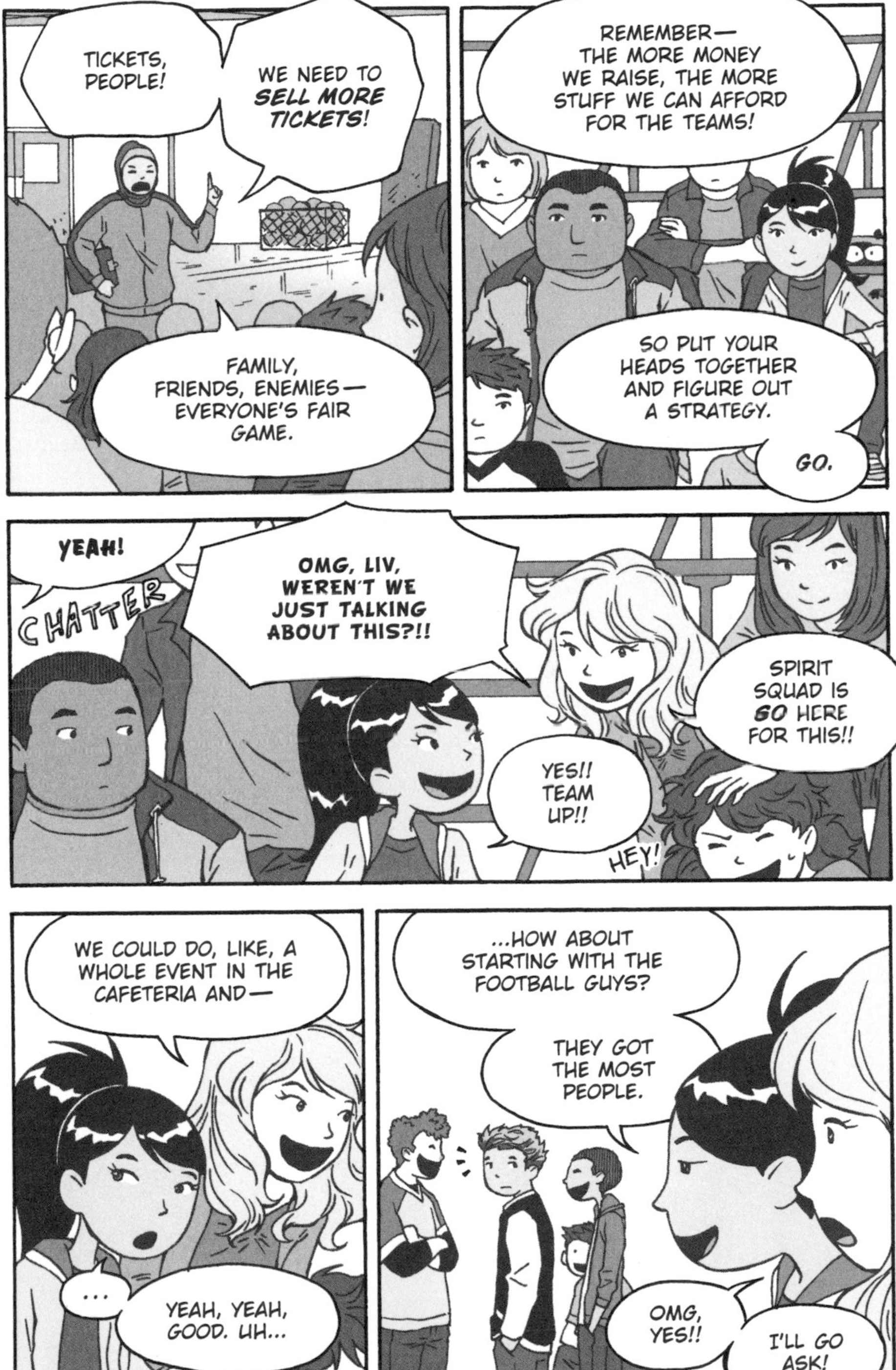
TICKETS, PEOPLE!
WE NEED TO SELL MORE TICKETS!
FAMILY, FRIENDS, ENEMIES— EVERYONE'S FAIR GAME.
REMEMBER— THE MORE MONEY WE RAISE, THE MORE STUFF WE CAN AFFORD FOR THE TEAMS!
SO PUT YOUR HEADS TOGETHER AND FIGURE OUT A STRATEGY.
GO.
YEAH!
CHATTER
OMG, LIV, WEREN'T WE JUST TALKING ABOUT THIS?!!
SPIRIT SQUAD IS SO HERE FOR THIS!!
YES!! TEAM UP!!
HEY!
WE COULD DO, LIKE, A WHOLE EVENT IN THE CAFETERIA AND—
...
YEAH, YEAH, GOOD. UH...
...HOW ABOUT STARTING WITH THE FOOTBALL GUYS?
THEY GOT THE MOST PEOPLE.
OMG, YES!!
I'LL GO ASK!

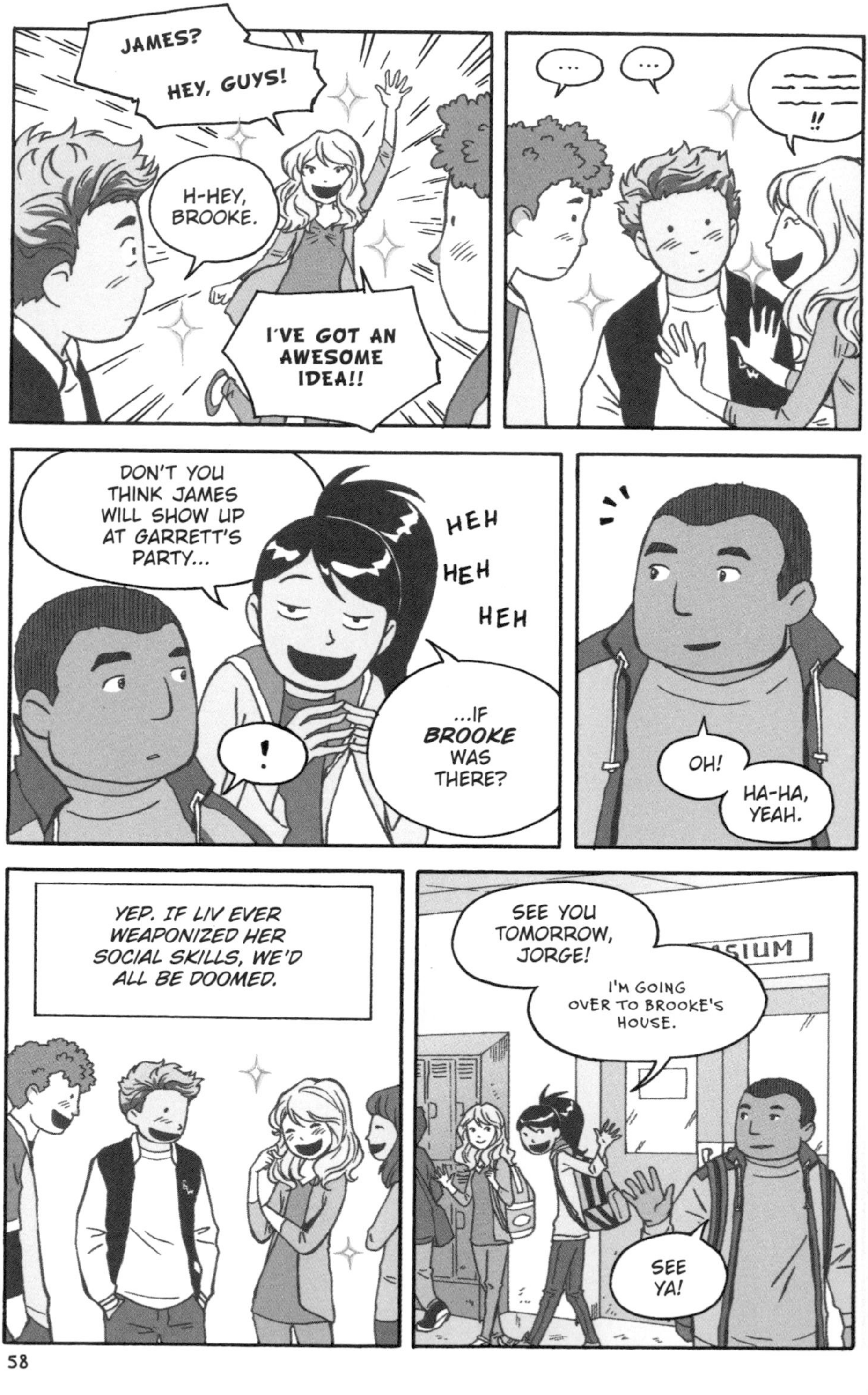
JAMES?
HEY, GUYS!
H-HEY, BROOKE.
I'VE GOT AN AWESOME IDEA!!
...
...
!!
DON'T YOU THINK JAMES WILL SHOW UP AT GARRETT'S PARTY...
HEH
HEH
HEH
!
...IF *BROOKE* WAS THERE?
OH!
HA-HA, YEAH.
YEP. IF LIV EVER WEAPONIZED HER SOCIAL SKILLS, WE'D ALL BE DOOMED.
SEE YOU TOMORROW, JORGE!
I'M GOING OVER TO BROOKE'S HOUSE.
SEE YA!

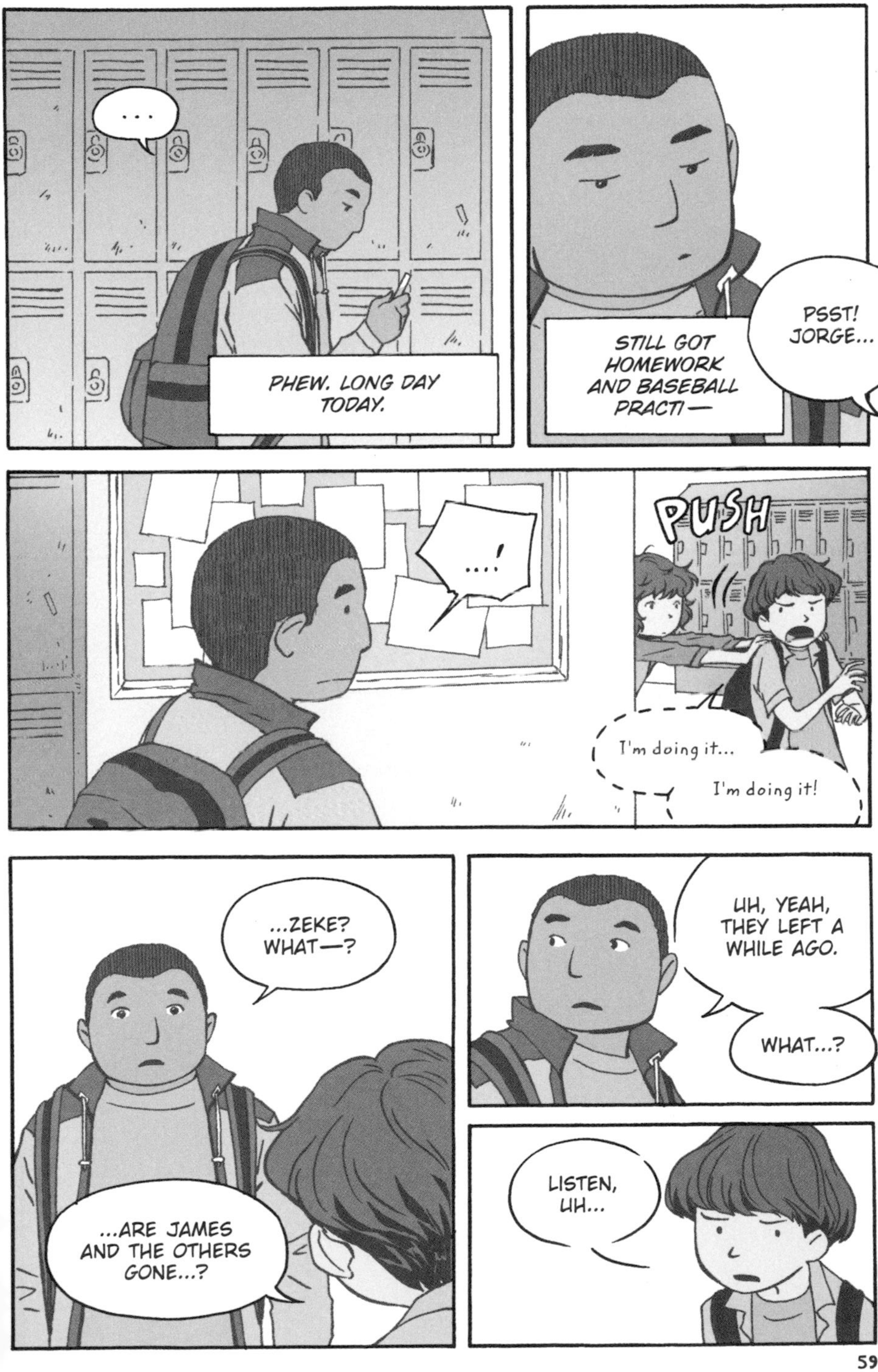
. . .
PHEW. LONG DAY TODAY.
STILL GOT HOMEWORK AND BASEBALL PRACTI—
PSST! JORGE...
...!
PUSH
I'm doing it...
I'm doing it!
...ZEKE? WHAT—?
...ARE JAMES AND THE OTHERS GONE...?
UH, YEAH, THEY LEFT A WHILE AGO.
WHAT...?
LISTEN, UH...

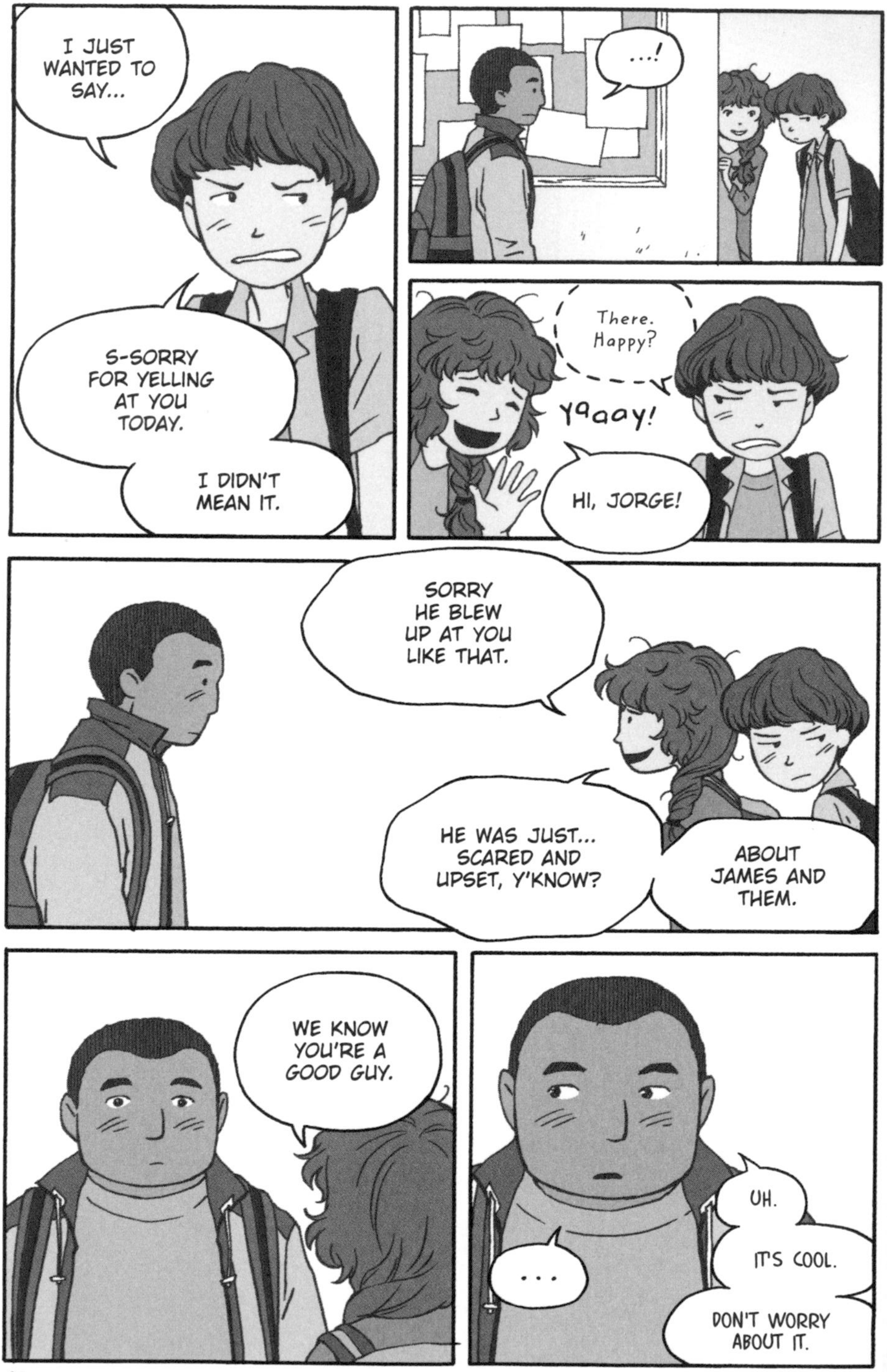
I JUST WANTED TO SAY...
S-SORRY FOR YELLING AT YOU TODAY.
I DIDN'T MEAN IT.
...!
There. Happy?
Yaaay!
HI, JORGE!
SORRY HE BLEW UP AT YOU LIKE THAT.
HE WAS JUST... SCARED AND UPSET, Y'KNOW?
ABOUT JAMES AND THEM.
WE KNOW YOU'RE A GOOD GUY.
...
UH.
IT'S COOL.
DON'T WORRY ABOUT IT.

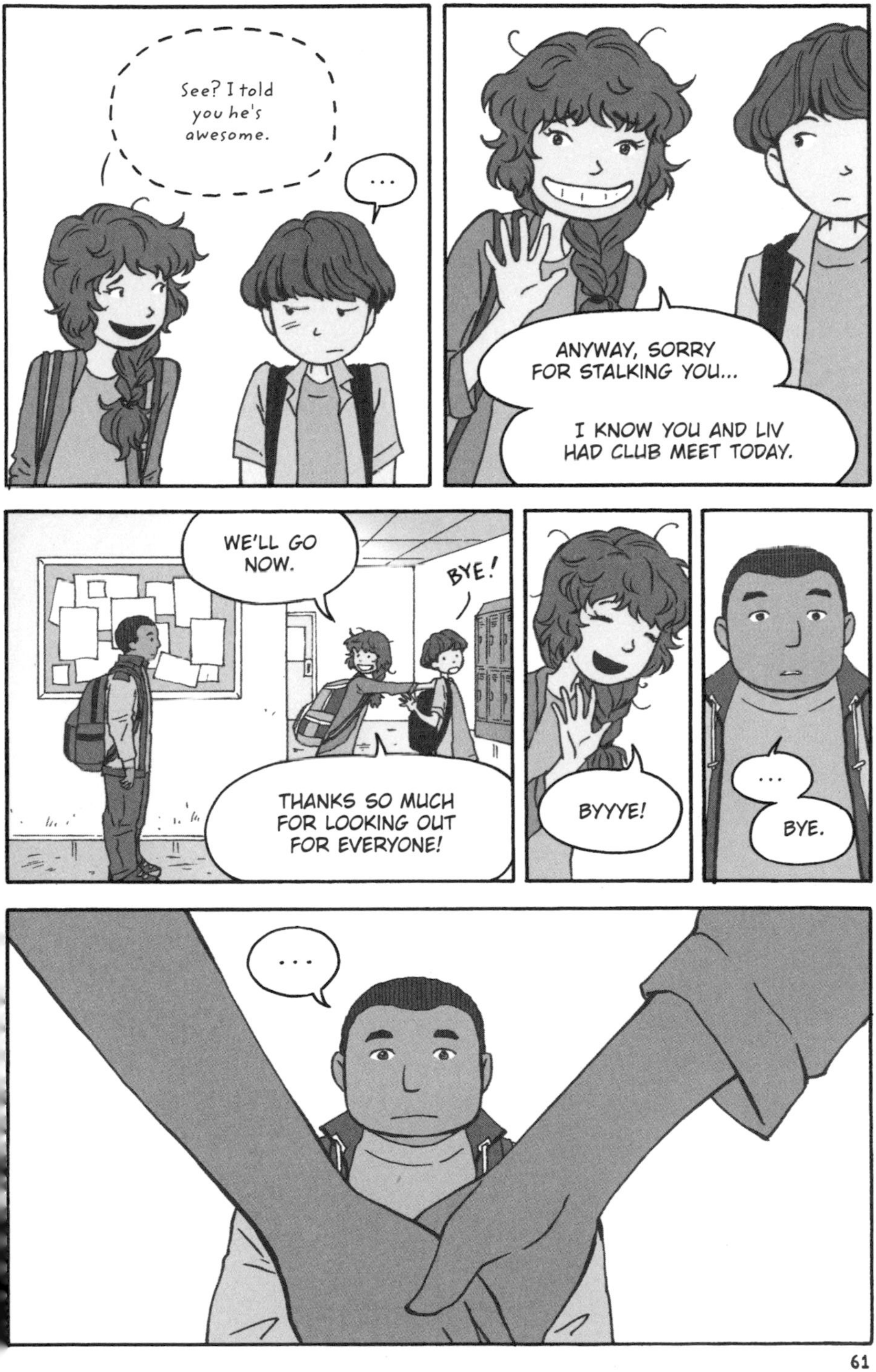
See? I told you he's awesome.
...
ANYWAY, SORRY FOR STALKING YOU...
I KNOW YOU AND LIV HAD CLUB MEET TODAY.
WE'LL GO NOW.
BYE!
THANKS SO MUCH FOR LOOKING OUT FOR EVERYONE!
BYYYE!
...
BYE.
...

CHAPTER 4

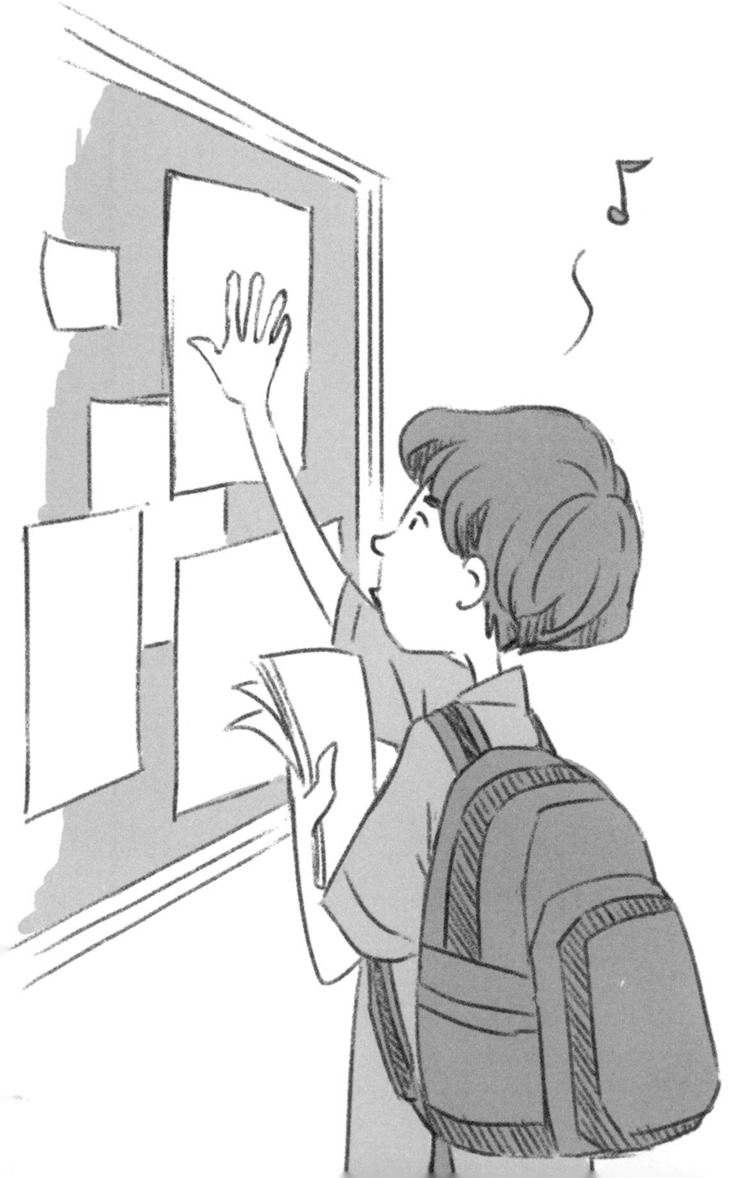

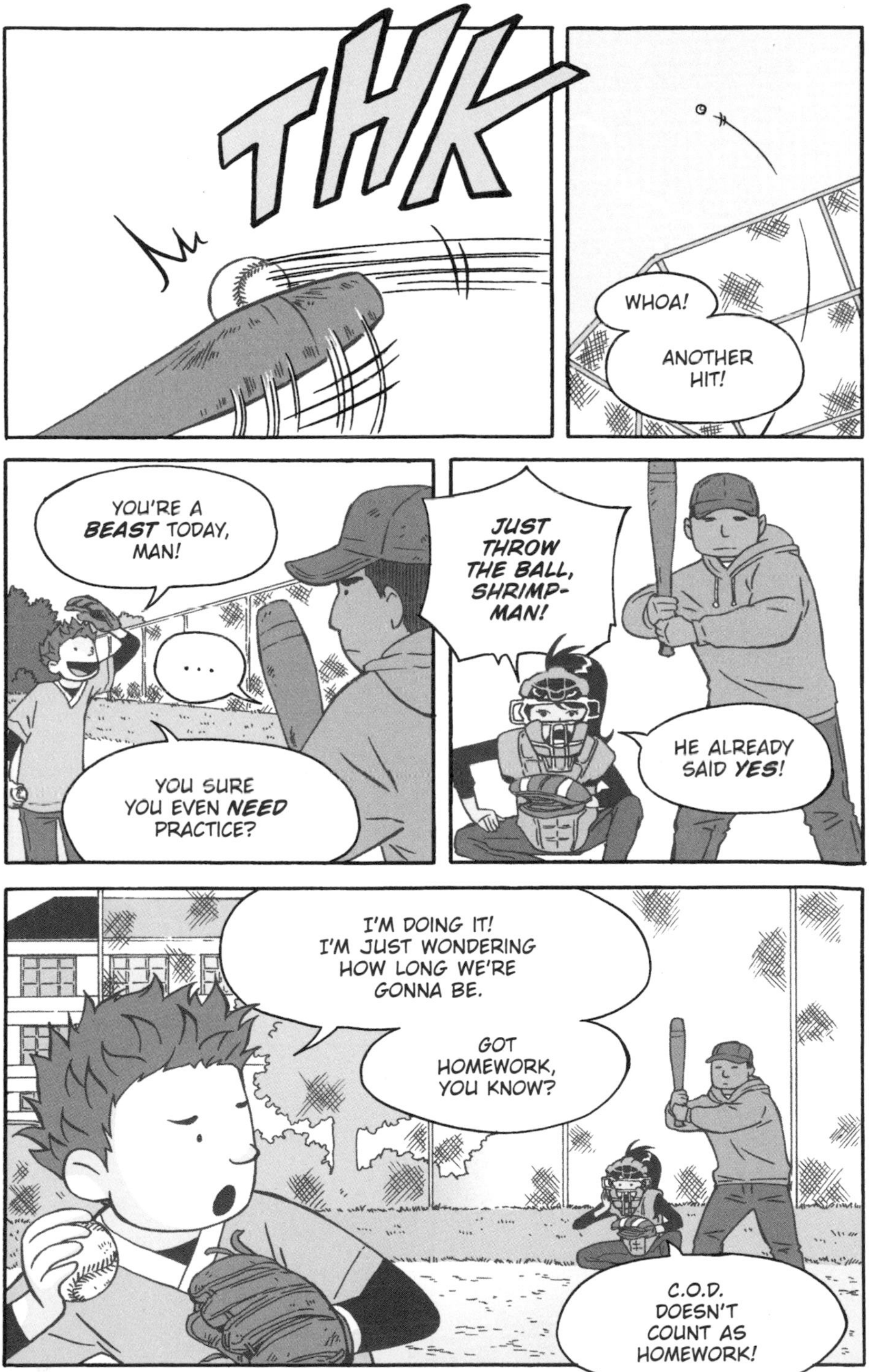
THK
WHOA!
ANOTHER HIT!
YOU'RE A **BEAST** TODAY, MAN!
...
YOU SURE YOU EVEN **NEED** PRACTICE?
JUST THROW THE BALL, SHRIMP-MAN!
HE ALREADY SAID **YES**!
I'M DOING IT! I'M JUST WONDERING HOW LONG WE'RE GONNA BE.
GOT HOMEWORK, YOU KNOW?
C.O.D. DOESN'T COUNT AS HOMEWORK!

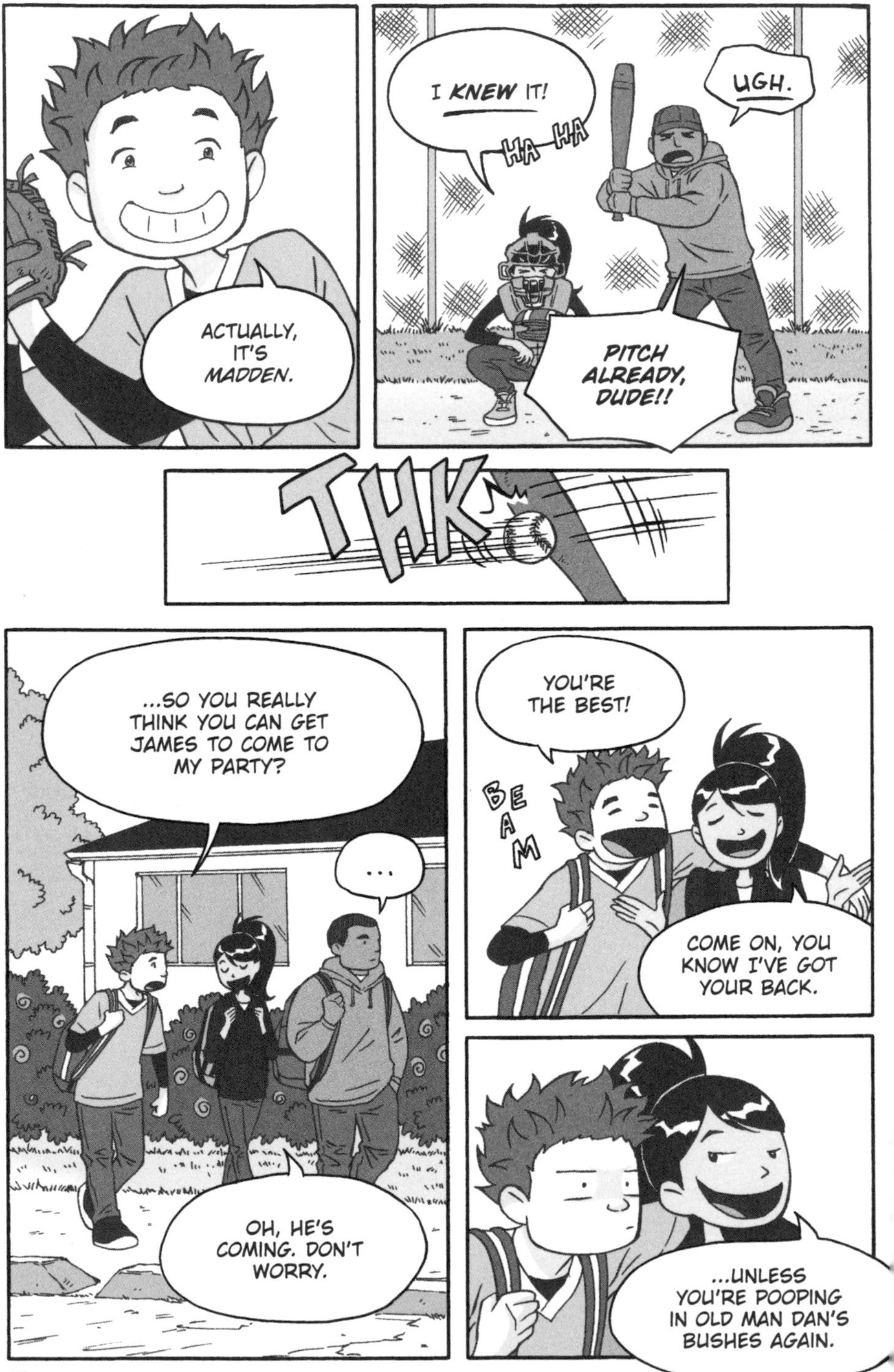
ACTUALLY, IT'S MADDEN.
I KNEW IT!
HA HA
UGH.
PITCH ALREADY, DUDE!!
THK
...SO YOU REALLY THINK YOU CAN GET JAMES TO COME TO MY PARTY?
...
OH, HE'S COMING. DON'T WORRY.
YOU'RE THE BEST!
BEAM
COME ON, YOU KNOW I'VE GOT YOUR BACK.
...UNLESS YOU'RE POOPING IN OLD MAN DAN'S BUSHES AGAIN.

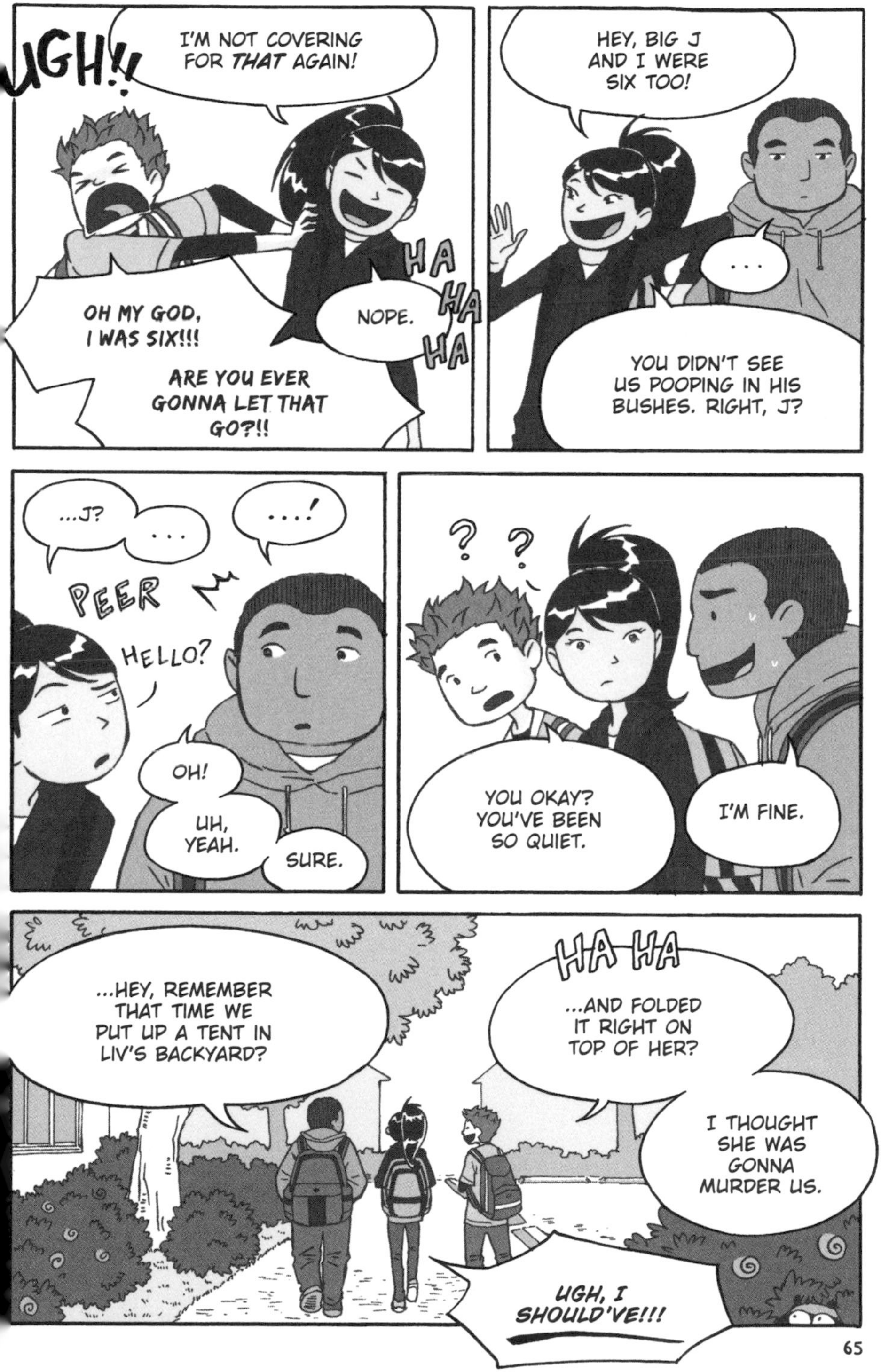
UGH!!
I'M NOT COVERING FOR *THAT* AGAIN!
OH MY GOD, I WAS SIX!!!
ARE YOU EVER GONNA LET THAT GO?!!
NOPE.
HA HA HA
HEY, BIG J AND I WERE SIX TOO!
. . .
YOU DIDN'T SEE US POOPING IN HIS BUSHES. RIGHT, J?
...J?
. . .
. . . !
PEER
HELLO?
OH!
UH, YEAH.
SURE.
? ?
YOU OKAY? YOU'VE BEEN SO QUIET.
I'M FINE.
...HEY, REMEMBER THAT TIME WE PUT UP A TENT IN LIV'S BACKYARD?
HA HA
...AND FOLDED IT RIGHT ON TOP OF HER?
I THOUGHT SHE WAS GONNA MURDER US.
UGH, I SHOULD'VE!!!

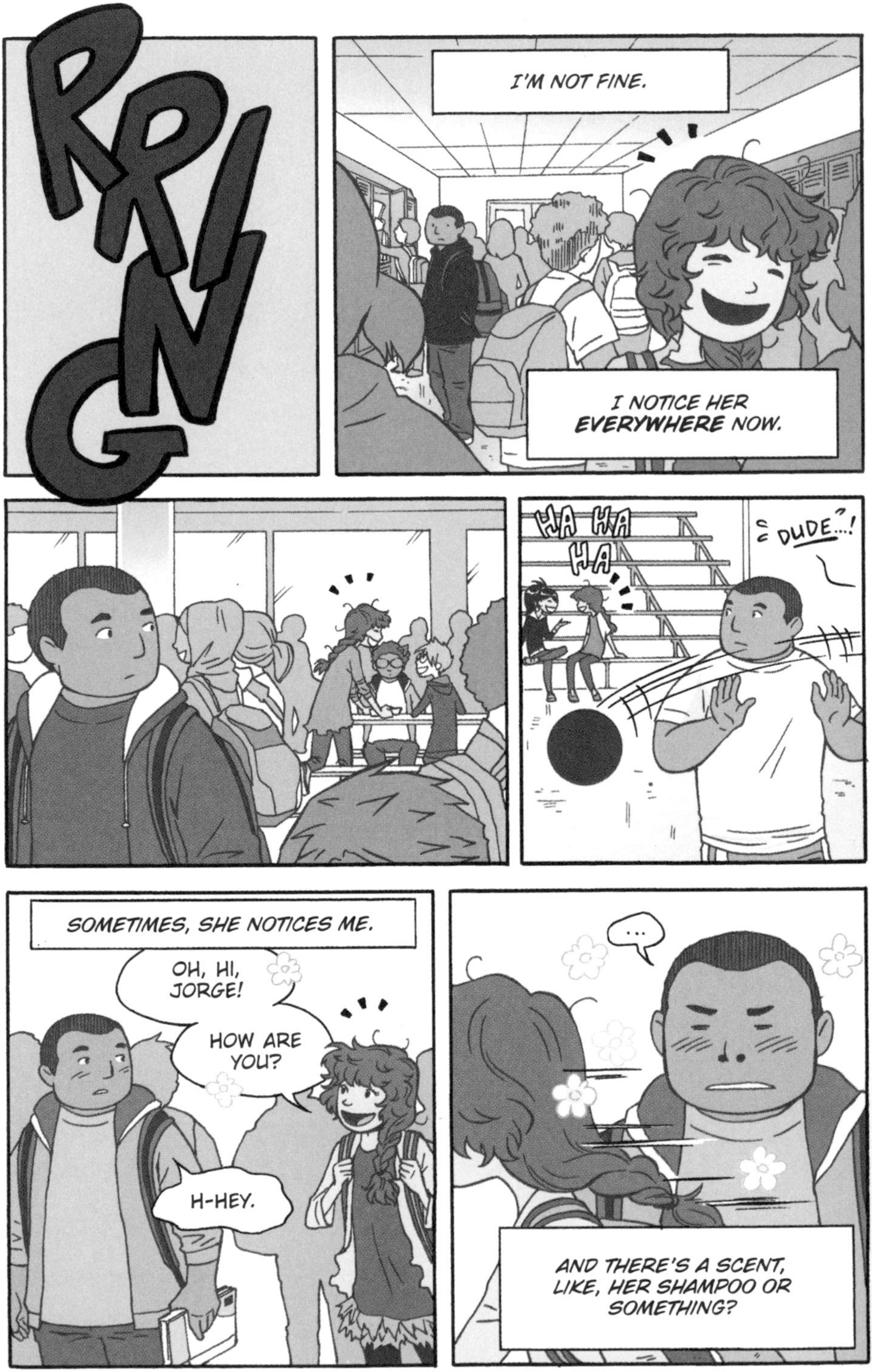
RRING
I'M NOT FINE.
I NOTICE HER EVERYWHERE NOW.
HA HA HA
DUDE...!
SOMETIMES, SHE NOTICES ME.
OH, HI, JORGE!
HOW ARE YOU?
H-HEY.
...
AND THERE'S A SCENT, LIKE, HER SHAMPOO OR SOMETHING?

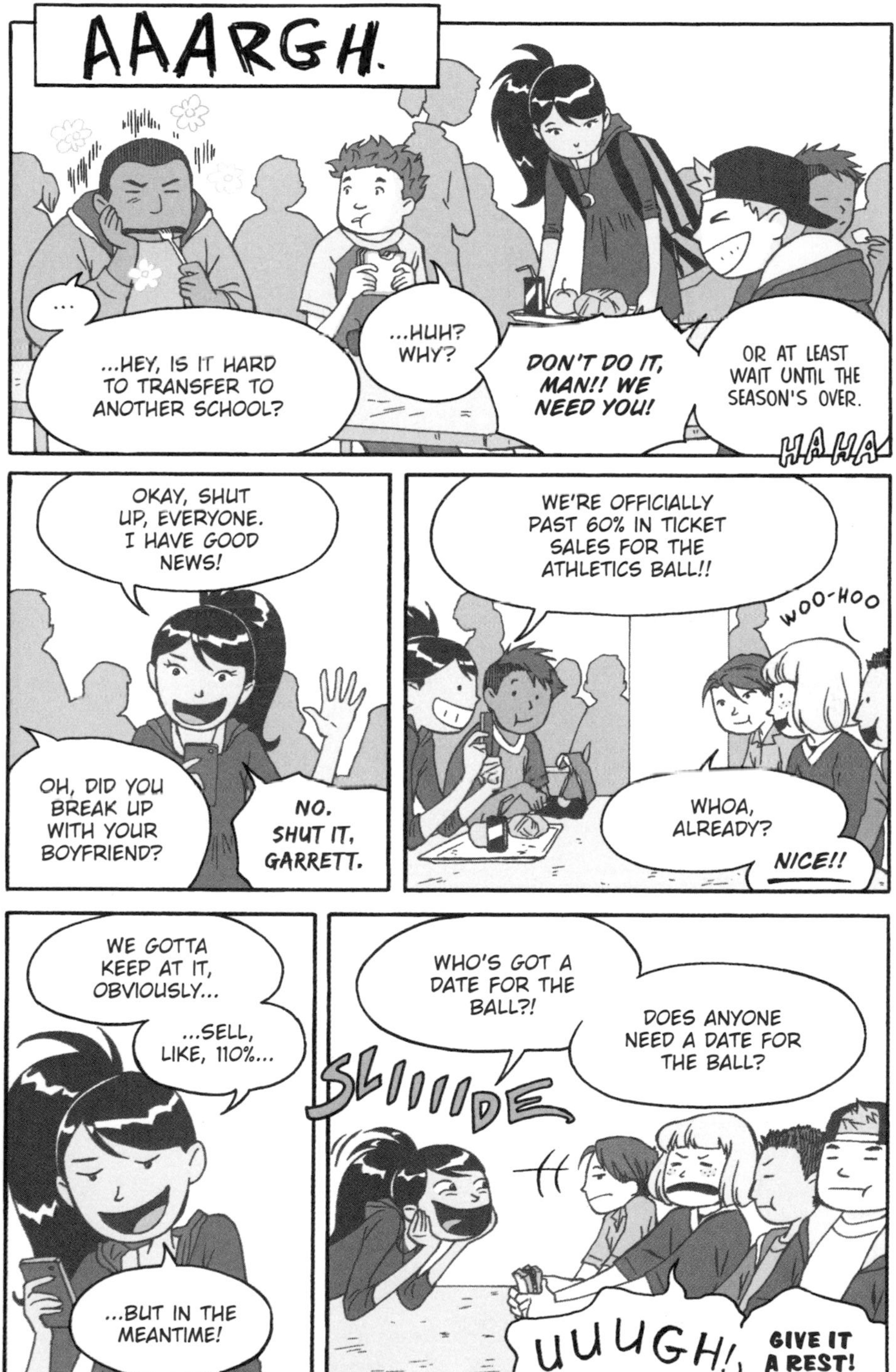
AAARGH.
...
...HEY, IS IT HARD TO TRANSFER TO ANOTHER SCHOOL?
...HUH? WHY?
DON'T DO IT, MAN!! WE NEED YOU!
OR AT LEAST WAIT UNTIL THE SEASON'S OVER.
HAHA
OKAY, SHUT UP, EVERYONE. I HAVE GOOD NEWS!
OH, DID YOU BREAK UP WITH YOUR BOYFRIEND?
NO. SHUT IT, GARRETT.
WE'RE OFFICIALLY PAST 60% IN TICKET SALES FOR THE ATHLETICS BALL!!
WOO-HOO
WHOA, ALREADY?
NICE!!
WE GOTTA KEEP AT IT, OBVIOUSLY...
...SELL, LIKE, 110%...
...BUT IN THE MEANTIME!
SLIIIIDE
WHO'S GOT A DATE FOR THE BALL?!
DOES ANYONE NEED A DATE FOR THE BALL?
UUUGH!
GIVE IT A REST!

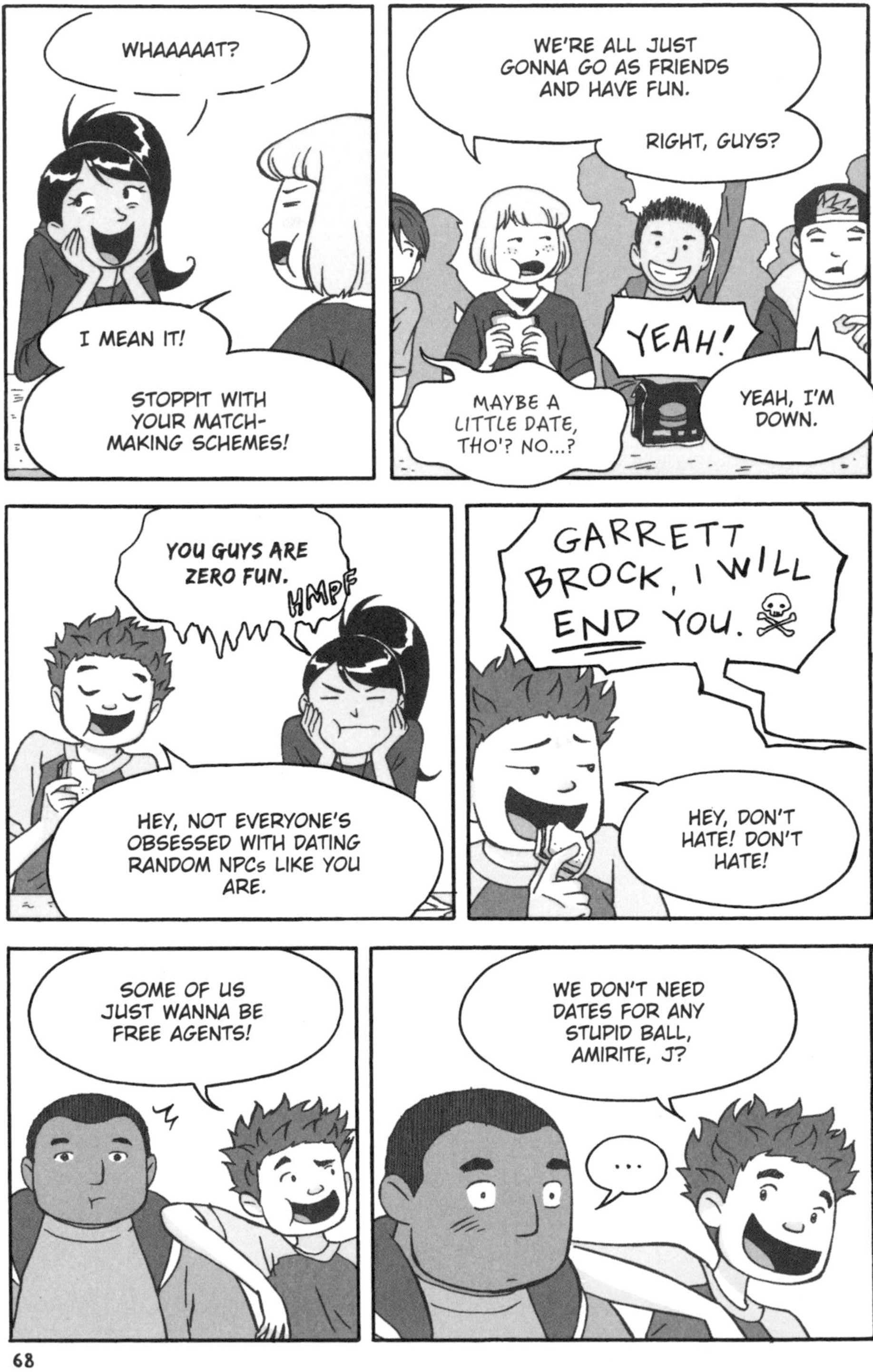
WHAAAAAT?
I MEAN IT!
STOPPIT WITH YOUR MATCH-MAKING SCHEMES!
WE'RE ALL JUST GONNA GO AS FRIENDS AND HAVE FUN.
RIGHT, GUYS?
YEAH!
MAYBE A LITTLE DATE, THO'? NO...?
YEAH, I'M DOWN.
YOU GUYS ARE ZERO FUN.
HMPF
HEY, NOT EVERYONE'S OBSESSED WITH DATING RANDOM NPCs LIKE YOU ARE.
GARRETT BROCK, I WILL END YOU.
HEY, DON'T HATE! DON'T HATE!
SOME OF US JUST WANNA BE FREE AGENTS!
WE DON'T NEED DATES FOR ANY STUPID BALL, AMIRITE, J?
...

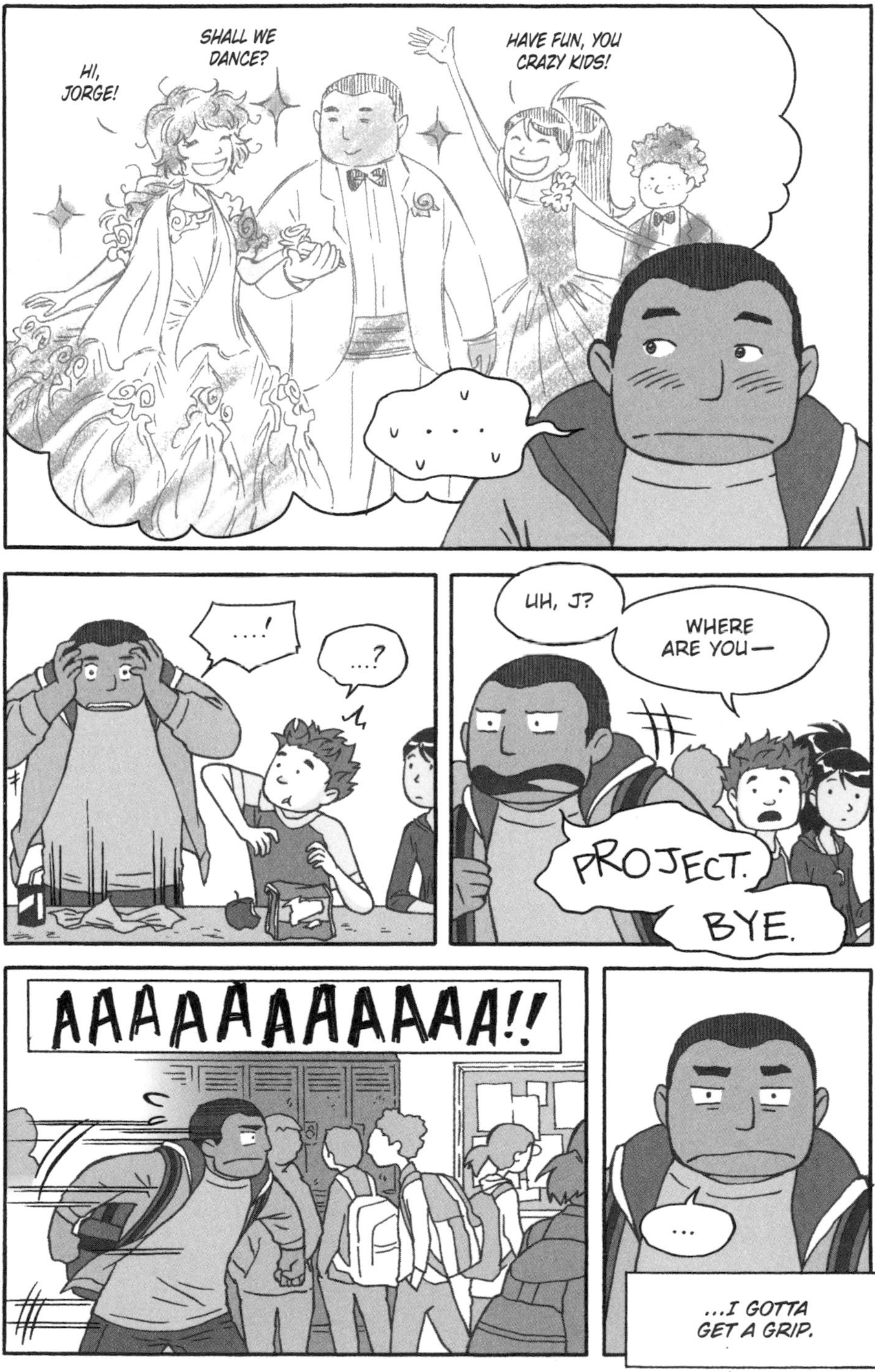
HI, JORGE!
SHALL WE DANCE?
HAVE FUN, YOU CRAZY KIDS!
...
...!
...?
UH, J?
WHERE ARE YOU—
PROJECT.
BYE.
AAAAAAAAAAA!!
...
...I GOTTA GET A GRIP.

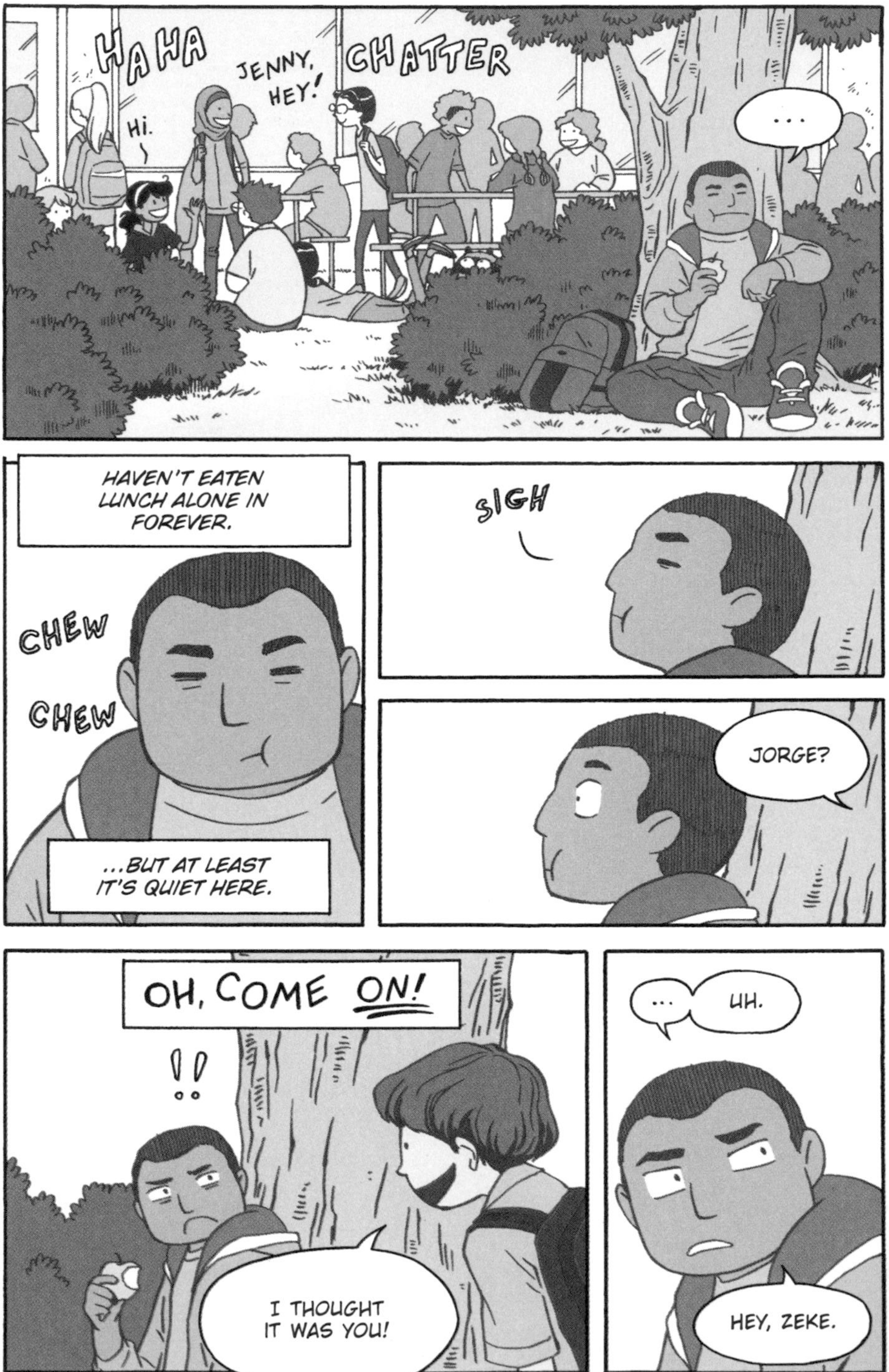
HAHA
JENNY, HEY!
CHATTER
HI.
...
HAVEN'T EATEN LUNCH ALONE IN FOREVER.
CHEW
CHEW
...BUT AT LEAST IT'S QUIET HERE.
SIGH
JORGE?
OH, COME ON!
!!
I THOUGHT IT WAS YOU!
...
UH.
HEY, ZEKE.

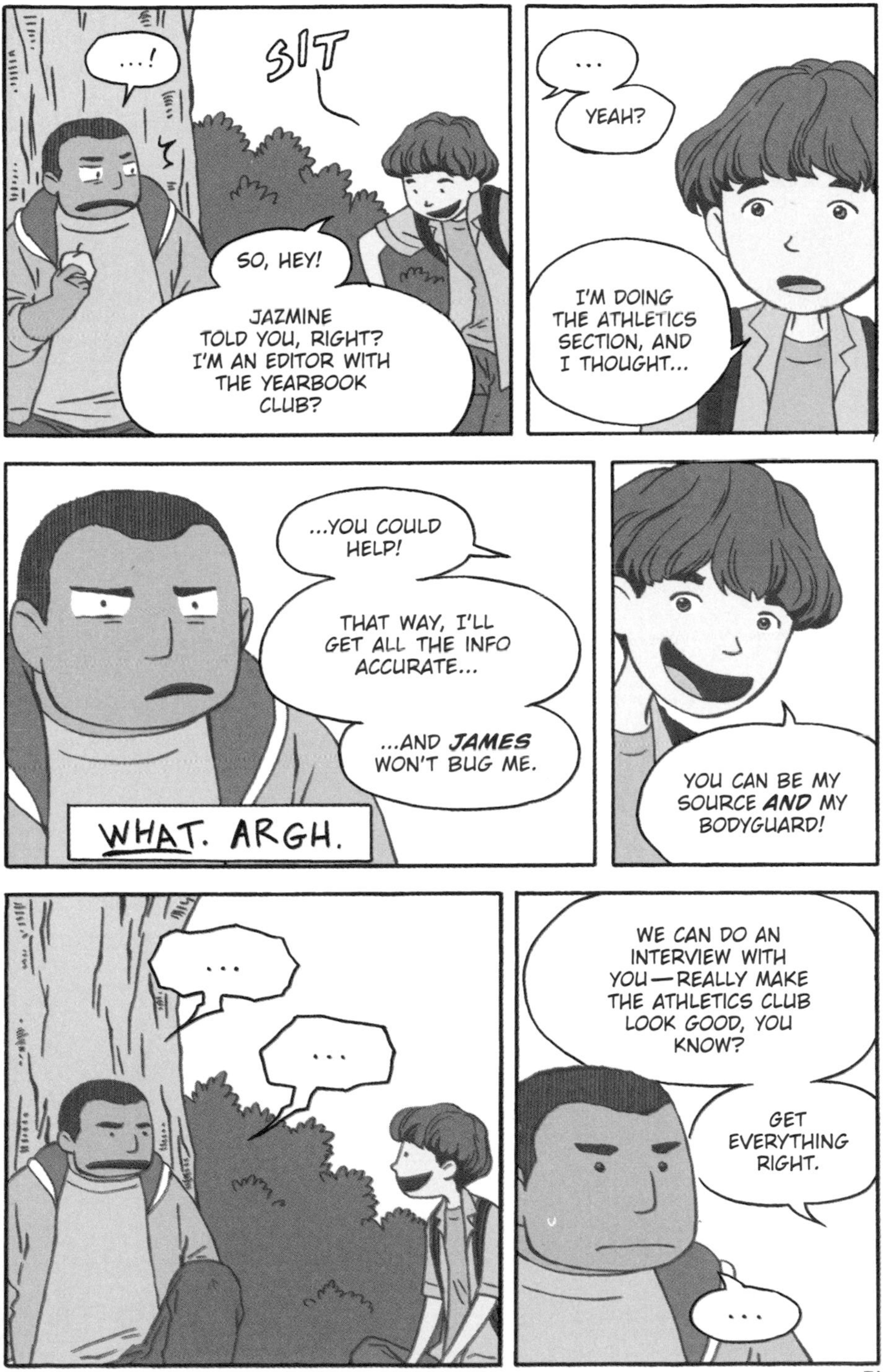
...!
SIT
SO, HEY!
JAZMINE TOLD YOU, RIGHT? I'M AN EDITOR WITH THE YEARBOOK CLUB?
...
YEAH?
I'M DOING THE ATHLETICS SECTION, AND I THOUGHT...
...YOU COULD HELP!
THAT WAY, I'LL GET ALL THE INFO ACCURATE...
...AND JAMES WON'T BUG ME.
WHAT. ARGH.
YOU CAN BE MY SOURCE AND MY BODYGUARD!
...
...
WE CAN DO AN INTERVIEW WITH YOU—REALLY MAKE THE ATHLETICS CLUB LOOK GOOD, YOU KNOW?
GET EVERYTHING RIGHT.
...

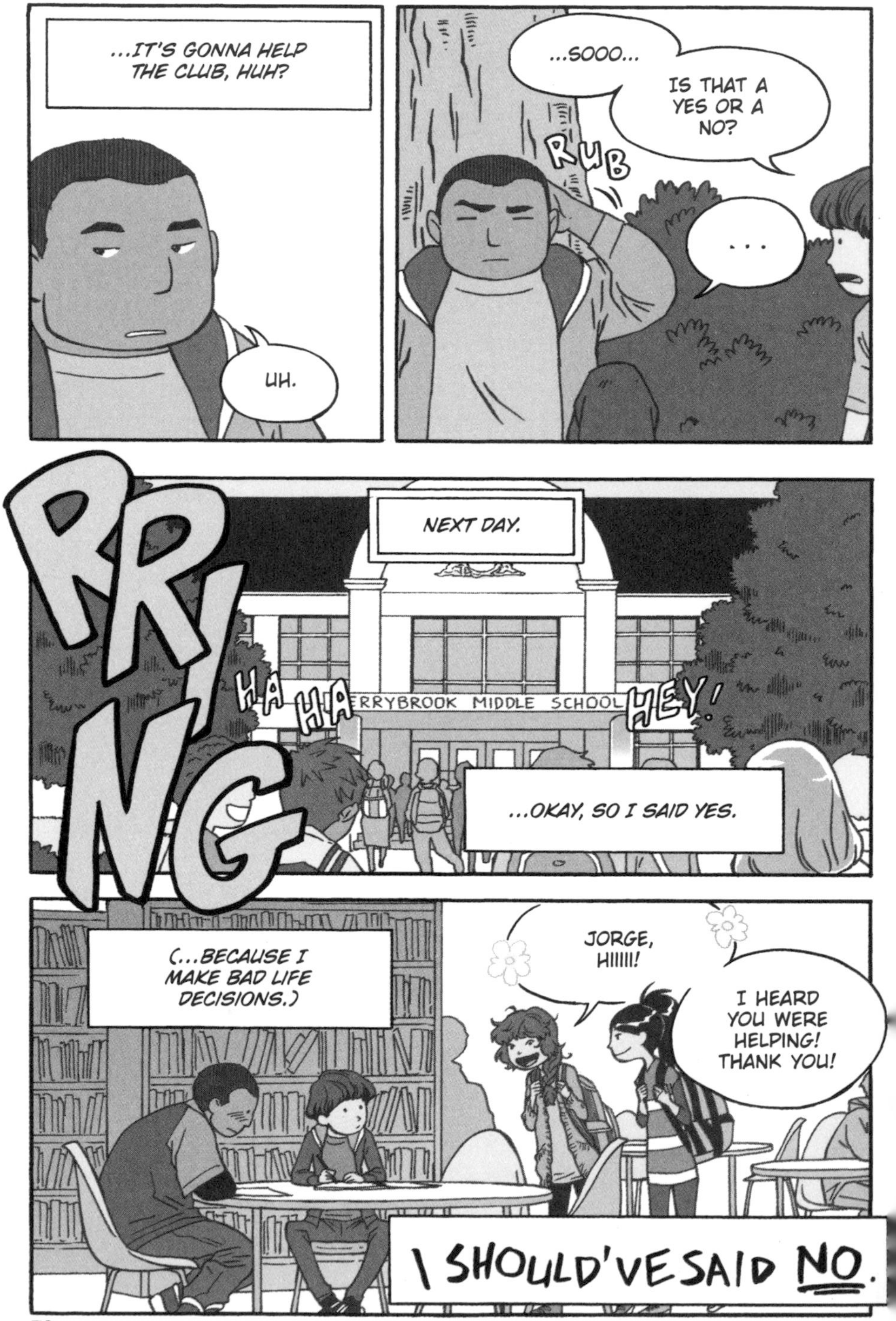
...IT'S GONNA HELP THE CLUB, HUH?
UH.
...SOOO...
IS THAT A YES OR A NO?
RUB
. . .
PRRING
NEXT DAY.
HA
HA
ERRYBROOK MIDDLE SCHOOL
HEY!
...OKAY, SO I SAID YES.
(...BECAUSE I MAKE BAD LIFE DECISIONS.)
JORGE, HIIIII!
I HEARD YOU WERE HELPING! THANK YOU!
I SHOULD'VE SAID NO.

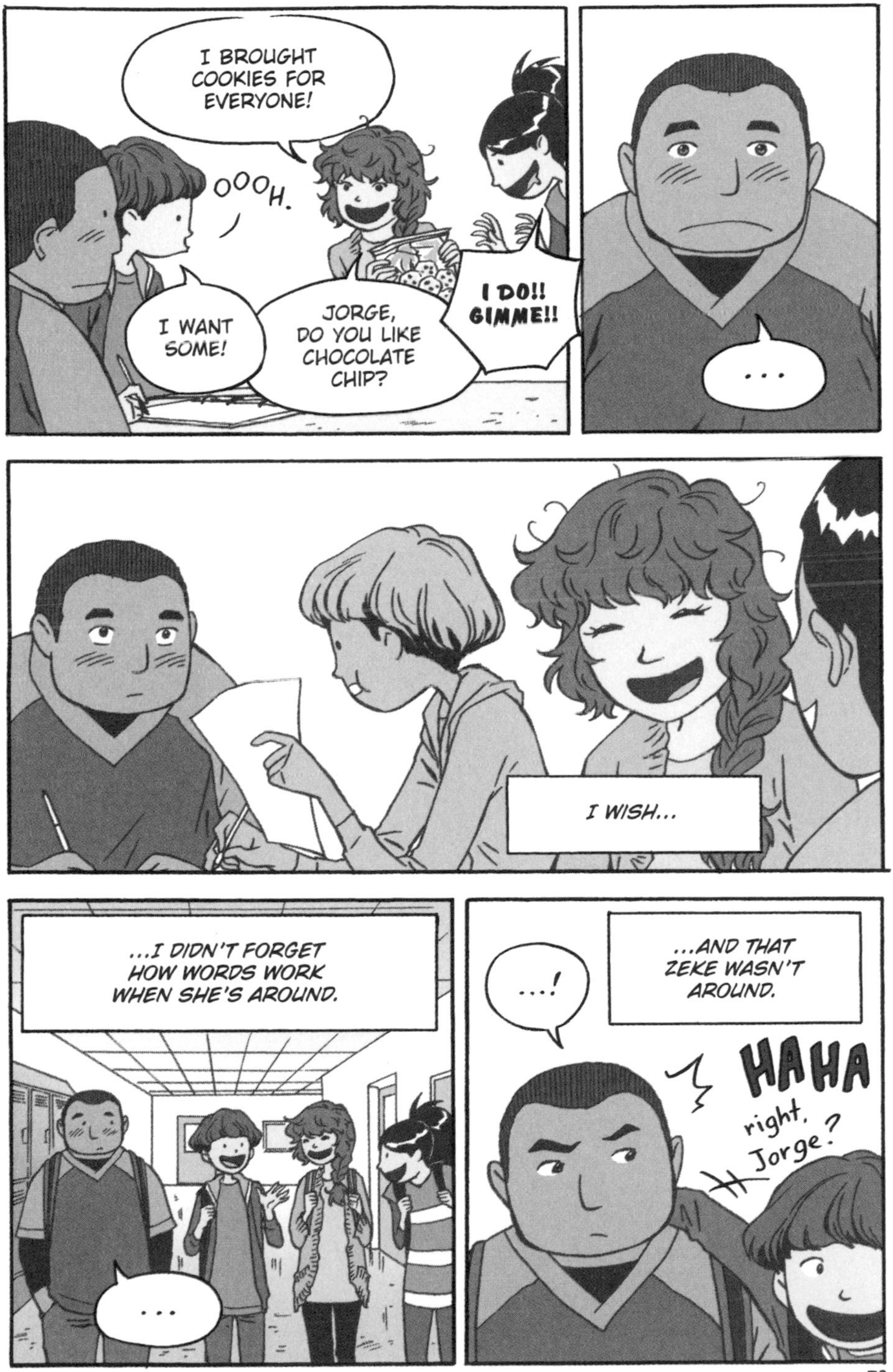

I BROUGHT COOKIES FOR EVERYONE!
OOOH.
I WANT SOME!
JORGE, DO YOU LIKE CHOCOLATE CHIP?
I DO!! GIMME!!
...
I WISH...
...I DIDN'T FORGET HOW WORDS WORK WHEN SHE'S AROUND.
...
...AND THAT ZEKE WASN'T AROUND.
...!
HAHA
right, Jorge?

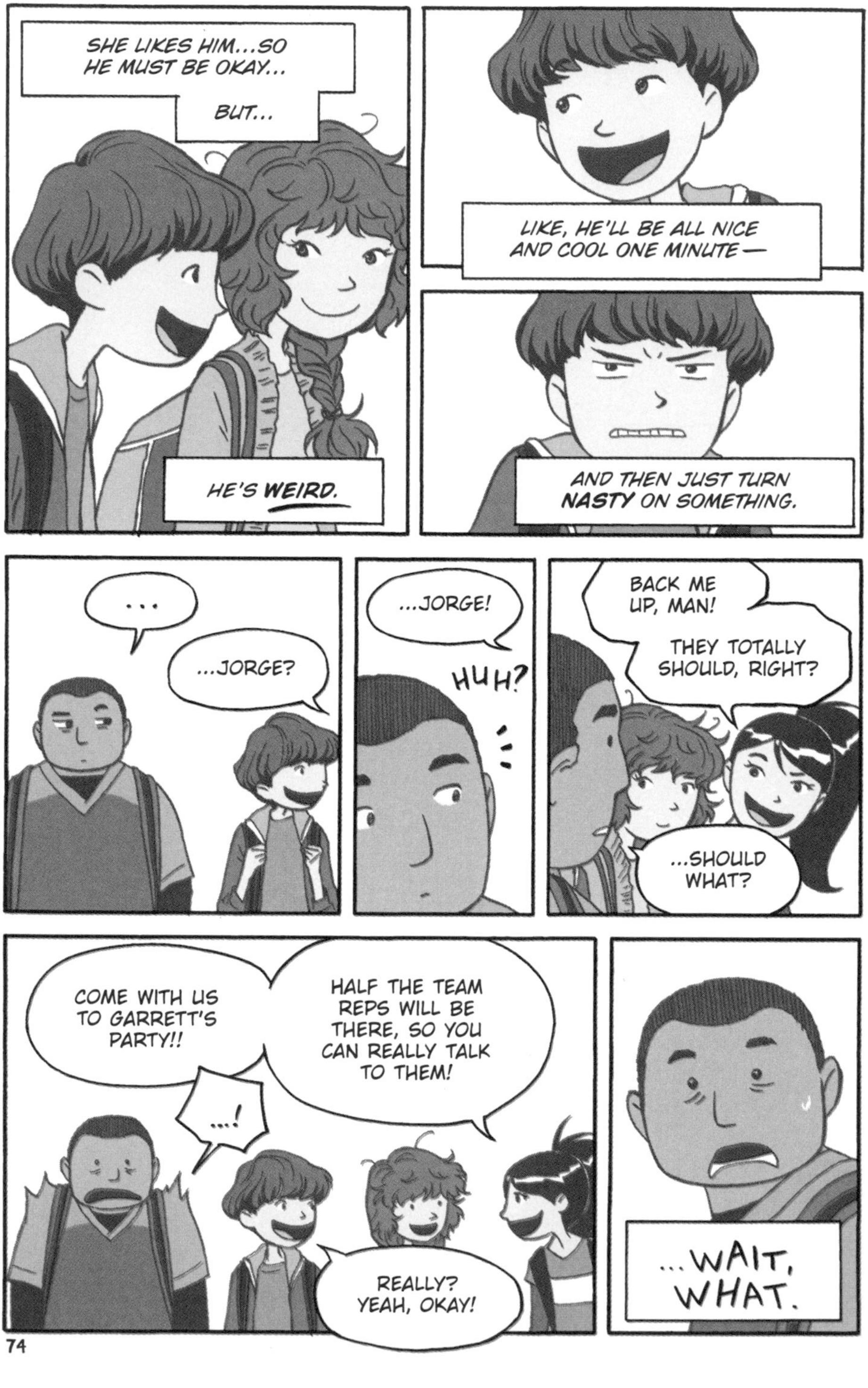
SHE LIKES HIM...SO HE MUST BE OKAY...
BUT...
HE'S **WEIRD.**
LIKE, HE'LL BE ALL NICE AND COOL ONE MINUTE—
AND THEN JUST TURN **NASTY** ON SOMETHING.
...
...JORGE?
...JORGE!
HUH?
BACK ME UP, MAN!
THEY TOTALLY SHOULD, RIGHT?
...SHOULD WHAT?
COME WITH US TO GARRETT'S PARTY!!
HALF THE TEAM REPS WILL BE THERE, SO YOU CAN REALLY TALK TO THEM!
...!
REALLY? YEAH, OKAY!
...WAIT, WHAT.

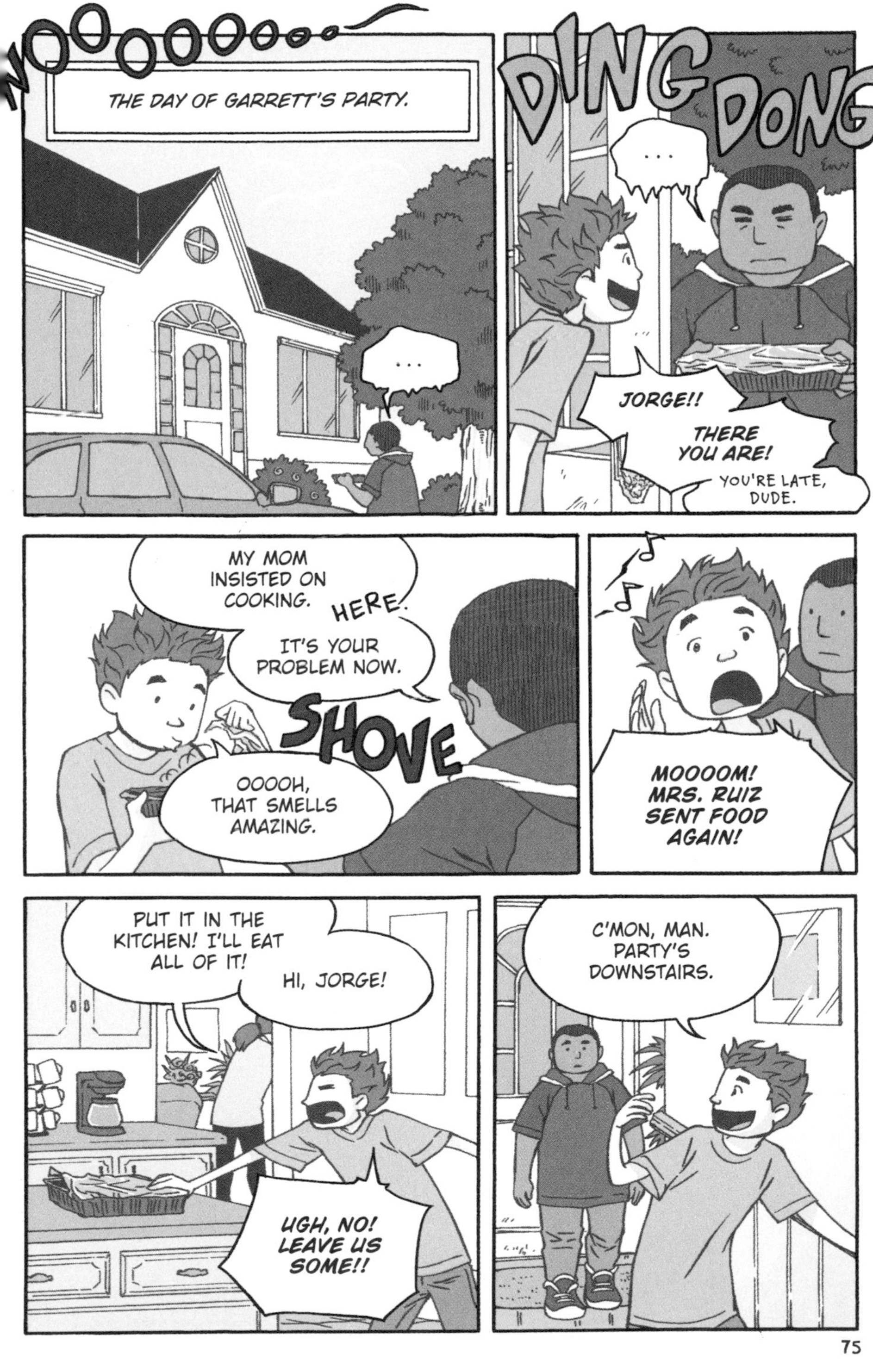
NOOOOOOOOO
THE DAY OF GARRETT'S PARTY.
...
DING DONG
...
JORGE!!
THERE YOU ARE!
YOU'RE LATE, DUDE.
MY MOM INSISTED ON COOKING.
HERE.
IT'S YOUR PROBLEM NOW.
SHOVE
OOOOH, THAT SMELLS AMAZING.
MOOOOM! MRS. RUIZ SENT FOOD AGAIN!
PUT IT IN THE KITCHEN! I'LL EAT ALL OF IT!
HI, JORGE!
UGH, NO! LEAVE US SOME!!
C'MON, MAN. PARTY'S DOWNSTAIRS.

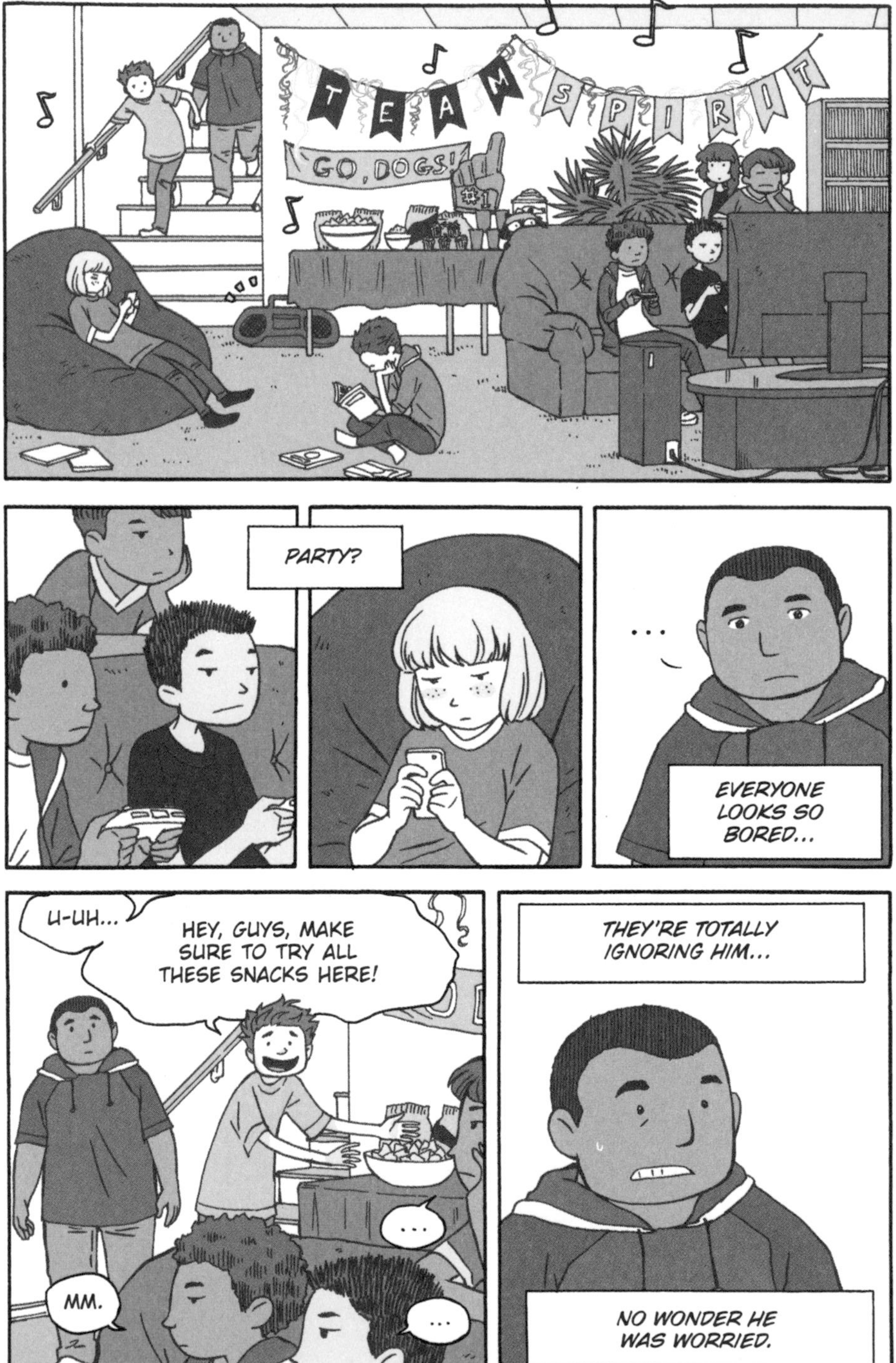

TEAM SPIRIT
GO, DOGS!
#1
PARTY?
...
EVERYONE LOOKS SO BORED...
U-UH...
HEY, GUYS, MAKE SURE TO TRY ALL THESE SNACKS HERE!
...
MM.
...
THEY'RE TOTALLY IGNORING HIM...
NO WONDER HE WAS WORRIED.

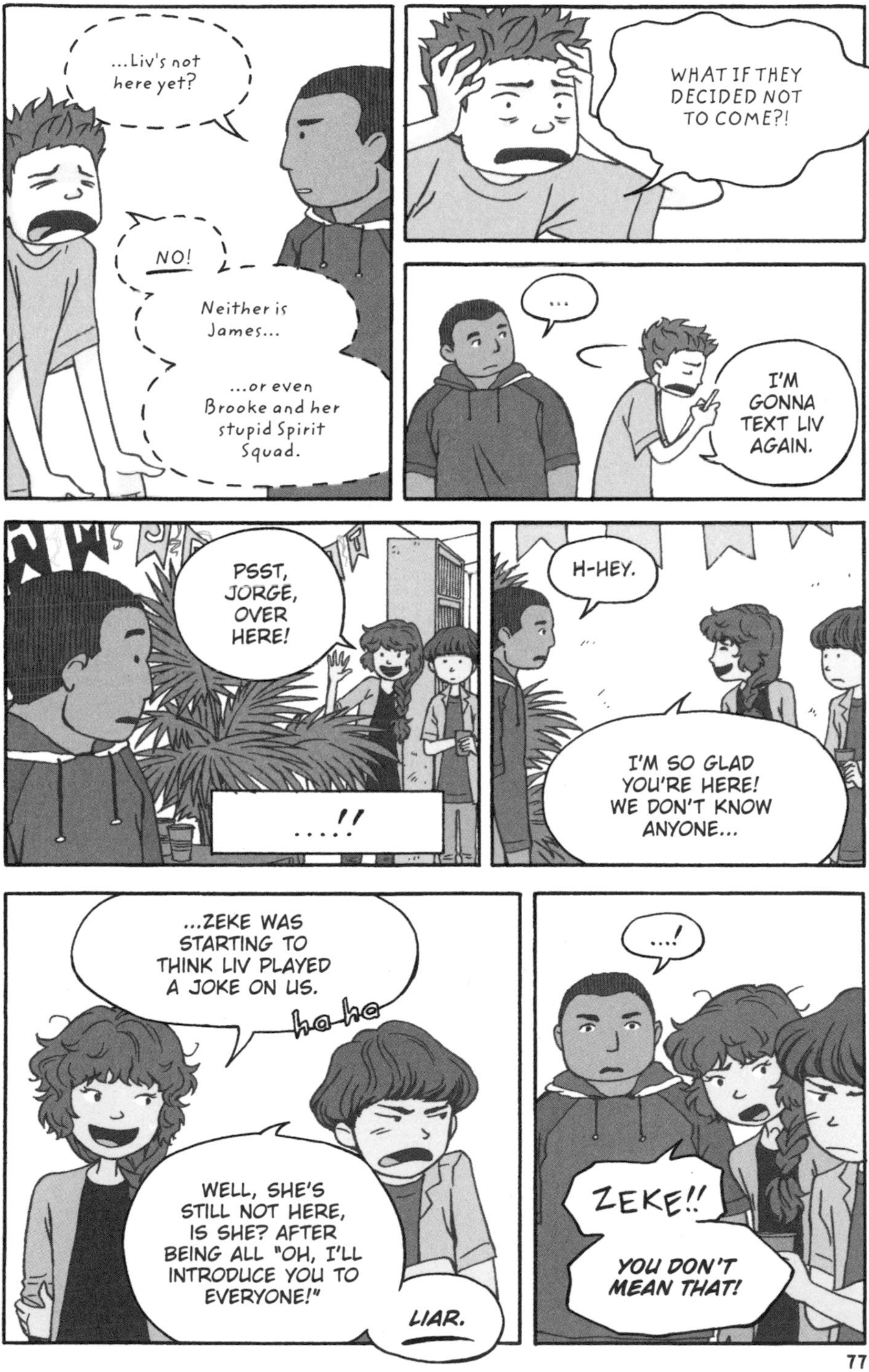
...Liv's not here yet?
NO!
Neither is James...
...or even Brooke and her stupid Spirit Squad.
WHAT IF THEY DECIDED NOT TO COME?!
...
I'M GONNA TEXT LIV AGAIN.
PSST, JORGE, OVER HERE!
....!!
H-HEY.
I'M SO GLAD YOU'RE HERE! WE DON'T KNOW ANYONE...
...ZEKE WAS STARTING TO THINK LIV PLAYED A JOKE ON US.
ha ha
WELL, SHE'S STILL NOT HERE, IS SHE? AFTER BEING ALL "OH, I'LL INTRODUCE YOU TO EVERYONE!"
LIAR.
...!
ZEKE!!
YOU DON'T MEAN THAT!

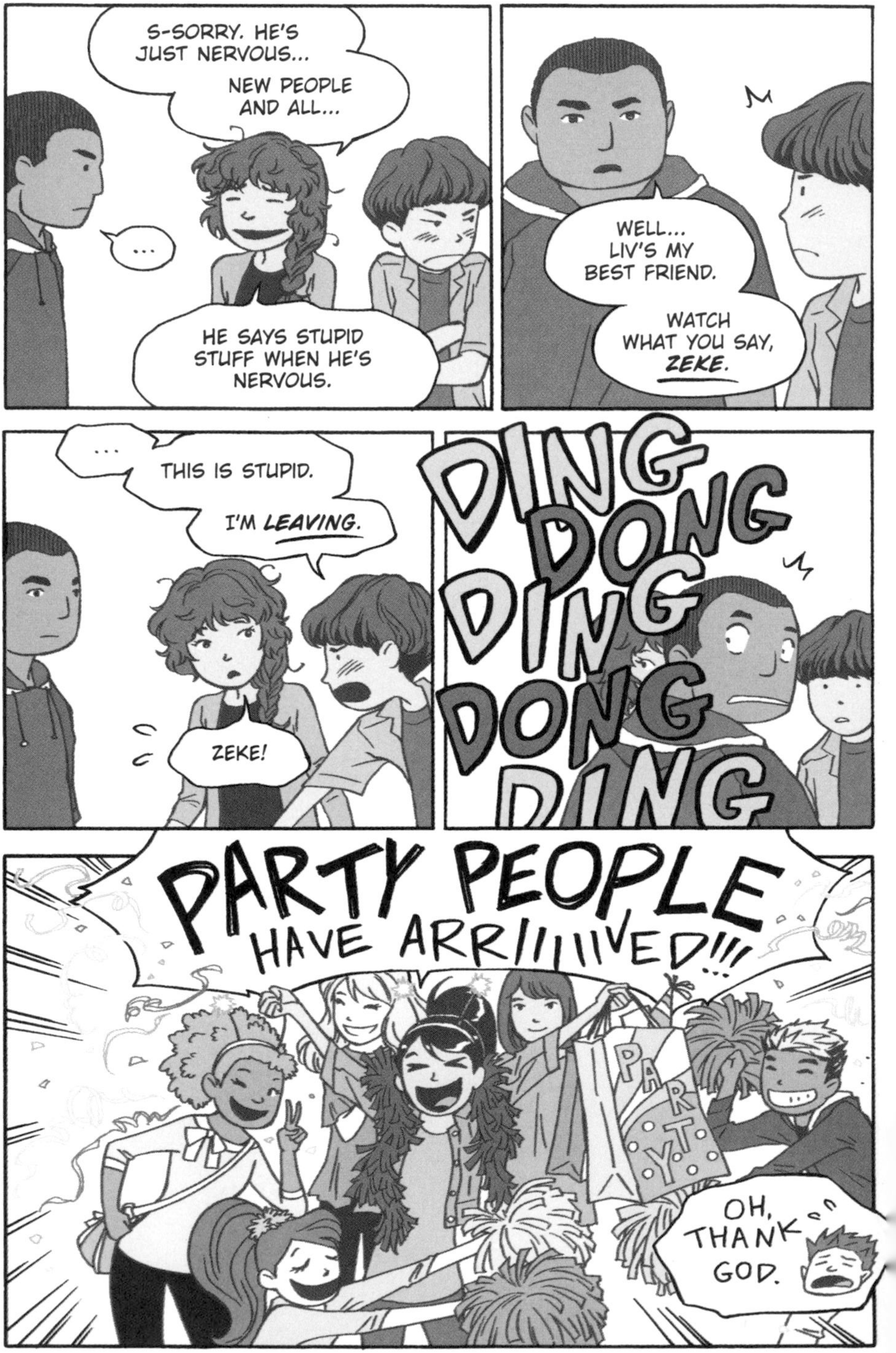
S-SORRY. HE'S JUST NERVOUS...
NEW PEOPLE AND ALL...
...
HE SAYS STUPID STUFF WHEN HE'S NERVOUS.
WELL... LIV'S MY BEST FRIEND.
WATCH WHAT YOU SAY, ZEKE.
...
THIS IS STUPID.
I'M LEAVING.
ZEKE!
DING DONG DING DONG DING
PARTY PEOPLE HAVE ARRIIIIIVED!!!
PARTY
OH, THANK GOD.

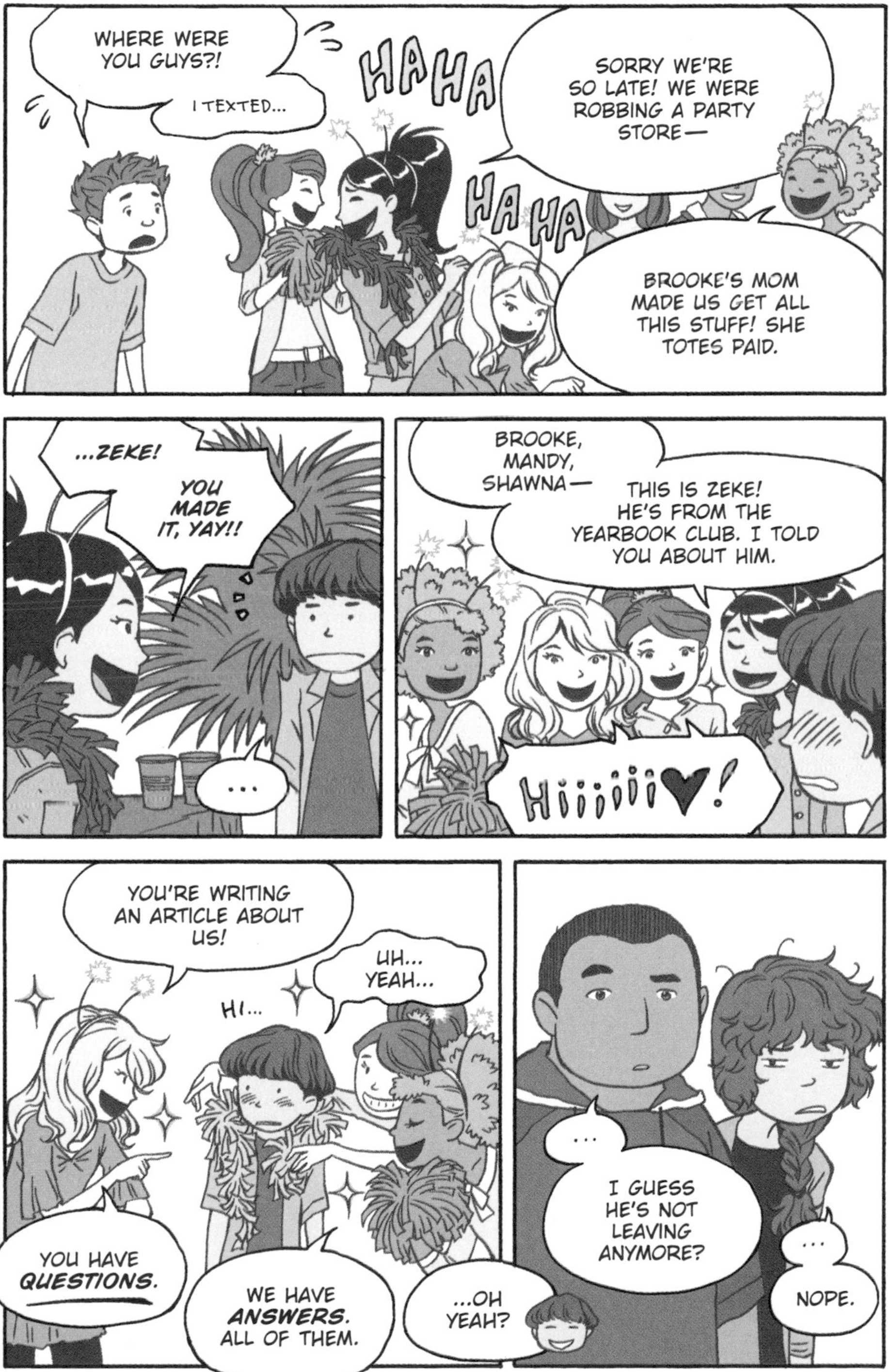
WHERE WERE YOU GUYS?!
I TEXTED...
HAHA
SORRY WE'RE SO LATE! WE WERE ROBBING A PARTY STORE—
HAHA
BROOKE'S MOM MADE US GET ALL THIS STUFF! SHE TOTES PAID.
...ZEKE!
YOU MADE IT, YAY!!
...
BROOKE, MANDY, SHAWNA—
THIS IS ZEKE! HE'S FROM THE YEARBOOK CLUB. I TOLD YOU ABOUT HIM.
Hiiiiiii♥!
YOU'RE WRITING AN ARTICLE ABOUT US!
HI...
UH... YEAH...
YOU HAVE QUESTIONS.
WE HAVE ANSWERS. ALL OF THEM.
...OH YEAH?
...
I GUESS HE'S NOT LEAVING ANYMORE?
...
NOPE.

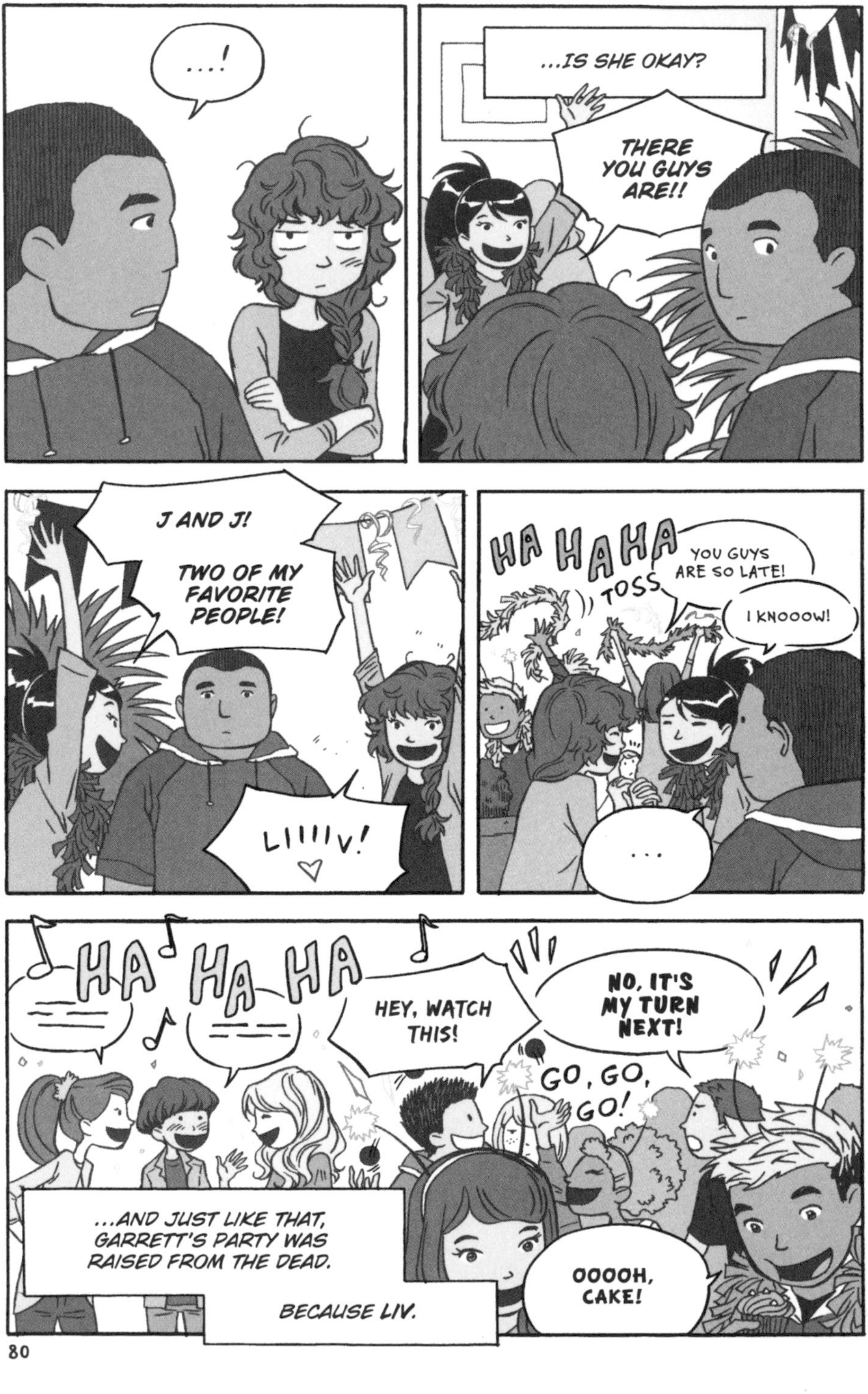
...!
...IS SHE OKAY?
THERE YOU GUYS ARE!!
J AND J!
TWO OF MY FAVORITE PEOPLE!
LIIIIV!
HA HA HAHA
TOSS
YOU GUYS ARE SO LATE!
I KNOOOW!
...
HA HA HA
HEY, WATCH THIS!
NO, IT'S MY TURN NEXT!
GO, GO, GO!
...AND JUST LIKE THAT, GARRETT'S PARTY WAS RAISED FROM THE DEAD.
BECAUSE LIV.
OOOOH, CAKE!

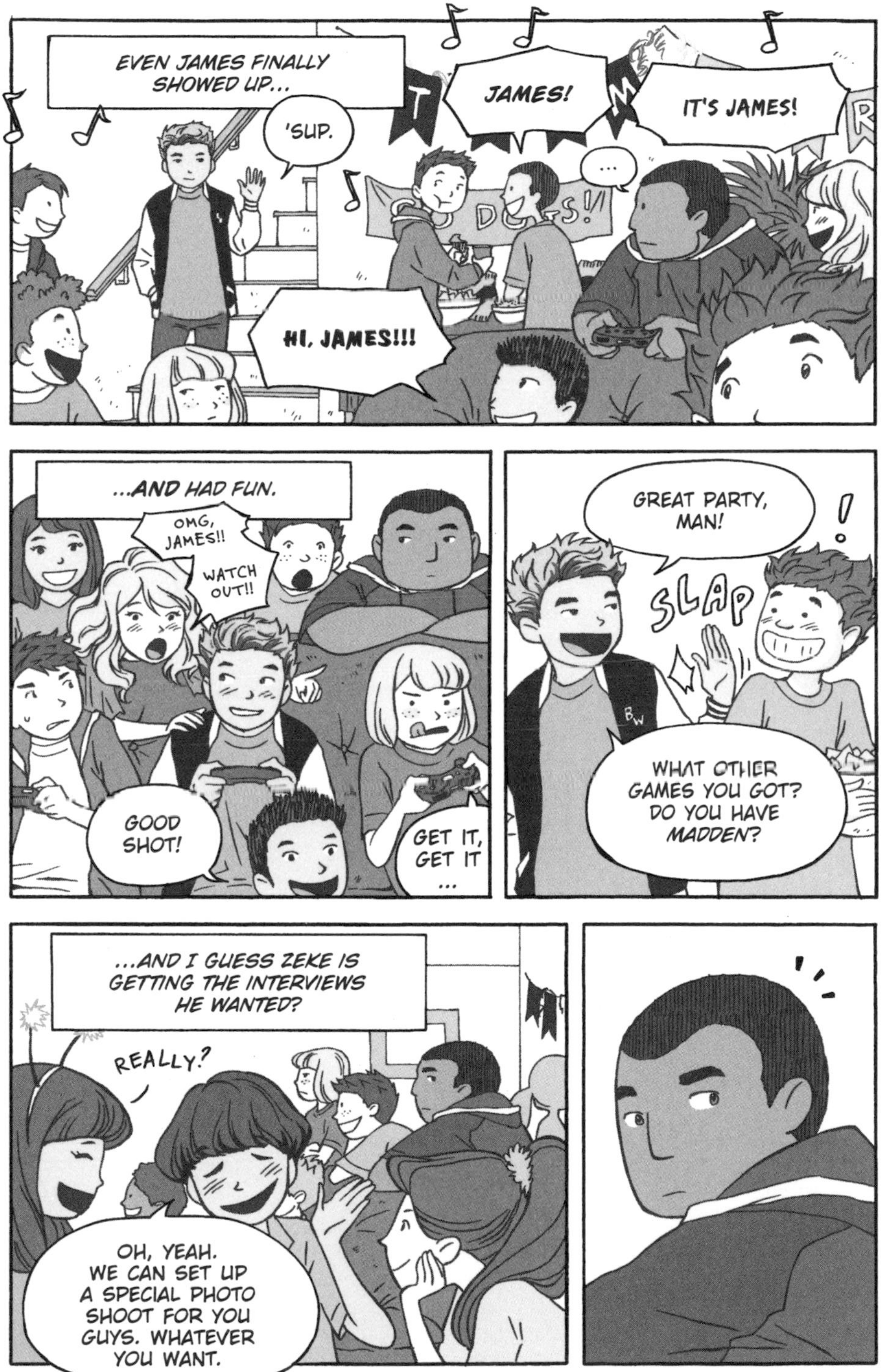

EVEN JAMES FINALLY SHOWED UP...
'SUP.
JAMES!
IT'S JAMES!
...
HI, JAMES!!!
...AND HAD FUN.
OMG, JAMES!!
WATCH OUT!!
GOOD SHOT!
GET IT, GET IT ...
GREAT PARTY, MAN!
!
SLAP
WHAT OTHER GAMES YOU GOT? DO YOU HAVE *MADDEN*?
...AND I GUESS ZEKE IS GETTING THE INTERVIEWS HE WANTED?
REALLY?
OH, YEAH. WE CAN SET UP A SPECIAL PHOTO SHOOT FOR YOU GUYS. WHATEVER YOU WANT.

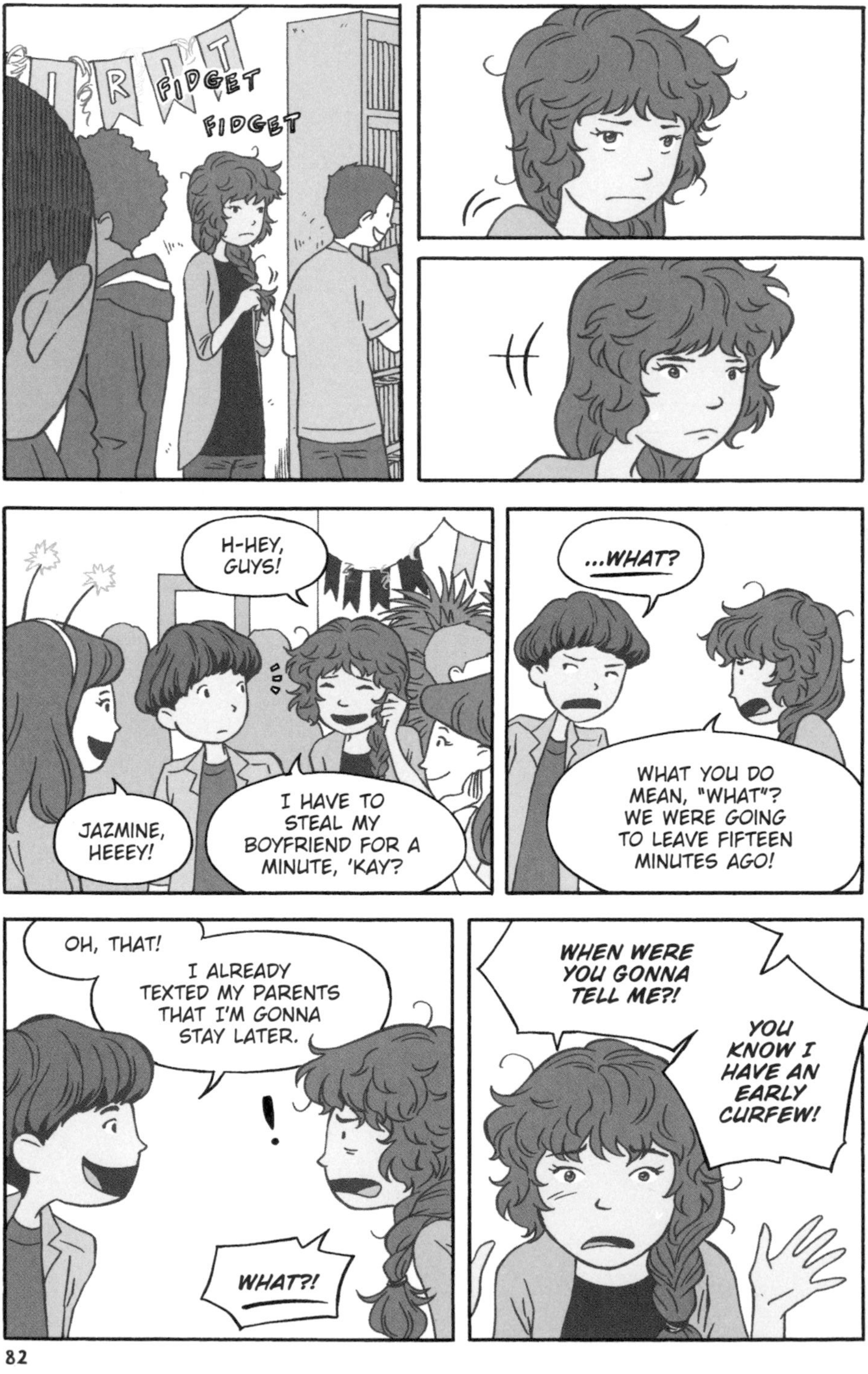

FIDGET
FIDGET
H-HEY, GUYS!
JAZMINE, HEEEY!
I HAVE TO STEAL MY BOYFRIEND FOR A MINUTE, 'KAY?
...WHAT?
WHAT YOU DO MEAN, "WHAT"? WE WERE GOING TO LEAVE FIFTEEN MINUTES AGO!
OH, THAT!
I ALREADY TEXTED MY PARENTS THAT I'M GONNA STAY LATER.
!
WHAT?!
WHEN WERE YOU GONNA TELL ME?!
YOU KNOW I HAVE AN EARLY CURFEW!

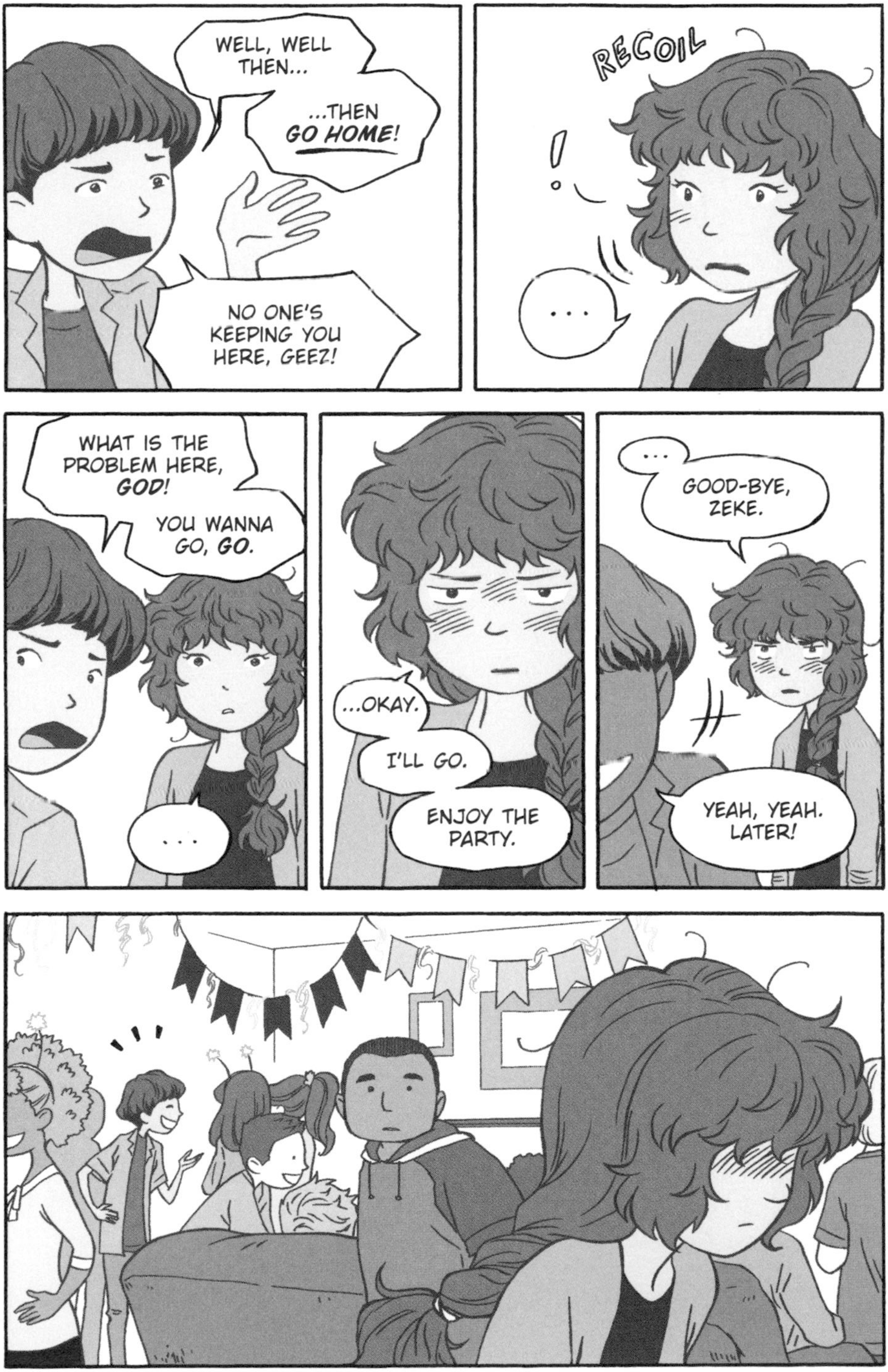
WELL, WELL THEN...
...THEN GO HOME!
NO ONE'S KEEPING YOU HERE, GEEZ!
RECOIL
!
...
WHAT IS THE PROBLEM HERE, GOD!
YOU WANNA GO, GO.
...
...OKAY.
I'LL GO.
ENJOY THE PARTY.
...
GOOD-BYE, ZEKE.
YEAH, YEAH. LATER!

CHAPTER 5

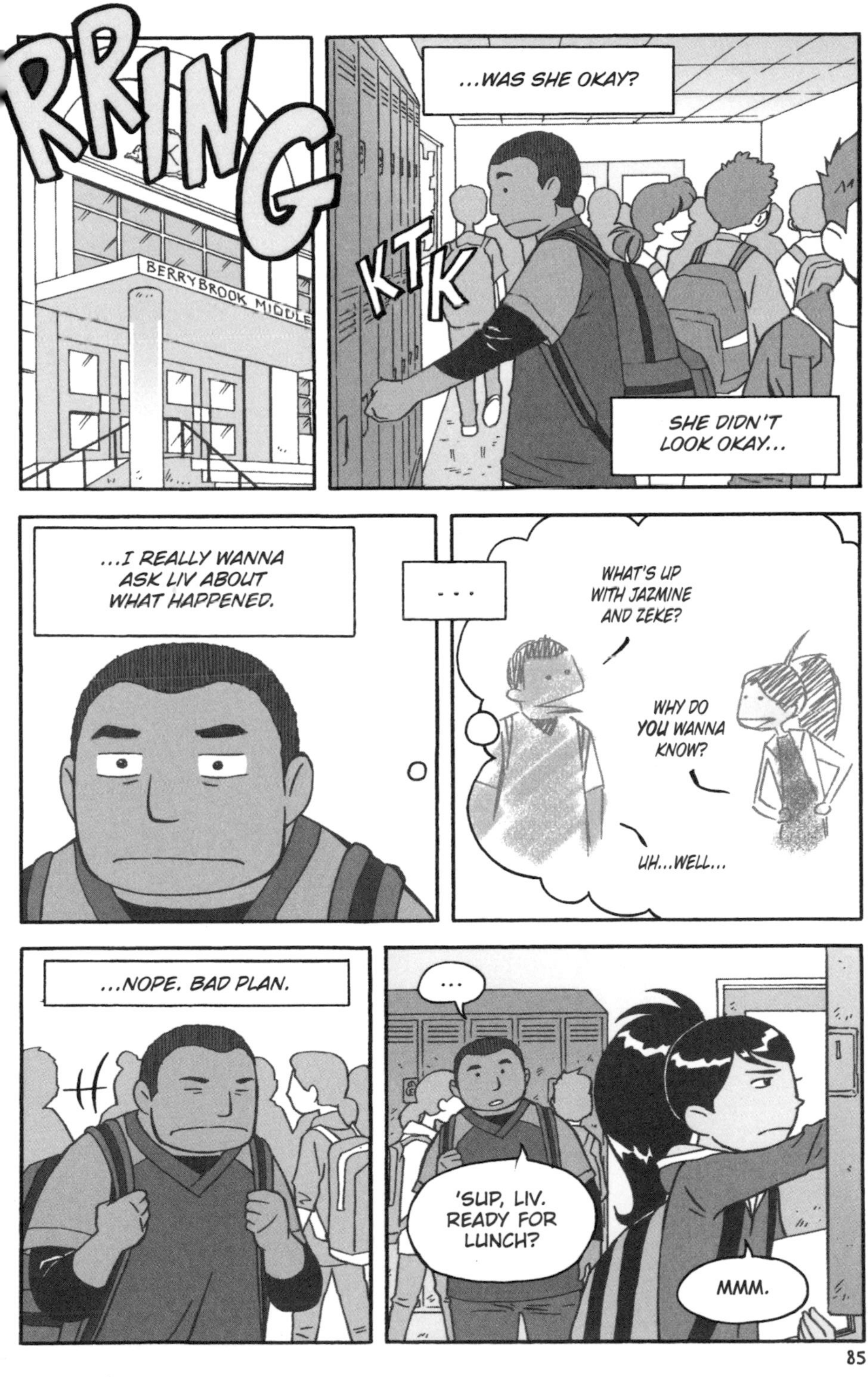
RRING
BERRYBROOK MIDDLE
...WAS SHE OKAY?
KTK
SHE DIDN'T LOOK OKAY...
...I REALLY WANNA ASK LIV ABOUT WHAT HAPPENED.
...
WHAT'S UP WITH JAZMINE AND ZEKE?
WHY DO YOU WANNA KNOW?
UH...WELL...
...NOPE. BAD PLAN.
...
'SUP, LIV. READY FOR LUNCH?
MMM.

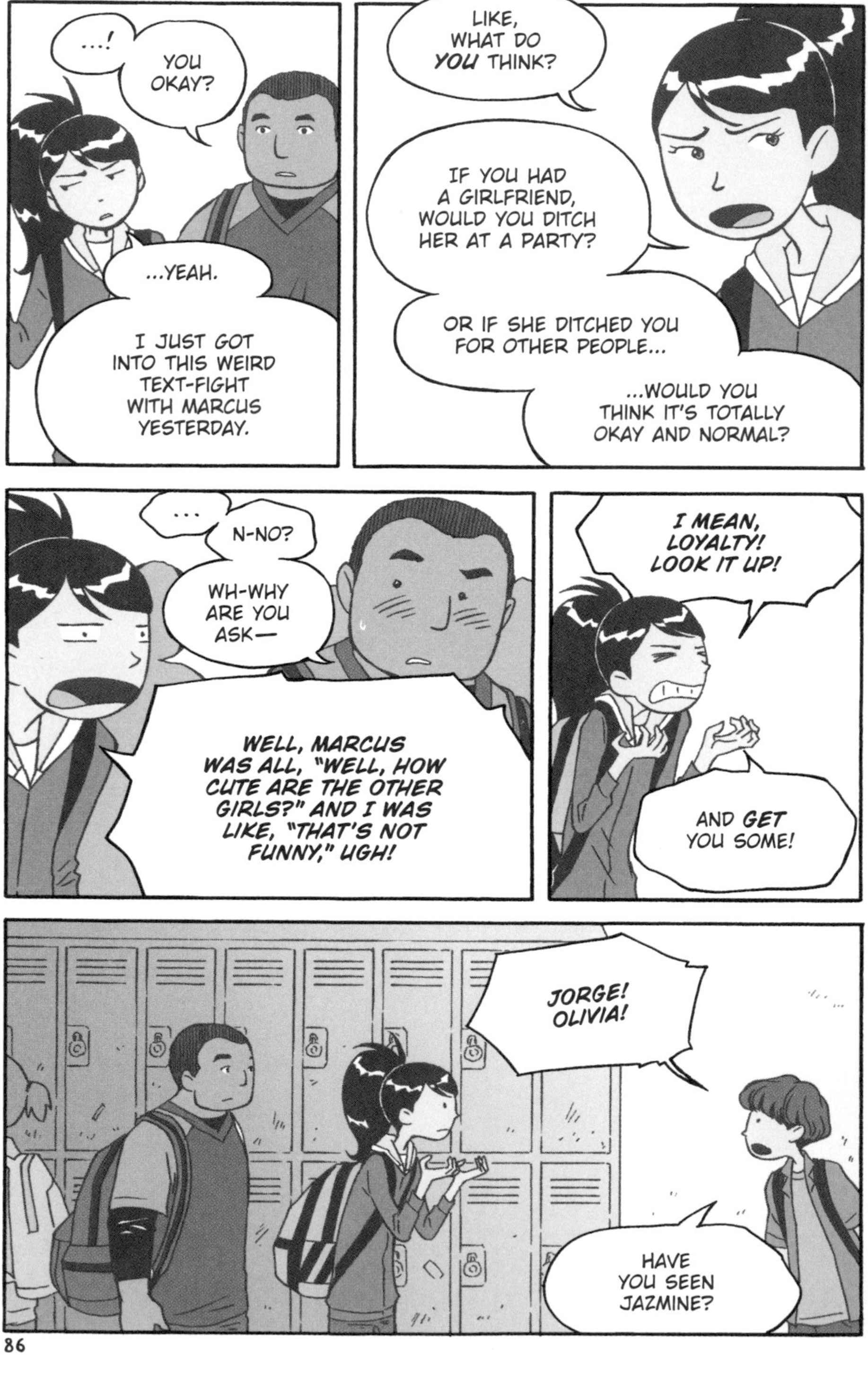
...!
YOU OKAY?
...YEAH.
I JUST GOT INTO THIS WEIRD TEXT-FIGHT WITH MARCUS YESTERDAY.
LIKE, WHAT DO *YOU* THINK?
IF YOU HAD A GIRLFRIEND, WOULD YOU DITCH HER AT A PARTY?
OR IF SHE DITCHED YOU FOR OTHER PEOPLE...
...WOULD YOU THINK IT'S TOTALLY OKAY AND NORMAL?
...
N-NO?
WH-WHY ARE YOU ASK—
WELL, MARCUS WAS ALL, "WELL, HOW CUTE ARE THE OTHER GIRLS?" AND I WAS LIKE, "THAT'S NOT FUNNY," UGH!
I MEAN, LOYALTY! LOOK IT UP!
AND *GET* YOU SOME!
JORGE! OLIVIA!
HAVE YOU SEEN JAZMINE?

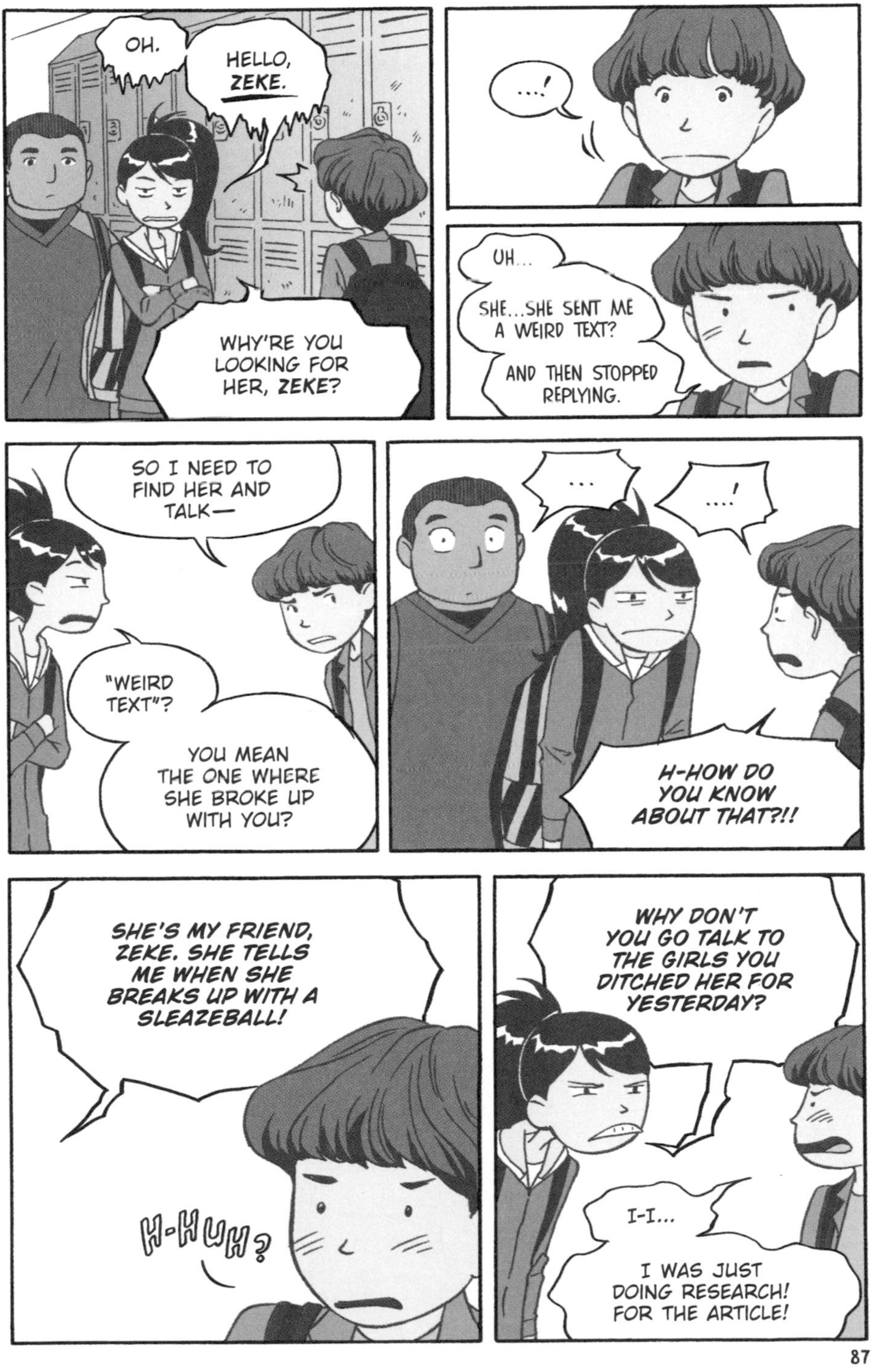
OH.
HELLO, ZEKE.
WHY'RE YOU LOOKING FOR HER, ZEKE?
....!
UH...
SHE...SHE SENT ME A WEIRD TEXT?
AND THEN STOPPED REPLYING.
SO I NEED TO FIND HER AND TALK—
"WEIRD TEXT"?
YOU MEAN THE ONE WHERE SHE BROKE UP WITH YOU?
...
....!
H-HOW DO YOU KNOW ABOUT THAT?!!
SHE'S MY FRIEND, ZEKE. SHE TELLS ME WHEN SHE BREAKS UP WITH A SLEAZEBALL!
H-HUH?
WHY DON'T YOU GO TALK TO THE GIRLS YOU DITCHED HER FOR YESTERDAY?
I-I...
I WAS JUST DOING RESEARCH! FOR THE ARTICLE!

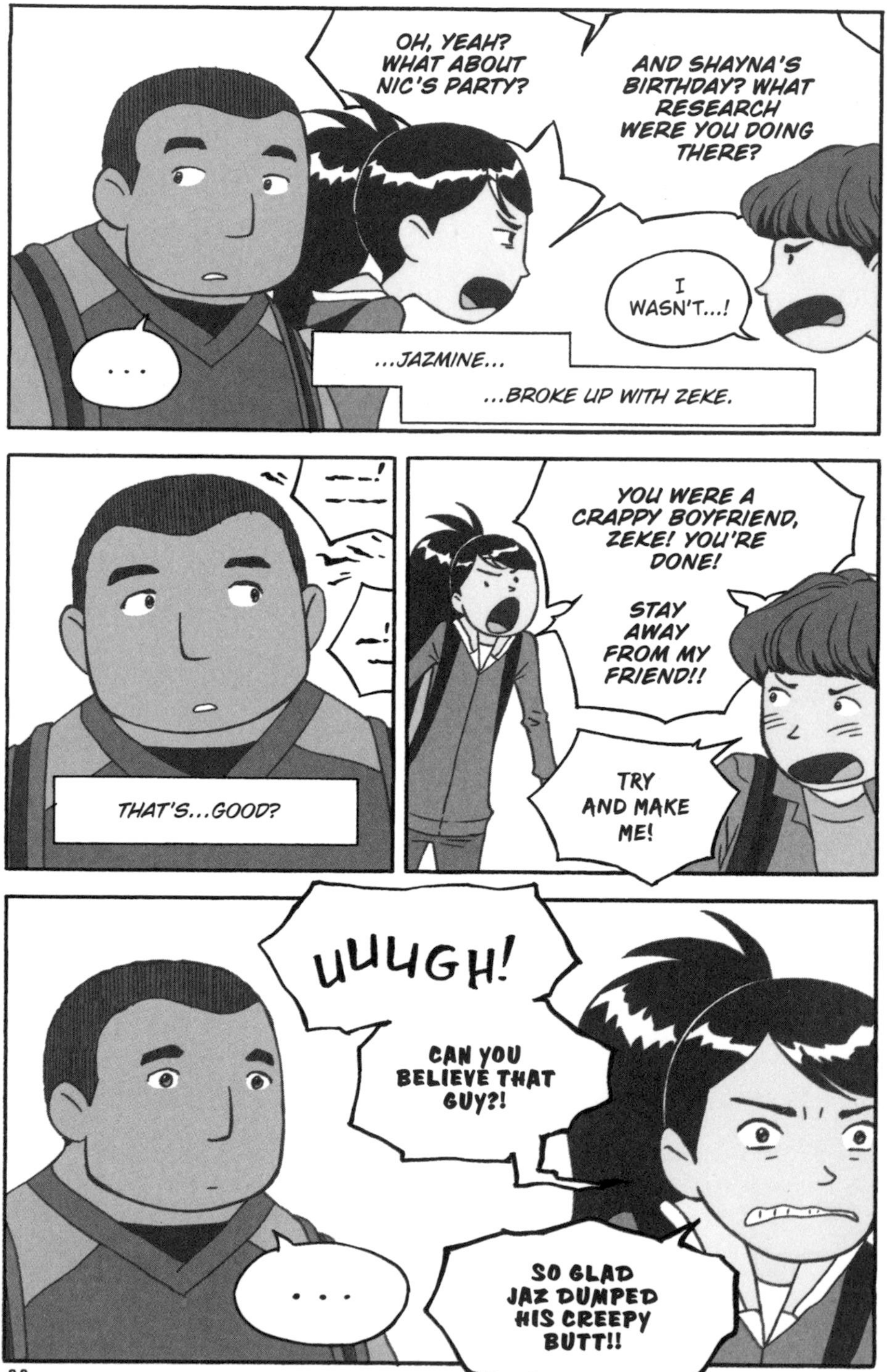

OH, YEAH? WHAT ABOUT NIC'S PARTY?
AND SHAYNA'S BIRTHDAY? WHAT RESEARCH WERE YOU DOING THERE?
I WASN'T...!
...
...JAZMINE...
...BROKE UP WITH ZEKE.
---!
-!
THAT'S...GOOD?
YOU WERE A CRAPPY BOYFRIEND, ZEKE! YOU'RE DONE!
STAY AWAY FROM MY FRIEND!!
TRY AND MAKE ME!
UUUGH!
CAN YOU BELIEVE THAT GUY?!
...
SO GLAD JAZ DUMPED HIS CREEPY BUTT!!

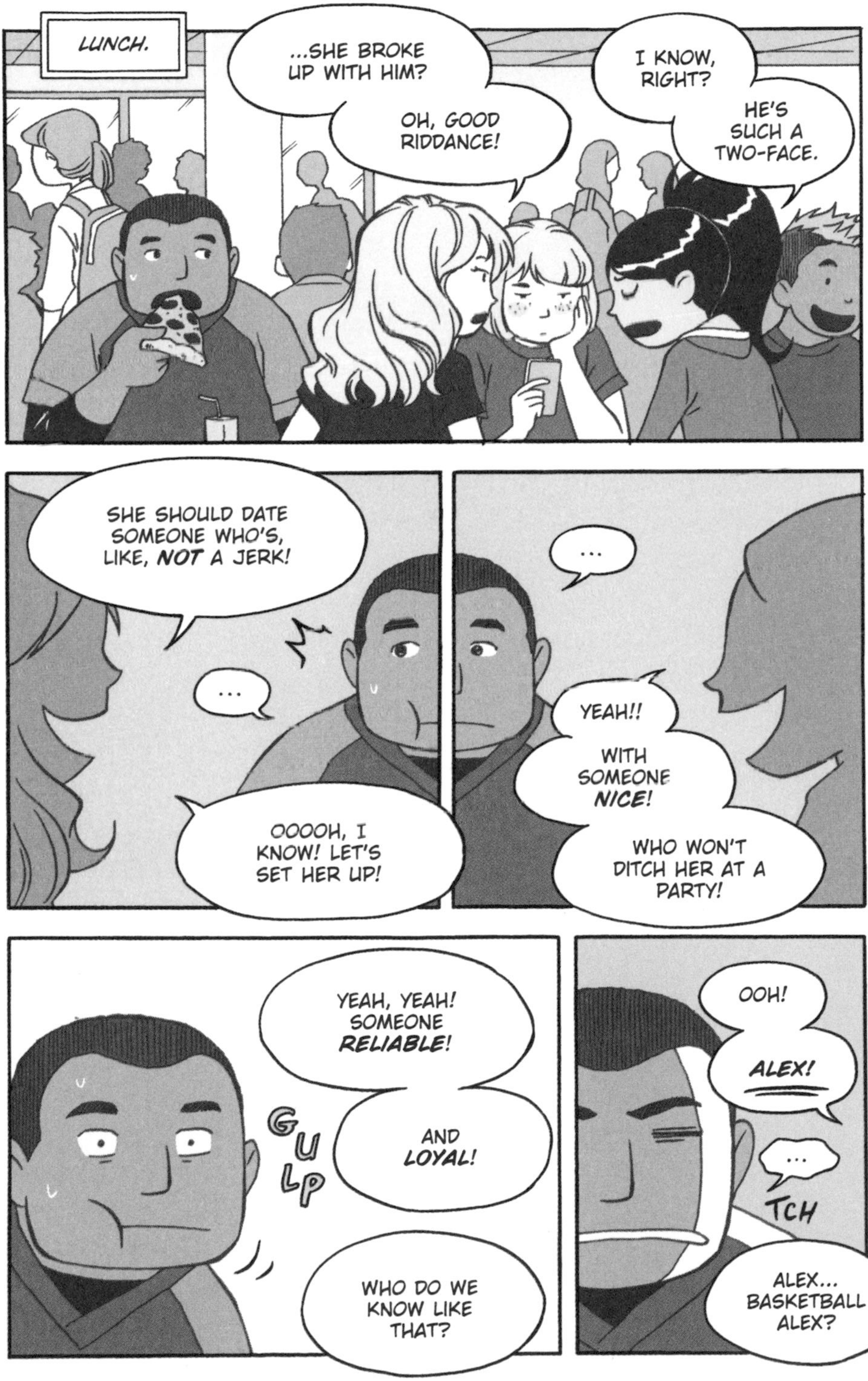
LUNCH.
...SHE BROKE UP WITH HIM?
OH, GOOD RIDDANCE!
I KNOW, RIGHT?
HE'S SUCH A TWO-FACE.
SHE SHOULD DATE SOMEONE WHO'S, LIKE, NOT A JERK!
...
OOOOH, I KNOW! LET'S SET HER UP!
...
YEAH!!
WITH SOMEONE NICE!
WHO WON'T DITCH HER AT A PARTY!
YEAH, YEAH! SOMEONE RELIABLE!
AND LOYAL!
GULP
WHO DO WE KNOW LIKE THAT?
OOH!
ALEX!
...
TCH
ALEX... BASKETBALL ALEX?

90

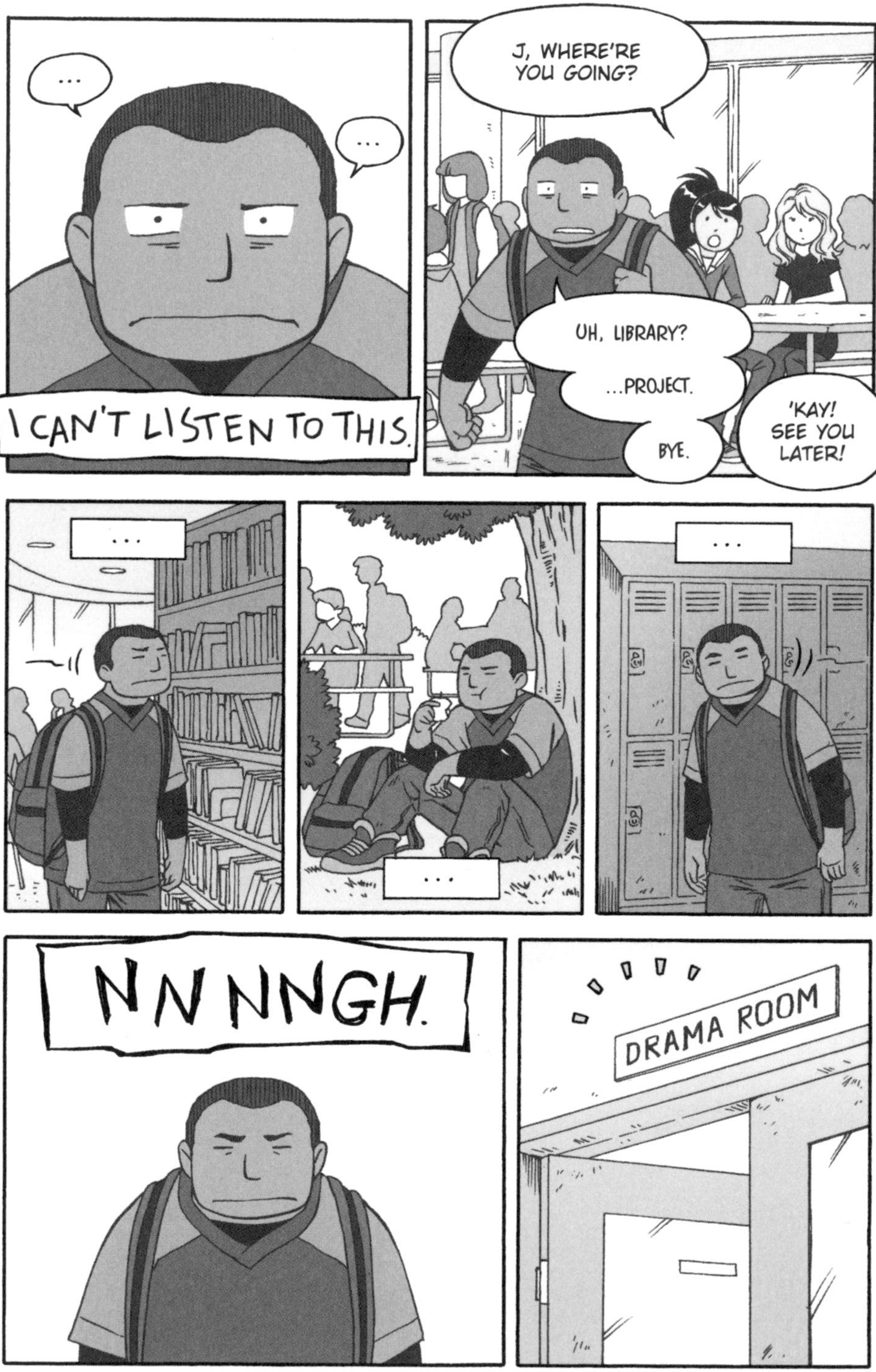
...
...
I CAN'T LISTEN TO THIS.
J, WHERE'RE YOU GOING?
UH, LIBRARY?
...PROJECT.
BYE.
'KAY! SEE YOU LATER!
...
...
...
NNNNGH.
DRAMA ROOM

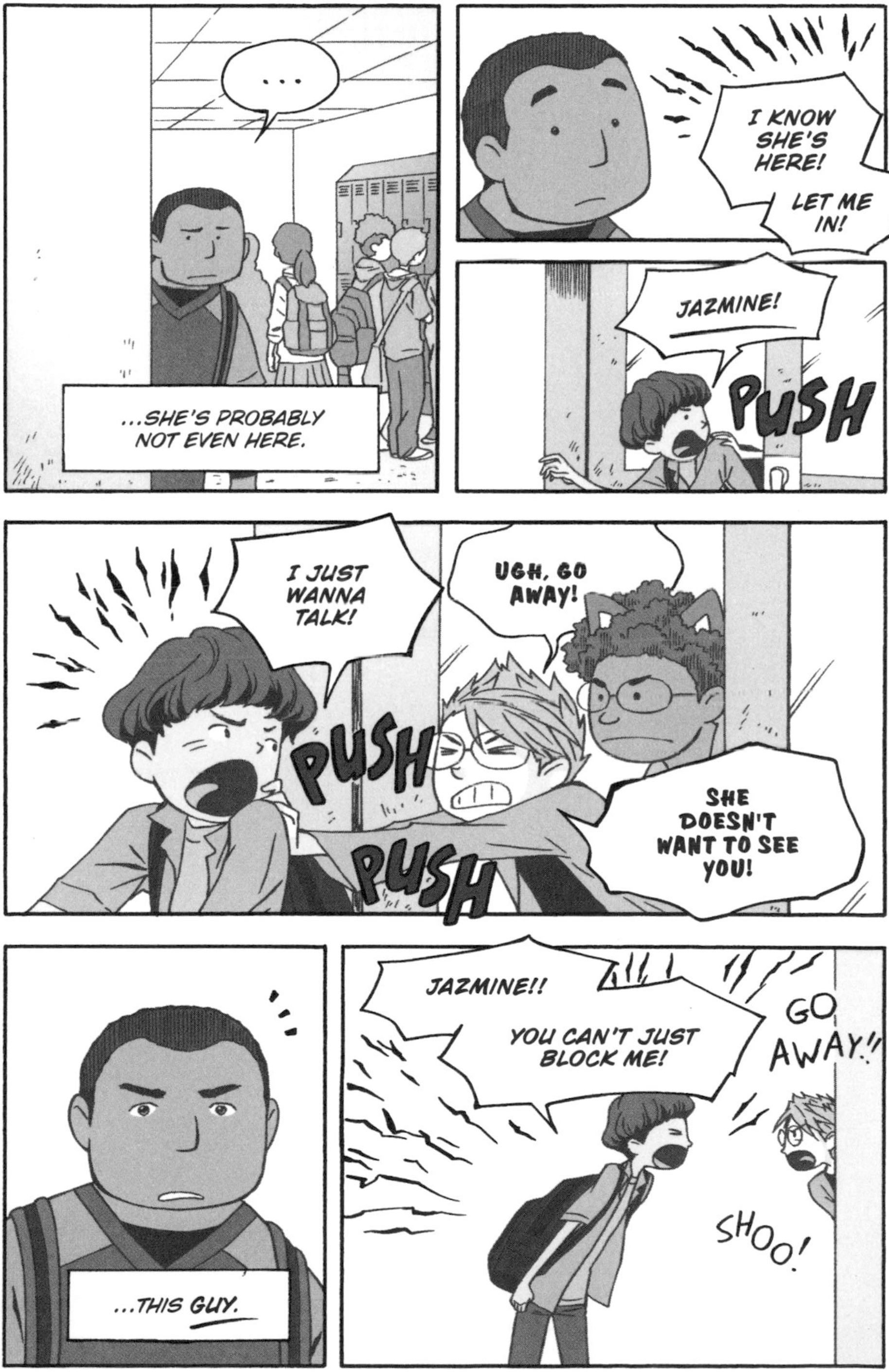
...
...SHE'S PROBABLY NOT EVEN HERE.
I KNOW SHE'S HERE!
LET ME IN!
JAZMINE!
PUSH
I JUST WANNA TALK!
UGH, GO AWAY!
PUSH
PUSH
SHE DOESN'T WANT TO SEE YOU!
...THIS GUY.
JAZMINE!!
YOU CAN'T JUST BLOCK ME!
GO AWAY!!
SHOO!

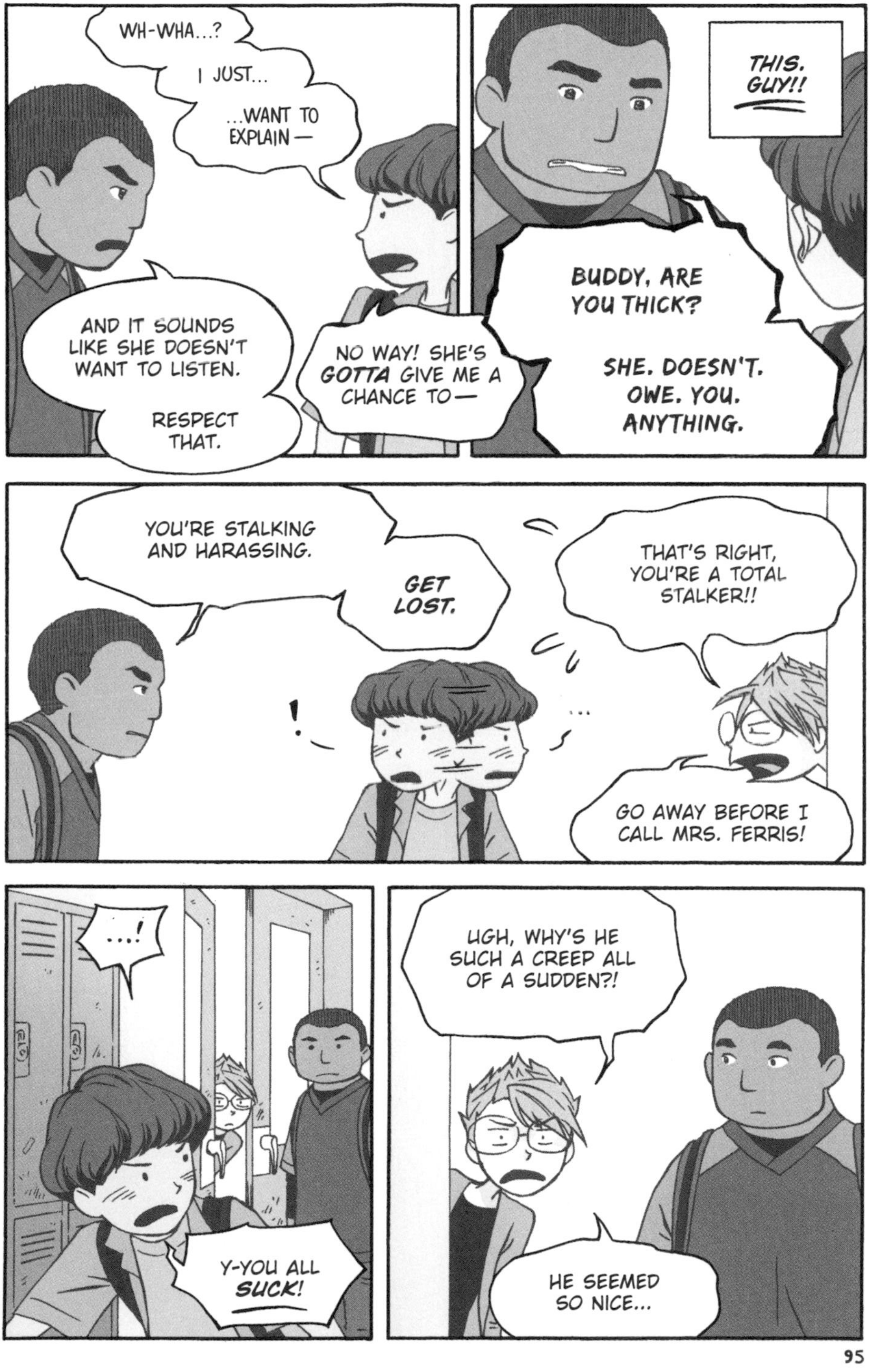
WH-WHA...?
I JUST...
...WANT TO EXPLAIN—
AND IT SOUNDS LIKE SHE DOESN'T WANT TO LISTEN.
RESPECT THAT.
NO WAY! SHE'S GOTTA GIVE ME A CHANCE TO—
THIS. GUY!!
BUDDY, ARE YOU THICK?
SHE. DOESN'T. OWE. YOU. ANYTHING.
YOU'RE STALKING AND HARASSING.
GET LOST.
!
...
THAT'S RIGHT, YOU'RE A TOTAL STALKER!!
GO AWAY BEFORE I CALL MRS. FERRIS!
....!
Y-YOU ALL SUCK!
UGH, WHY'S HE SUCH A CREEP ALL OF A SUDDEN?!
HE SEEMED SO NICE...

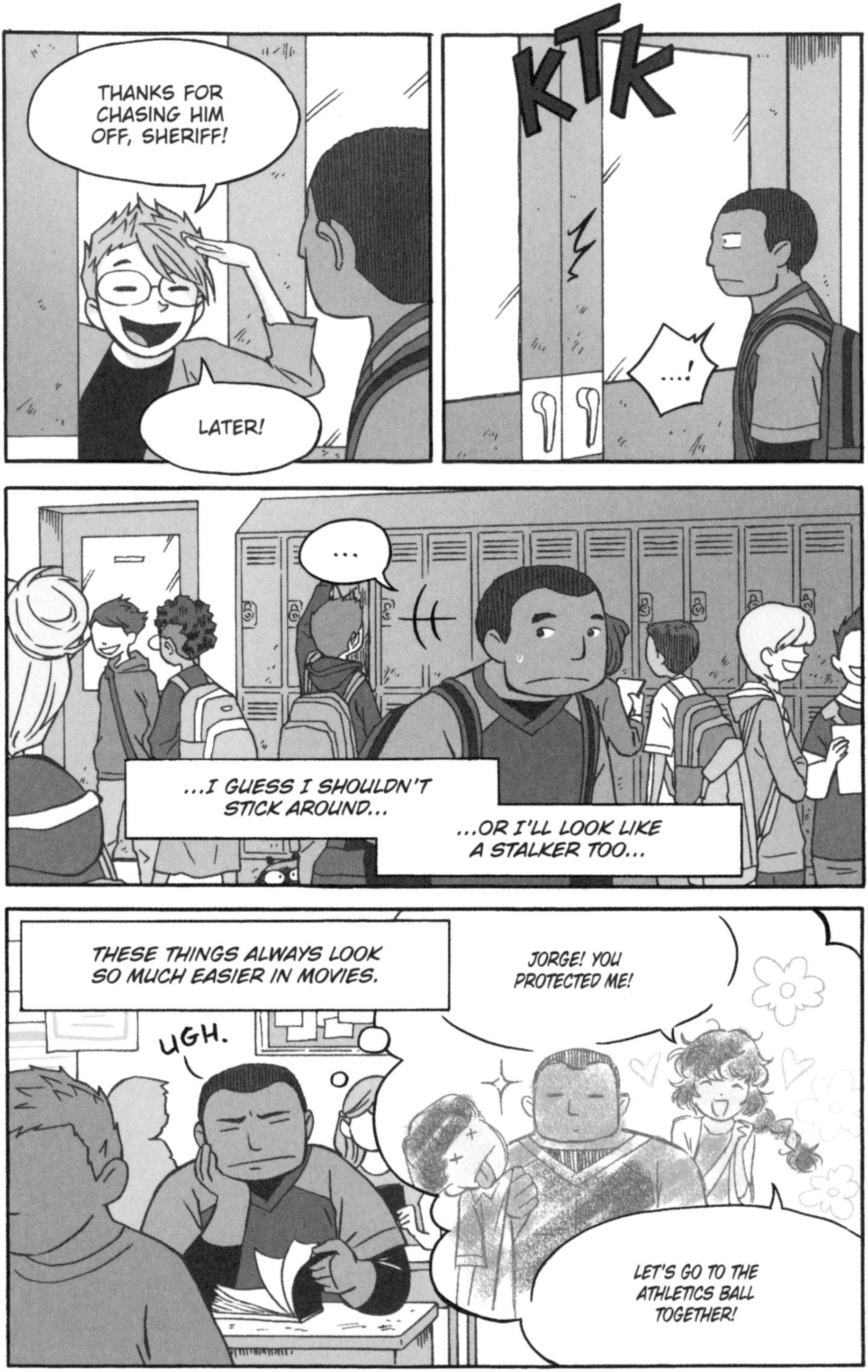

THANKS FOR CHASING HIM OFF, SHERIFF!
LATER!
KTK
...!
...
...I GUESS I SHOULDN'T STICK AROUND...
...OR I'LL LOOK LIKE A STALKER TOO...
THESE THINGS ALWAYS LOOK SO MUCH EASIER IN MOVIES.
UGH.
JORGE! YOU PROTECTED ME!
LET'S GO TO THE ATHLETICS BALL TOGETHER!

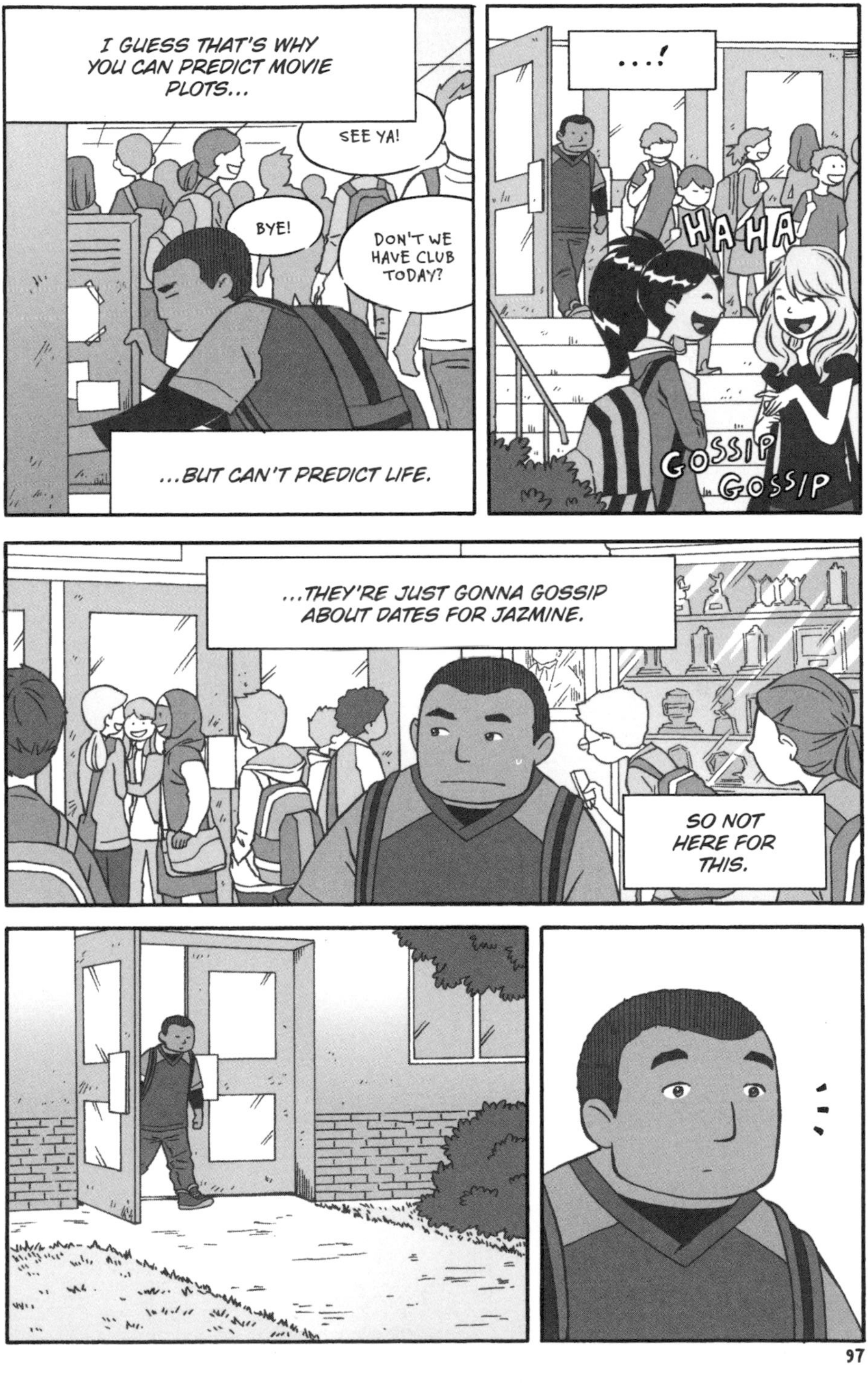

I GUESS THAT'S WHY YOU CAN PREDICT MOVIE PLOTS...
SEE YA!
BYE!
DON'T WE HAVE CLUB TODAY?
...BUT CAN'T PREDICT LIFE.
...!
HAHA
GOSSIP GOSSIP
...THEY'RE JUST GONNA GOSSIP ABOUT DATES FOR JAZMINE.
SO NOT HERE FOR THIS.

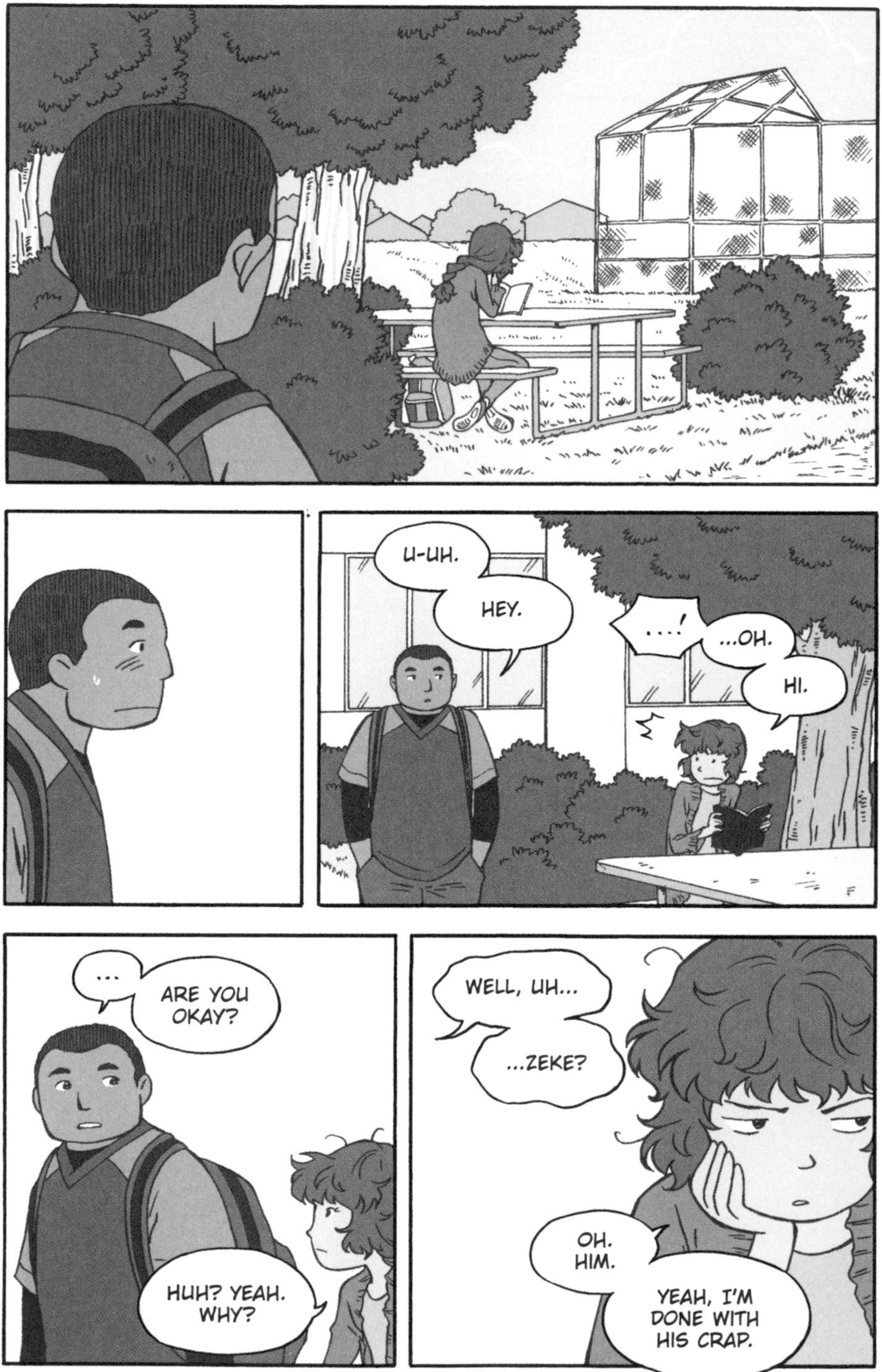
U-UH.
HEY.
....!
...OH.
HI.
...
ARE YOU OKAY?
HUH? YEAH. WHY?
WELL, UH...
...ZEKE?
OH. HIM.
YEAH, I'M DONE WITH HIS CRAP.

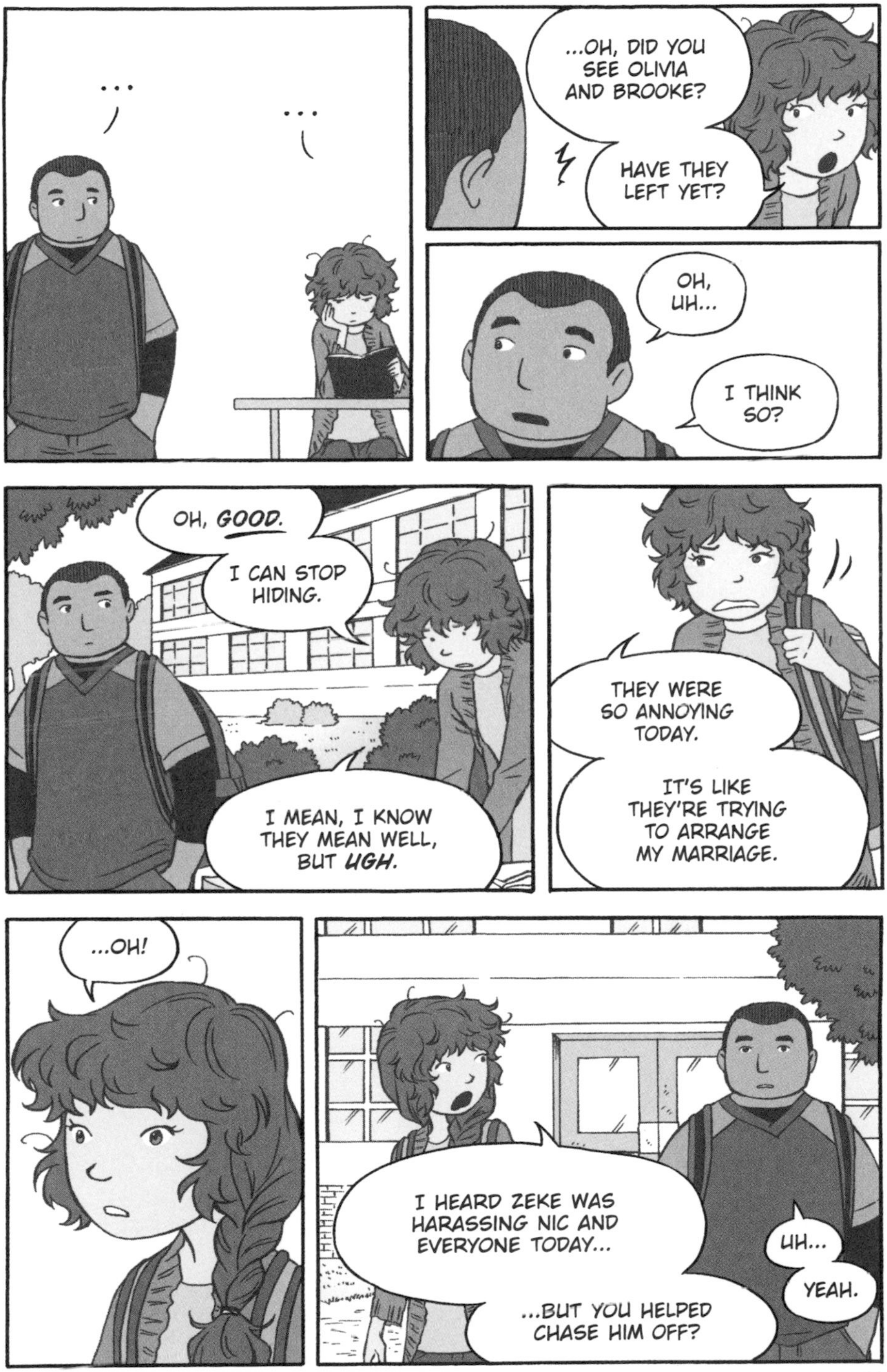
...
...
...OH, DID YOU SEE OLIVIA AND BROOKE?
HAVE THEY LEFT YET?
OH, UH...
I THINK SO?
OH, GOOD.
I CAN STOP HIDING.
I MEAN, I KNOW THEY MEAN WELL, BUT UGH.
THEY WERE SO ANNOYING TODAY.
IT'S LIKE THEY'RE TRYING TO ARRANGE MY MARRIAGE.
...OH!
I HEARD ZEKE WAS HARASSING NIC AND EVERYONE TODAY...
...BUT YOU HELPED CHASE HIM OFF?
UH...
YEAH.

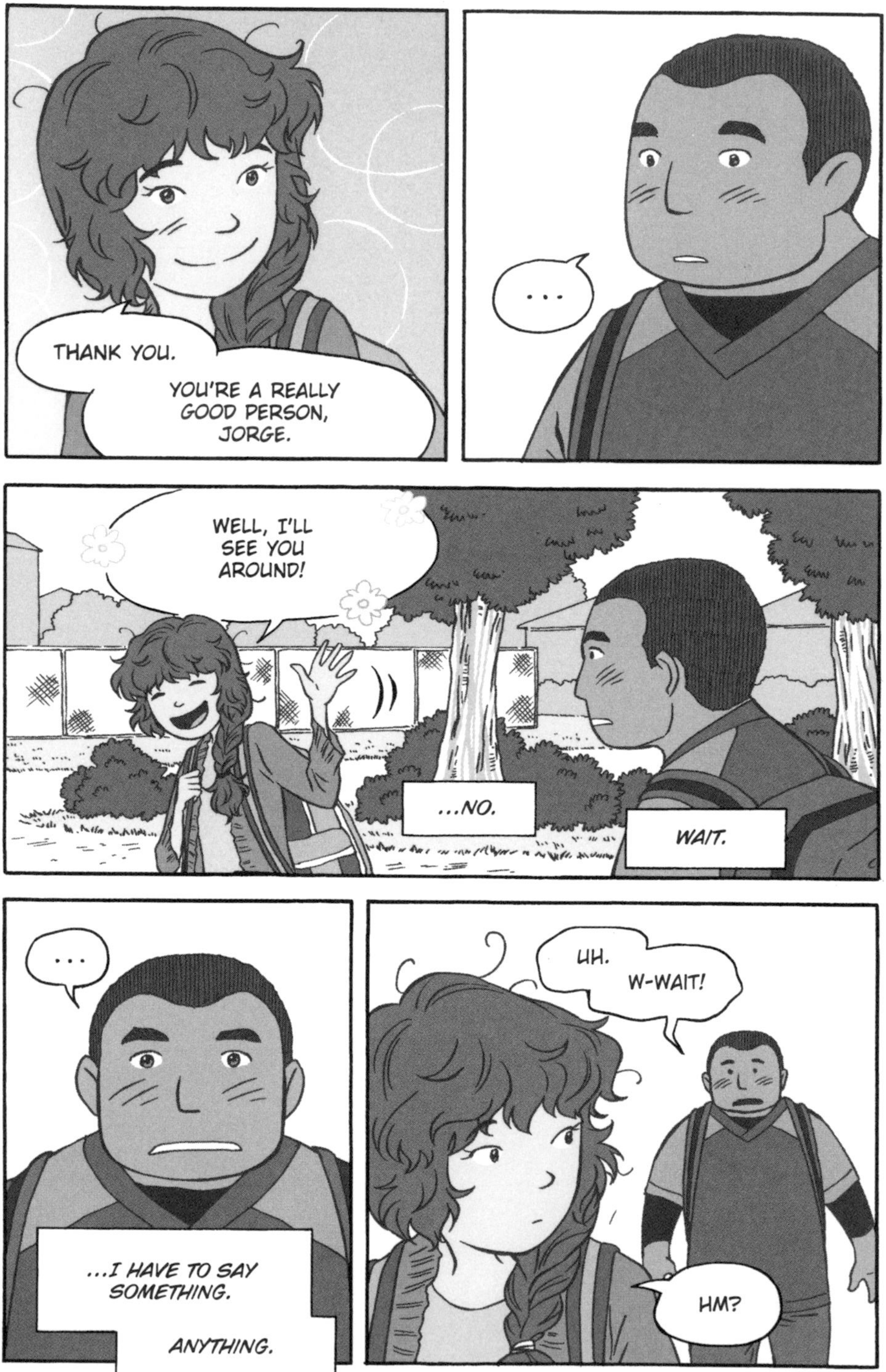
THANK YOU.
YOU'RE A REALLY GOOD PERSON, JORGE.
...
WELL, I'LL SEE YOU AROUND!
...NO.
WAIT.
...
...I HAVE TO SAY SOMETHING.
ANYTHING.
UH.
W-WAIT!
HM?

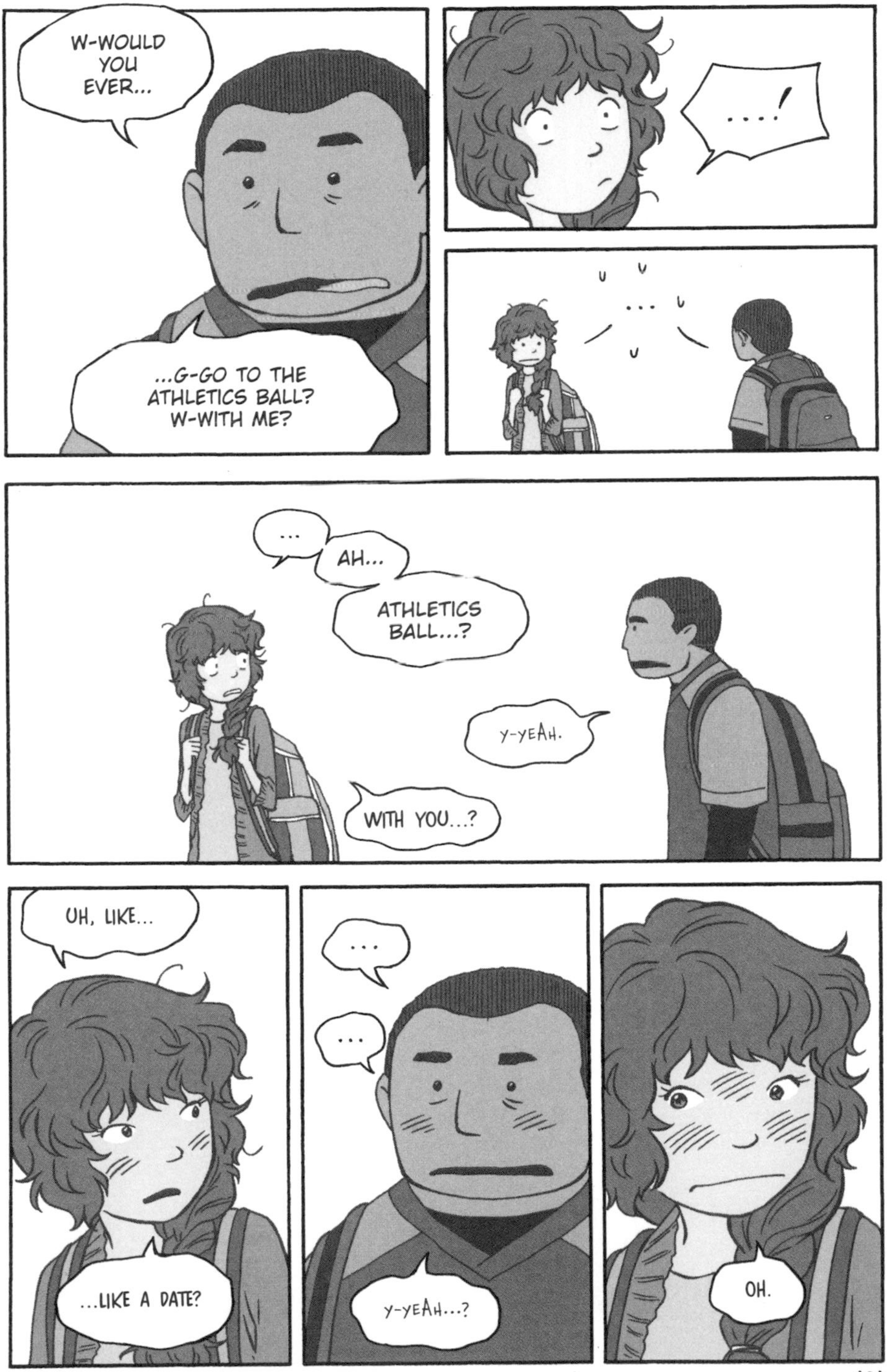
W-WOULD YOU EVER...
...G-GO TO THE ATHLETICS BALL? W-WITH ME?
....!
...
...
AH...
ATHLETICS BALL...?
Y-YEAH.
WITH YOU...?
UH, LIKE...
...LIKE A DATE?
...
...
Y-YEAH...?
OH.

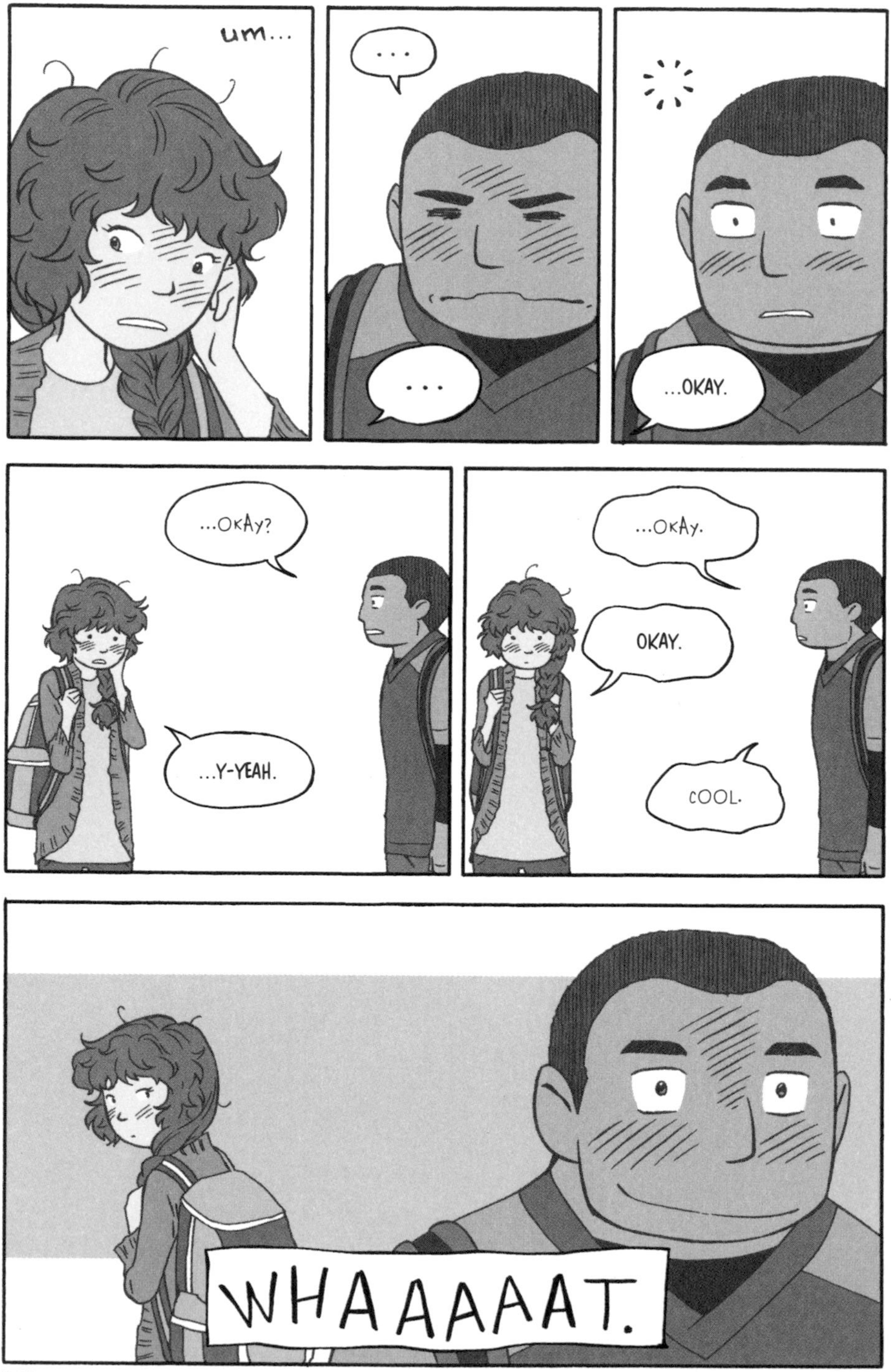
um...
...
...
...OKAY.
...OKAY?
...Y-YEAH.
...OKAY.
OKAY.
COOL.
WHAAAAAT.

CHAPTER 6

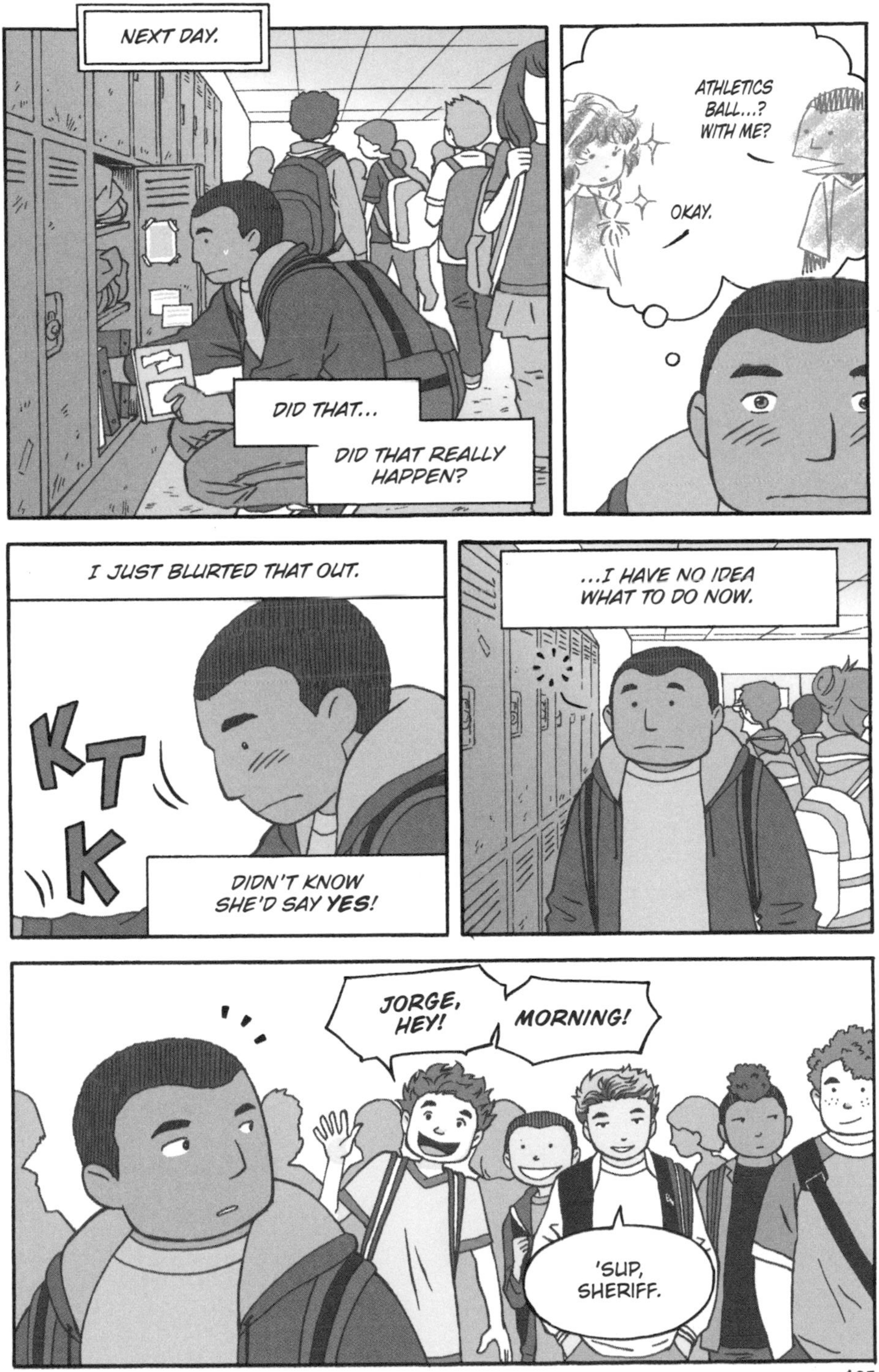
NEXT DAY.
DID THAT...
DID THAT REALLY HAPPEN?
ATHLETICS BALL...? WITH ME?
OKAY.
I JUST BLURTED THAT OUT.
KTK
DIDN'T KNOW SHE'D SAY YES!
...I HAVE NO IDEA WHAT TO DO NOW.
JORGE, HEY!
MORNING!
'SUP, SHERIFF.

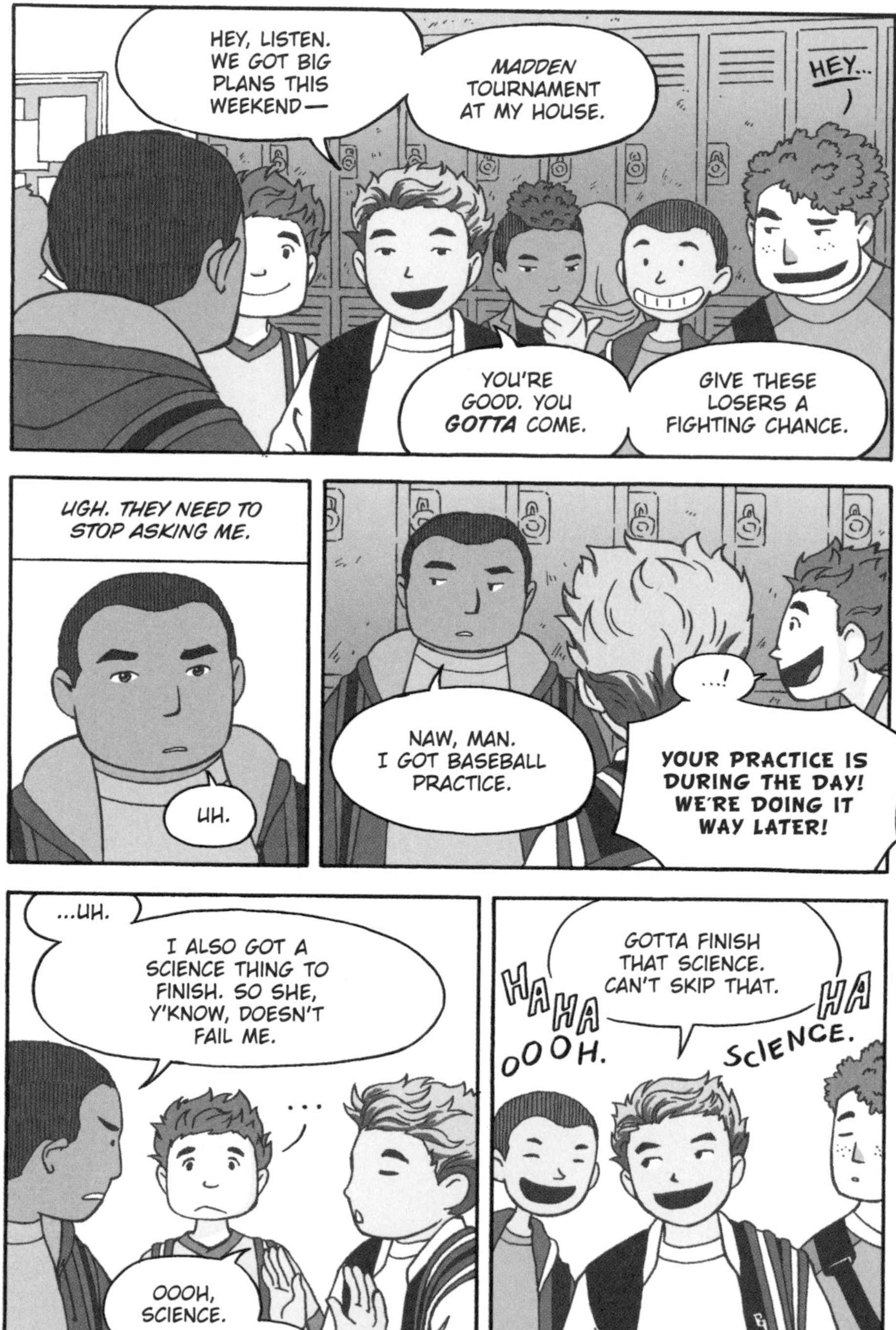
HEY, LISTEN. WE GOT BIG PLANS THIS WEEKEND—
MADDEN TOURNAMENT AT MY HOUSE.
HEY...
YOU'RE GOOD. YOU GOTTA COME.
GIVE THESE LOSERS A FIGHTING CHANCE.
UGH. THEY NEED TO STOP ASKING ME.
UH.
NAW, MAN. I GOT BASEBALL PRACTICE.
...!
YOUR PRACTICE IS DURING THE DAY! WE'RE DOING IT WAY LATER!
...UH.
I ALSO GOT A SCIENCE THING TO FINISH. SO SHE, Y'KNOW, DOESN'T FAIL ME.
...
OOOH, SCIENCE.
WELL.
HAHAHA
OOOH.
GOTTA FINISH THAT SCIENCE. CAN'T SKIP THAT.
HA
SCIENCE.

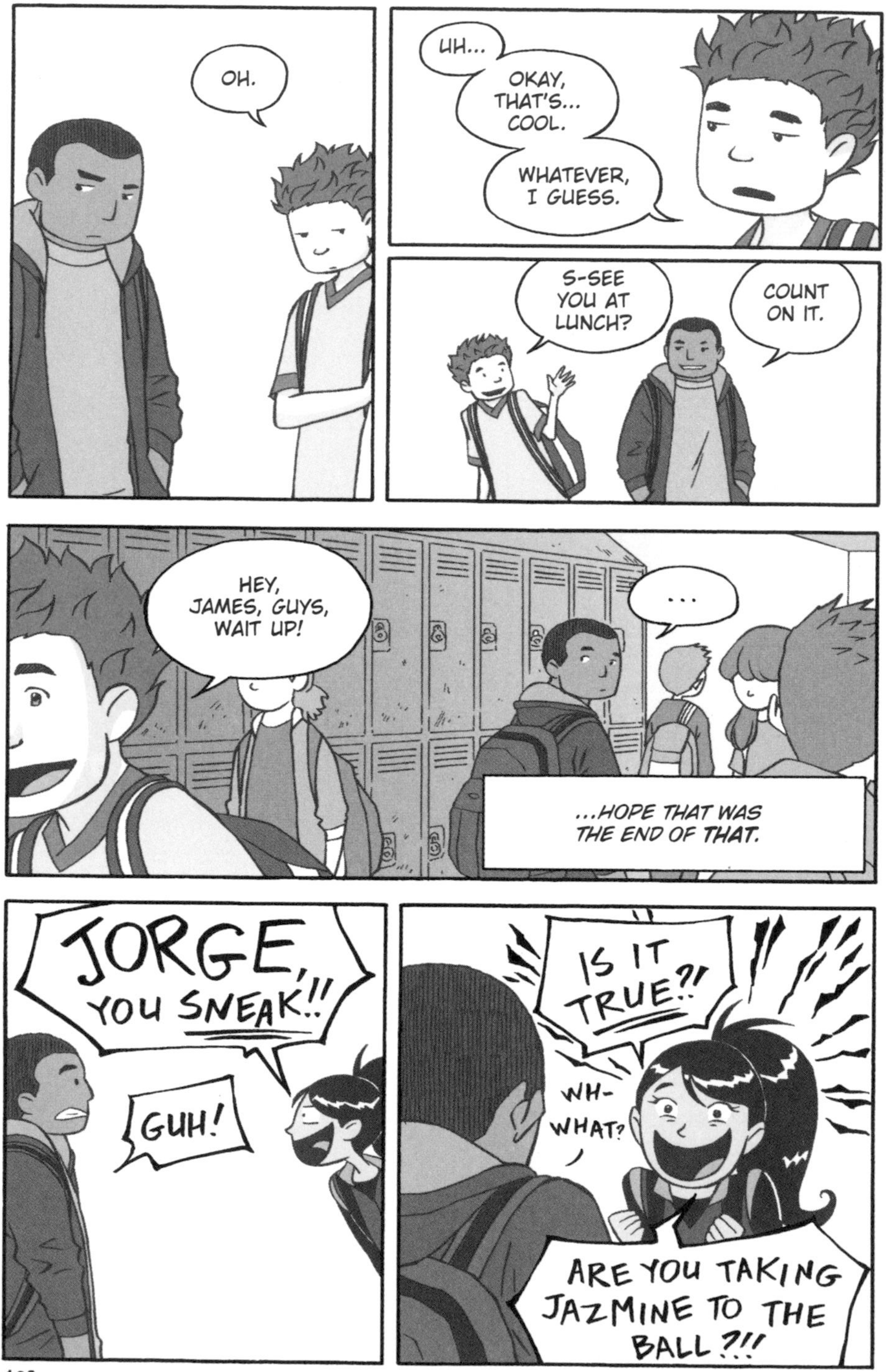
OH.
UH...
OKAY, THAT'S... COOL.
WHATEVER, I GUESS.
S-SEE YOU AT LUNCH?
COUNT ON IT.
HEY, JAMES, GUYS, WAIT UP!
...
...HOPE THAT WAS THE END OF THAT.
JORGE, YOU SNEAK!!
GUH!
IS IT TRUE?!
WH-WHAT?
ARE YOU TAKING JAZMINE TO THE BALL?!!

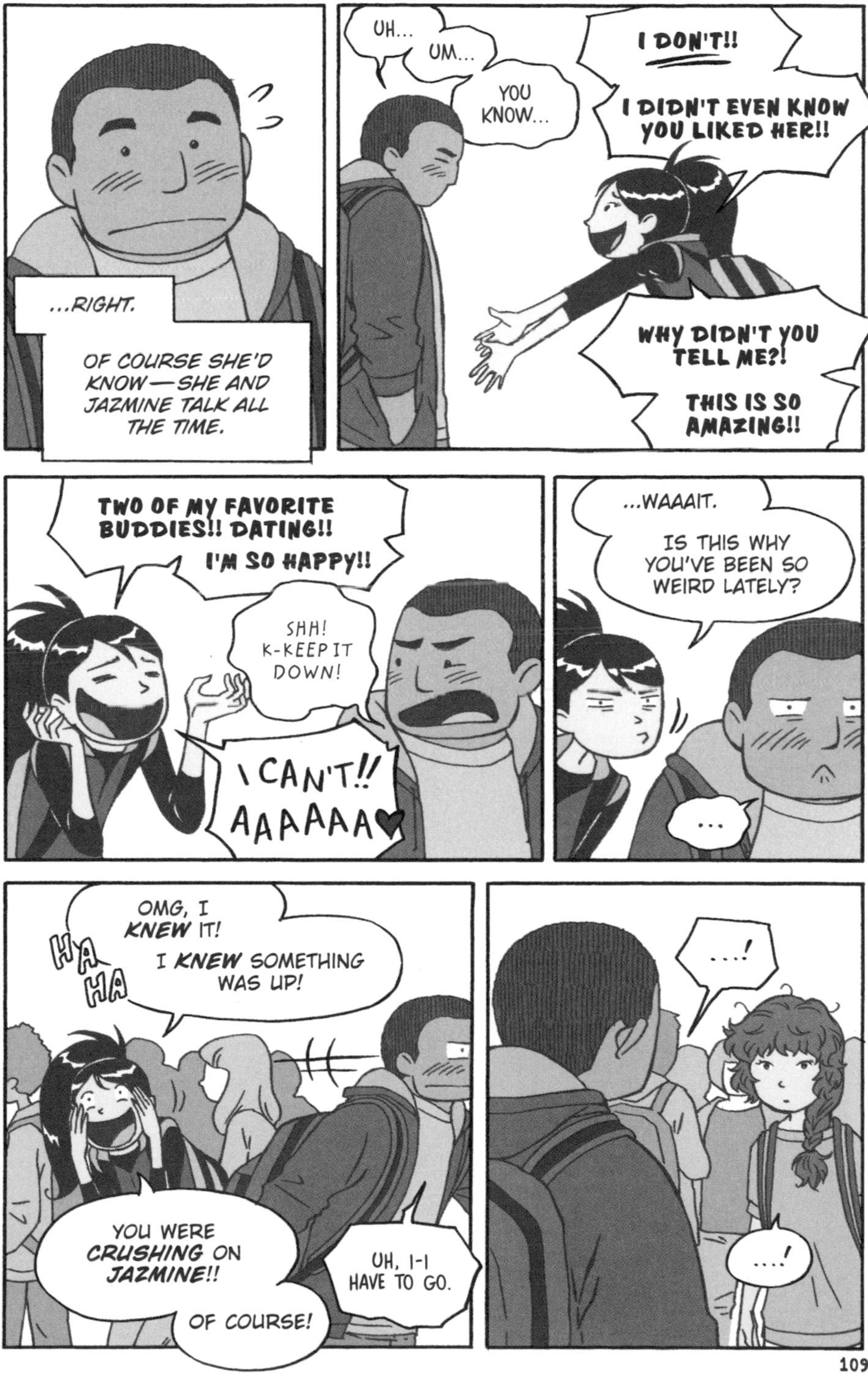
...RIGHT.
OF COURSE SHE'D KNOW—SHE AND JAZMINE TALK ALL THE TIME.
UH...
UM...
YOU KNOW...
I DON'T!!
I DIDN'T EVEN KNOW YOU LIKED HER!!
WHY DIDN'T YOU TELL ME?!
THIS IS SO AMAZING!!
TWO OF MY FAVORITE BUDDIES!! DATING!!
I'M SO HAPPY!!
SHH! K-KEEP IT DOWN!
I CAN'T!! AAAAAA♥
...WAAAIT.
IS THIS WHY YOU'VE BEEN SO WEIRD LATELY?
...
HA HA
OMG, I KNEW IT!
I KNEW SOMETHING WAS UP!
YOU WERE CRUSHING ON JAZMINE!!
OF COURSE!
UH, I-I HAVE TO GO.
...!
...!

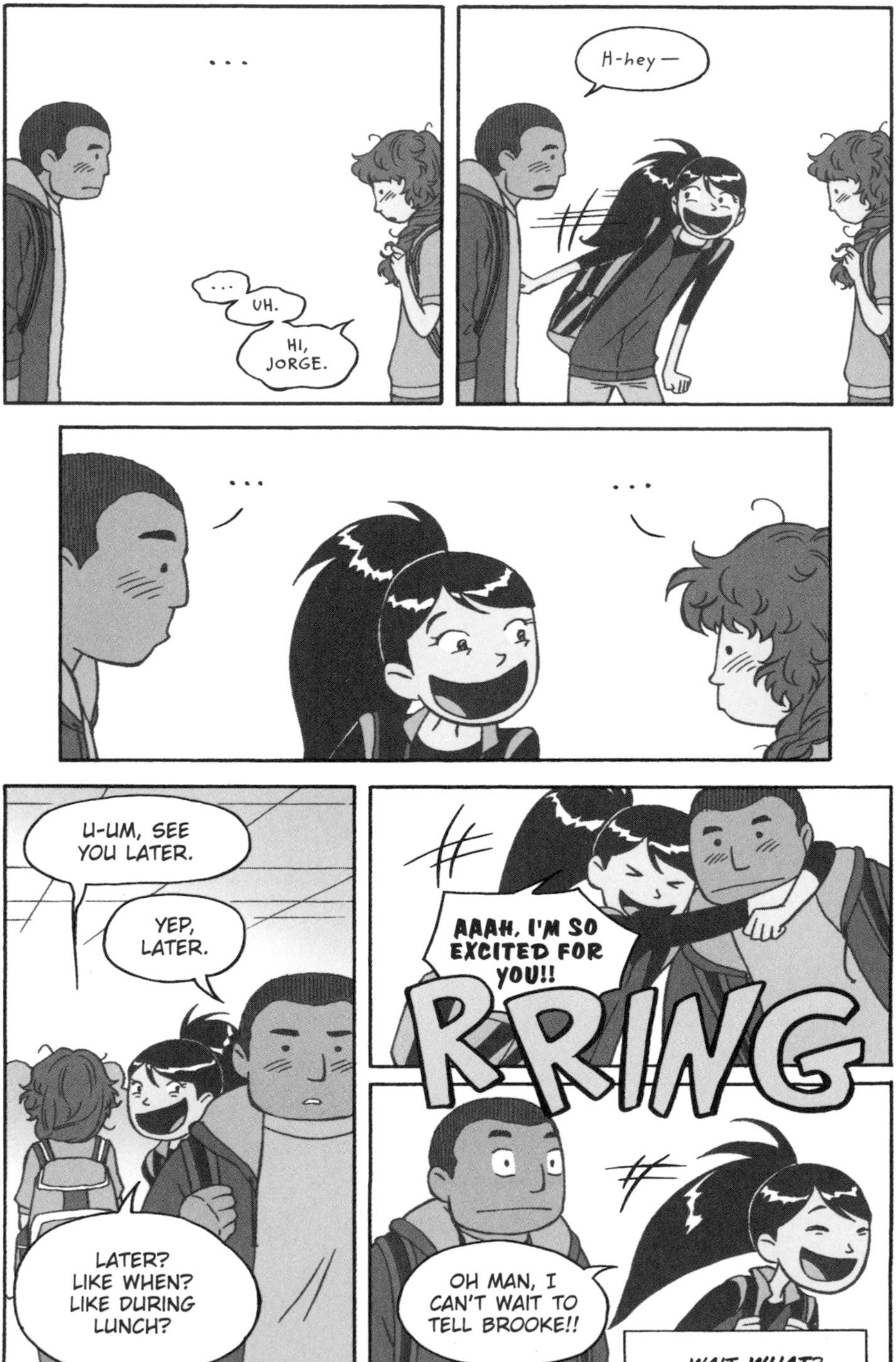
...
... UH.
HI, JORGE.
H-hey—
...
...
U-UM, SEE YOU LATER.
YEP, LATER.
LATER? LIKE WHEN? LIKE DURING LUNCH?
AAAH, I'M SO EXCITED FOR YOU!!
RRING
OH MAN, I CAN'T WAIT TO TELL BROOKE!!
...WAIT, WHAT?

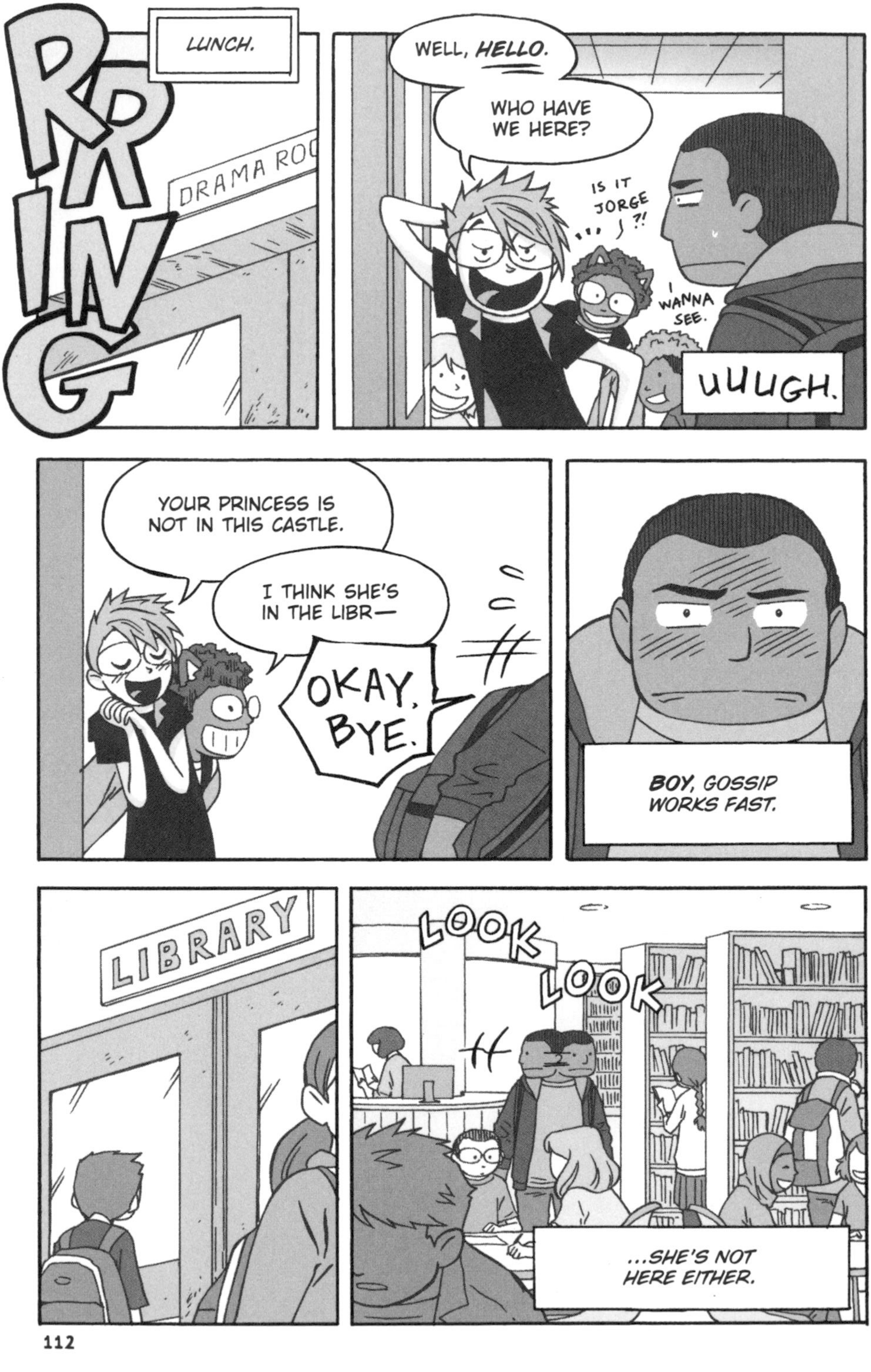
RRRING
LUNCH.
DRAMA ROO
WELL, HELLO.
WHO HAVE WE HERE?
IS IT JORGE ?!
I WANNA SEE.
UUUGH.
YOUR PRINCESS IS NOT IN THIS CASTLE.
I THINK SHE'S IN THE LIBR—
OKAY. BYE.
BOY, GOSSIP WORKS FAST.
LIBRARY
LOOK
LOOK
...SHE'S NOT HERE EITHER.

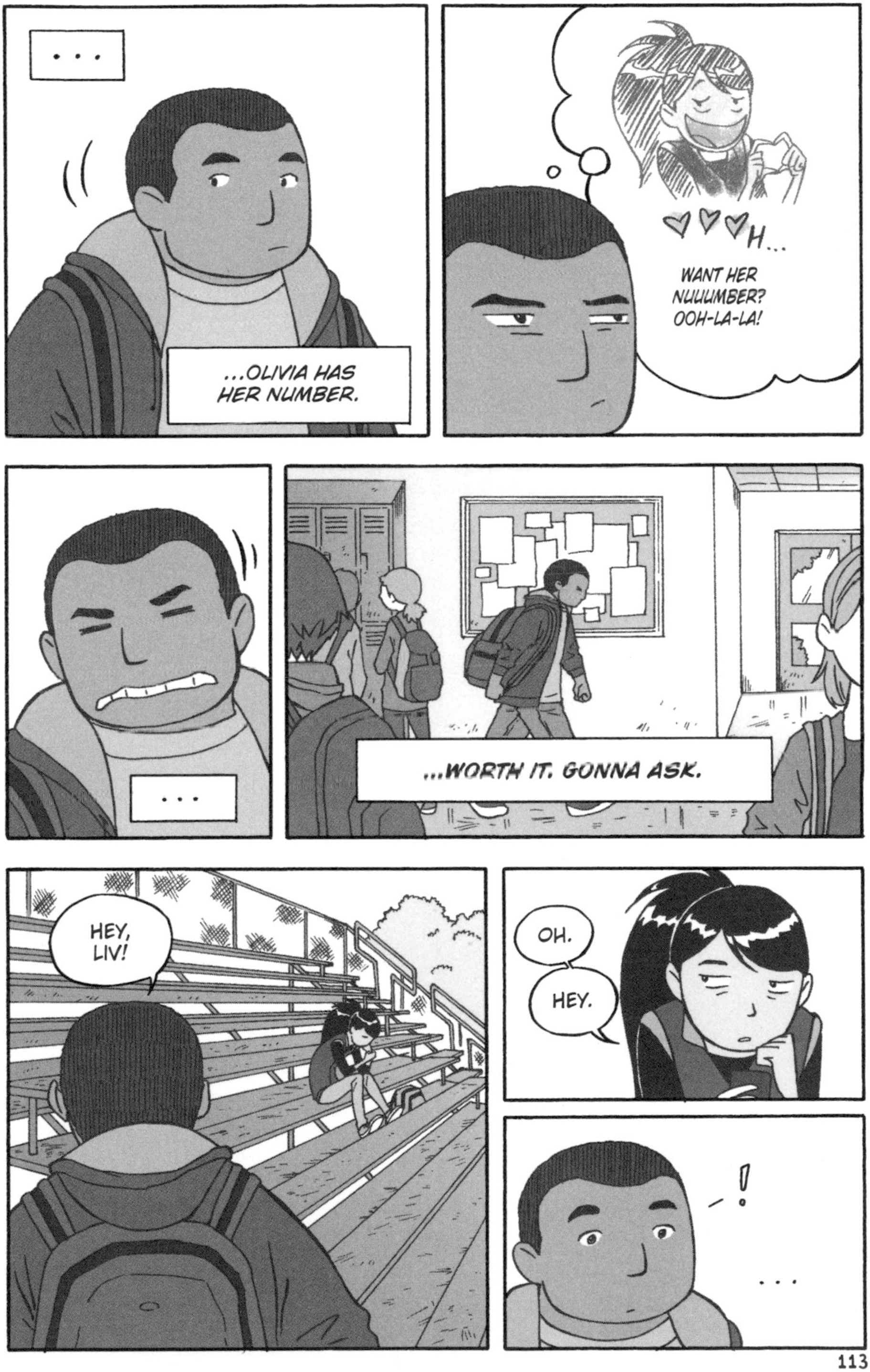
. . .
...OLIVIA HAS HER NUMBER.
♥♥♥H...
WANT HER NUUUMBER? OOH-LA-LA!
. . .
...WORTH IT. GONNA ASK.
HEY, LIV!
OH.
HEY.
!
. . .

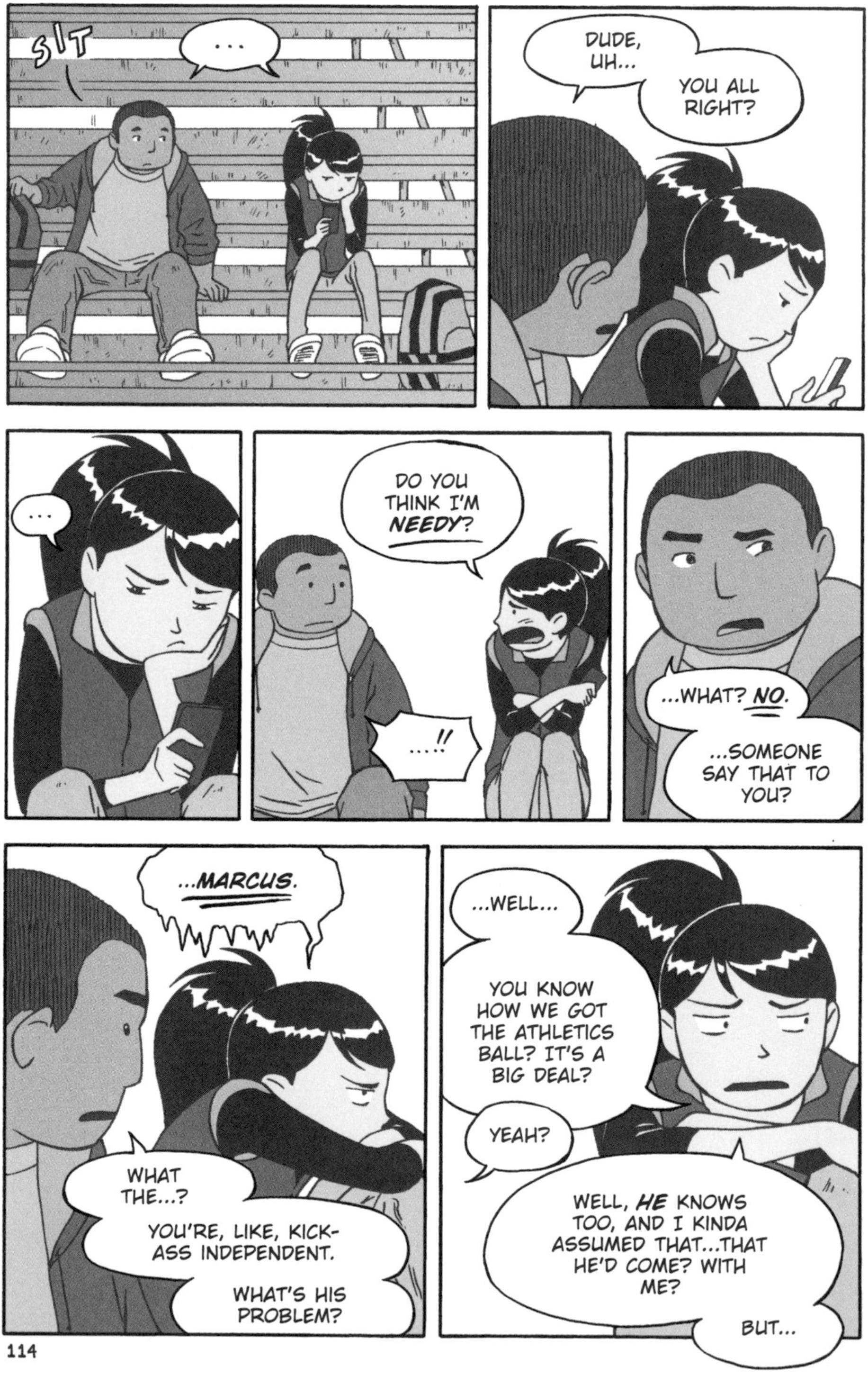
SIT
...
DUDE, UH...
YOU ALL RIGHT?
...
DO YOU THINK I'M NEEDY?
....!!
...WHAT? NO.
...SOMEONE SAY THAT TO YOU?
...MARCUS.
WHAT THE...?
YOU'RE, LIKE, KICK-ASS INDEPENDENT.
WHAT'S HIS PROBLEM?
...WELL...
YOU KNOW HOW WE GOT THE ATHLETICS BALL? IT'S A BIG DEAL?
YEAH?
WELL, HE KNOWS TOO, AND I KINDA ASSUMED THAT...THAT HE'D COME? WITH ME?
BUT...

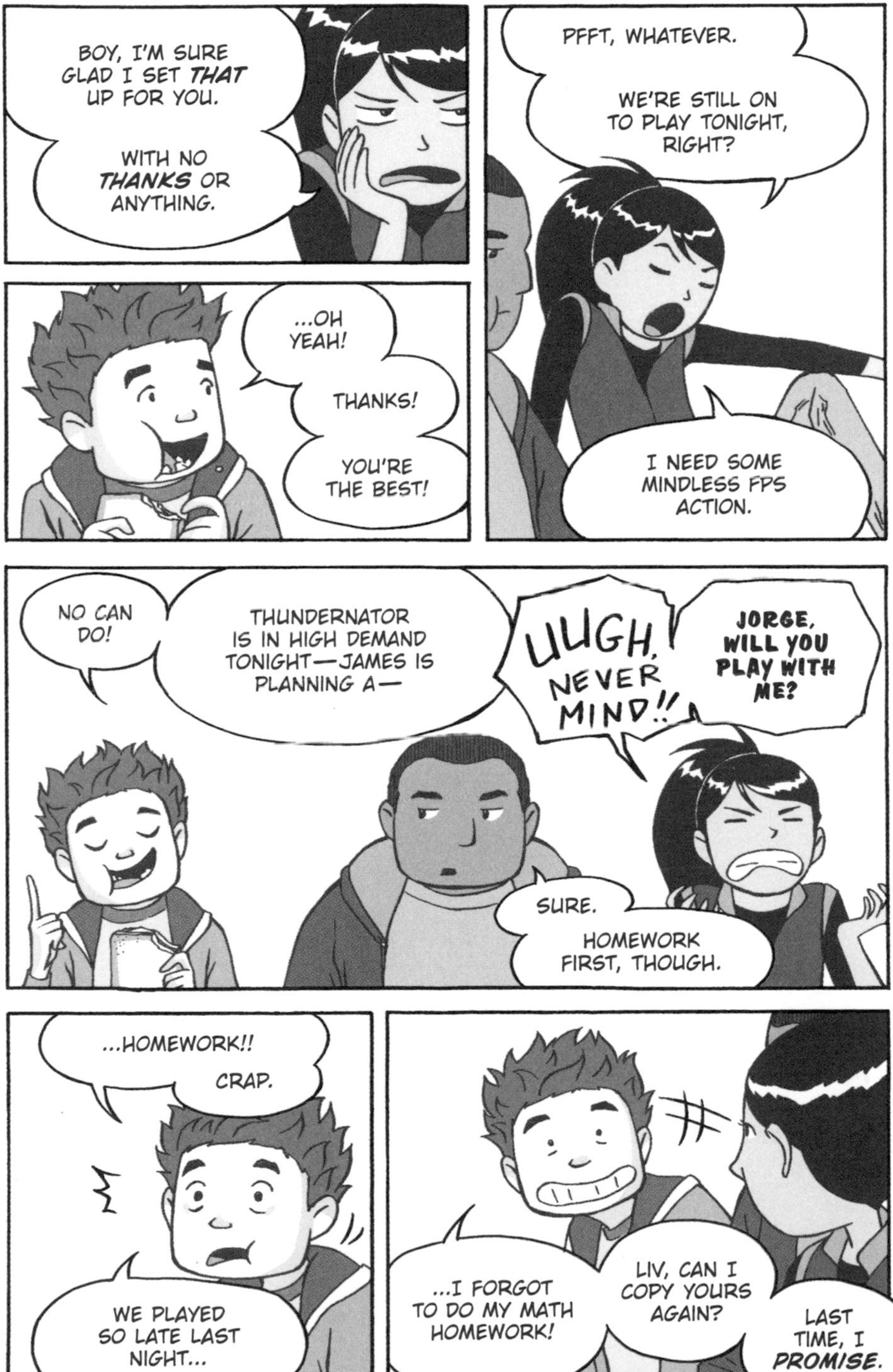
BOY, I'M SURE GLAD I SET *THAT* UP FOR YOU.
WITH NO *THANKS* OR ANYTHING.
PFFT, WHATEVER.
WE'RE STILL ON TO PLAY TONIGHT, RIGHT?
...OH YEAH!
THANKS!
YOU'RE THE BEST!
I NEED SOME MINDLESS FPS ACTION.
NO CAN DO!
THUNDERNATOR IS IN HIGH DEMAND TONIGHT—JAMES IS PLANNING A—
UUGH, NEVER MIND!!
JORGE, WILL YOU PLAY WITH ME?
SURE.
HOMEWORK FIRST, THOUGH.
...HOMEWORK!!
CRAP.
WE PLAYED SO LATE LAST NIGHT...
...I FORGOT TO DO MY MATH HOMEWORK!
LIV, CAN I COPY YOURS AGAIN?
LAST TIME, I ***PROMISE***.

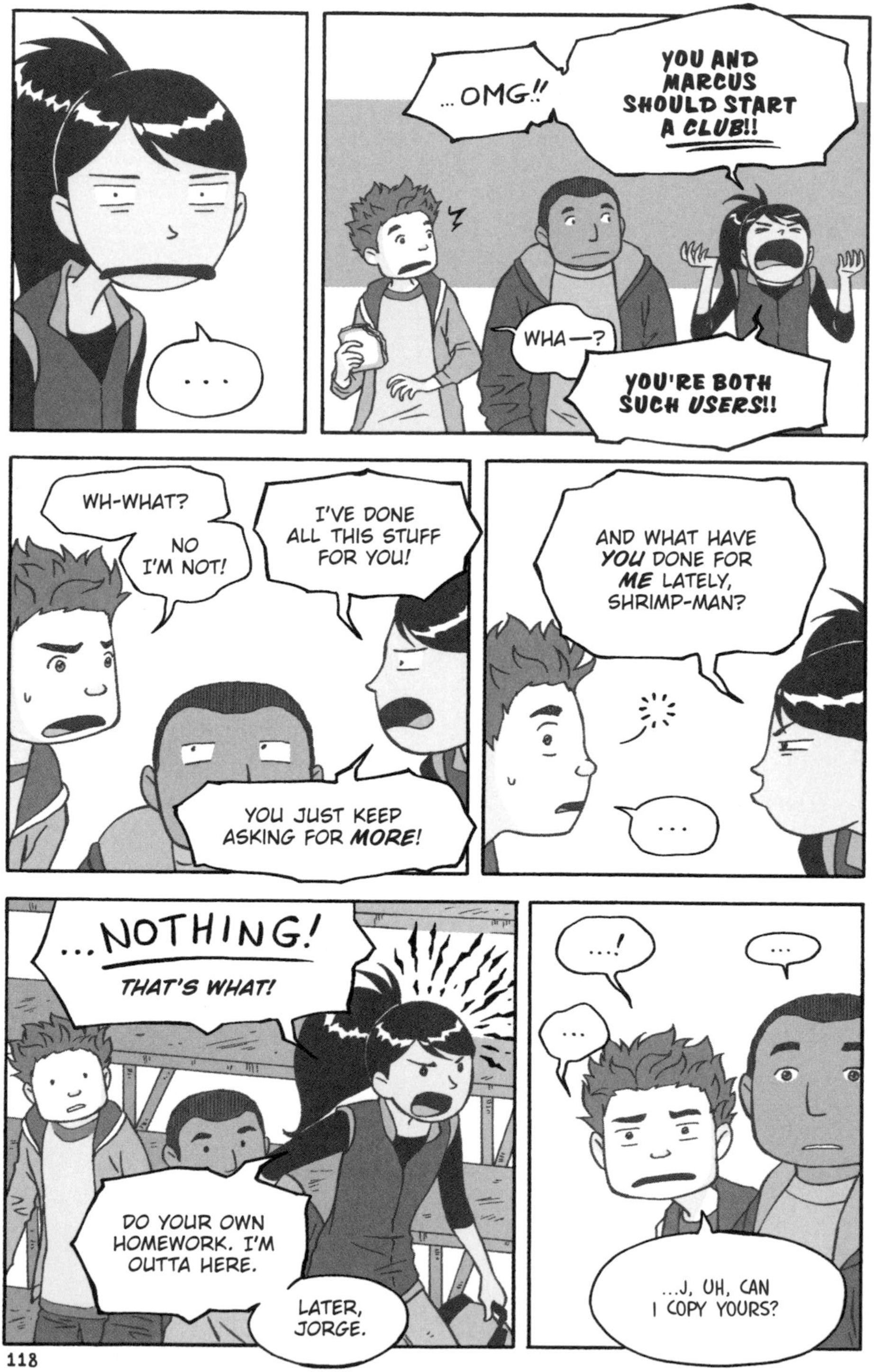
. . .
...OMG!!
YOU AND MARCUS SHOULD START A CLUB!!
WHA—?
YOU'RE BOTH SUCH USERS!!
WH-WHAT?
NO I'M NOT!
I'VE DONE ALL THIS STUFF FOR YOU!
YOU JUST KEEP ASKING FOR MORE!
AND WHAT HAVE YOU DONE FOR ME LATELY, SHRIMP-MAN?
. . .
...NOTHING!
THAT'S WHAT!
DO YOUR OWN HOMEWORK. I'M OUTTA HERE.
LATER, JORGE.
...!
...
...
...J, UH, CAN I COPY YOURS?

120

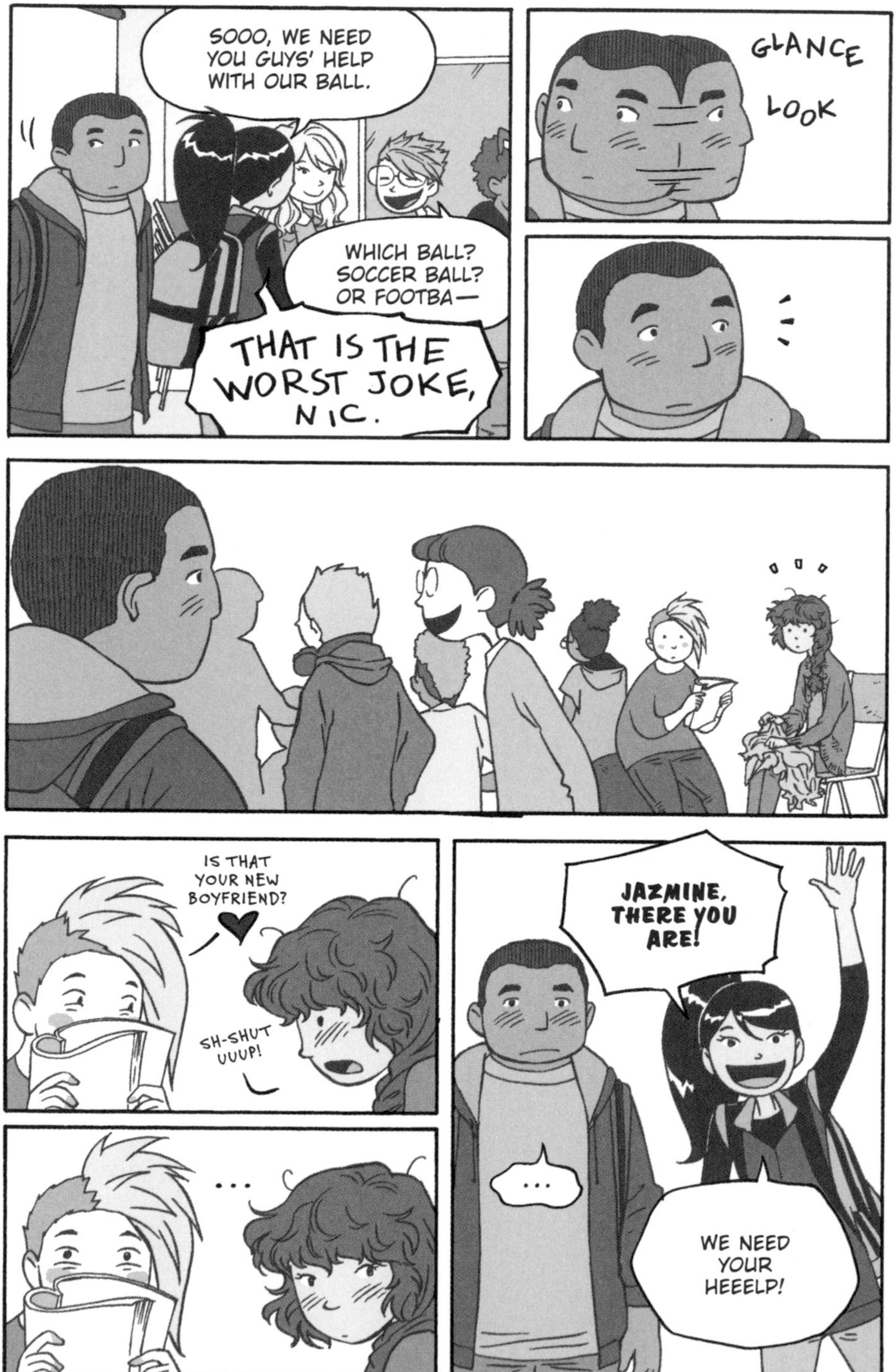

SOOO, WE NEED YOU GUYS' HELP WITH OUR BALL.
WHICH BALL? SOCCER BALL? OR FOOTBA—
THAT IS THE WORST JOKE, NIC.
GLANCE
LOOK
IS THAT YOUR NEW BOYFRIEND?
SH-SHUT UUUP!
...
JAZMINE, THERE YOU ARE!
...
WE NEED YOUR HEEELP!

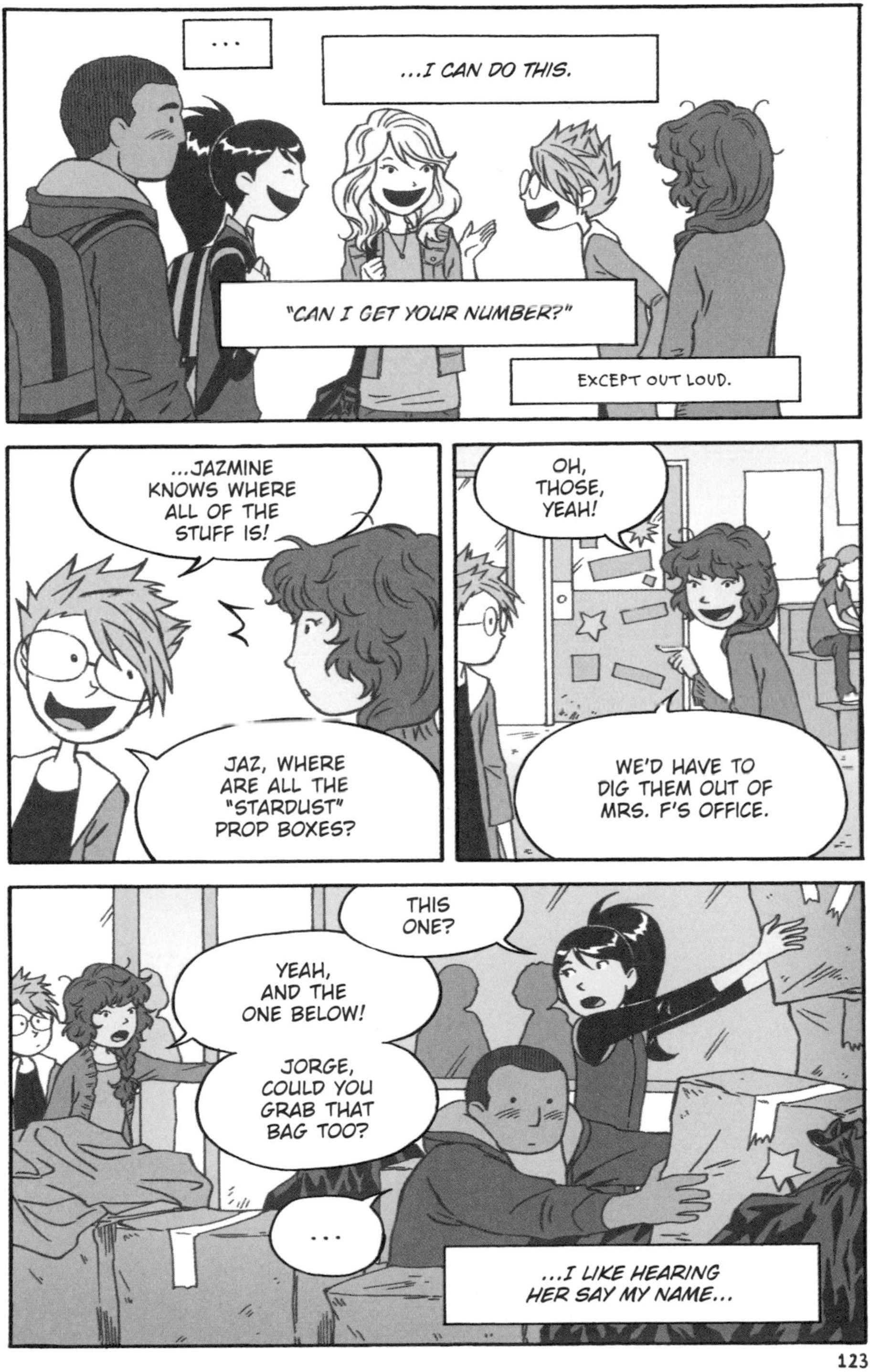
...
...I CAN DO THIS.
"CAN I GET YOUR NUMBER?"
EXCEPT OUT LOUD.
...JAZMINE KNOWS WHERE ALL OF THE STUFF IS!
JAZ, WHERE ARE ALL THE "STARDUST" PROP BOXES?
OH, THOSE, YEAH!
WE'D HAVE TO DIG THEM OUT OF MRS. F'S OFFICE.
THIS ONE?
YEAH, AND THE ONE BELOW!
JORGE, COULD YOU GRAB THAT BAG TOO?
...
...I LIKE HEARING HER SAY MY NAME...

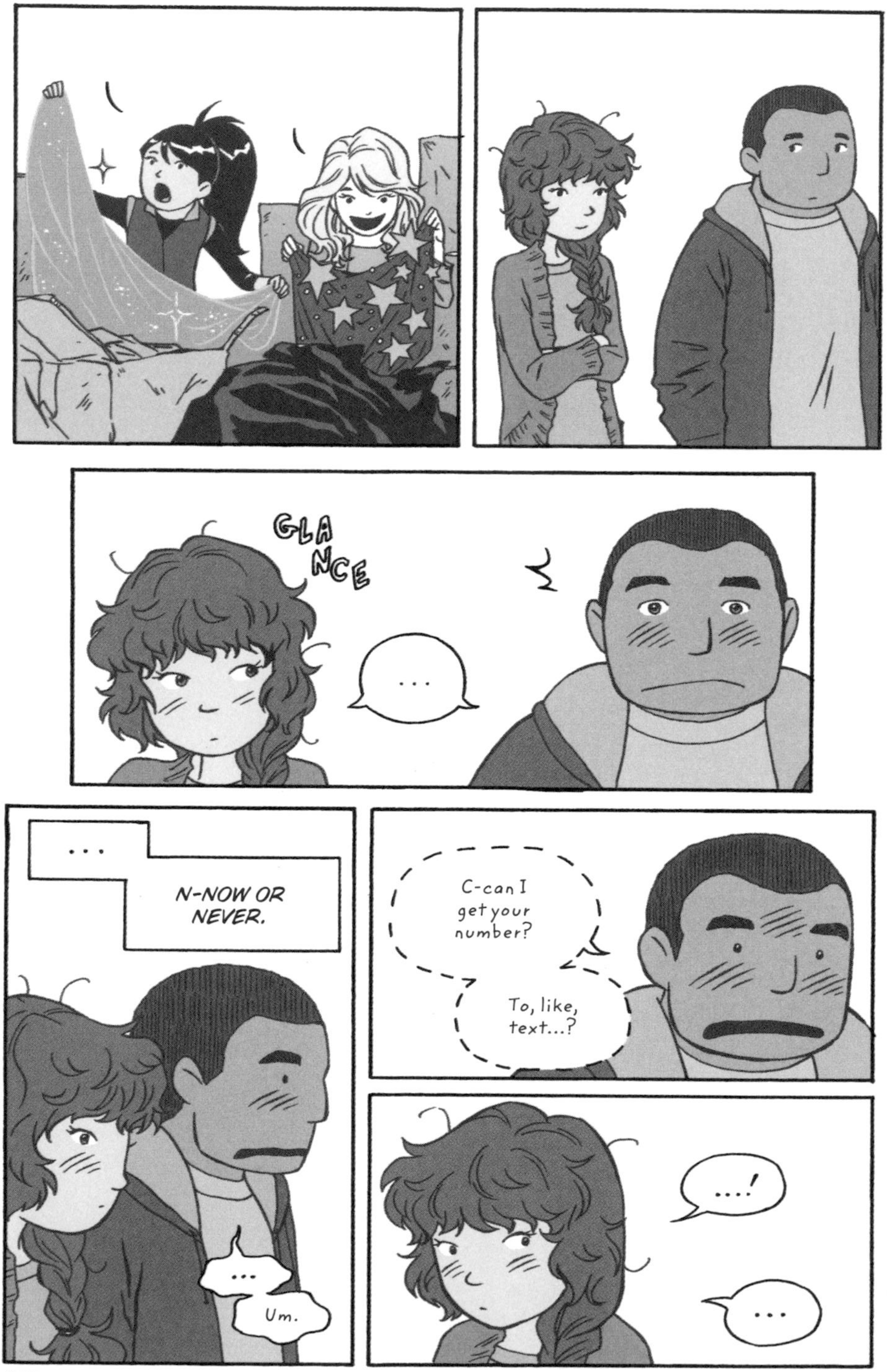
GLANCE
...
...
N-NOW OR NEVER.
...
Um.
C-can I get your number?
To, like, text...?
....!
...

CHAPTER 7

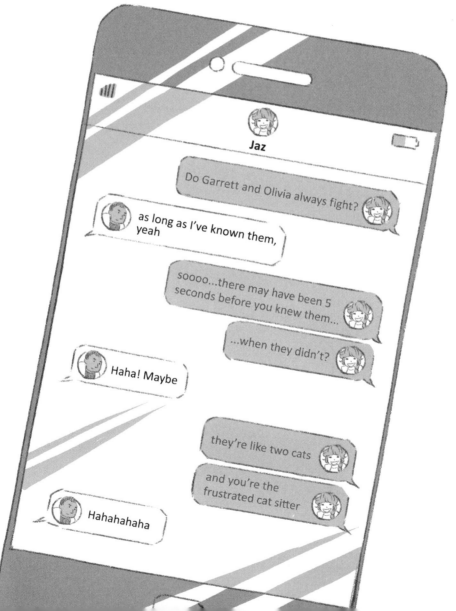

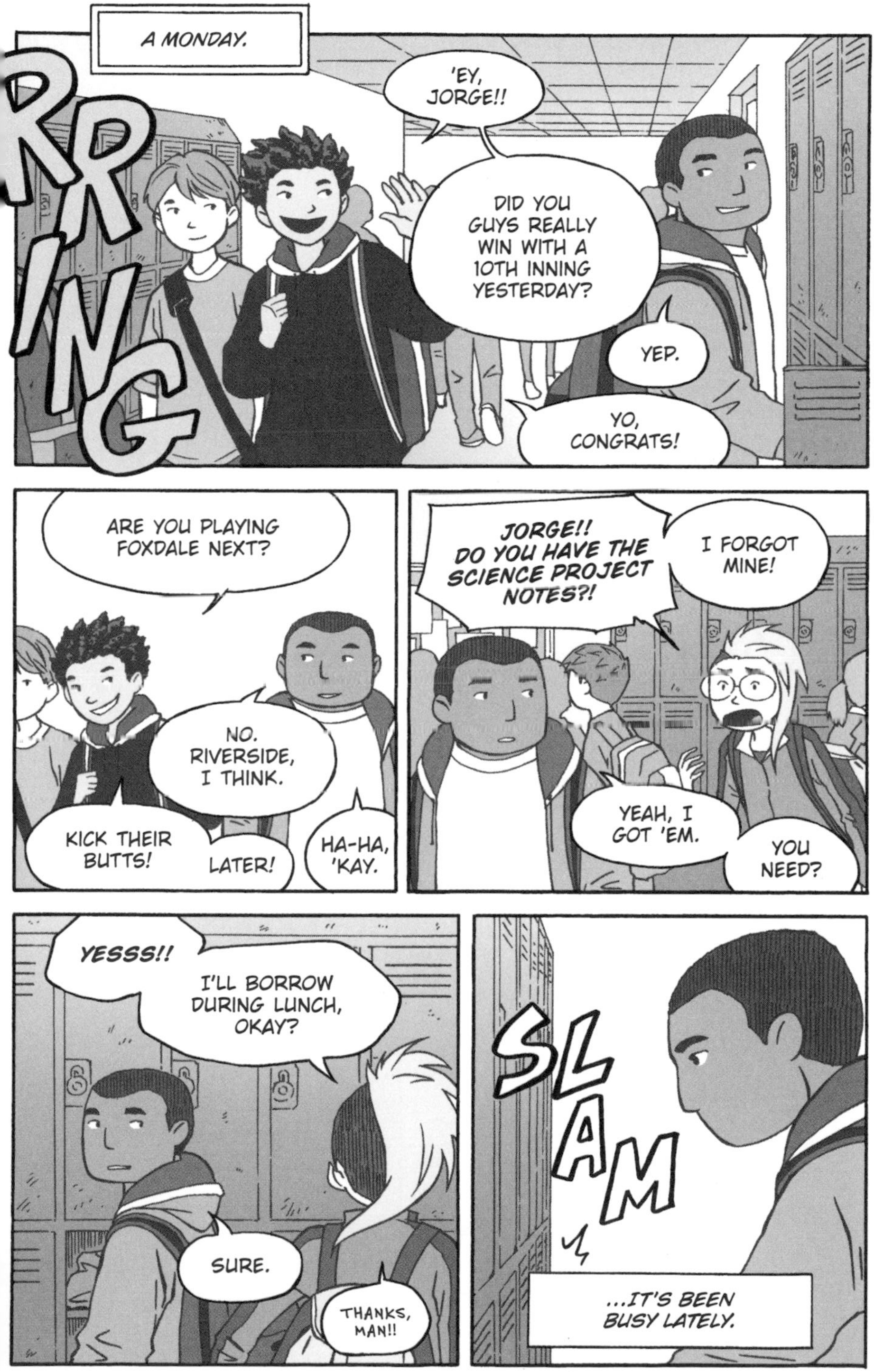
A MONDAY.
RRRING
'EY, JORGE!!
DID YOU GUYS REALLY WIN WITH A 10TH INNING YESTERDAY?
YEP.
YO, CONGRATS!
ARE YOU PLAYING FOXDALE NEXT?
NO. RIVERSIDE, I THINK.
KICK THEIR BUTTS!
LATER!
HA-HA, 'KAY.
JORGE!! DO YOU HAVE THE SCIENCE PROJECT NOTES?!
I FORGOT MINE!
YEAH, I GOT 'EM.
YOU NEED?
YESSS!!
I'LL BORROW DURING LUNCH, OKAY?
SURE.
THANKS, MAN!!
SLAM
...IT'S BEEN BUSY LATELY.

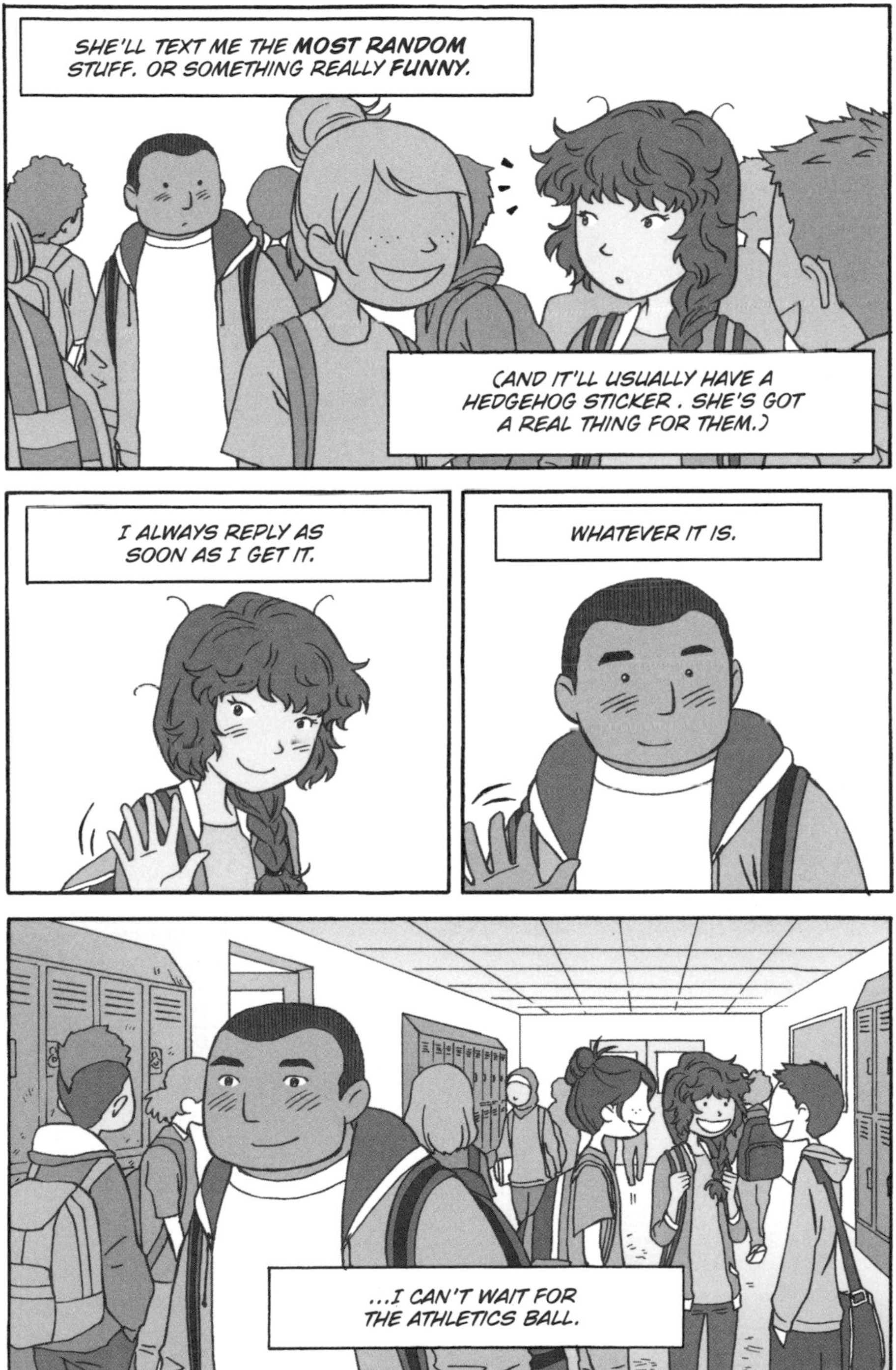
SHE'LL TEXT ME THE **MOST RANDOM** STUFF. OR SOMETHING REALLY **FUNNY.**
(AND IT'LL USUALLY HAVE A HEDGEHOG STICKER . SHE'S GOT A REAL THING FOR THEM.)
I ALWAYS REPLY AS SOON AS I GET IT.
WHATEVER IT IS.
...I CAN'T WAIT FOR THE ATHLETICS BALL.

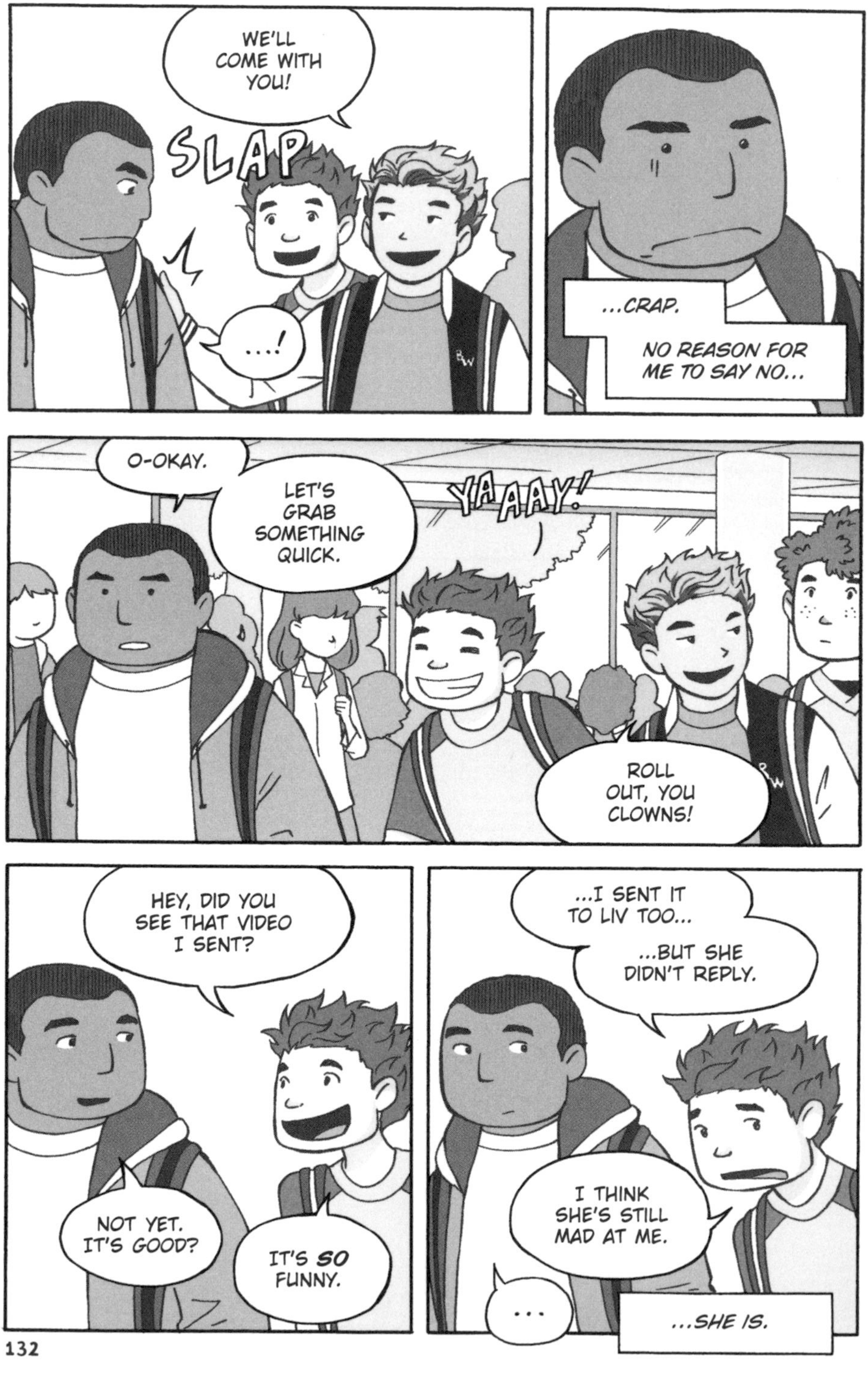
WE'LL COME WITH YOU!
SLAP
....!
...CRAP.
NO REASON FOR ME TO SAY NO...
O-OKAY.
LET'S GRAB SOMETHING QUICK.
YAAAAY!
ROLL OUT, YOU CLOWNS!
HEY, DID YOU SEE THAT VIDEO I SENT?
NOT YET. IT'S GOOD?
IT'S SO FUNNY.
...I SENT IT TO LIV TOO...
...BUT SHE DIDN'T REPLY.
I THINK SHE'S STILL MAD AT ME.
...
...SHE IS.

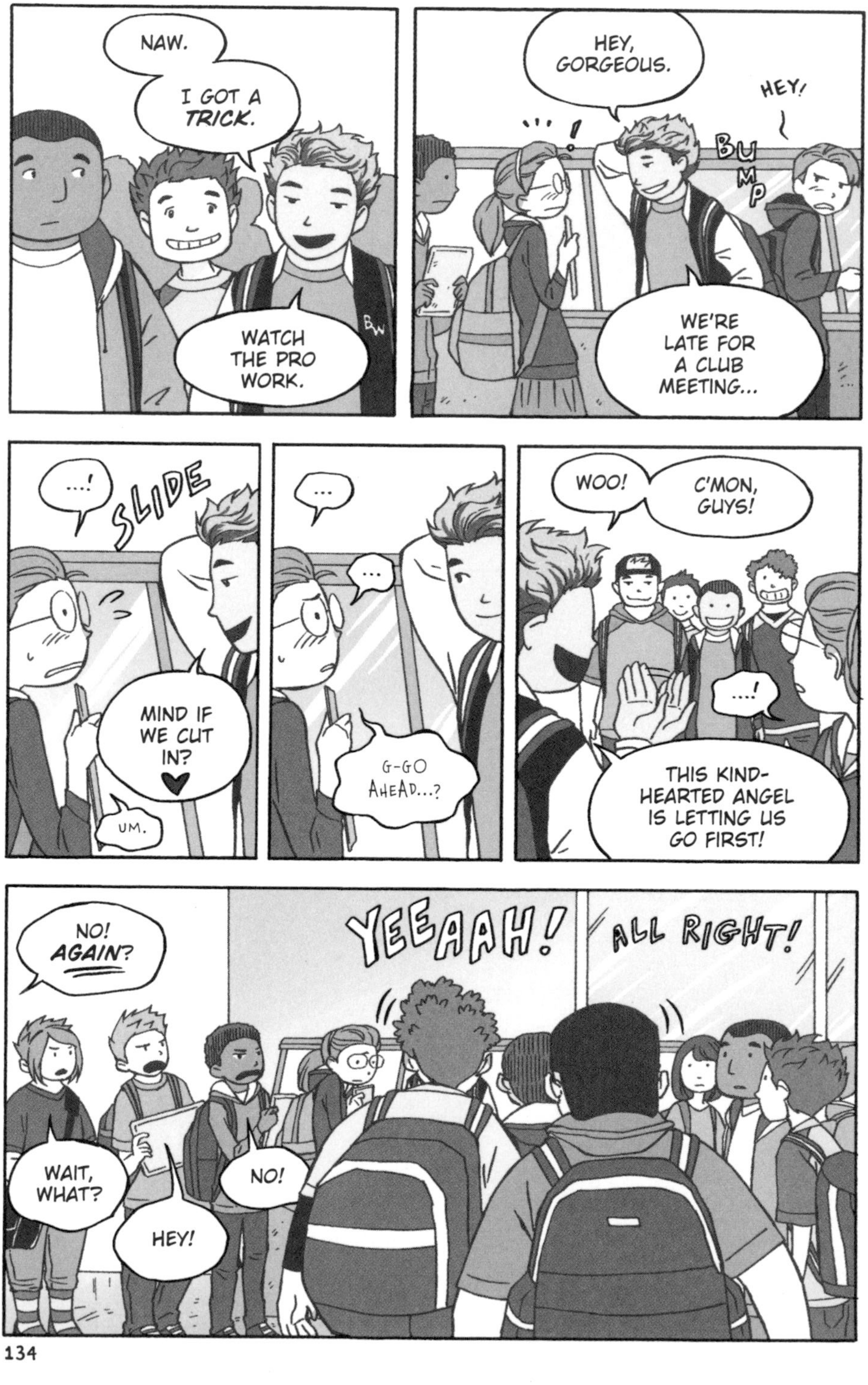
NAW.
I GOT A TRICK.
WATCH THE PRO WORK.
HEY, GORGEOUS.
...!
HEY!
BUMP
WE'RE LATE FOR A CLUB MEETING...
...!
SLIDE
MIND IF WE CUT IN?
UM.
...
...
G-GO AHEAD...?
WOO!
C'MON, GUYS!
...!
THIS KIND-HEARTED ANGEL IS LETTING US GO FIRST!
NO! AGAIN?
YEEAAH!
ALL RIGHT!
WAIT, WHAT?
HEY!
NO!

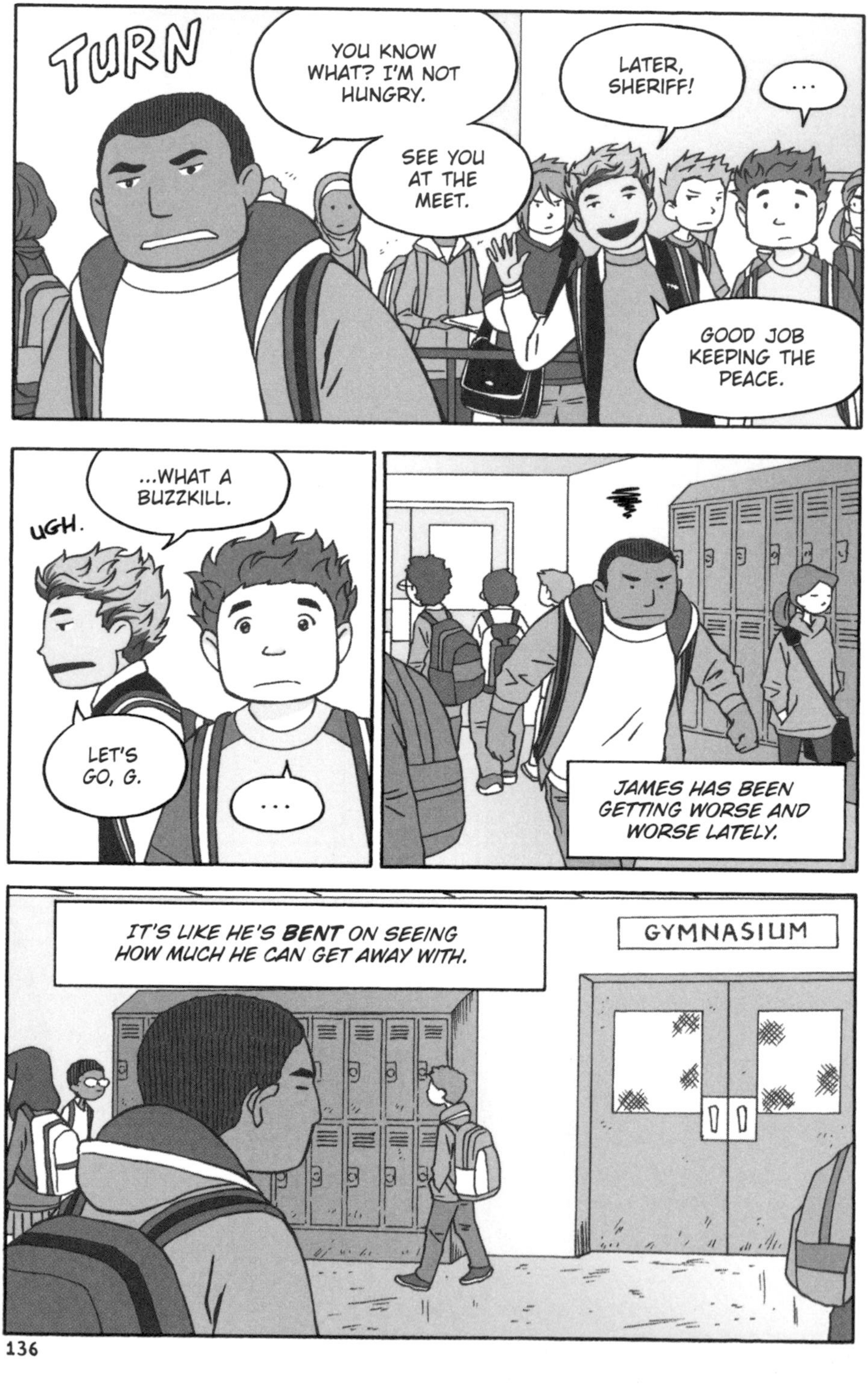
TURN
YOU KNOW WHAT? I'M NOT HUNGRY.
SEE YOU AT THE MEET.
LATER, SHERIFF!
...
GOOD JOB KEEPING THE PEACE.
...WHAT A BUZZKILL.
UGH.
LET'S GO, G.
...
JAMES HAS BEEN GETTING WORSE AND WORSE LATELY.
IT'S LIKE HE'S BENT ON SEEING HOW MUCH HE CAN GET AWAY WITH.
GYMNASIUM

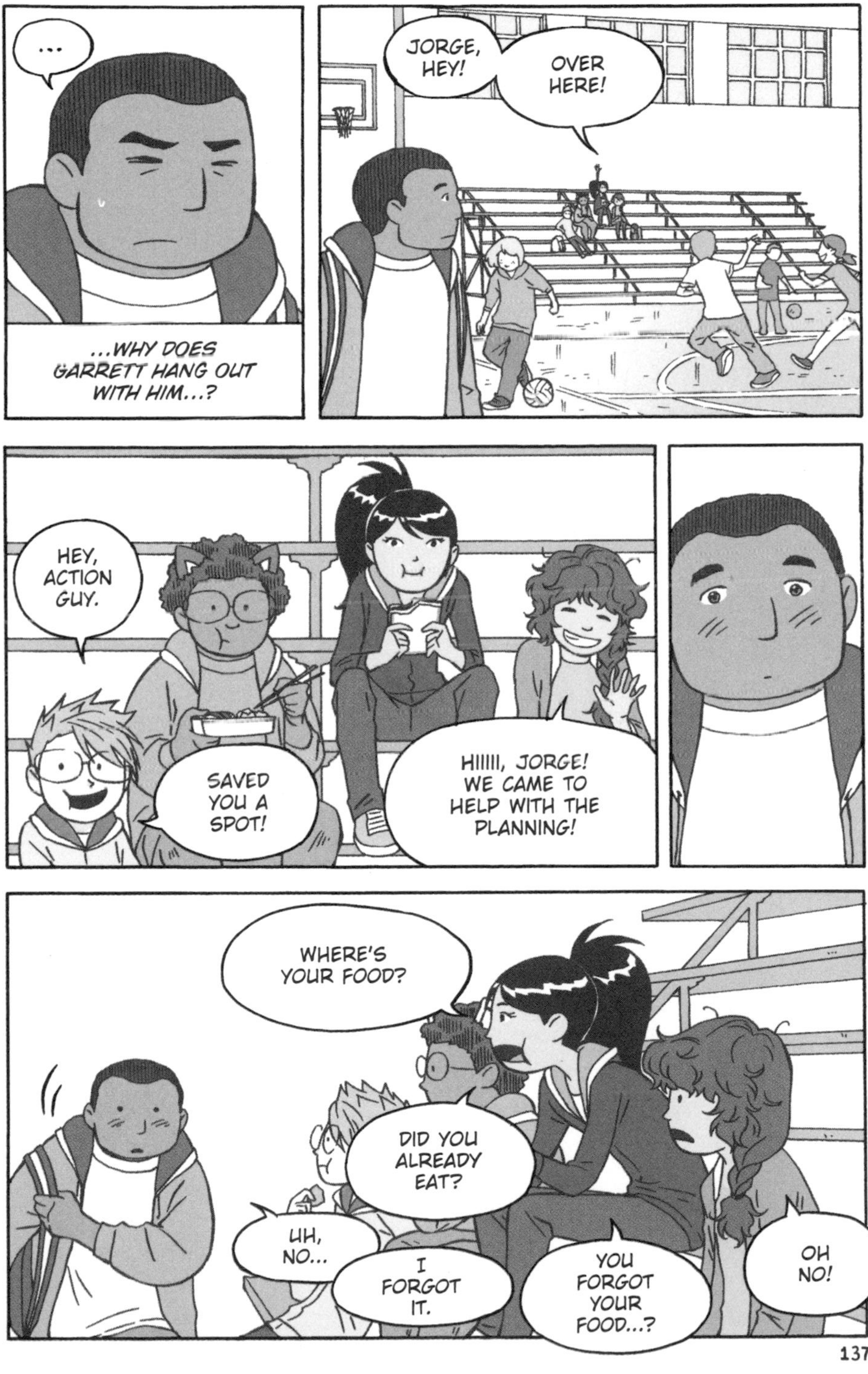
...
...WHY DOES GARRETT HANG OUT WITH HIM...?
JORGE, HEY!
OVER HERE!
HEY, ACTION GUY.
SAVED YOU A SPOT!
HIIIII, JORGE! WE CAME TO HELP WITH THE PLANNING!
WHERE'S YOUR FOOD?
DID YOU ALREADY EAT?
UH, NO...
I FORGOT IT.
YOU FORGOT YOUR FOOD...?
OH NO!

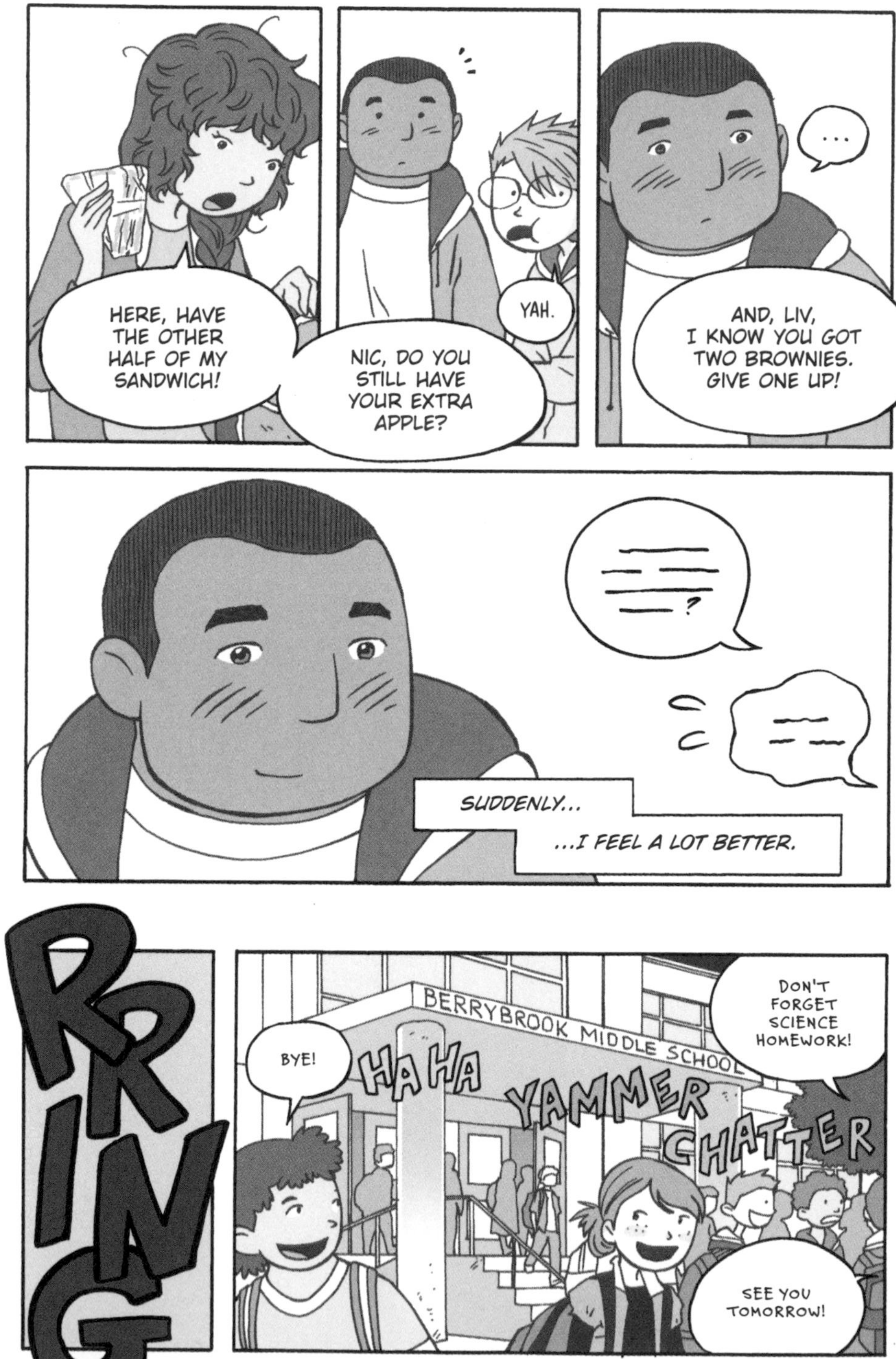
HERE, HAVE THE OTHER HALF OF MY SANDWICH!
YAH.
NIC, DO YOU STILL HAVE YOUR EXTRA APPLE?
...
AND, LIV, I KNOW YOU GOT TWO BROWNIES. GIVE ONE UP!
SUDDENLY...
...I FEEL A LOT BETTER.
RRING
BERRYBROOK MIDDLE SCHOOL
BYE!
HAHA
YAMMER
CHATTER
DON'T FORGET SCIENCE HOMEWORK!
SEE YOU TOMORROW!

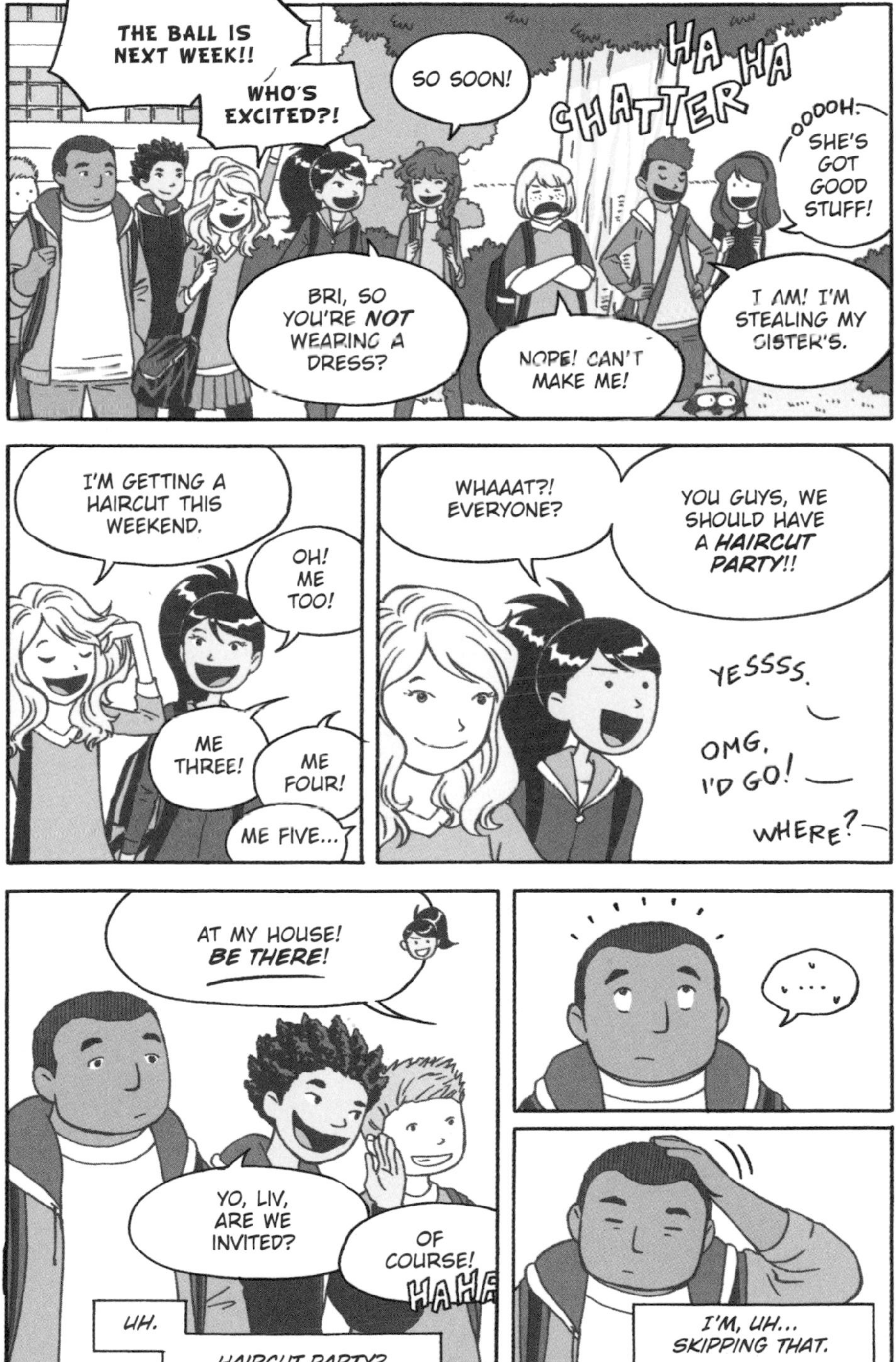
THE BALL IS NEXT WEEK!!
WHO'S EXCITED?!
SO SOON!
HA HA
CHATTER
OOOOH.
SHE'S GOT GOOD STUFF!
BRI, SO YOU'RE NOT WEARING A DRESS?
NOPE! CAN'T MAKE ME!
I AM! I'M STEALING MY SISTER'S.
I'M GETTING A HAIRCUT THIS WEEKEND.
OH! ME TOO!
ME THREE!
ME FOUR!
ME FIVE...
WHAAAT?! EVERYONE?
YOU GUYS, WE SHOULD HAVE A HAIRCUT PARTY!!
YESSSS.
OMG. I'D GO!
WHERE?
AT MY HOUSE! BE THERE!
YO, LIV, ARE WE INVITED?
OF COURSE!
HAHA
UH.
HAIRCUT PARTY?
I'M, UH... SKIPPING THAT.

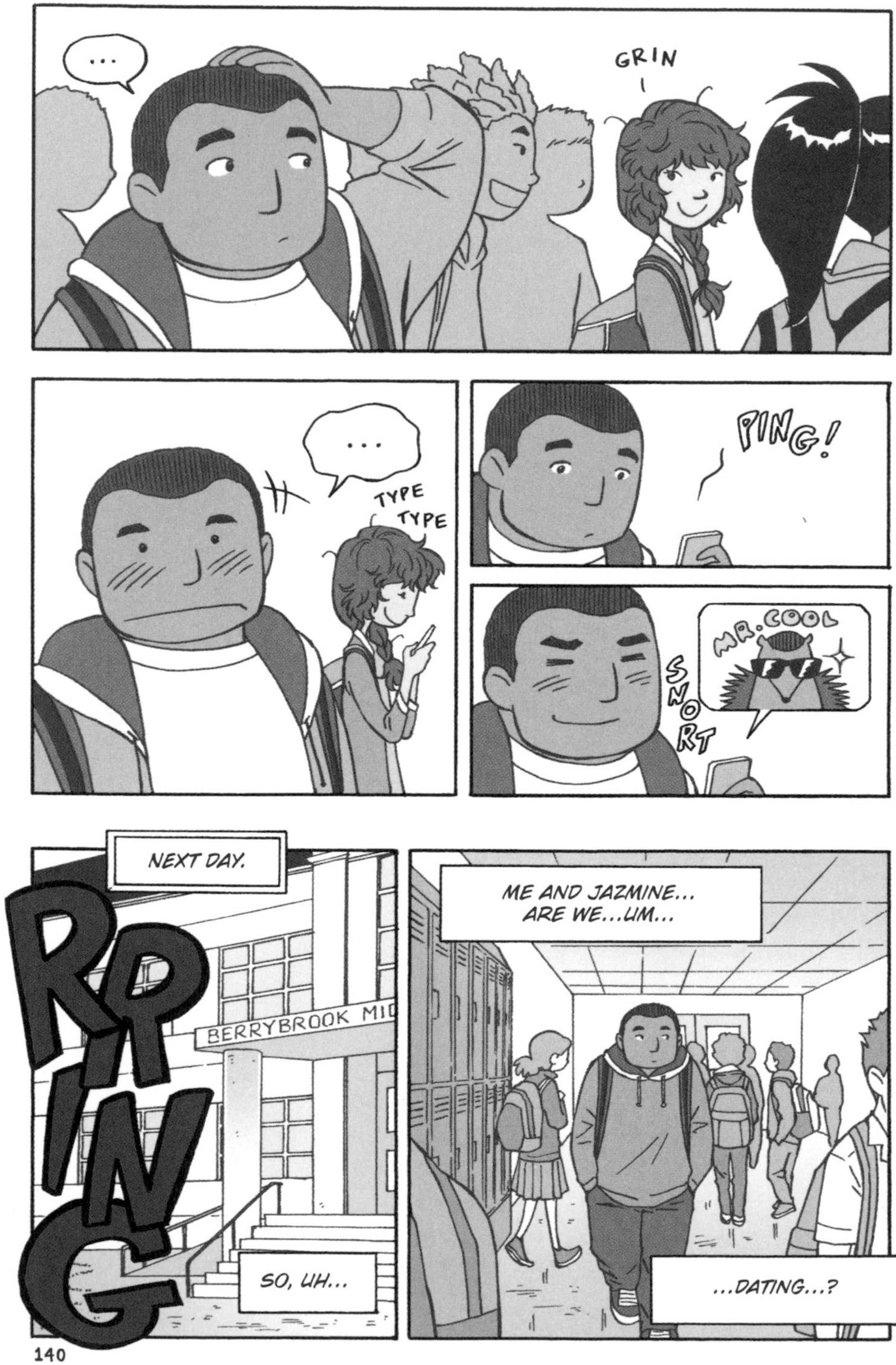

...
GRIN
...
TYPE TYPE
PING!
MR. COOL
SNORT
NEXT DAY.
RRING
BERRYBROOK MID
SO, UH...
ME AND JAZMINE... ARE WE...UM...
...DATING...?

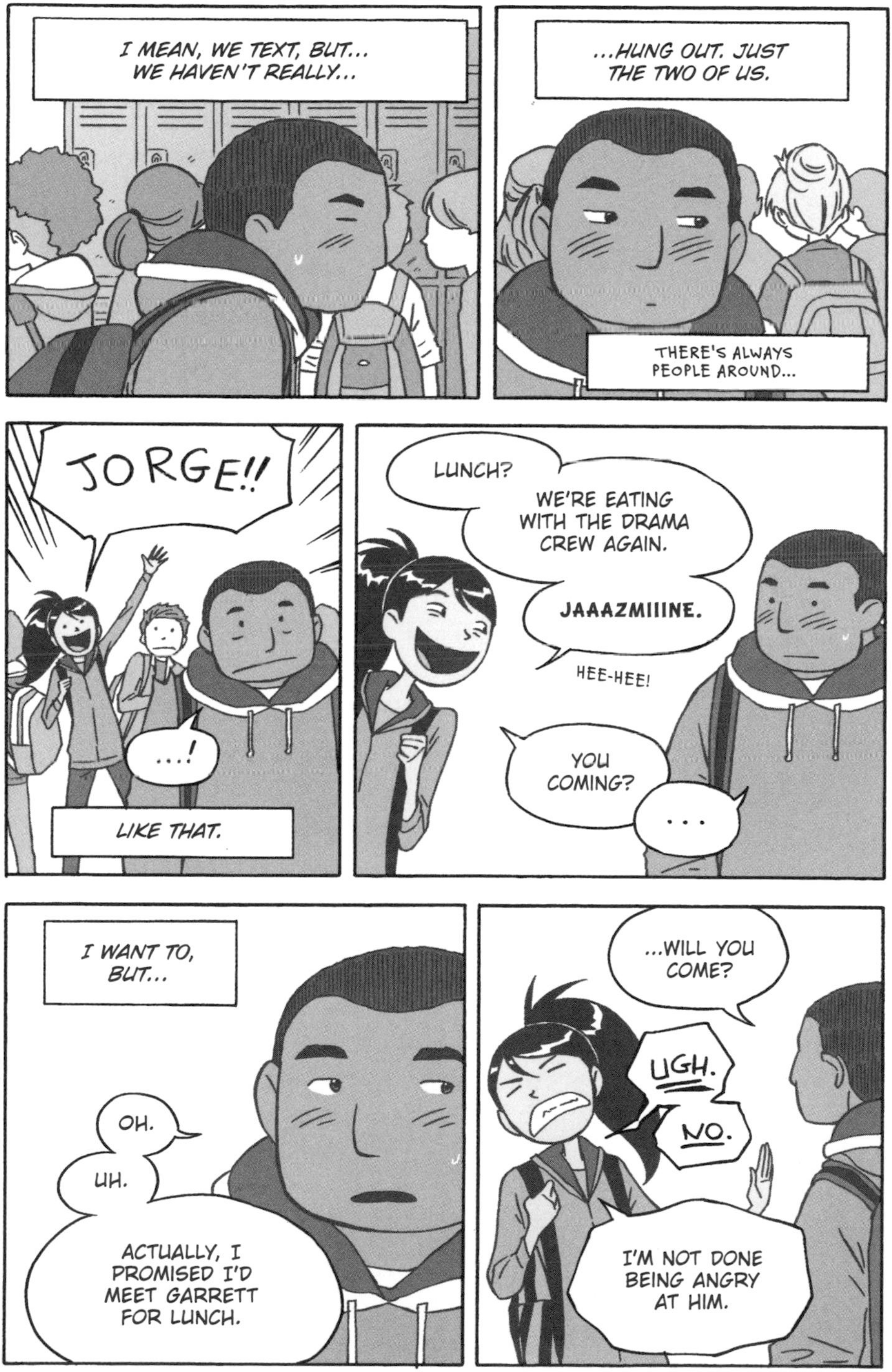
I MEAN, WE TEXT, BUT...
WE HAVEN'T REALLY...
...HUNG OUT. JUST
THE TWO OF US.
THERE'S ALWAYS
PEOPLE AROUND...
JORGE!!
...!
LIKE THAT.
LUNCH?
WE'RE EATING
WITH THE DRAMA
CREW AGAIN.
JAAAZMIIINE.
HEE-HEE!
YOU
COMING?
...
I WANT TO,
BUT...
OH.
UH.
ACTUALLY, I
PROMISED I'D
MEET GARRETT
FOR LUNCH.
...WILL YOU
COME?
UGH.
NO.
I'M NOT DONE
BEING ANGRY
AT HIM.

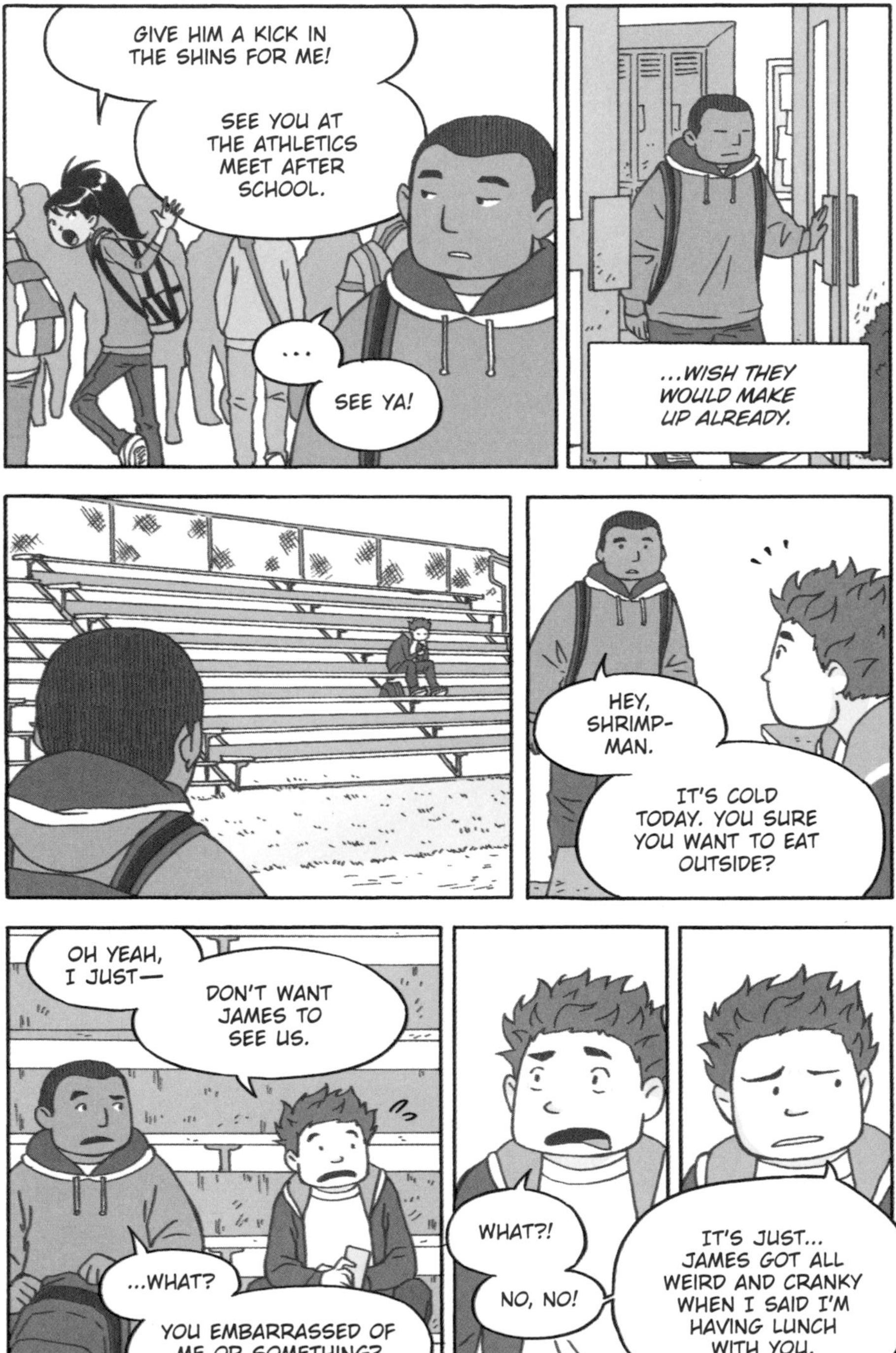
GIVE HIM A KICK IN THE SHINS FOR ME!
SEE YOU AT THE ATHLETICS MEET AFTER SCHOOL.
...
SEE YA!
...WISH THEY WOULD MAKE UP ALREADY.
HEY, SHRIMP-MAN.
IT'S COLD TODAY. YOU SURE YOU WANT TO EAT OUTSIDE?
OH YEAH, I JUST—
DON'T WANT JAMES TO SEE US.
...WHAT?
YOU EMBARRASSED OF ME OR SOMETHING?
WHAT?!
NO, NO!
IT'S JUST... JAMES GOT ALL WEIRD AND CRANKY WHEN I SAID I'M HAVING LUNCH WITH YOU.

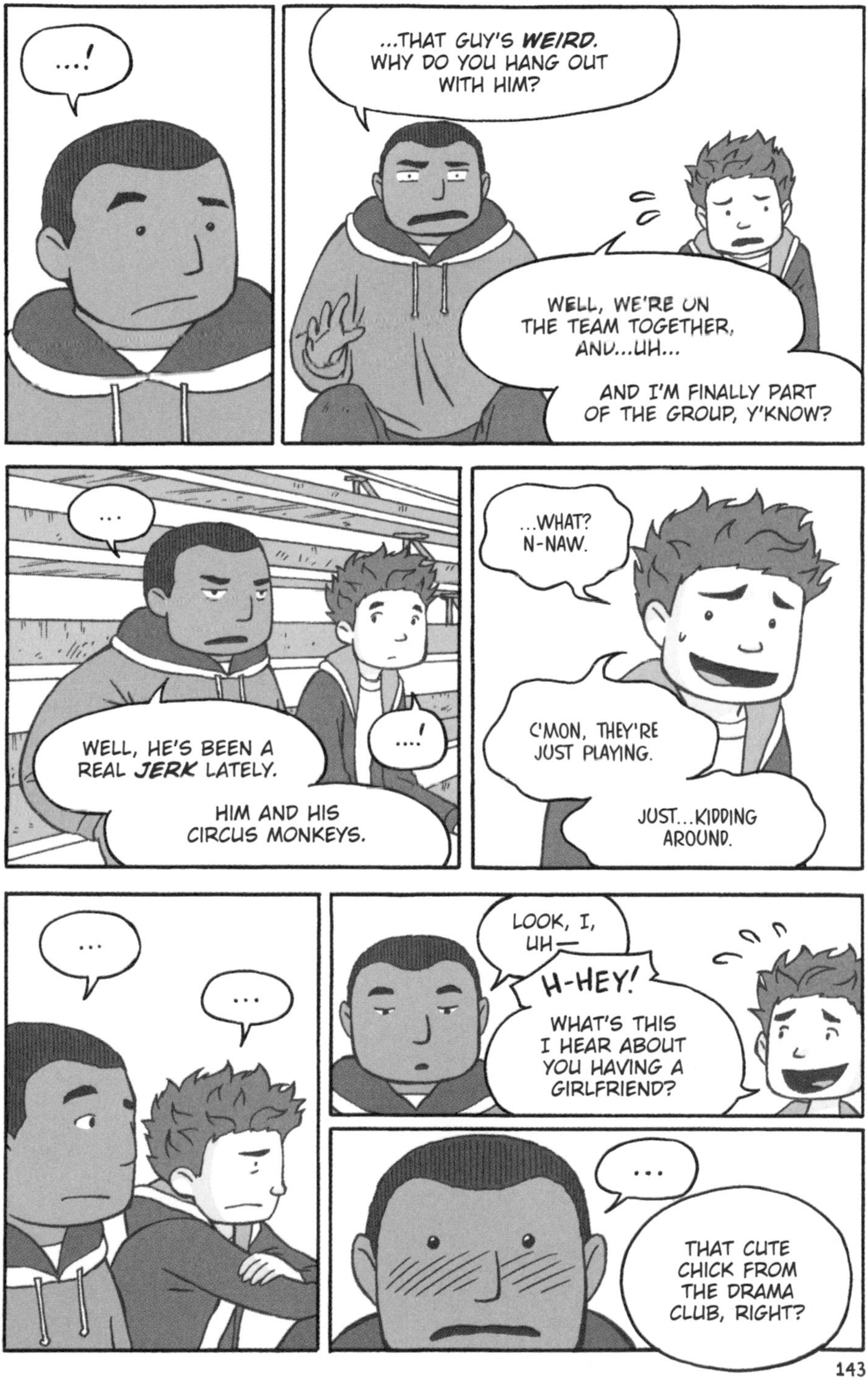
...!
...THAT GUY'S WEIRD. WHY DO YOU HANG OUT WITH HIM?
WELL, WE'RE ON THE TEAM TOGETHER, AND...UH...
AND I'M FINALLY PART OF THE GROUP, Y'KNOW?
...
WELL, HE'S BEEN A REAL JERK LATELY.
HIM AND HIS CIRCUS MONKEYS.
...!
...WHAT? N-NAW.
C'MON, THEY'RE JUST PLAYING.
JUST...KIDDING AROUND.
...
...
LOOK, I, UH—
H-HEY!
WHAT'S THIS I HEAR ABOUT YOU HAVING A GIRLFRIEND?
...
THAT CUTE CHICK FROM THE DRAMA CLUB, RIGHT?

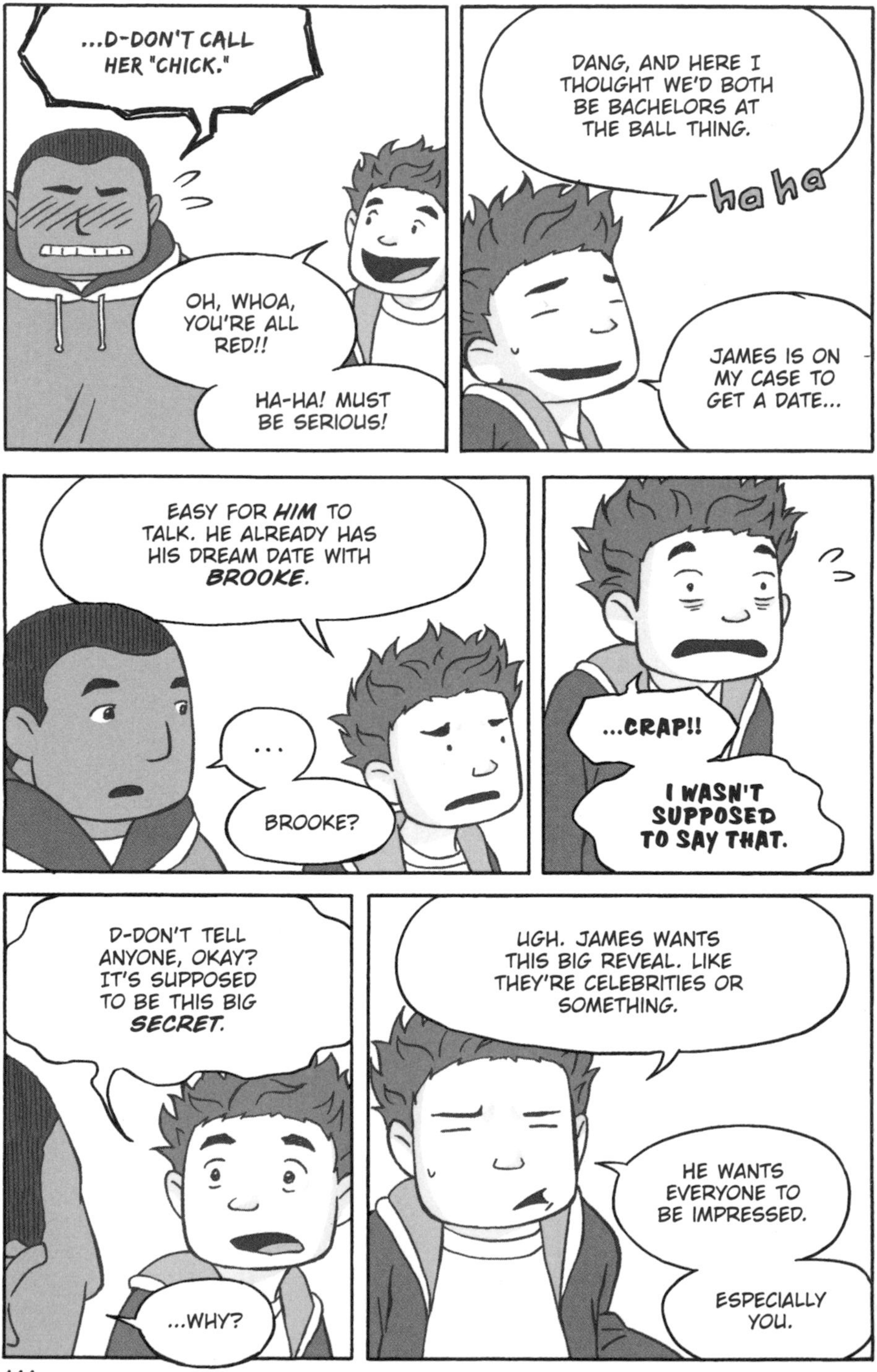
...D-DON'T CALL HER "CHICK."
OH, WHOA, YOU'RE ALL RED!!
HA-HA! MUST BE SERIOUS!
DANG, AND HERE I THOUGHT WE'D BOTH BE BACHELORS AT THE BALL THING.
ha ha
JAMES IS ON MY CASE TO GET A DATE...
EASY FOR HIM TO TALK. HE ALREADY HAS HIS DREAM DATE WITH BROOKE.
...
BROOKE?
...CRAP!!
I WASN'T SUPPOSED TO SAY THAT.
D-DON'T TELL ANYONE, OKAY? IT'S SUPPOSED TO BE THIS BIG SECRET.
...WHY?
UGH. JAMES WANTS THIS BIG REVEAL. LIKE THEY'RE CELEBRITIES OR SOMETHING.
HE WANTS EVERYONE TO BE IMPRESSED.
ESPECIALLY YOU.

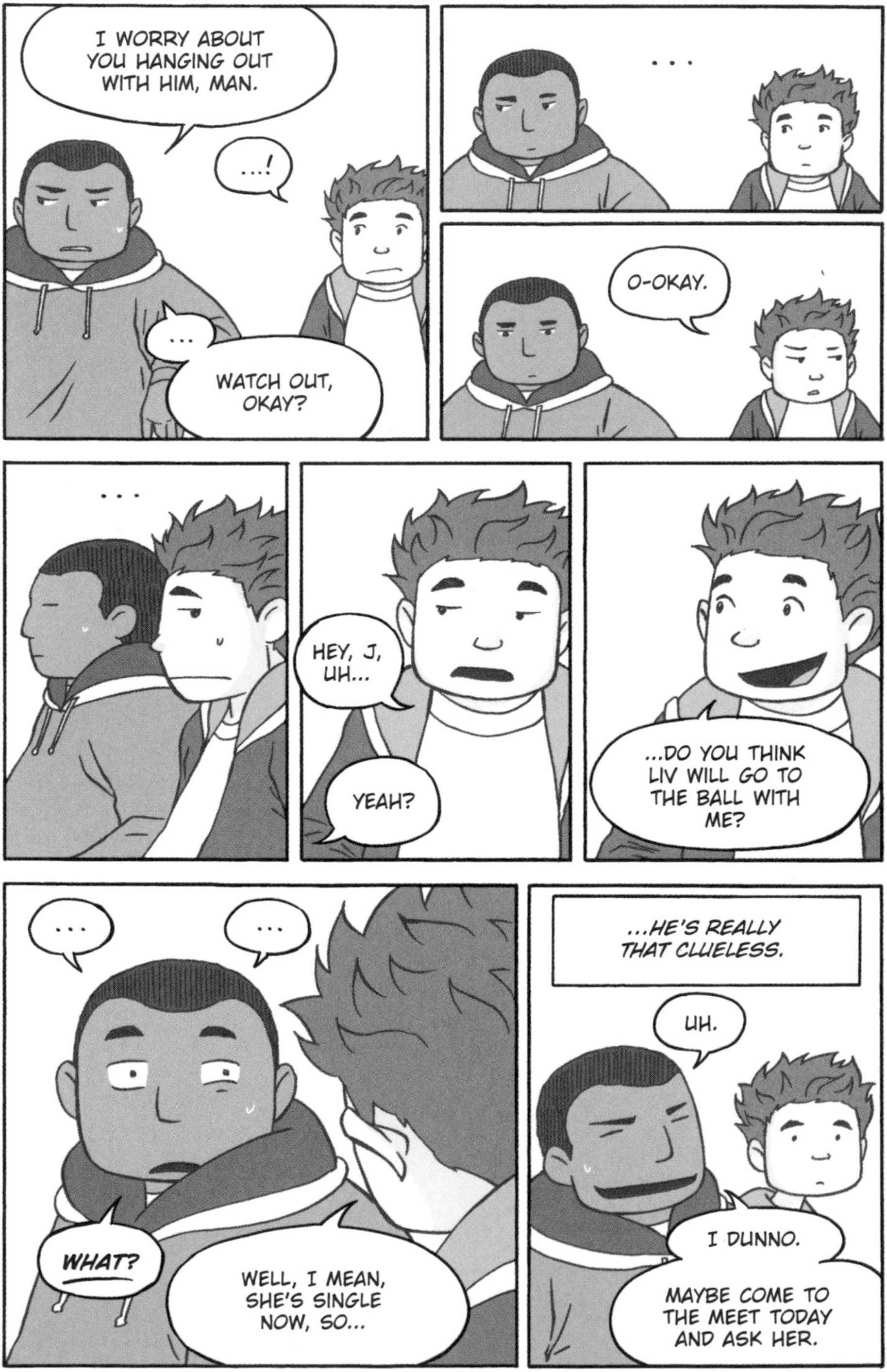
I WORRY ABOUT YOU HANGING OUT WITH HIM, MAN.
...!
...
WATCH OUT, OKAY?
. . .
O-OKAY.
. . .
HEY, J, UH...
YEAH?
...DO YOU THINK LIV WILL GO TO THE BALL WITH ME?
. . .
. . .
WHAT?
WELL, I MEAN, SHE'S SINGLE NOW, SO...
...HE'S REALLY THAT CLUELESS.
UH.
I DUNNO.
MAYBE COME TO THE MEET TODAY AND ASK HER.

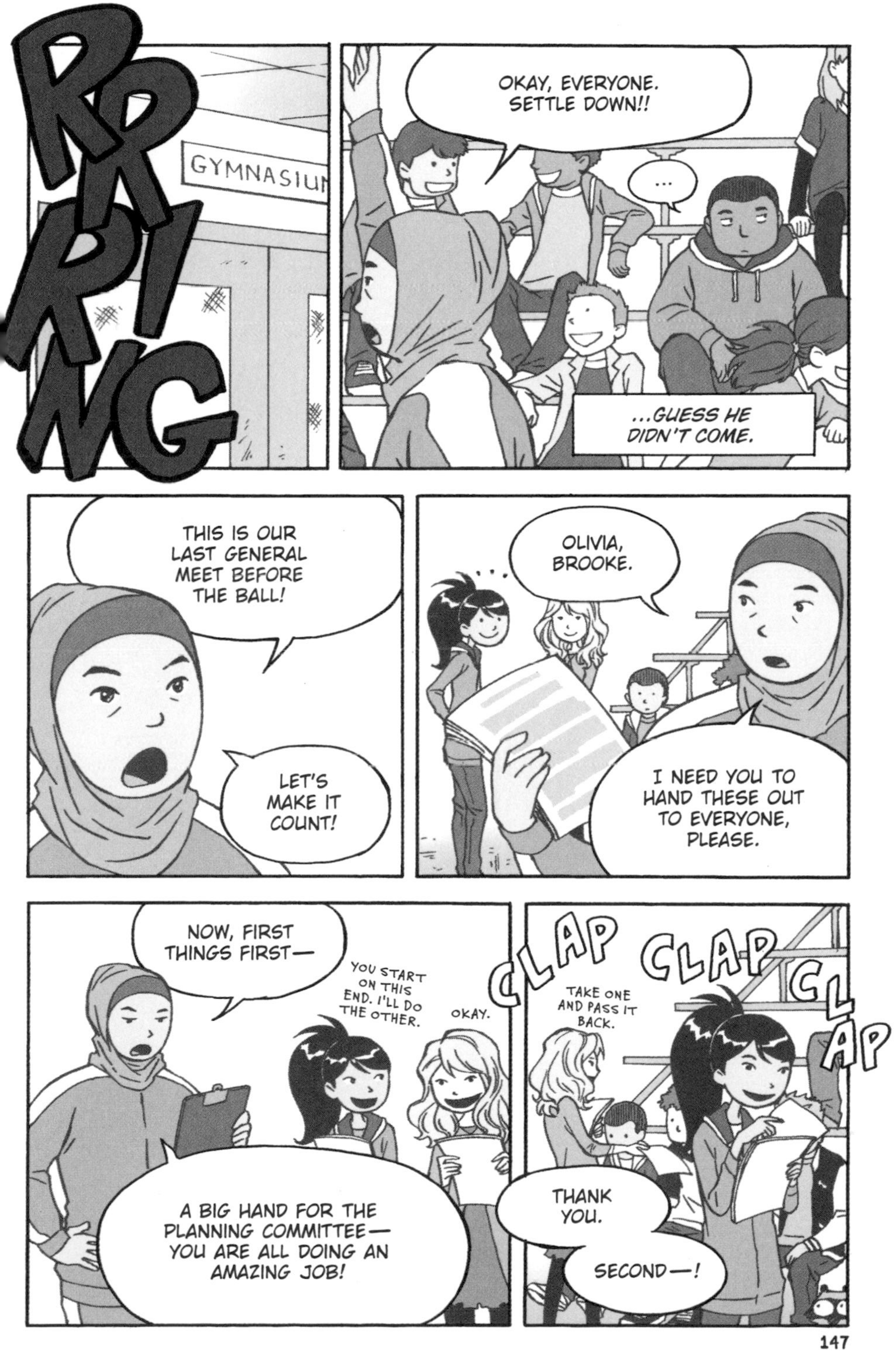
RRRIIING
GYMNASIUM
OKAY, EVERYONE. SETTLE DOWN!!
...
...GUESS HE DIDN'T COME.
THIS IS OUR LAST GENERAL MEET BEFORE THE BALL!
LET'S MAKE IT COUNT!
OLIVIA, BROOKE.
I NEED YOU TO HAND THESE OUT TO EVERYONE, PLEASE.
NOW, FIRST THINGS FIRST—
YOU START ON THIS END. I'LL DO THE OTHER.
OKAY.
A BIG HAND FOR THE PLANNING COMMITTEE—YOU ARE ALL DOING AN AMAZING JOB!
CLAP CLAP CLAP
TAKE ONE AND PASS IT BACK.
THANK YOU.
SECOND—!

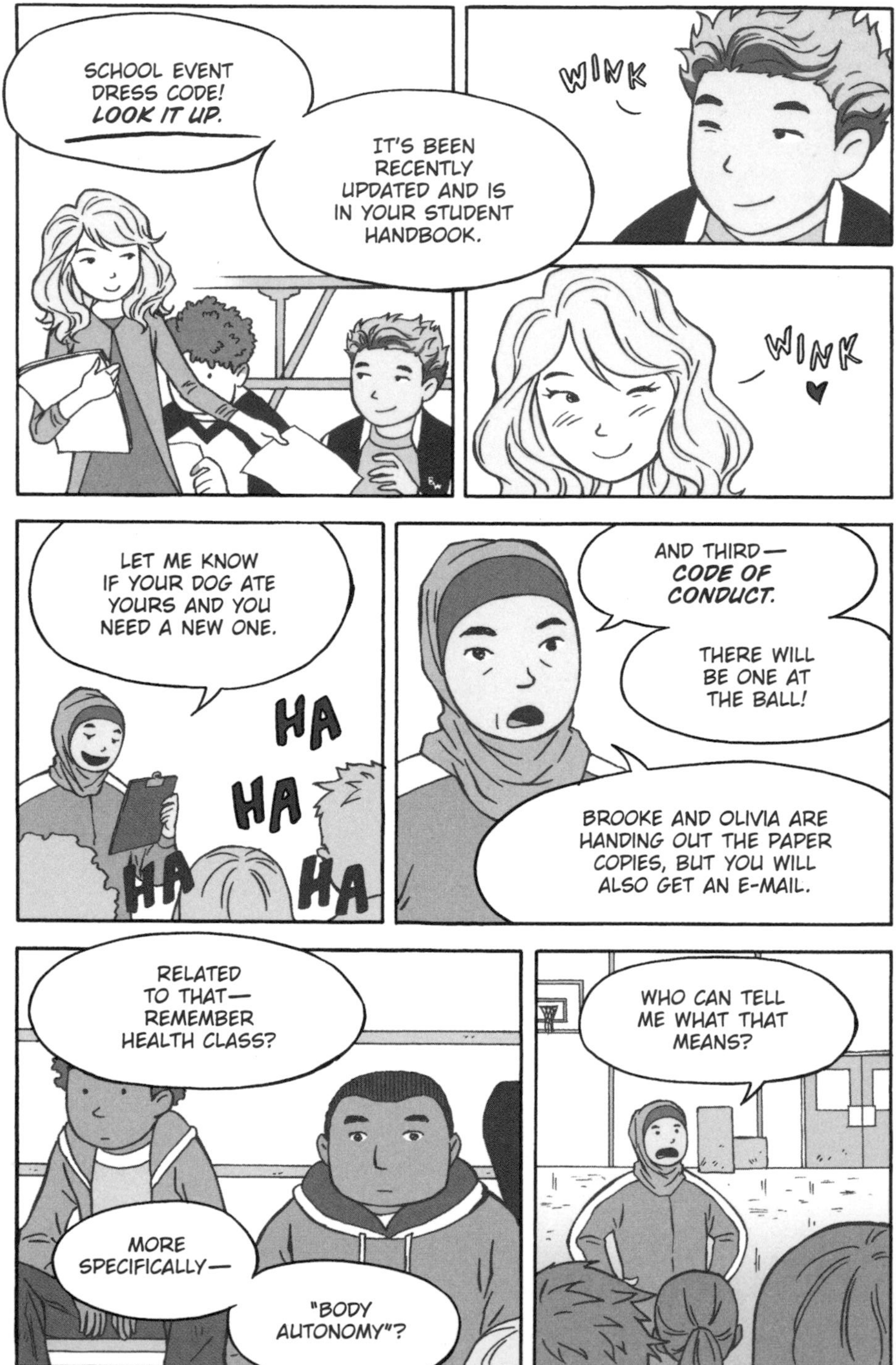
SCHOOL EVENT DRESS CODE! LOOK IT UP.
IT'S BEEN RECENTLY UPDATED AND IS IN YOUR STUDENT HANDBOOK.
WINK
WINK
LET ME KNOW IF YOUR DOG ATE YOURS AND YOU NEED A NEW ONE.
HA HA HA HA
AND THIRD— CODE OF CONDUCT.
THERE WILL BE ONE AT THE BALL!
BROOKE AND OLIVIA ARE HANDING OUT THE PAPER COPIES, BUT YOU WILL ALSO GET AN E-MAIL.
RELATED TO THAT— REMEMBER HEALTH CLASS?
MORE SPECIFICALLY—
"BODY AUTONOMY"?
WHO CAN TELL ME WHAT THAT MEANS?

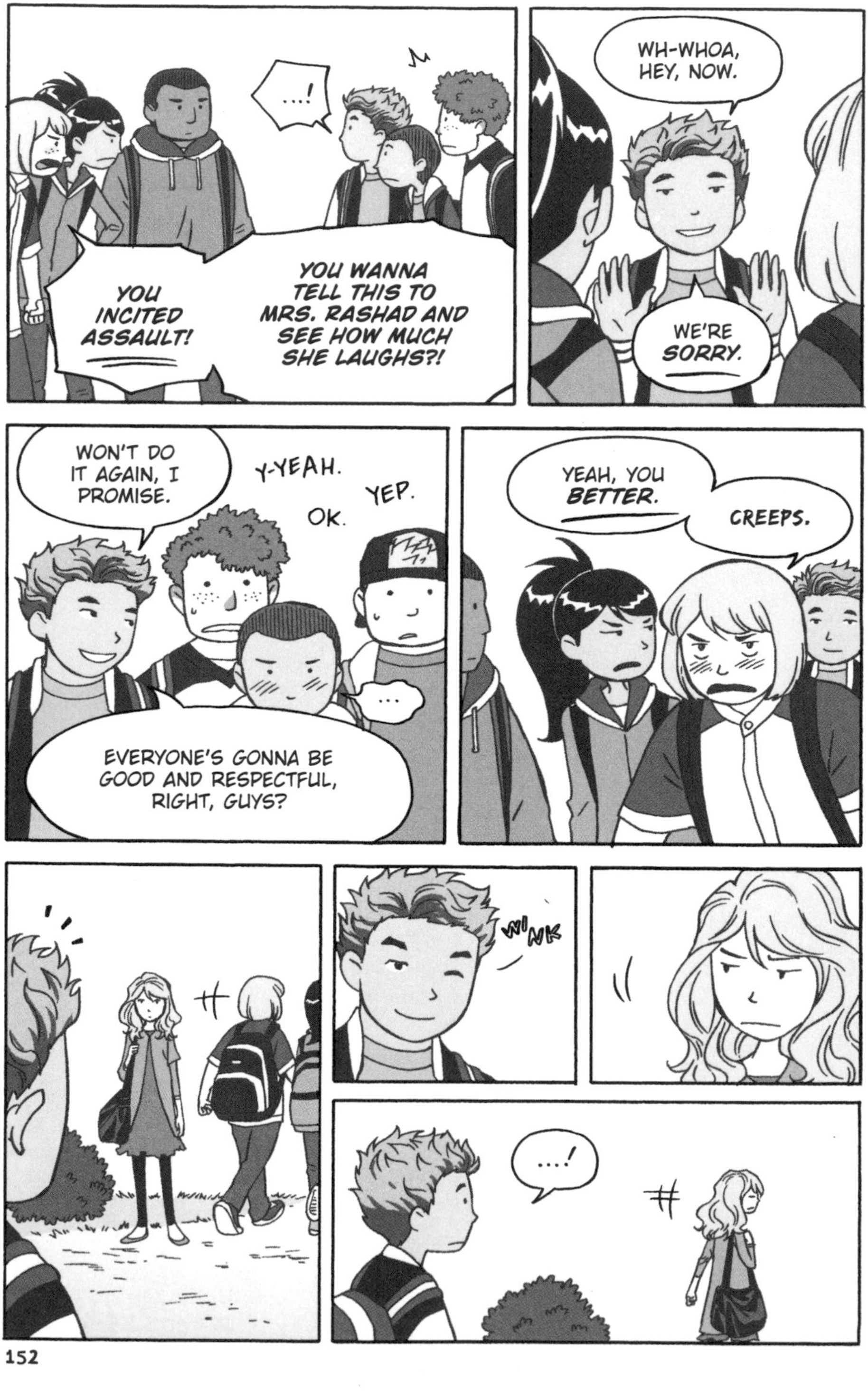
...!
YOU INCITED ASSAULT!
YOU WANNA TELL THIS TO MRS. RASHAD AND SEE HOW MUCH SHE LAUGHS?!
WH-WHOA, HEY, NOW.
WE'RE SORRY.
WON'T DO IT AGAIN, I PROMISE.
Y-YEAH.
OK.
YEP.
...
EVERYONE'S GONNA BE GOOD AND RESPECTFUL, RIGHT, GUYS?
YEAH, YOU BETTER.
CREEPS.
WINK
...!

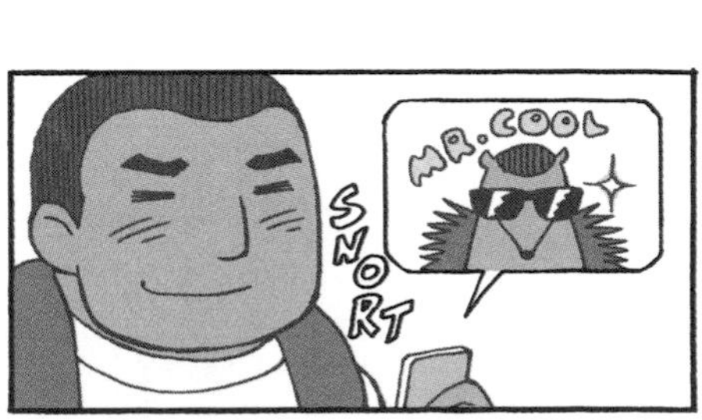
SNORT
MR. COOL

CHAPTER 8

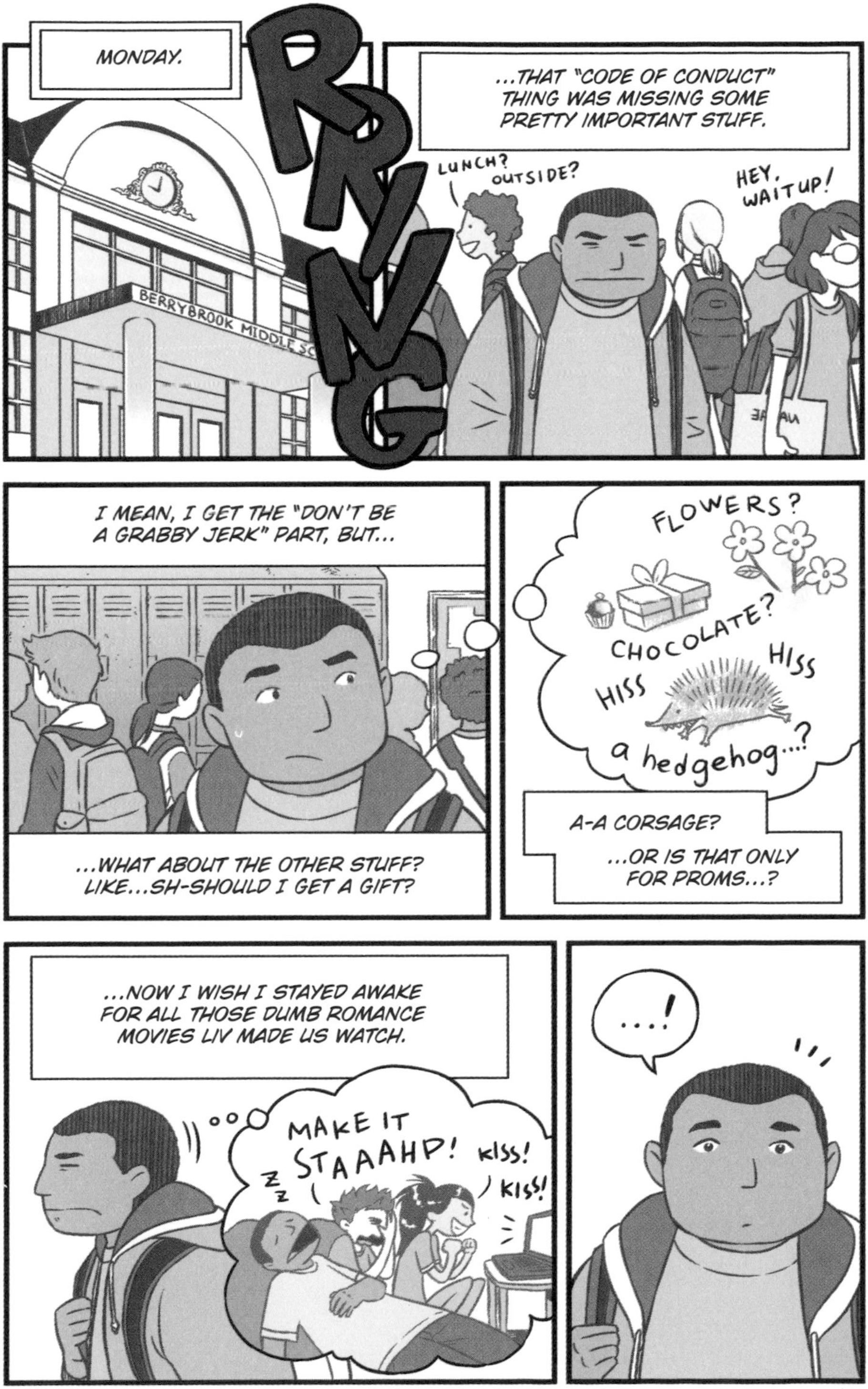
MONDAY.
RRRING
...THAT "CODE OF CONDUCT" THING WAS MISSING SOME PRETTY IMPORTANT STUFF.
LUNCH? OUTSIDE?
HEY, WAIT UP!
BERRYBROOK MIDDLE SC
I MEAN, I GET THE "DON'T BE A GRABBY JERK" PART, BUT...
...WHAT ABOUT THE OTHER STUFF? LIKE...SH-SHOULD I GET A GIFT?
FLOWERS?
CHOCOLATE?
HISS
HISS
a hedgehog...?
A-A CORSAGE?
...OR IS THAT ONLY FOR PROMS...?
...NOW I WISH I STAYED AWAKE FOR ALL THOSE DUMB ROMANCE MOVIES LIV MADE US WATCH.
MAKE IT STAAAHP!
KISS!
KISS!
Z Z
...!

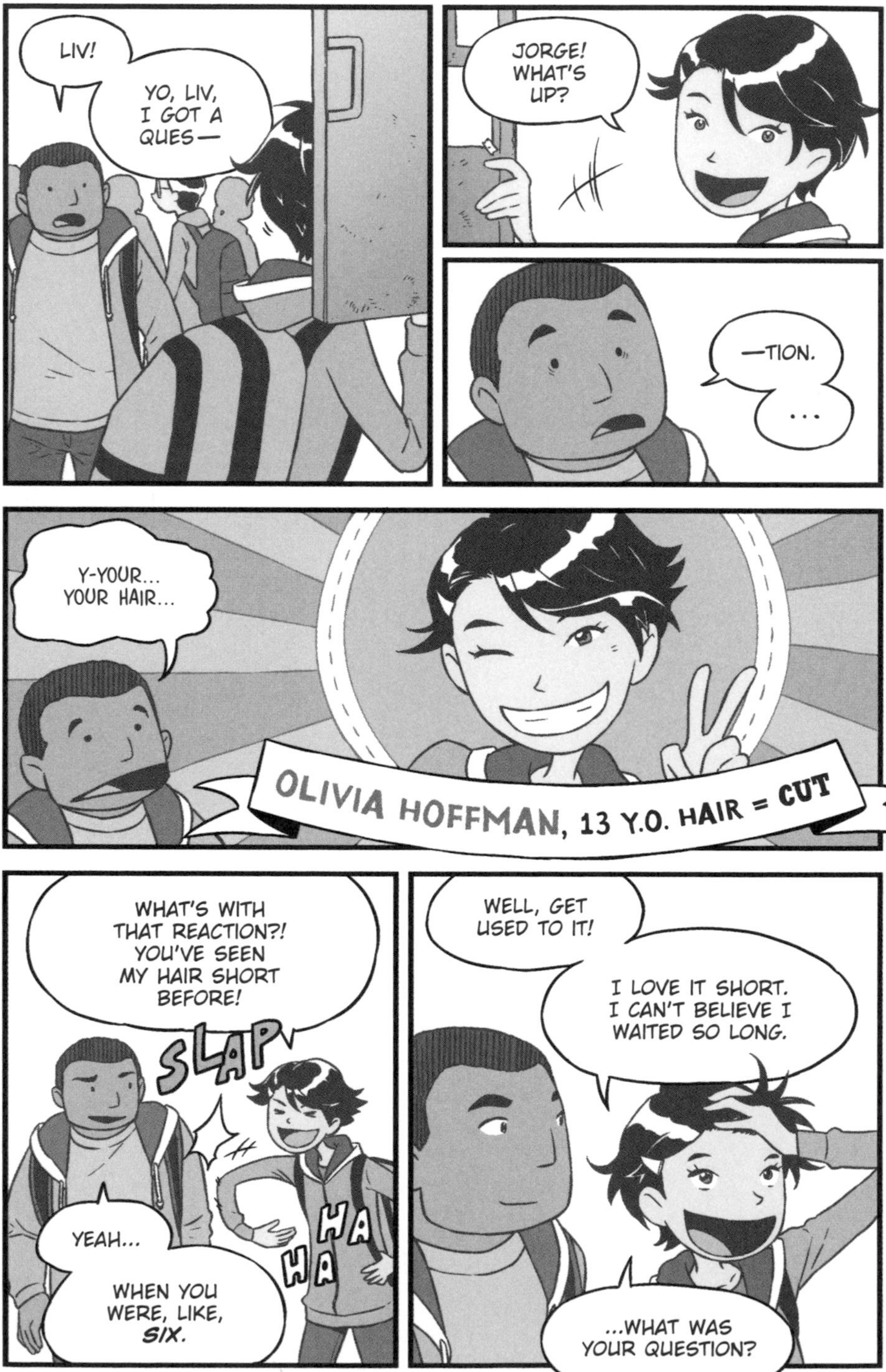
LIV!
YO, LIV, I GOT A QUES—
JORGE! WHAT'S UP?
—TION.
...
Y-YOUR... YOUR HAIR...
OLIVIA HOFFMAN, 13 Y.O. HAIR = CUT
WHAT'S WITH THAT REACTION?! YOU'VE SEEN MY HAIR SHORT BEFORE!
SLAP
HA HA
YEAH...
WHEN YOU WERE, LIKE, SIX.
WELL, GET USED TO IT!
I LOVE IT SHORT. I CAN'T BELIEVE I WAITED SO LONG.
...WHAT WAS YOUR QUESTION?

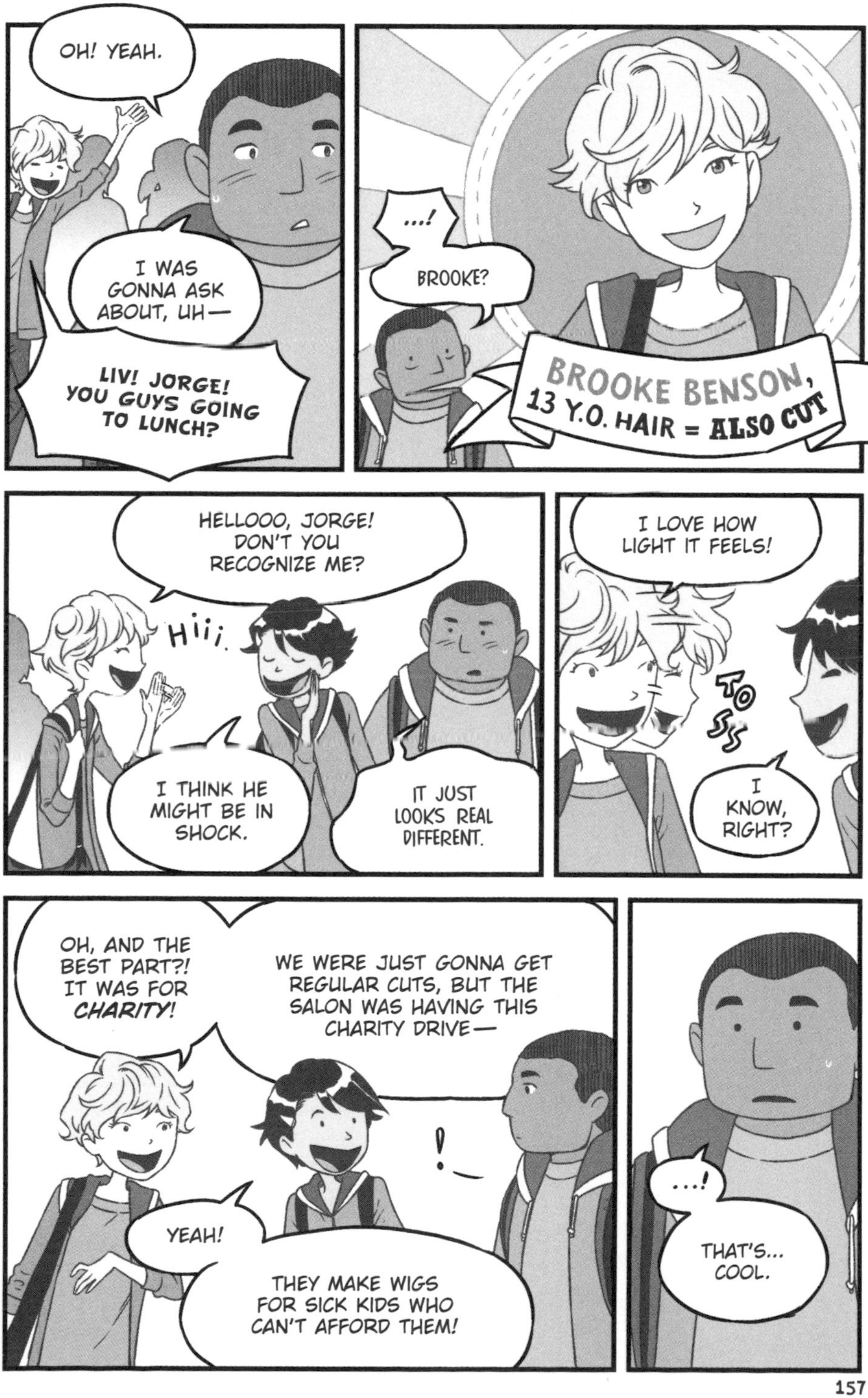
OH! YEAH.
I WAS GONNA ASK ABOUT, UH—
LIV! JORGE! YOU GUYS GOING TO LUNCH?
...!
BROOKE?
BROOKE BENSON, 13 Y.O. HAIR = ALSO CUT
HELLOOO, JORGE! DON'T YOU RECOGNIZE ME?
Hiii.
I THINK HE MIGHT BE IN SHOCK.
IT JUST LOOKS REAL DIFFERENT.
I LOVE HOW LIGHT IT FEELS!
TOSS
I KNOW, RIGHT?
OH, AND THE BEST PART?! IT WAS FOR CHARITY!
WE WERE JUST GONNA GET REGULAR CUTS, BUT THE SALON WAS HAVING THIS CHARITY DRIVE—
!
YEAH!
THEY MAKE WIGS FOR SICK KIDS WHO CAN'T AFFORD THEM!
...!
THAT'S... COOL.

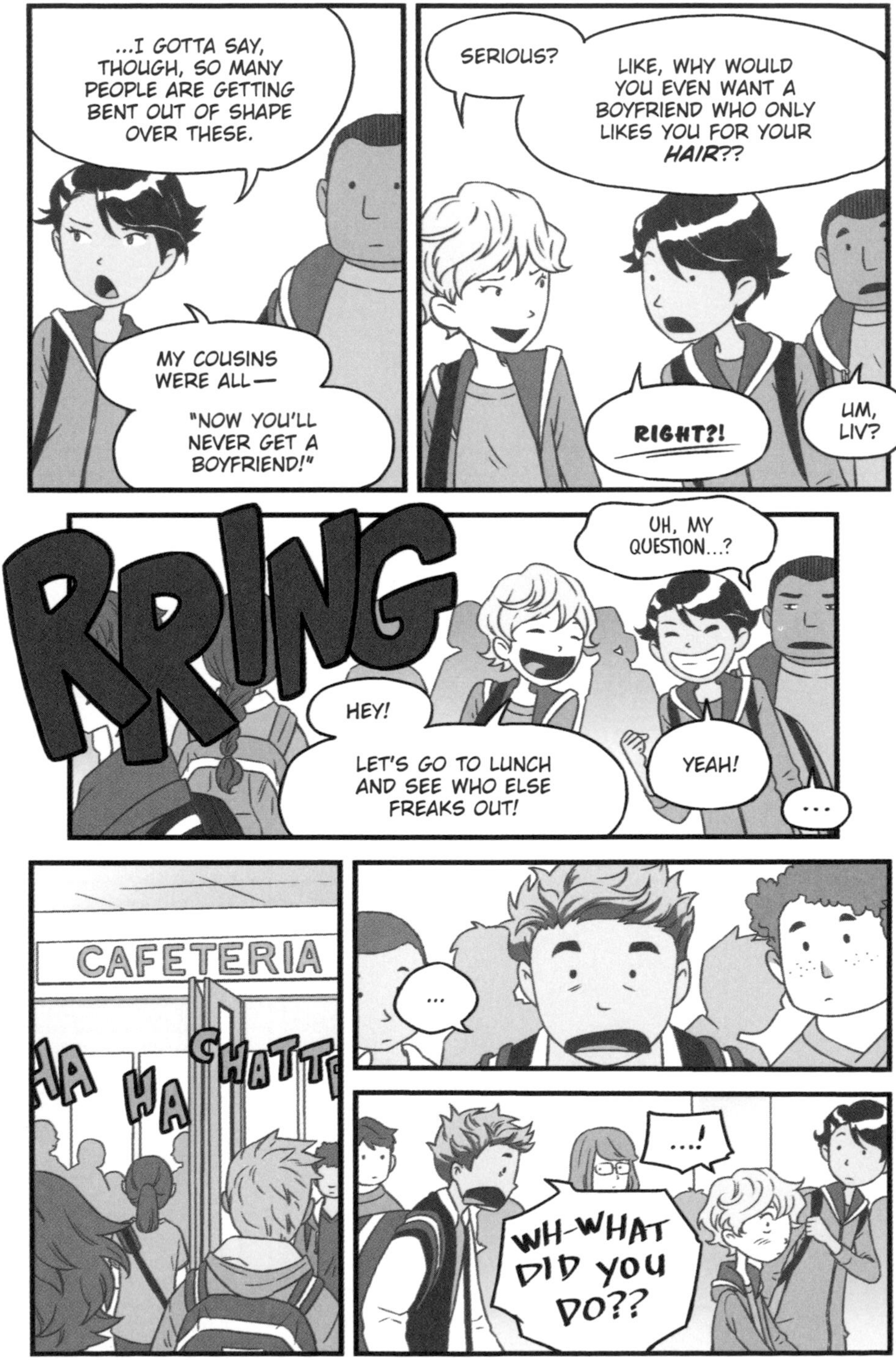
...I GOTTA SAY, THOUGH, SO MANY PEOPLE ARE GETTING BENT OUT OF SHAPE OVER THESE.
MY COUSINS WERE ALL—
"NOW YOU'LL NEVER GET A BOYFRIEND!"
SERIOUS?
LIKE, WHY WOULD YOU EVEN WANT A BOYFRIEND WHO ONLY LIKES YOU FOR YOUR *HAIR*??
RIGHT?!
UM, LIV?
RRING
UH, MY QUESTION...?
HEY!
LET'S GO TO LUNCH AND SEE WHO ELSE FREAKS OUT!
YEAH!
...
CAFETERIA
HA
HA
CHATT
...
...!
WH-WHAT DID YOU DO??

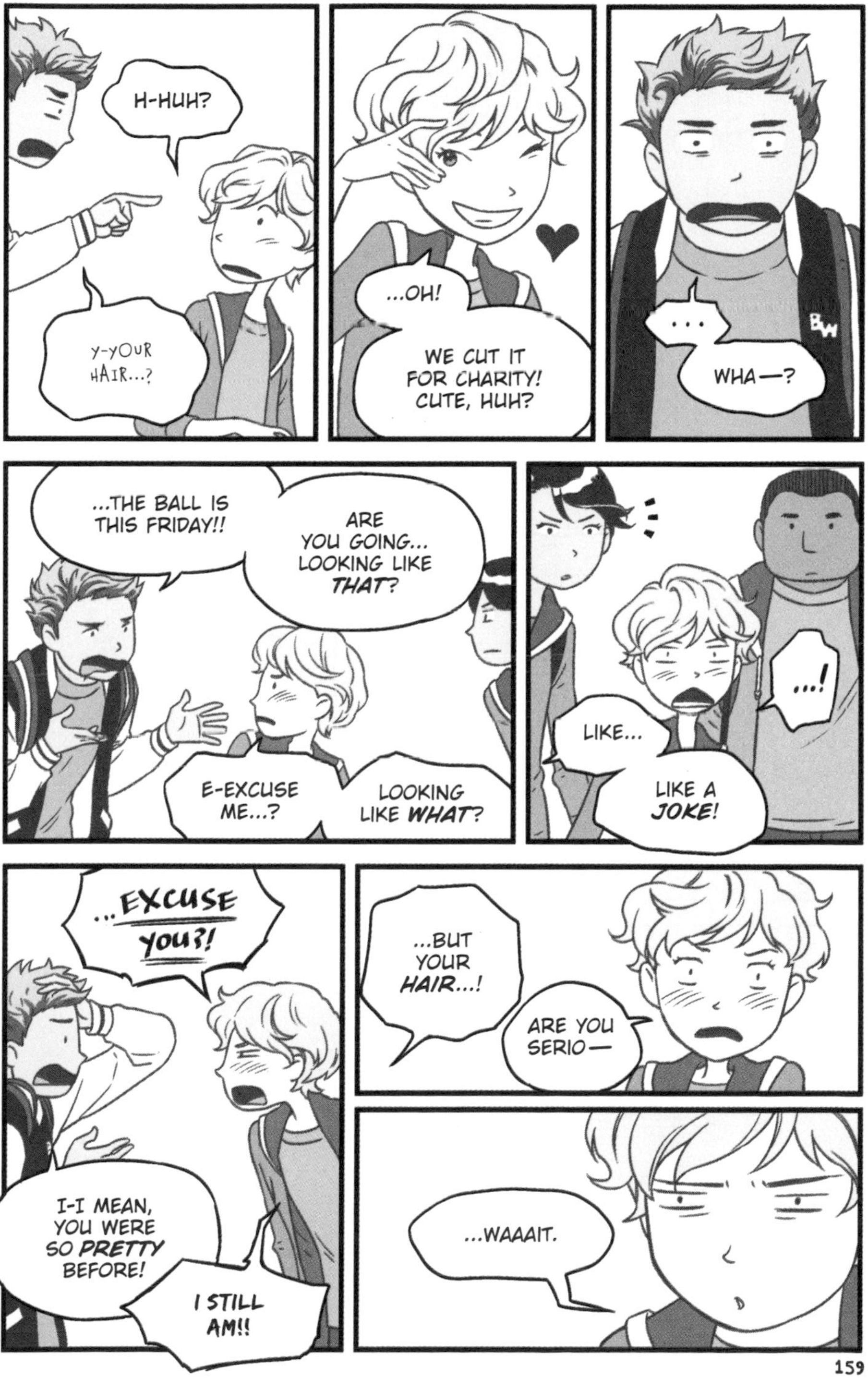
H-HUH?
Y-YOUR HAIR...?
...OH!
WE CUT IT FOR CHARITY! CUTE, HUH?
...
WHA—?
...THE BALL IS THIS FRIDAY!!
ARE YOU GOING... LOOKING LIKE THAT?
E-EXCUSE ME...?
LOOKING LIKE WHAT?
...!
LIKE...
LIKE A JOKE!
...EXCUSE YOU?!
I-I MEAN, YOU WERE SO PRETTY BEFORE!
I STILL AM!!
...BUT YOUR HAIR...!
ARE YOU SERIO—
...WAAAIT.

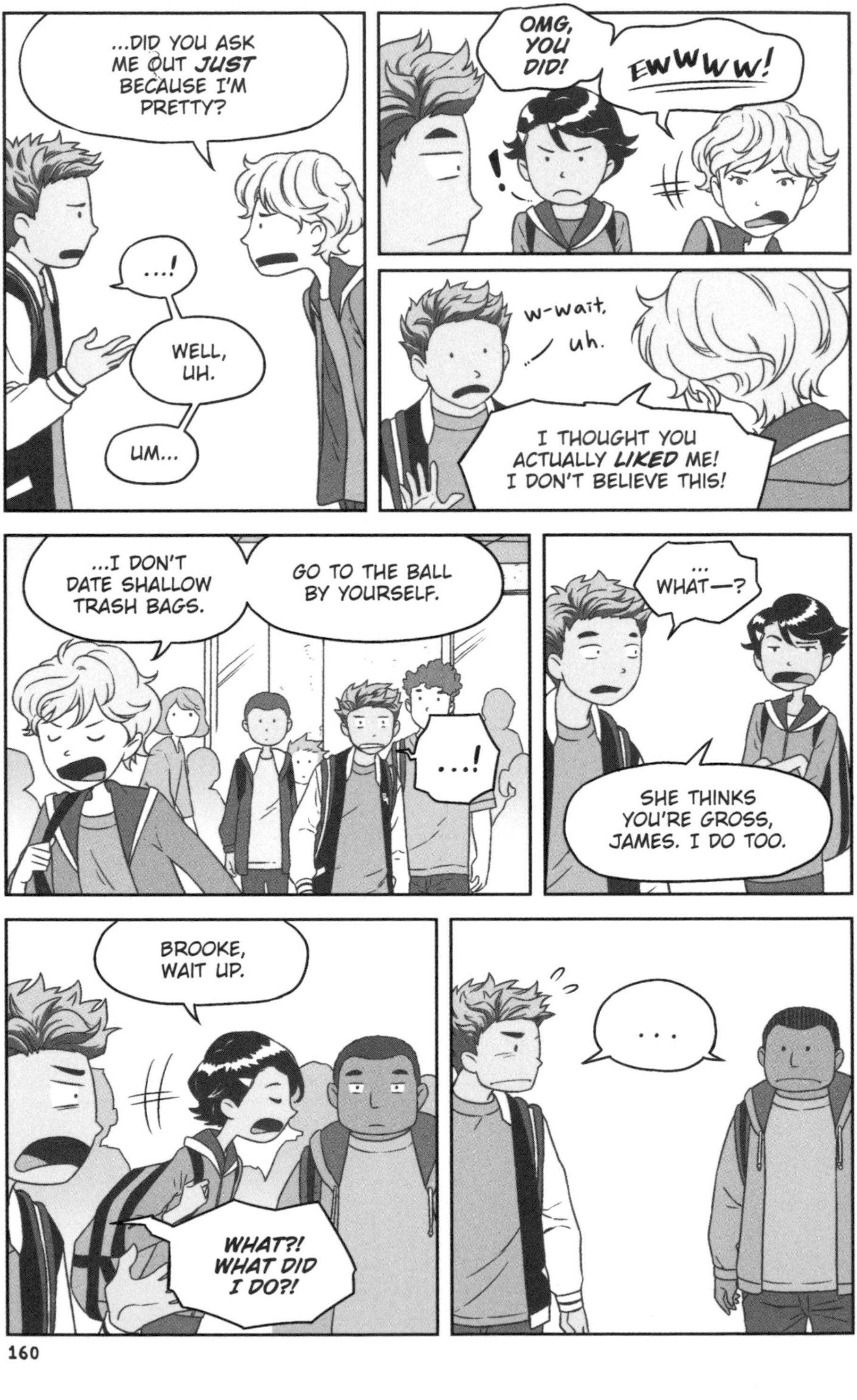
...DID YOU ASK ME OUT JUST BECAUSE I'M PRETTY?
....!
WELL, UH.
UM...
OMG, YOU DID!
EWWWWW!
W-wait, uh.
I THOUGHT YOU ACTUALLY LIKED ME! I DON'T BELIEVE THIS!
...I DON'T DATE SHALLOW TRASH BAGS.
GO TO THE BALL BY YOURSELF.
....!
... WHAT—?
SHE THINKS YOU'RE GROSS, JAMES. I DO TOO.
BROOKE, WAIT UP.
WHAT?! WHAT DID I DO?!
. . .

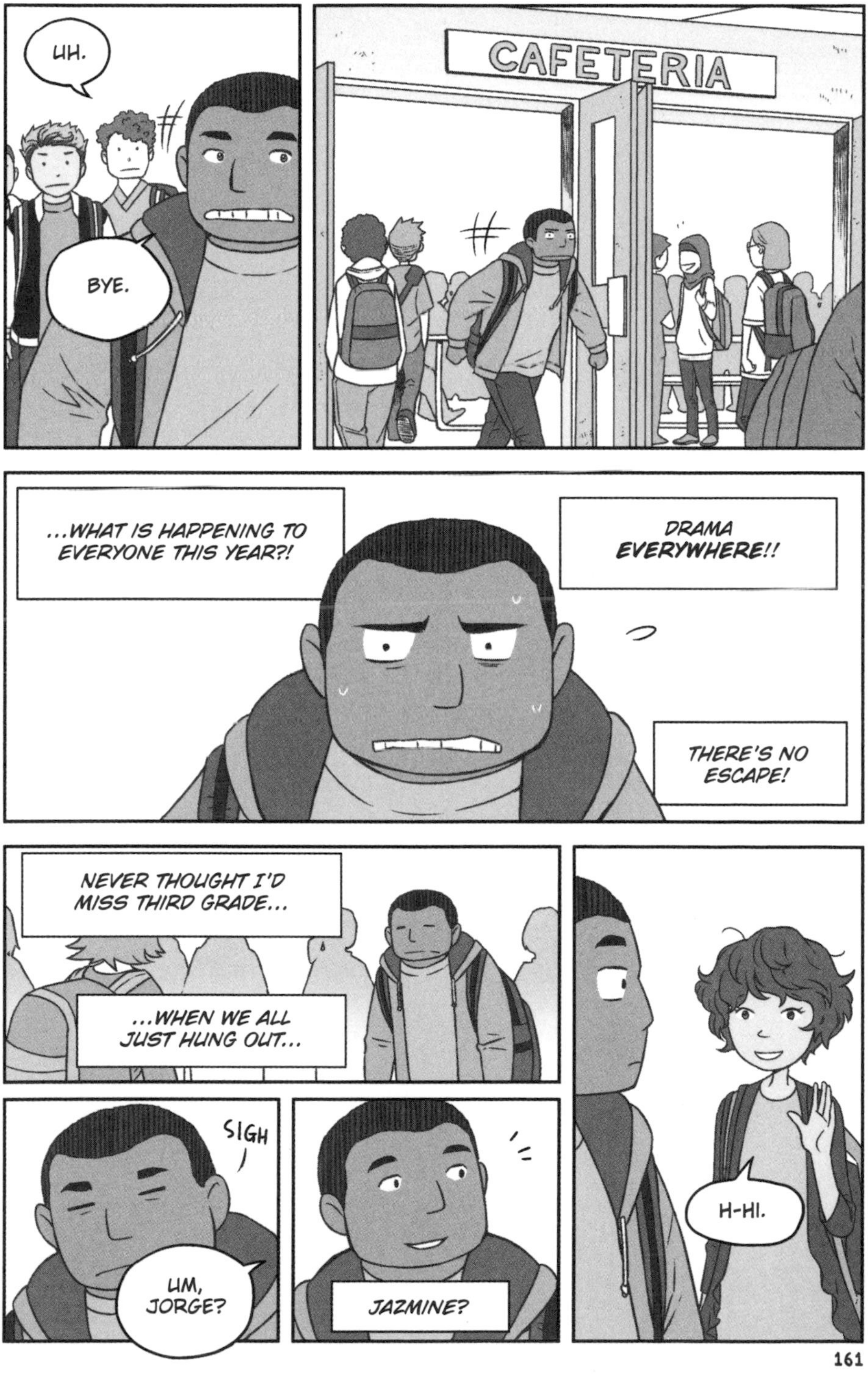
UH.
BYE.
CAFETERIA
...WHAT IS HAPPENING TO EVERYONE THIS YEAR?!
DRAMA EVERYWHERE!!
THERE'S NO ESCAPE!
NEVER THOUGHT I'D MISS THIRD GRADE...
...WHEN WE ALL JUST HUNG OUT...
SIGH
UM, JORGE?
JAZMINE?
H-HI.

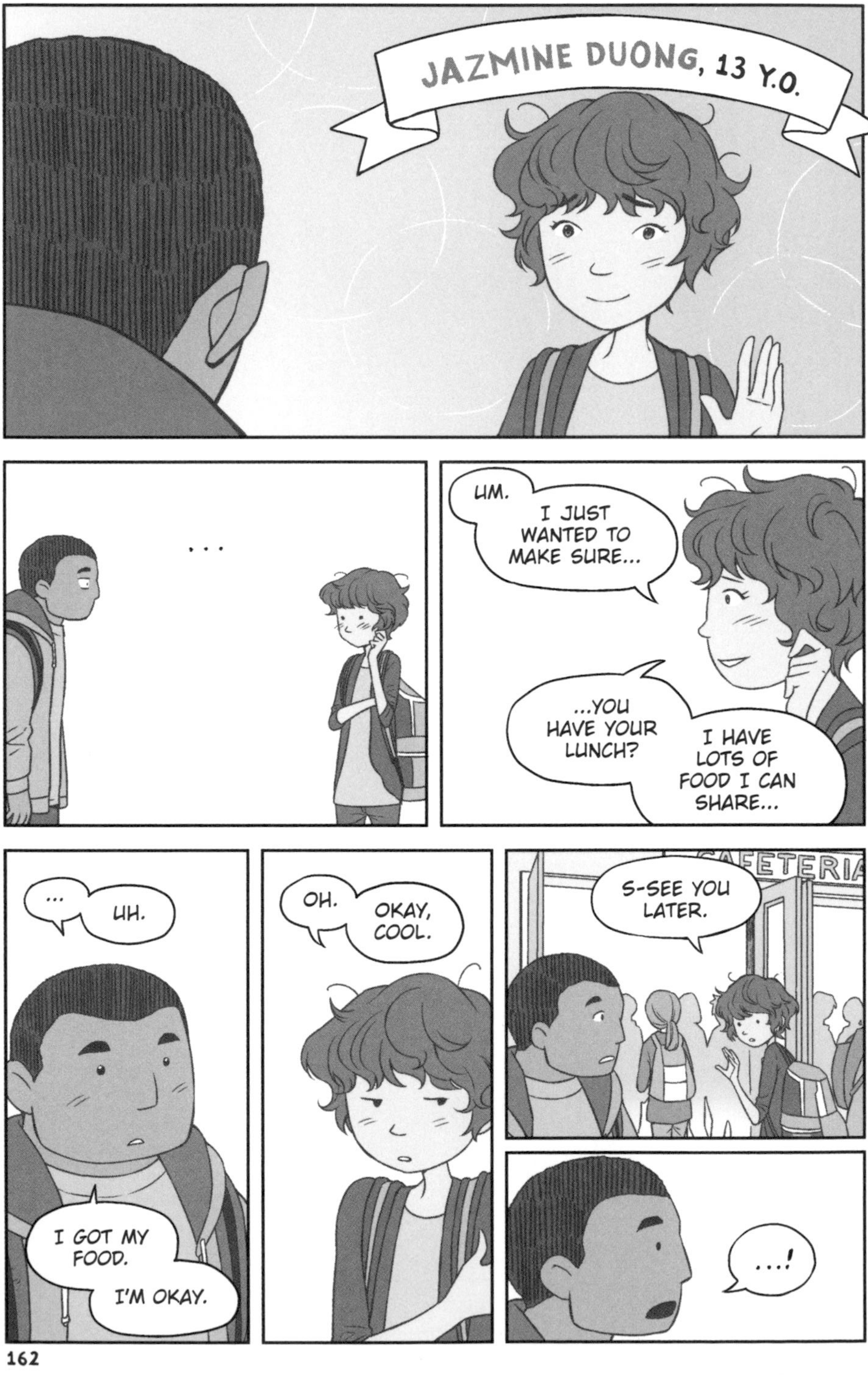
JAZMINE DUONG, 13 Y.O.
...
UM.
I JUST WANTED TO MAKE SURE...
...YOU HAVE YOUR LUNCH?
I HAVE LOTS OF FOOD I CAN SHARE...
...
UH.
I GOT MY FOOD.
I'M OKAY.
OH.
OKAY, COOL.
CAFETERIA
S-SEE YOU LATER.
...!

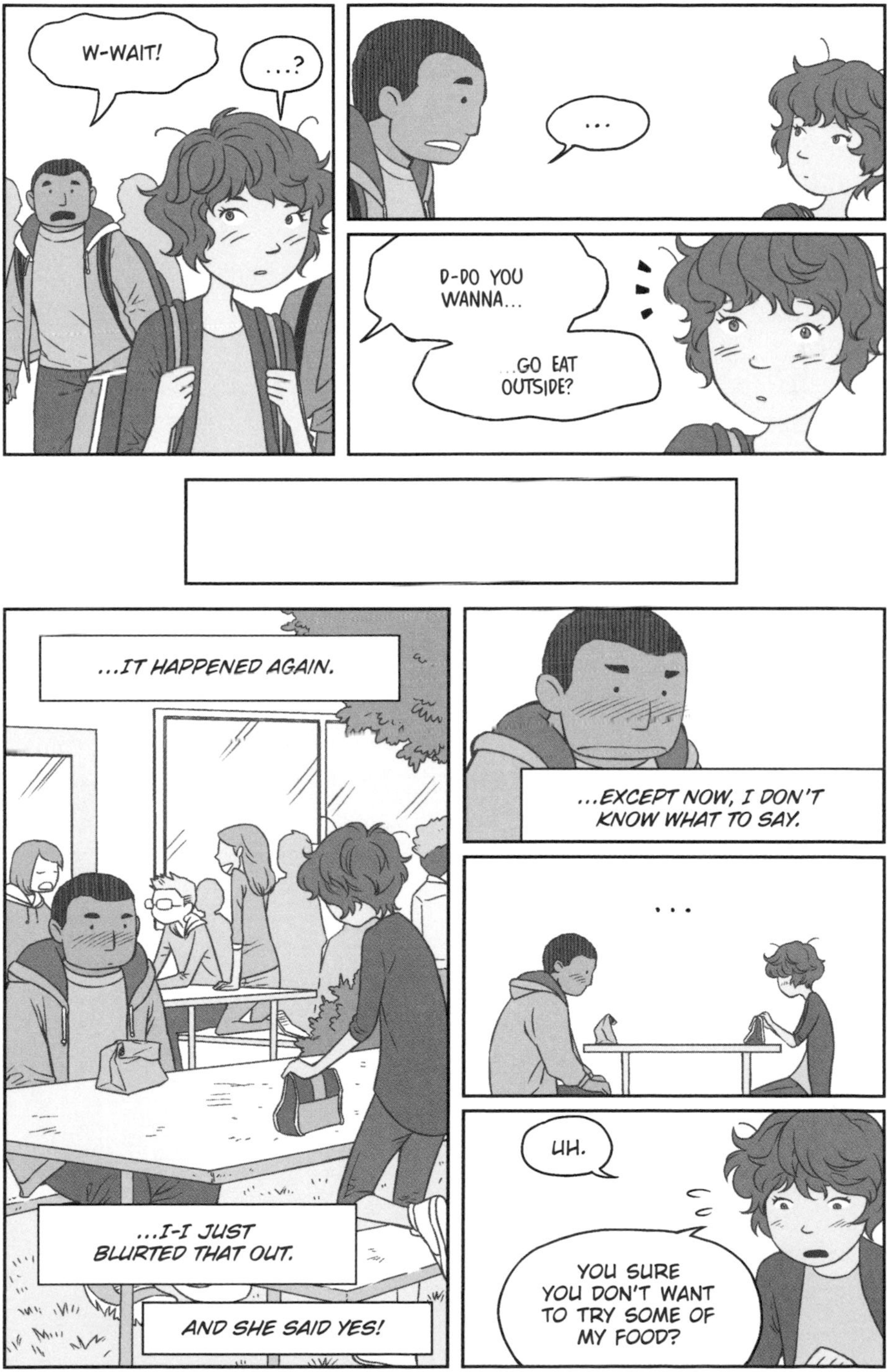
W-WAIT!
...?
...
D-DO YOU WANNA...
...GO EAT OUTSIDE?
...IT HAPPENED AGAIN.
...I-I JUST BLURTED THAT OUT.
AND SHE SAID YES!
...EXCEPT NOW, I DON'T KNOW WHAT TO SAY.
...
UH.
YOU SURE YOU DON'T WANT TO TRY SOME OF MY FOOD?

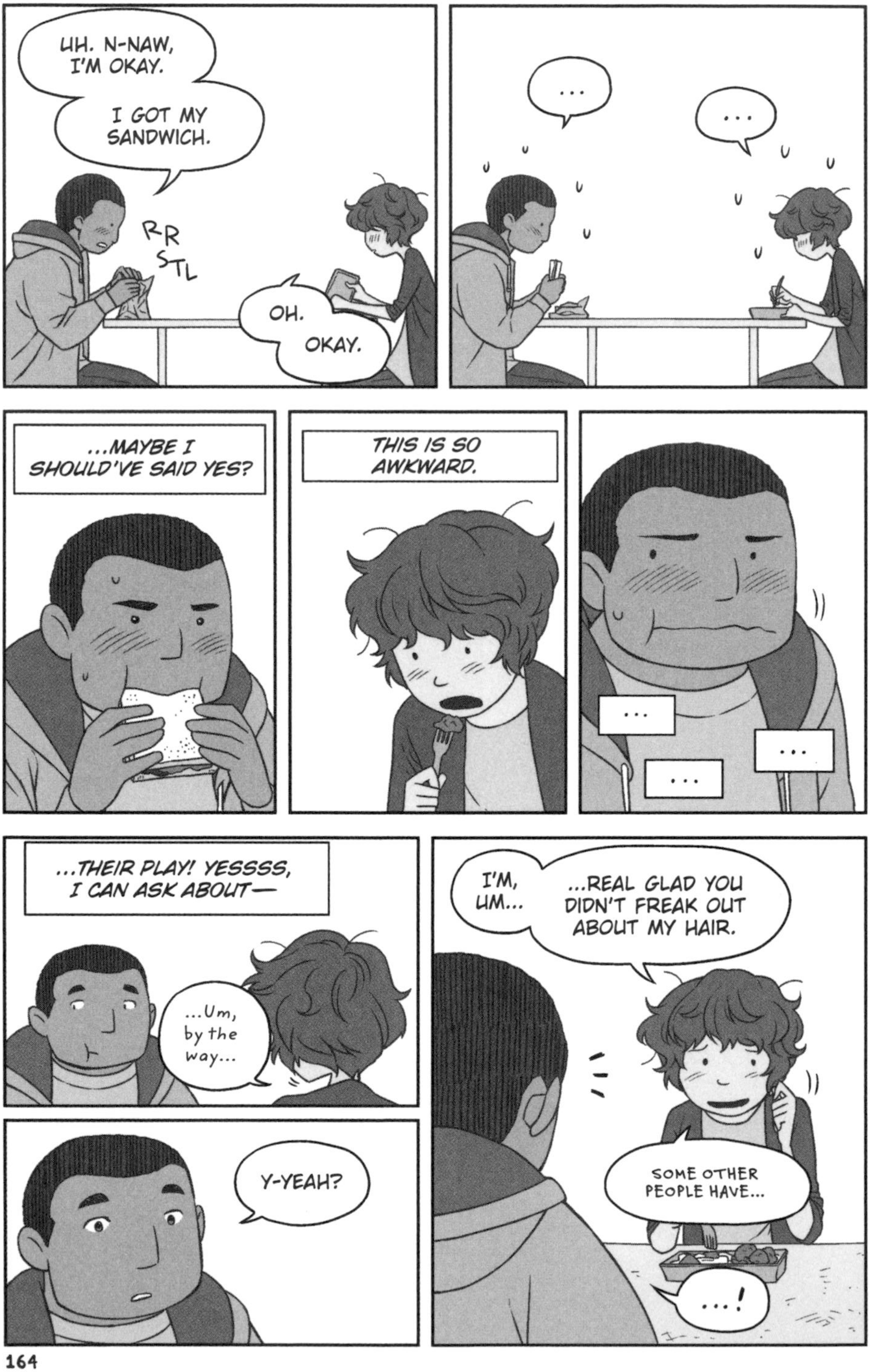
UH. N-NAW, I'M OKAY.
I GOT MY SANDWICH.
RRSTL
OH.
OKAY.
...
...
...MAYBE I SHOULD'VE SAID YES?
THIS IS SO AWKWARD.
...
...
...
...THEIR PLAY! YESSSS, I CAN ASK ABOUT—
...Um, by the way...
Y-YEAH?
I'M, UM...
...REAL GLAD YOU DIDN'T FREAK OUT ABOUT MY HAIR.
SOME OTHER PEOPLE HAVE...
...!

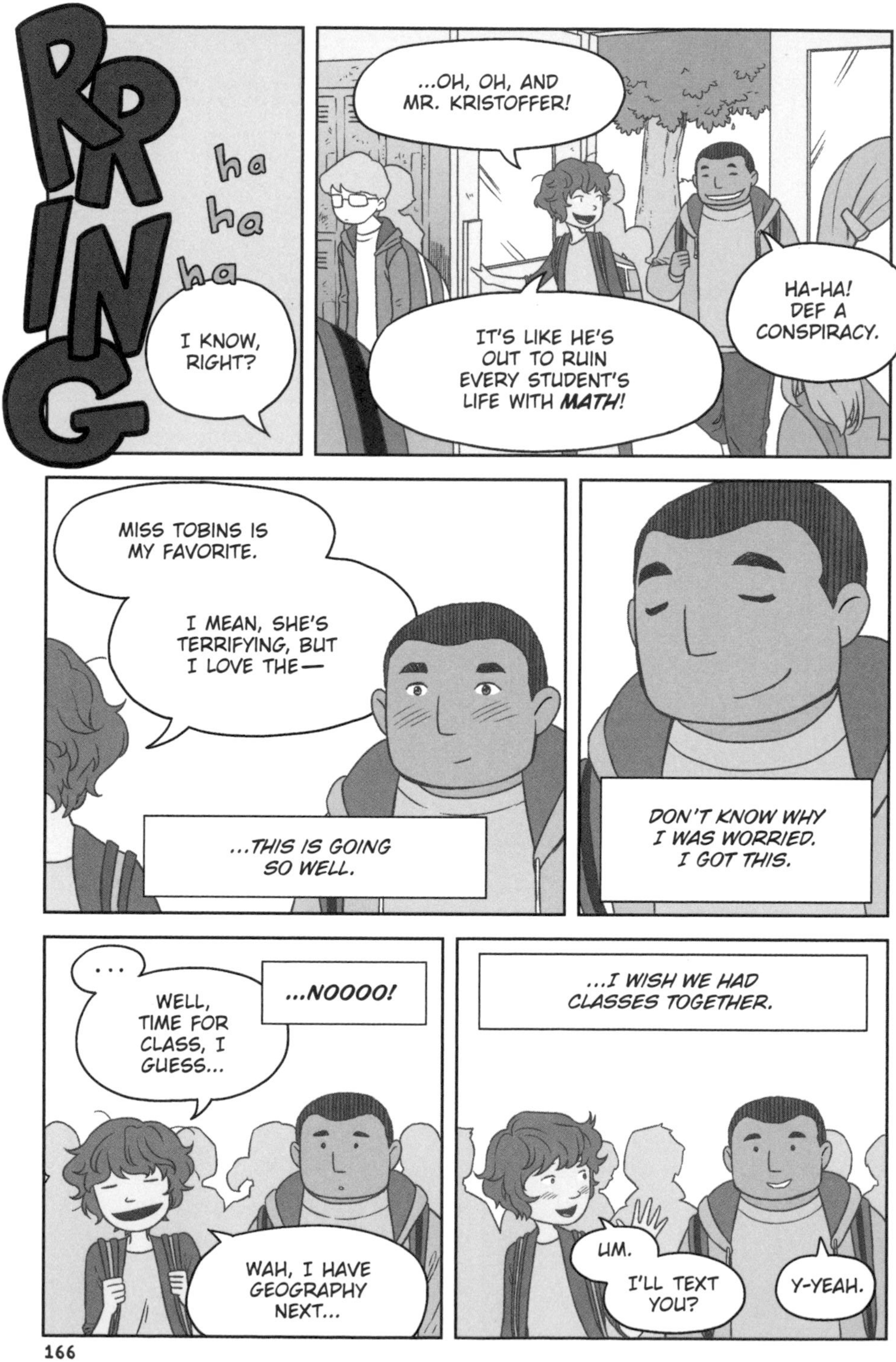
RRING
ha ha ha
I KNOW, RIGHT?
...OH, OH, AND MR. KRISTOFFER!
IT'S LIKE HE'S OUT TO RUIN EVERY STUDENT'S LIFE WITH MATH!
HA-HA! DEF A CONSPIRACY.
MISS TOBINS IS MY FAVORITE.
I MEAN, SHE'S TERRIFYING, BUT I LOVE THE—
...THIS IS GOING SO WELL.
DON'T KNOW WHY I WAS WORRIED. I GOT THIS.
...
WELL, TIME FOR CLASS, I GUESS...
...NOOOO!
WAH, I HAVE GEOGRAPHY NEXT...
...I WISH WE HAD CLASSES TOGETHER.
UM.
I'LL TEXT YOU?
Y-YEAH.

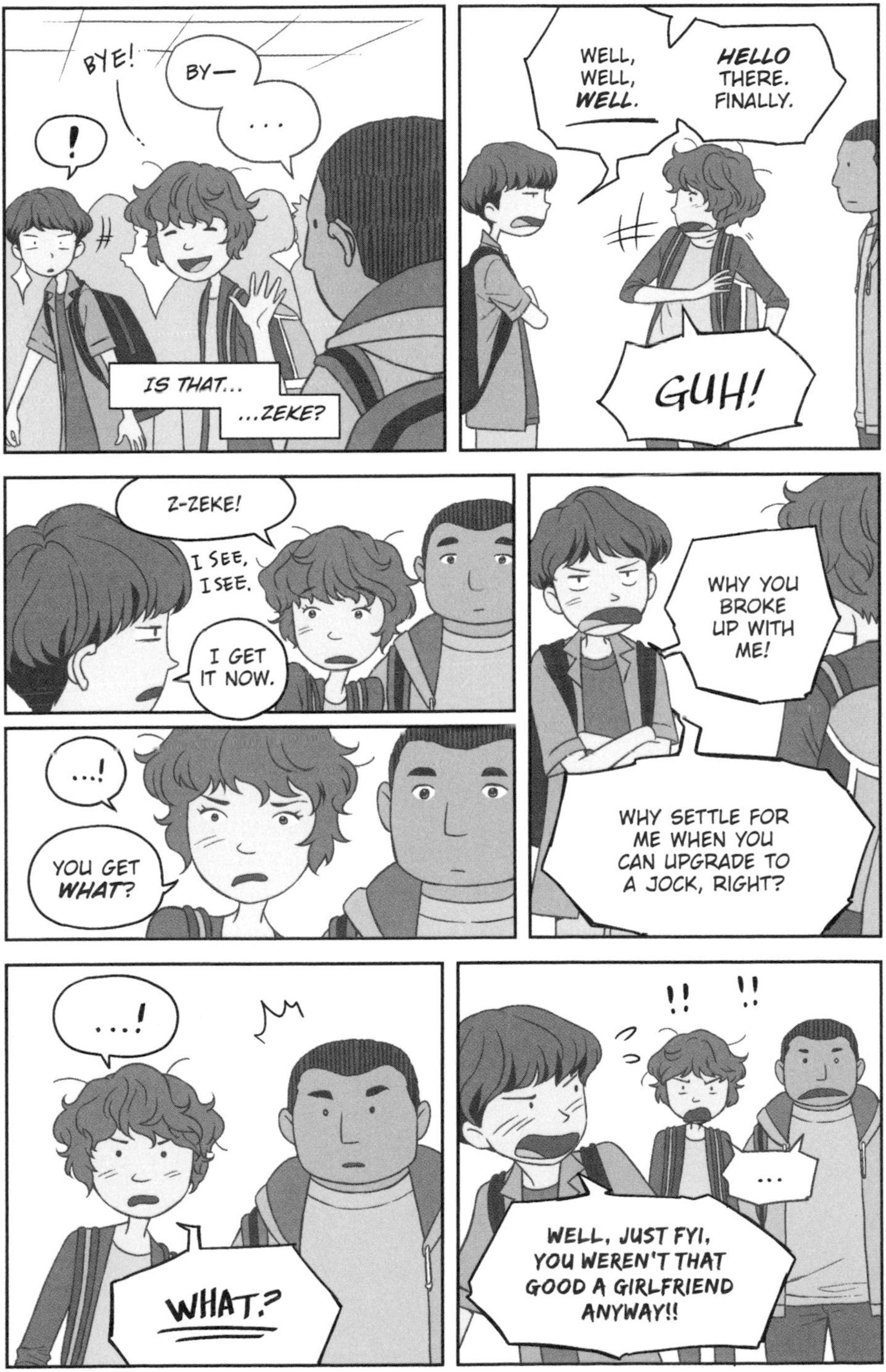
BYE!
BY—
...
!
IS THAT...
...ZEKE?
WELL, WELL, WELL.
HELLO THERE. FINALLY.
GUH!
Z-ZEKE!
I SEE, I SEE.
I GET IT NOW.
...!
YOU GET WHAT?
WHY YOU BROKE UP WITH ME!
WHY SETTLE FOR ME WHEN YOU CAN UPGRADE TO A JOCK, RIGHT?
...!
WHAT.?
!!
!!
...
WELL, JUST FYI, YOU WEREN'T THAT GOOD A GIRLFRIEND ANYWAY!!

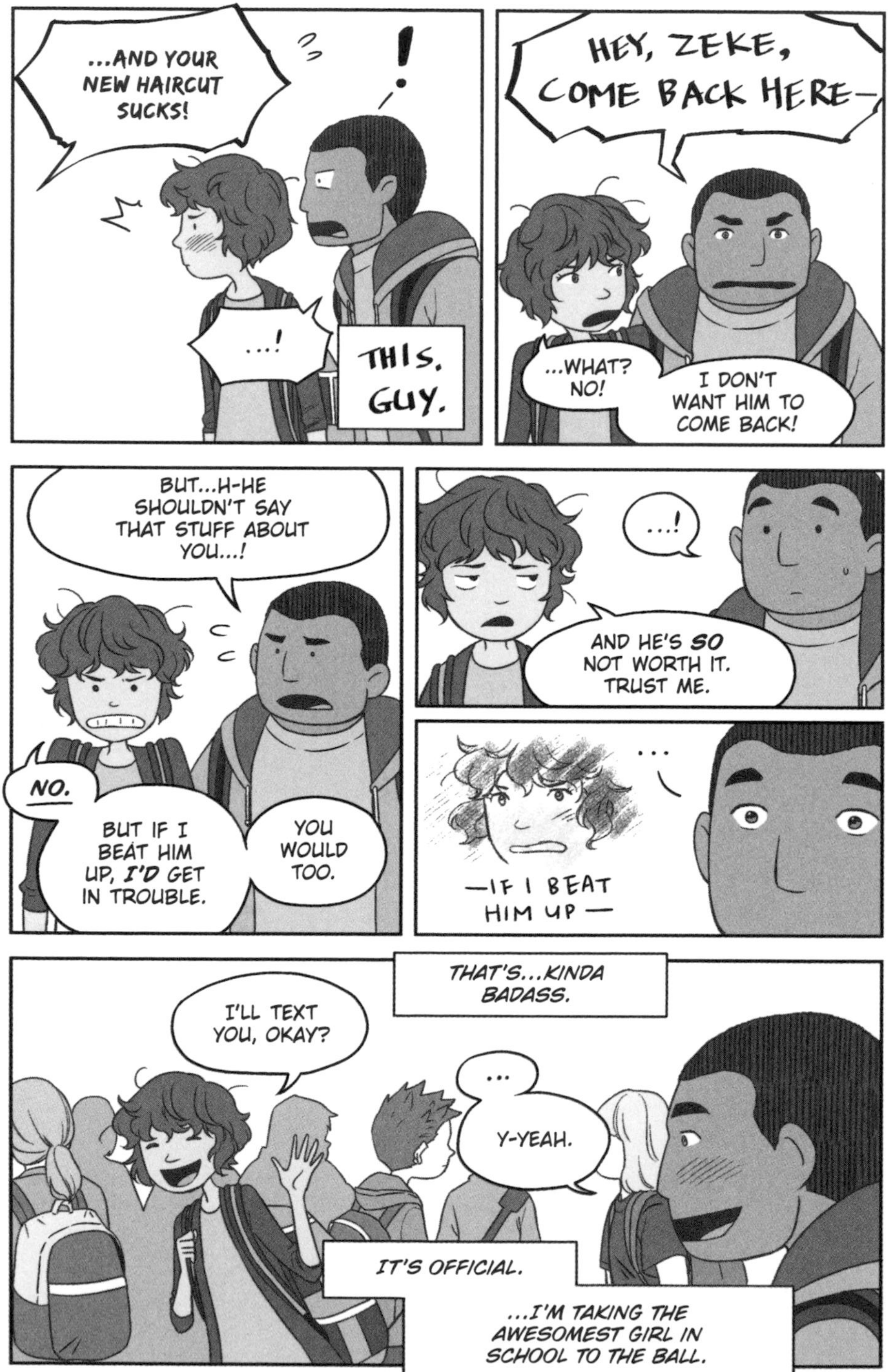
...AND YOUR NEW HAIRCUT SUCKS!
!
...!
THIS. GUY.
HEY, ZEKE, COME BACK HERE—
...WHAT? NO!
I DON'T WANT HIM TO COME BACK!
BUT...H-HE SHOULDN'T SAY THAT STUFF ABOUT YOU...!
NO.
BUT IF I BEAT HIM UP, I'D GET IN TROUBLE.
YOU WOULD TOO.
...!
AND HE'S SO NOT WORTH IT. TRUST ME.
...
—IF I BEAT HIM UP—
THAT'S...KINDA BADASS.
I'LL TEXT YOU, OKAY?
...
Y-YEAH.
IT'S OFFICIAL.
...I'M TAKING THE AWESOMEST GIRL IN SCHOOL TO THE BALL.

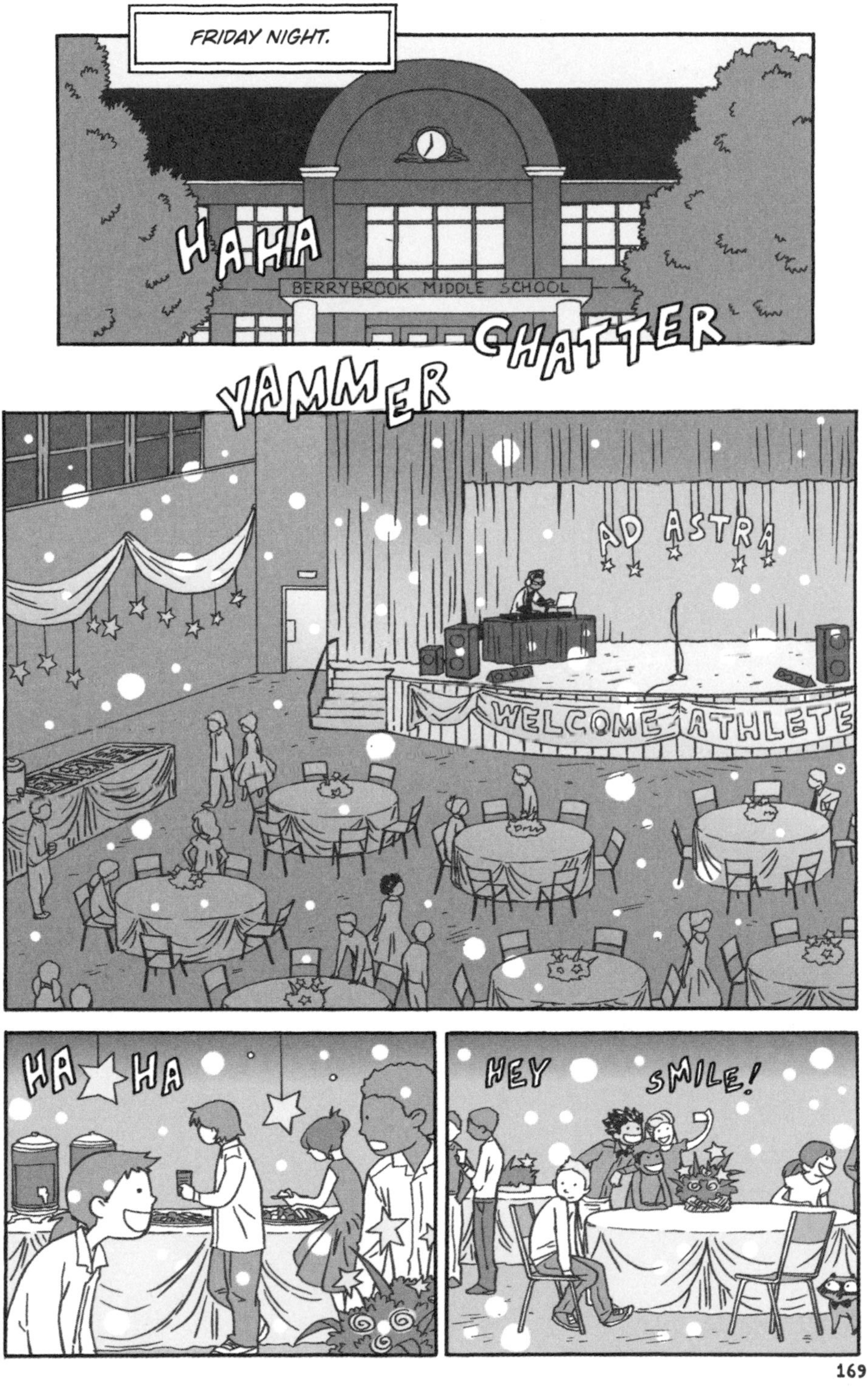
FRIDAY NIGHT.
HAHA
BERRYBROOK MIDDLE SCHOOL
CHATTER
YAMMER
AD ASTRA
WELCOME ATHLETE
HA HA
HEY
SMILE!

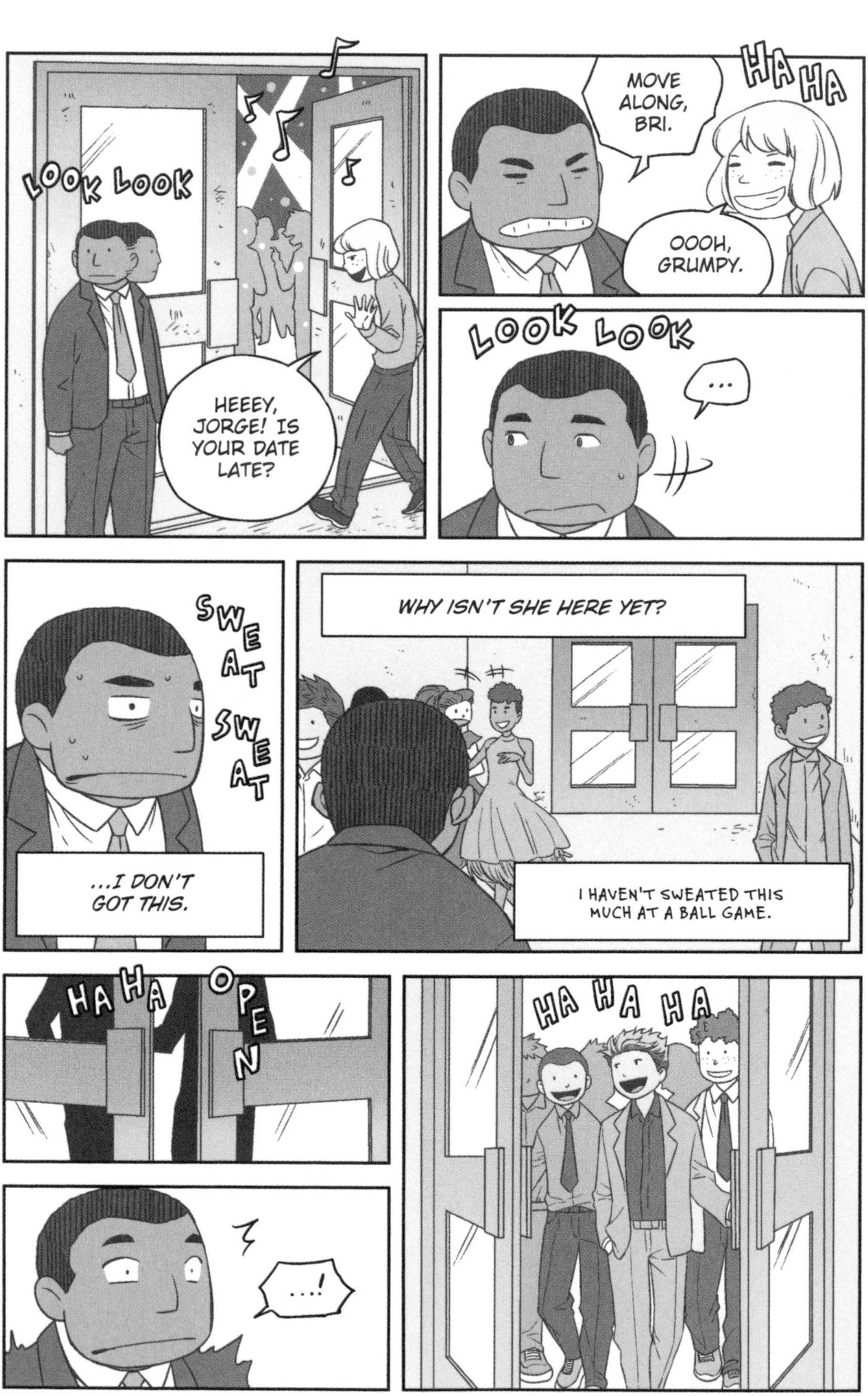
LOOK LOOK
HEEEY, JORGE! IS YOUR DATE LATE?
MOVE ALONG, BRI.
HA HA
OOOH, GRUMPY.
LOOK LOOK
...
SWEAT SWEAT
...I DON'T GOT THIS.
WHY ISN'T SHE HERE YET?
I HAVEN'T SWEATED THIS MUCH AT A BALL GAME.
HAHA
OPEN
...!
HA HA HA HA

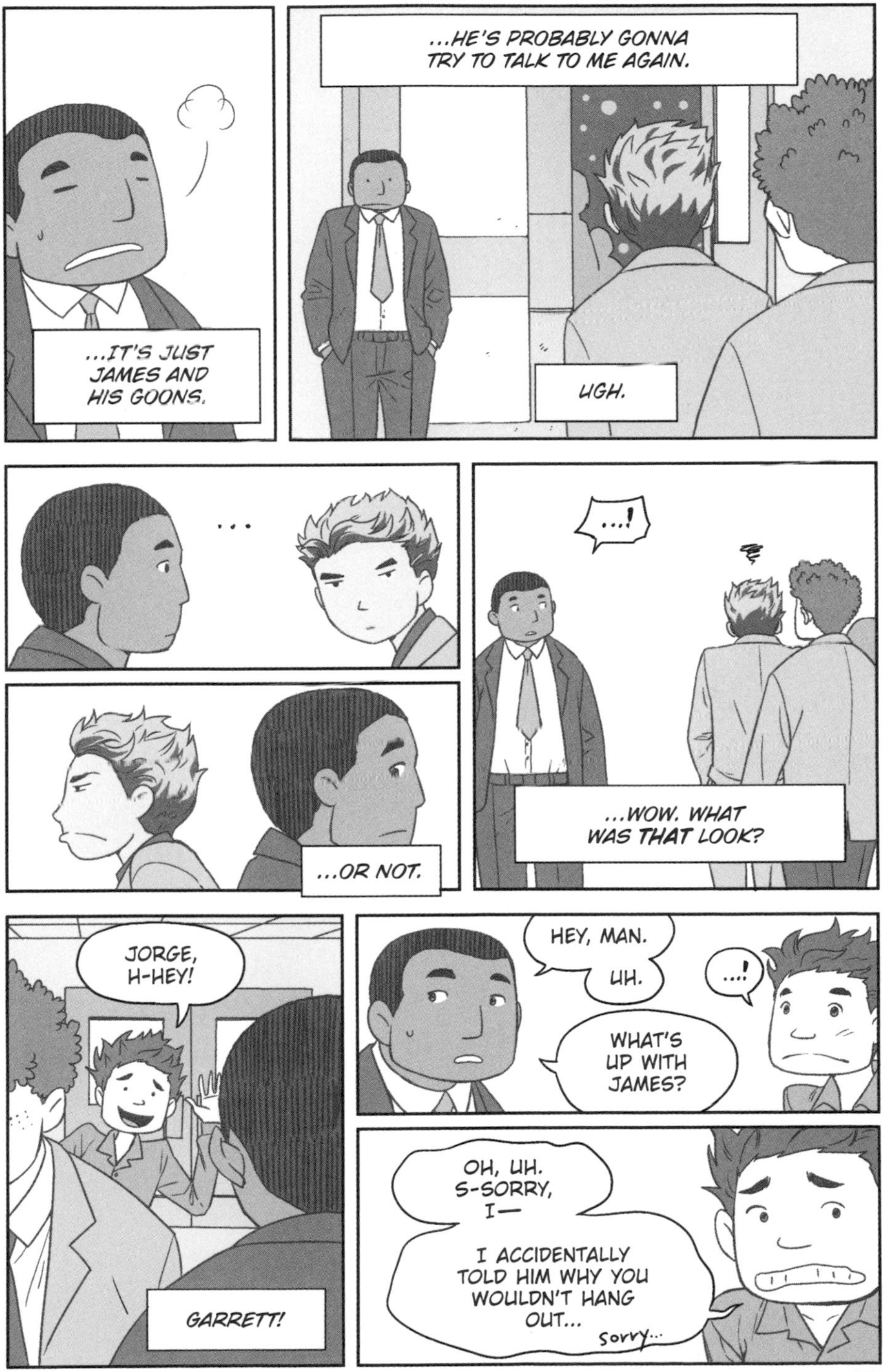
...IT'S JUST JAMES AND HIS GOONS.
...HE'S PROBABLY GONNA TRY TO TALK TO ME AGAIN.
UGH.
...
...!
...OR NOT.
...WOW. WHAT WAS THAT LOOK?
JORGE, H-HEY!
GARRETT!
HEY, MAN.
UH.
WHAT'S UP WITH JAMES?
...!
OH, UH. S-SORRY, I—
I ACCIDENTALLY TOLD HIM WHY YOU WOULDN'T HANG OUT...
sorry...

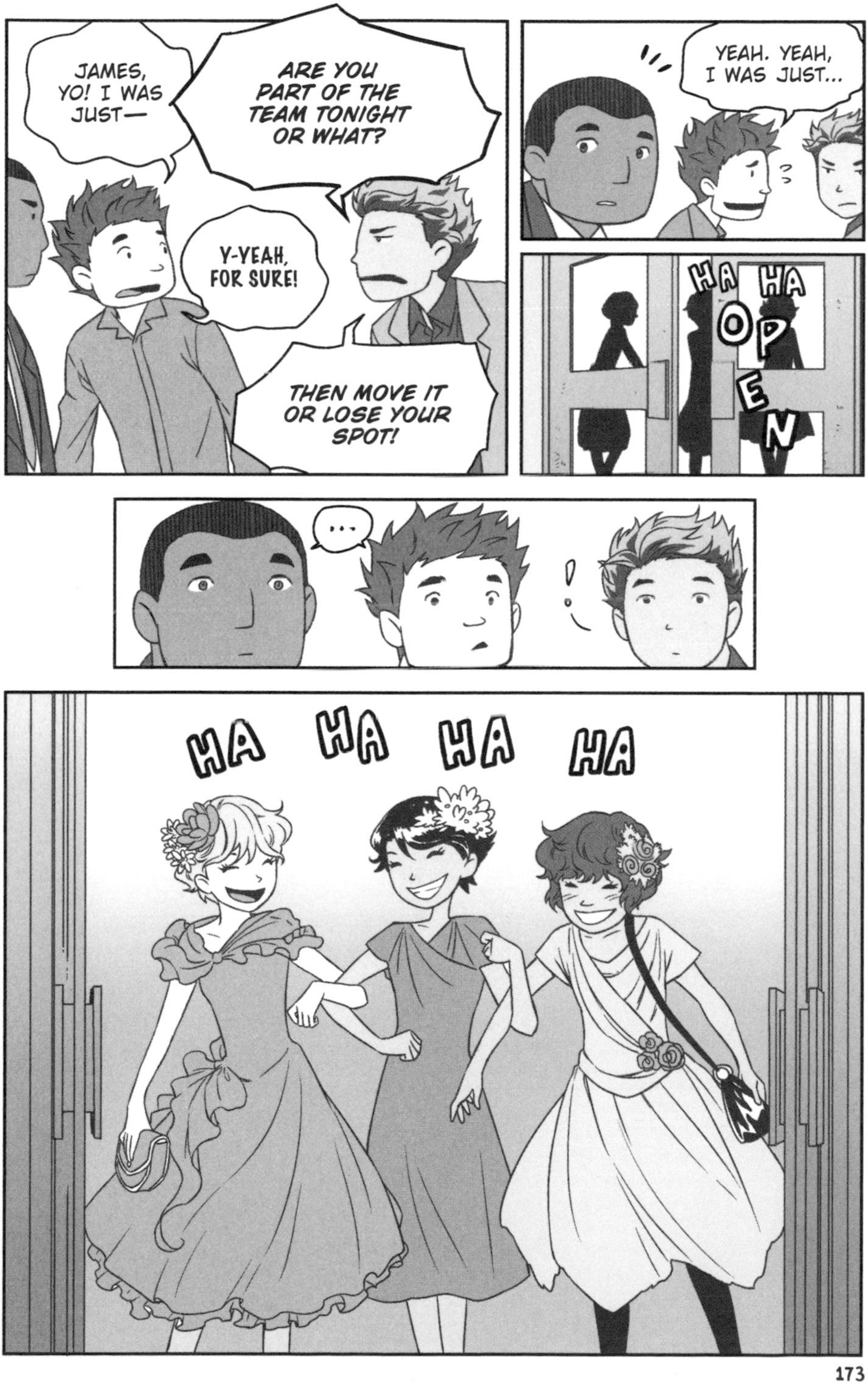
JAMES, YO! I WAS JUST—
ARE YOU PART OF THE TEAM TONIGHT OR WHAT?
Y-YEAH, FOR SURE!
THEN MOVE IT OR LOSE YOUR SPOT!
YEAH. YEAH, I WAS JUST...
HA HA
OPEN
...
HA HA HA HA

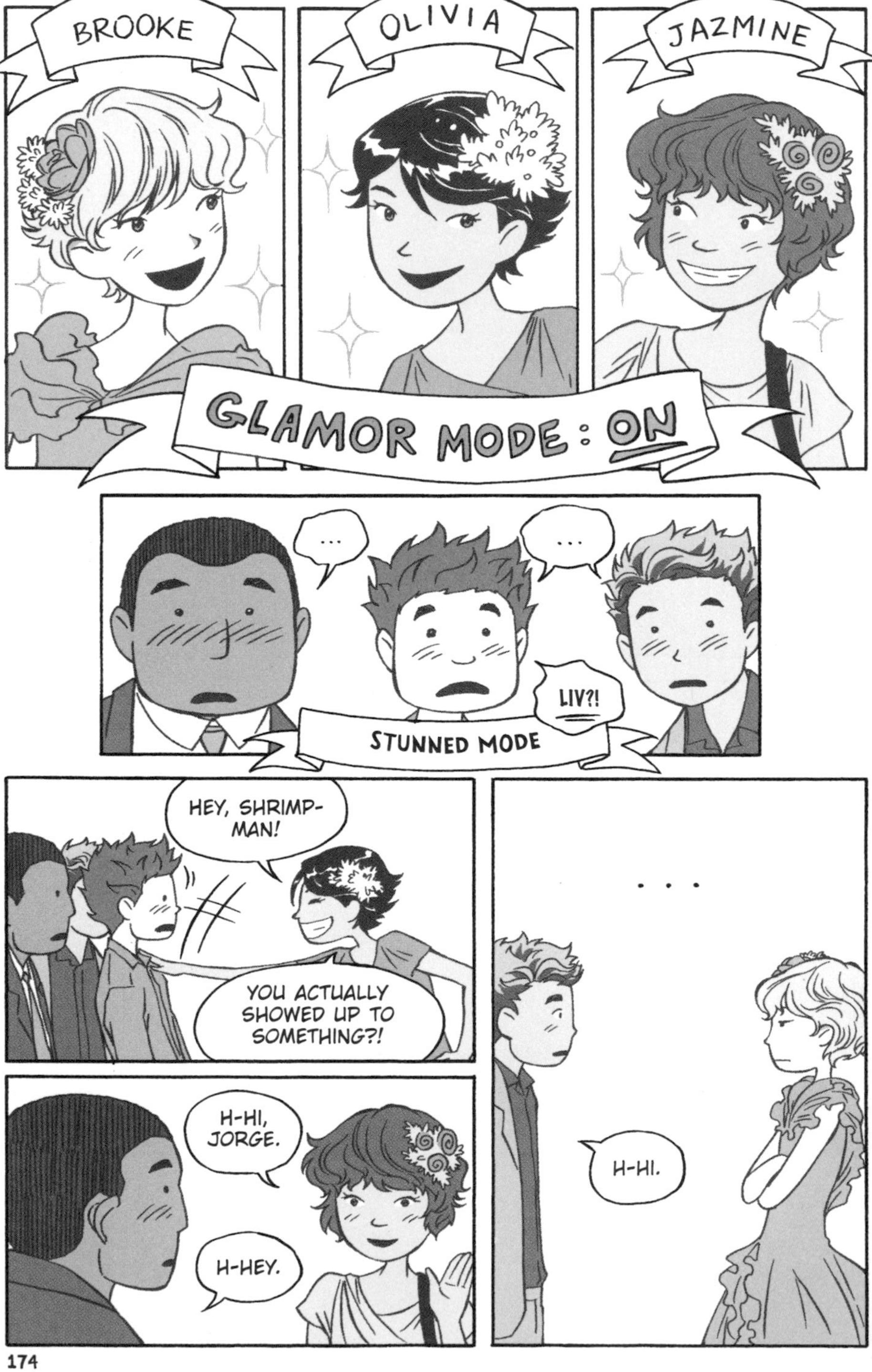
BROOKE
OLIVIA
JAZMINE
GLAMOR MODE: ON
...
...
LIV?!
STUNNED MODE
HEY, SHRIMP-MAN!
YOU ACTUALLY SHOWED UP TO SOMETHING?!
. . .
H-HI, JORGE.
H-HEY.
H-HI.

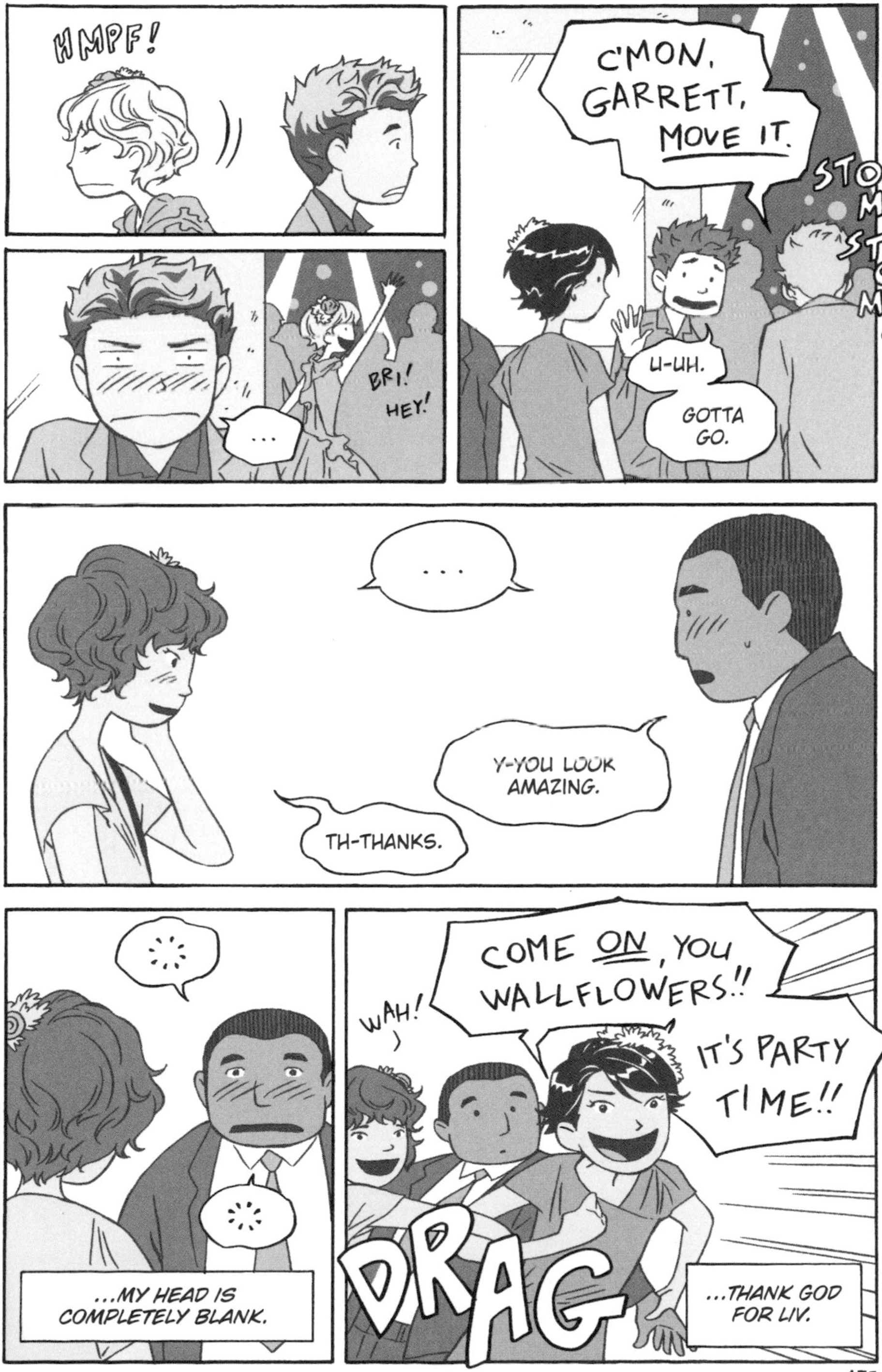
HMPF!
BRI! HEY!
...
C'MON, GARRETT, MOVE IT.
STOMP STOMP
U-UH.
GOTTA GO.
...
Y-YOU LOOK AMAZING.
TH-THANKS.
...MY HEAD IS COMPLETELY BLANK.
COME ON, YOU WALLFLOWERS!!
WAH!
IT'S PARTY TIME!!
DRAG
...THANK GOD FOR LIV.

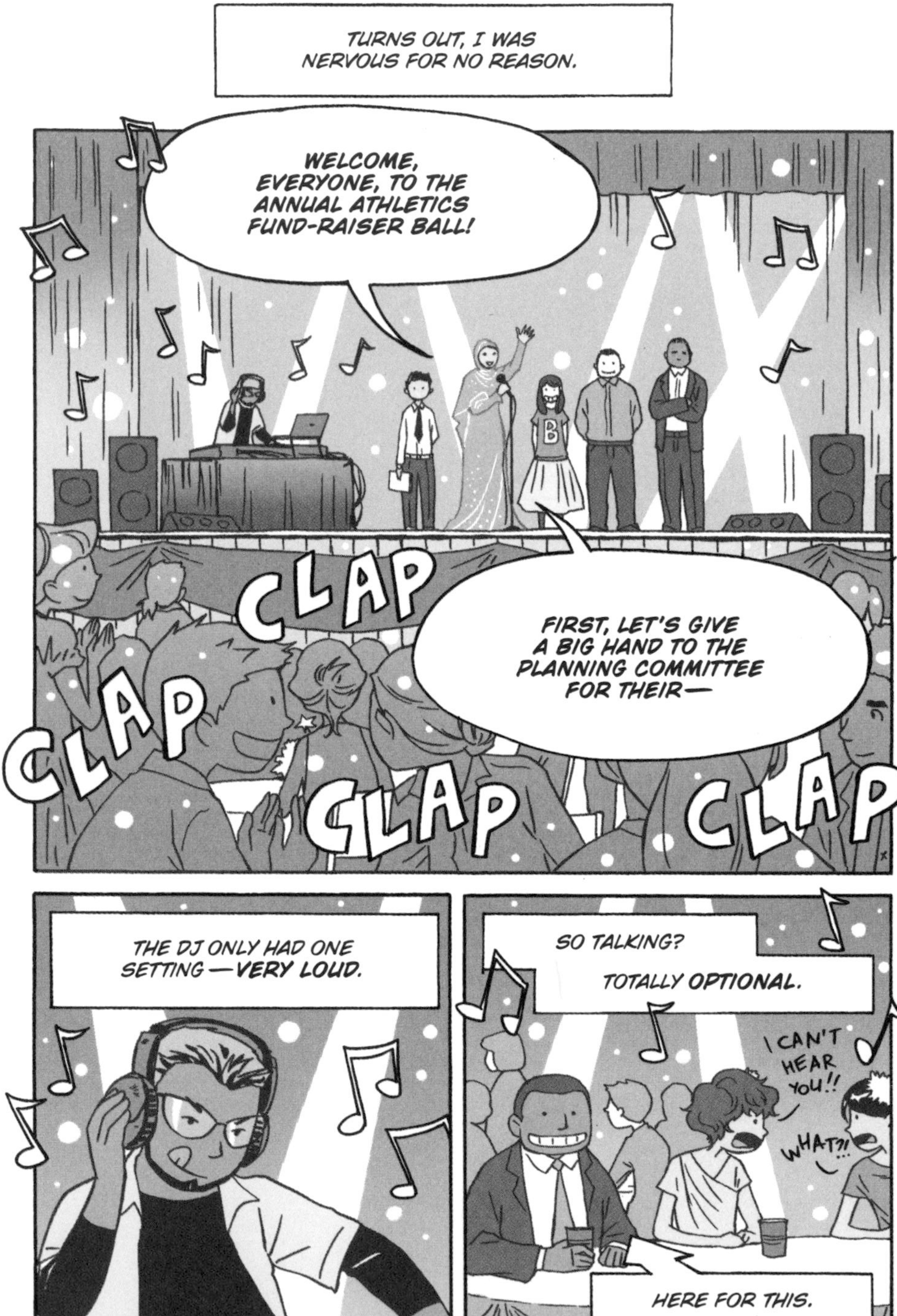
TURNS OUT, I WAS NERVOUS FOR NO REASON.
WELCOME, EVERYONE, TO THE ANNUAL ATHLETICS FUND-RAISER BALL!
FIRST, LET'S GIVE A BIG HAND TO THE PLANNING COMMITTEE FOR THEIR—
CLAP
CLAP
CLAP
CLAP
THE DJ ONLY HAD ONE SETTING—VERY LOUD.
SO TALKING?
TOTALLY OPTIONAL.
I CAN'T HEAR YOU!!
WHAT?!!
HERE FOR THIS.

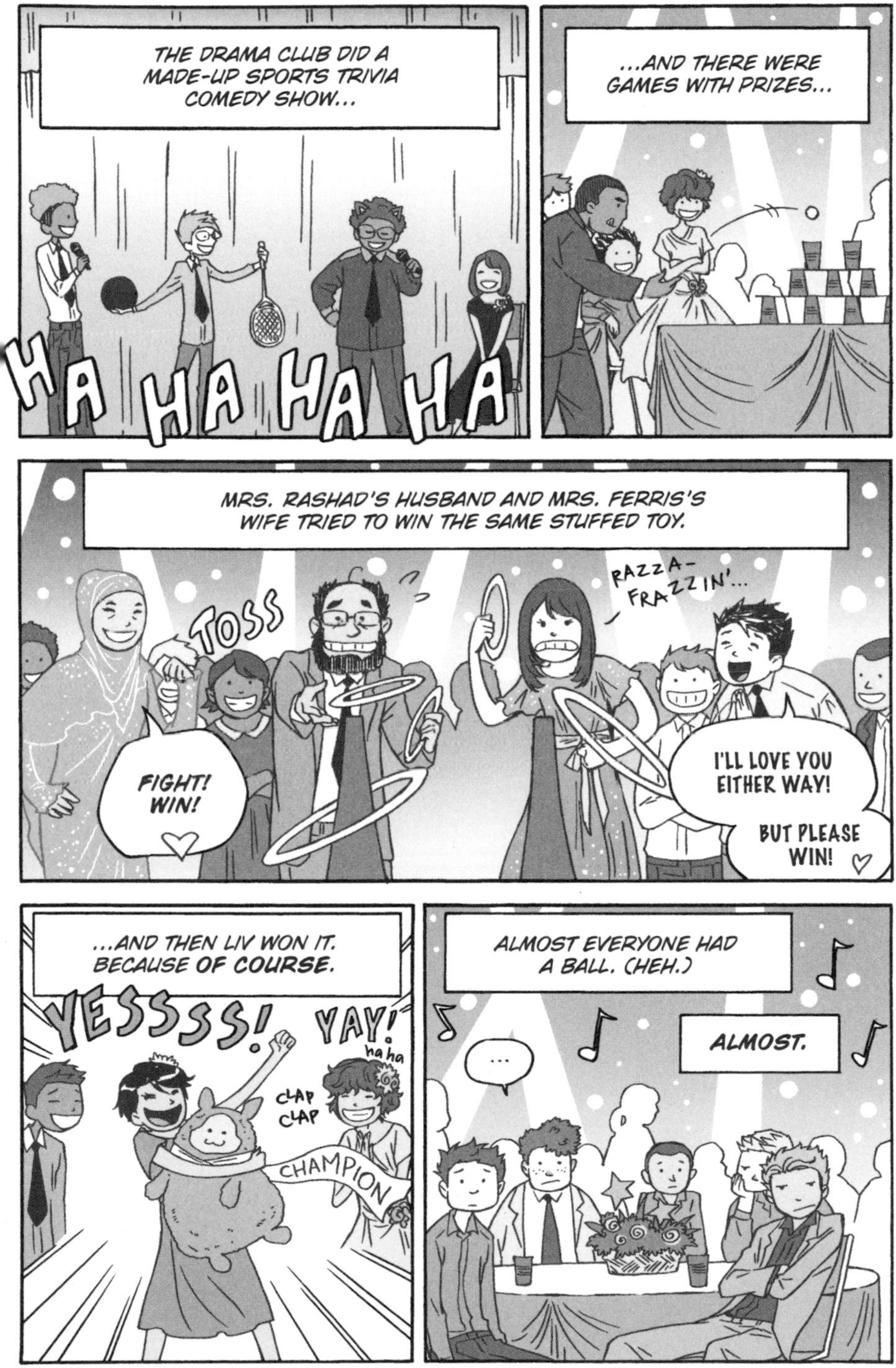
THE DRAMA CLUB DID A MADE-UP SPORTS TRIVIA COMEDY SHOW...
HA HA HA HA
...AND THERE WERE GAMES WITH PRIZES...
MRS. RASHAD'S HUSBAND AND MRS. FERRIS'S WIFE TRIED TO WIN THE SAME STUFFED TOY.
TOSS
RAZZA-FRAZZIN'...
FIGHT! WIN!
I'LL LOVE YOU EITHER WAY!
BUT PLEASE WIN!
...AND THEN LIV WON IT. BECAUSE OF COURSE.
YESSSSS!
YAY!
ha ha
CLAP CLAP
CHAMPION
ALMOST EVERYONE HAD A BALL. (HEH.)
ALMOST.
...

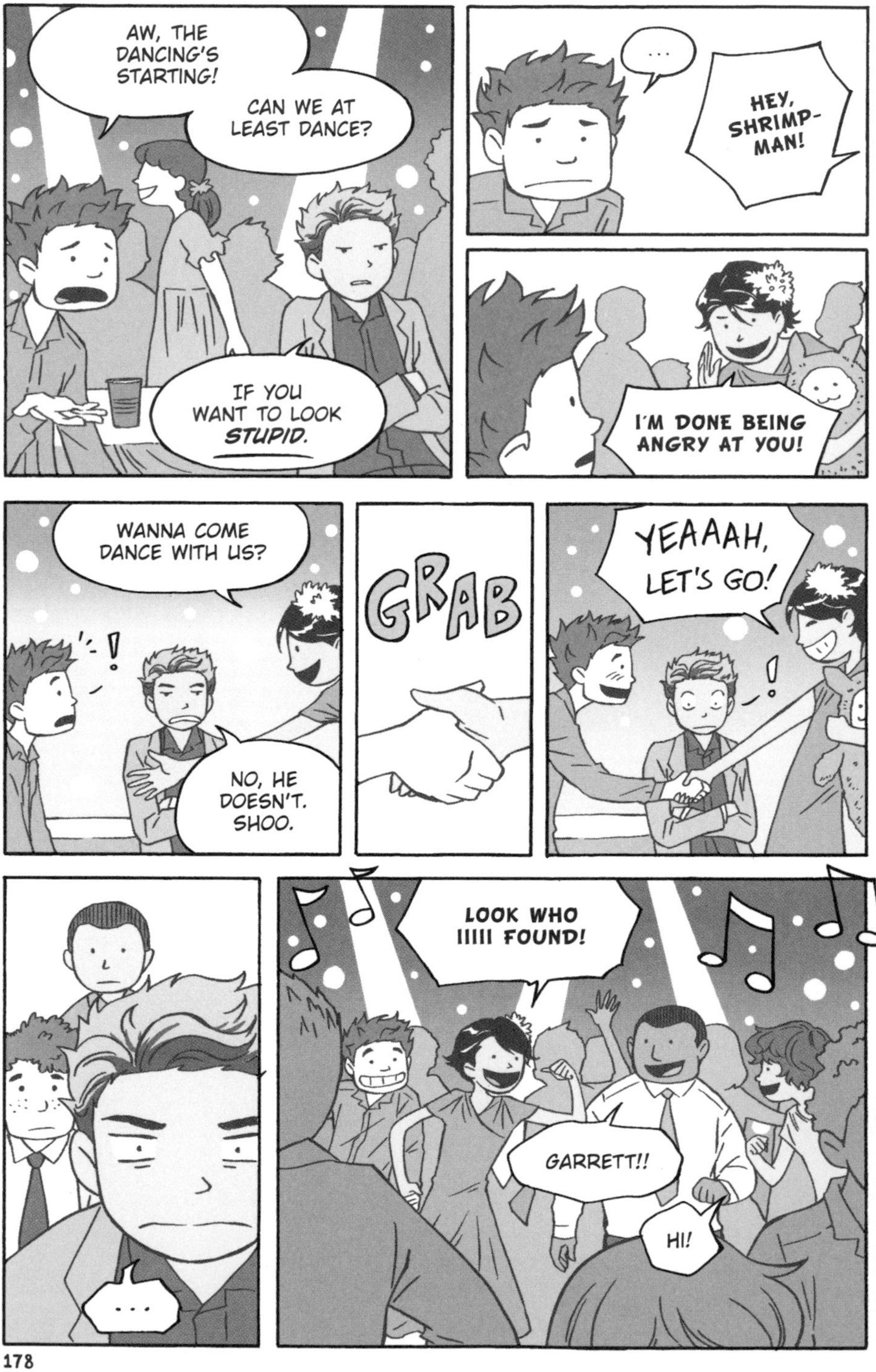
AW, THE DANCING'S STARTING!
CAN WE AT LEAST DANCE?
IF YOU WANT TO LOOK STUPID.
...
HEY, SHRIMP-MAN!
I'M DONE BEING ANGRY AT YOU!
WANNA COME DANCE WITH US?
NO, HE DOESN'T. SHOO.
GRAB
YEAAAH, LET'S GO!
...
LOOK WHO IIIII FOUND!
GARRETT!!
HI!

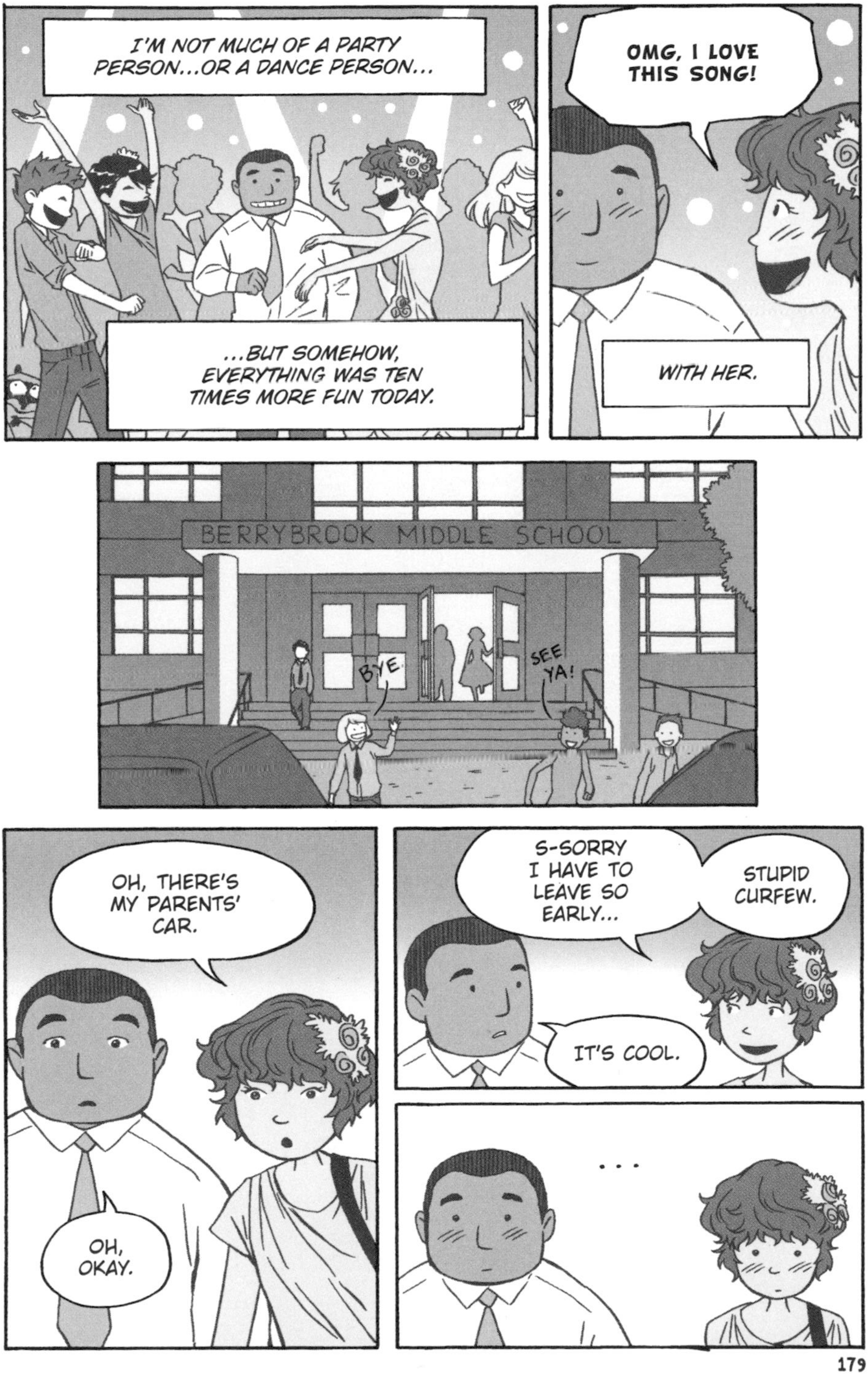

I'M NOT MUCH OF A PARTY PERSON...OR A DANCE PERSON...
...BUT SOMEHOW, EVERYTHING WAS TEN TIMES MORE FUN TODAY.
OMG, I LOVE THIS SONG!
WITH HER.
BERRYBROOK MIDDLE SCHOOL
BYE.
SEE YA!
OH, THERE'S MY PARENTS' CAR.
OH, OKAY.
S-SORRY I HAVE TO LEAVE SO EARLY...
STUPID CURFEW.
IT'S COOL.
. . .

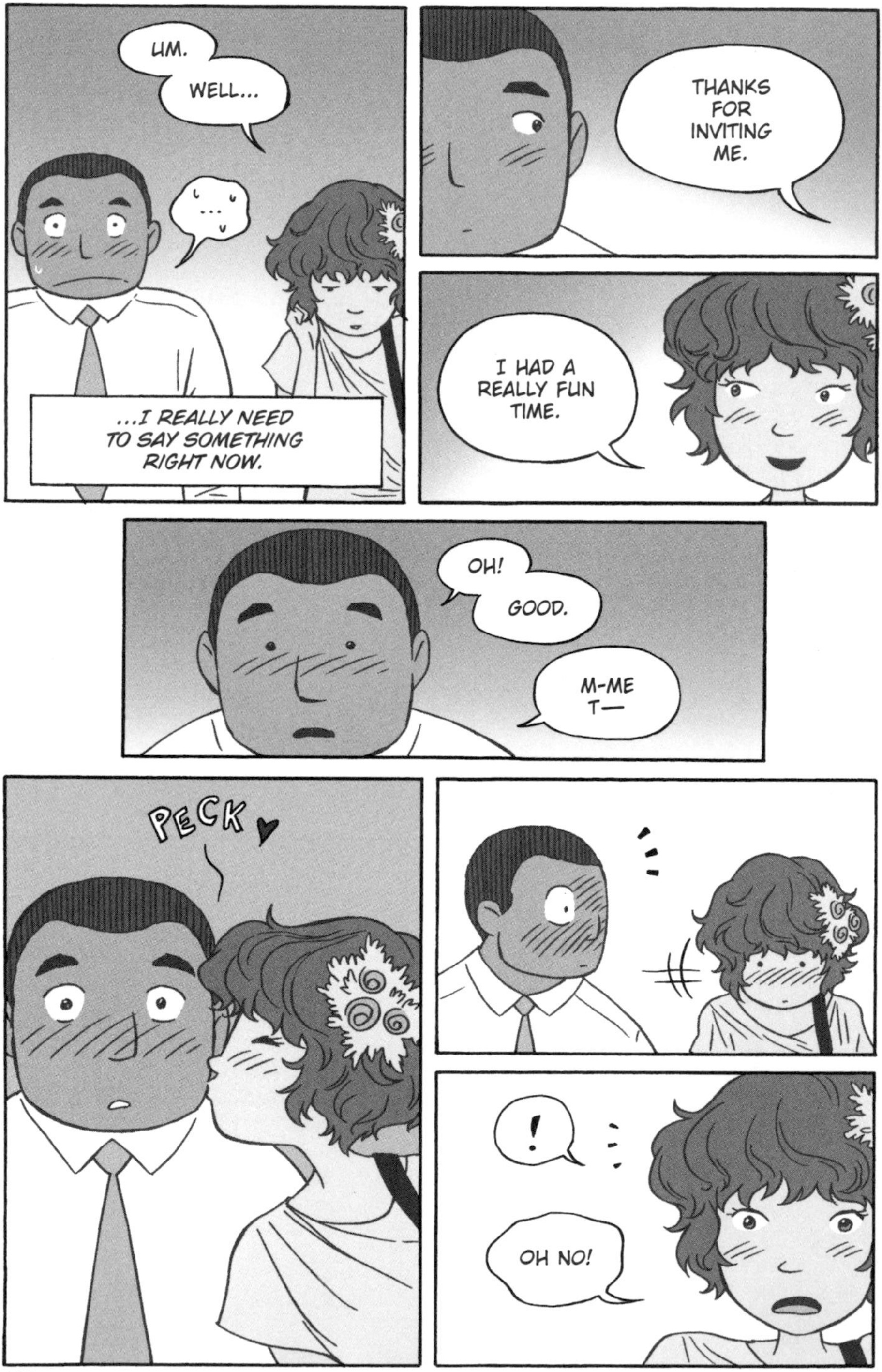
UM.
WELL...
...
...I REALLY NEED TO SAY SOMETHING RIGHT NOW.
THANKS FOR INVITING ME.
I HAD A REALLY FUN TIME.
OH!
GOOD.
M-ME T—
PECK
!
OH NO!

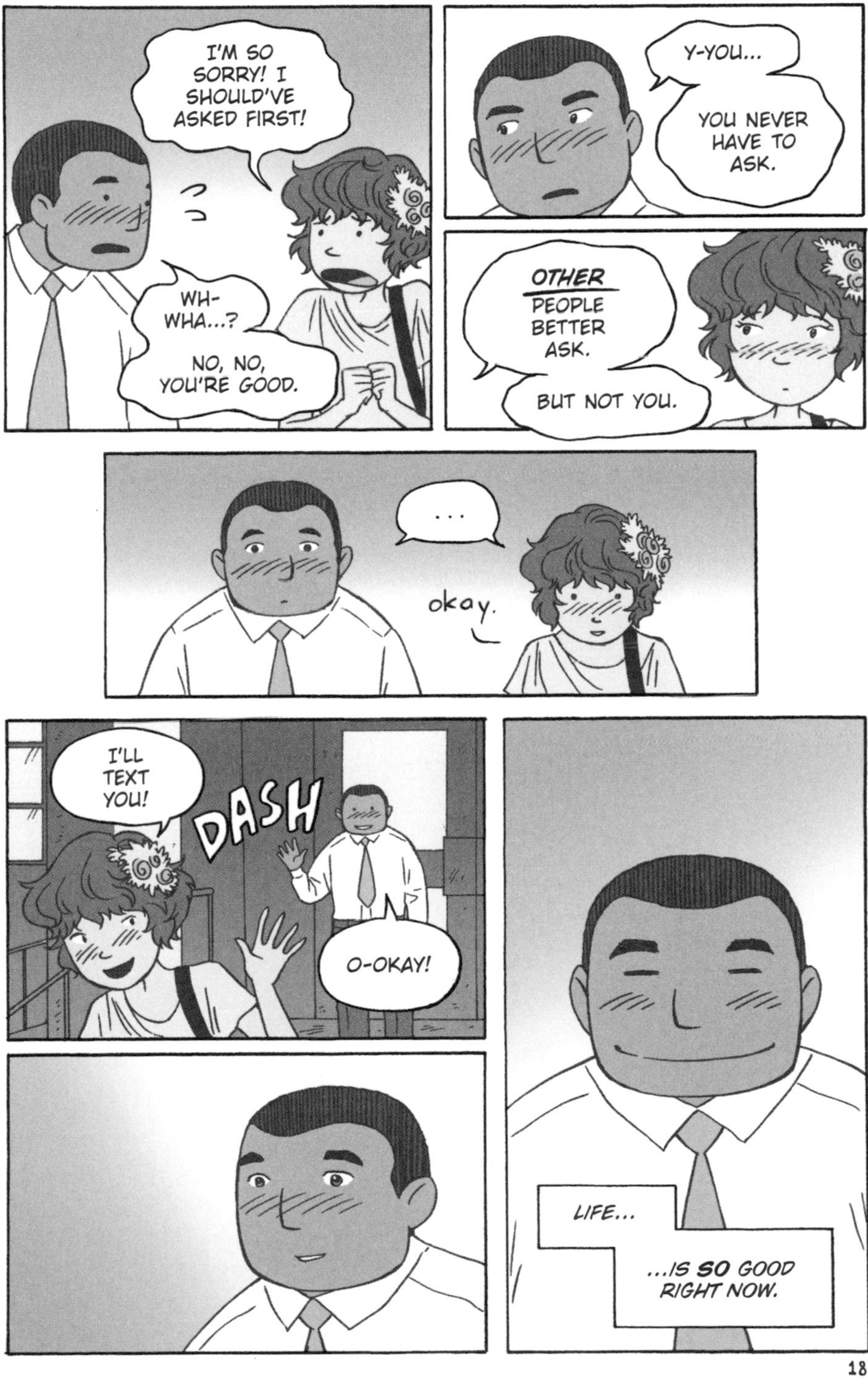
I'M SO SORRY! I SHOULD'VE ASKED FIRST!
WH- WHA...?
NO, NO, YOU'RE GOOD.
Y-YOU...
YOU NEVER HAVE TO ASK.
OTHER PEOPLE BETTER ASK.
BUT NOT YOU.
...
okay.
I'LL TEXT YOU!
DASH
O-OKAY!
LIFE...
...IS SO GOOD RIGHT NOW.

CHAPTER 9

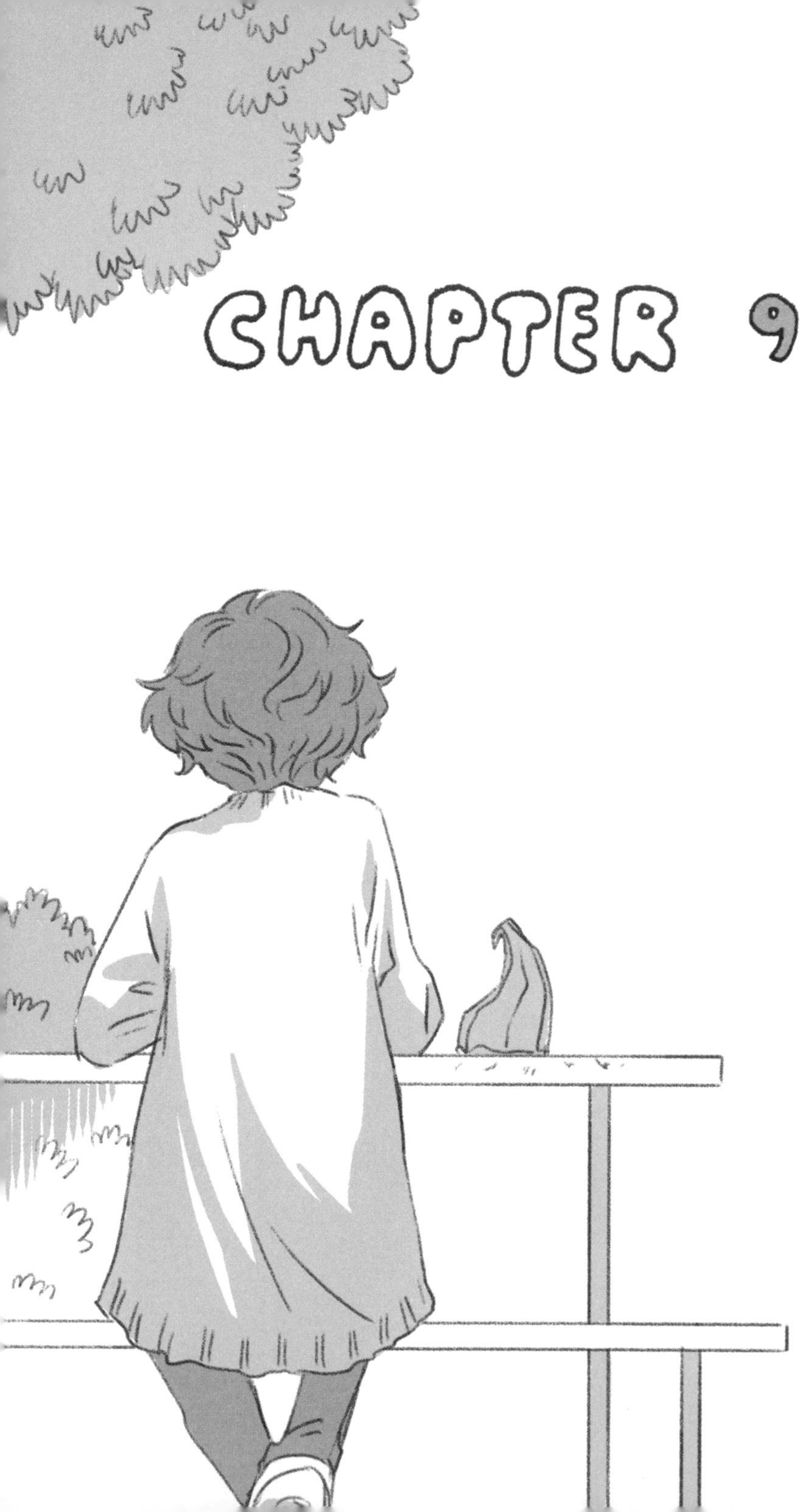

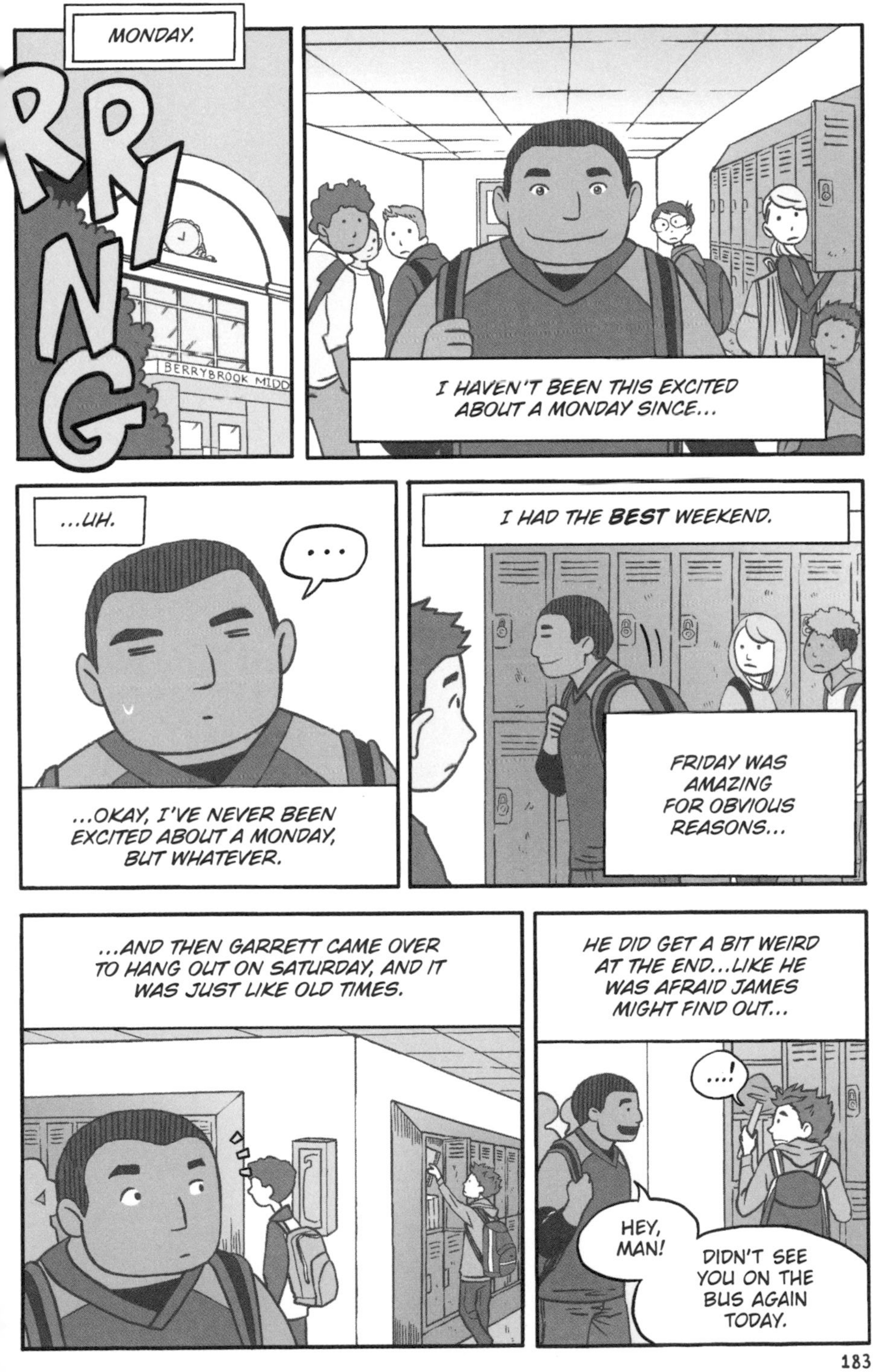
MONDAY.
RRRING
BERRYBROOK MIDD
I HAVEN'T BEEN THIS EXCITED ABOUT A MONDAY SINCE...
...UH.
. . .
...OKAY, I'VE NEVER BEEN EXCITED ABOUT A MONDAY, BUT WHATEVER.
I HAD THE **BEST** WEEKEND.
FRIDAY WAS AMAZING FOR OBVIOUS REASONS...
...AND THEN GARRETT CAME OVER TO HANG OUT ON SATURDAY, AND IT WAS JUST LIKE OLD TIMES.
HE DID GET A BIT WEIRD AT THE END...LIKE HE WAS AFRAID JAMES MIGHT FIND OUT...
...!
HEY, MAN!
DIDN'T SEE YOU ON THE BUS AGAIN TODAY.

185

187

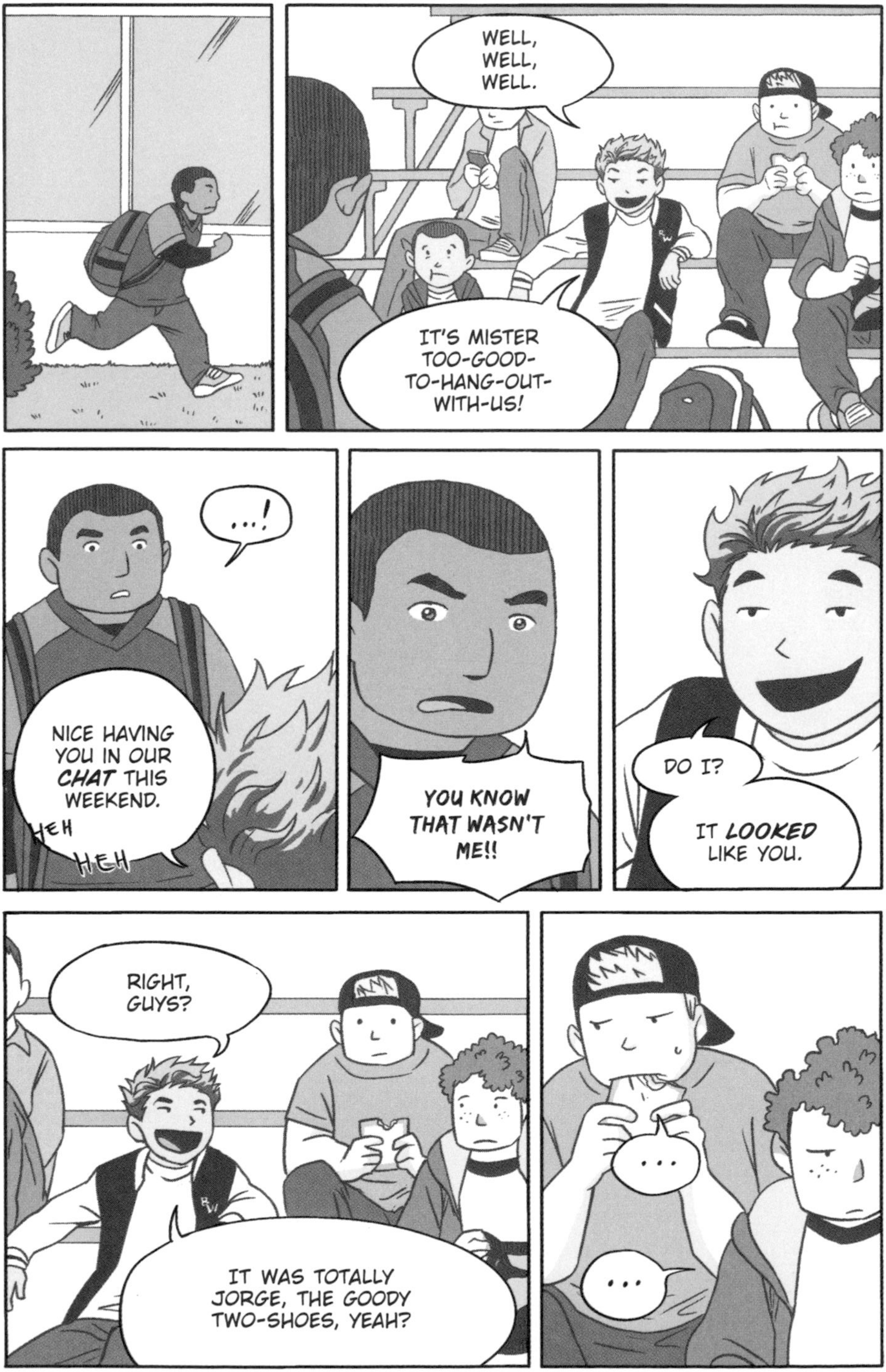
WELL, WELL, WELL.
IT'S MISTER TOO-GOOD-TO-HANG-OUT-WITH-US!
...!
NICE HAVING YOU IN OUR *CHAT* THIS WEEKEND.
HEH HEH
YOU KNOW THAT WASN'T ME!!
DO I?
IT ***LOOKED*** LIKE YOU.
RIGHT, GUYS?
IT WAS TOTALLY JORGE, THE GOODY TWO-SHOES, YEAH?
...
...

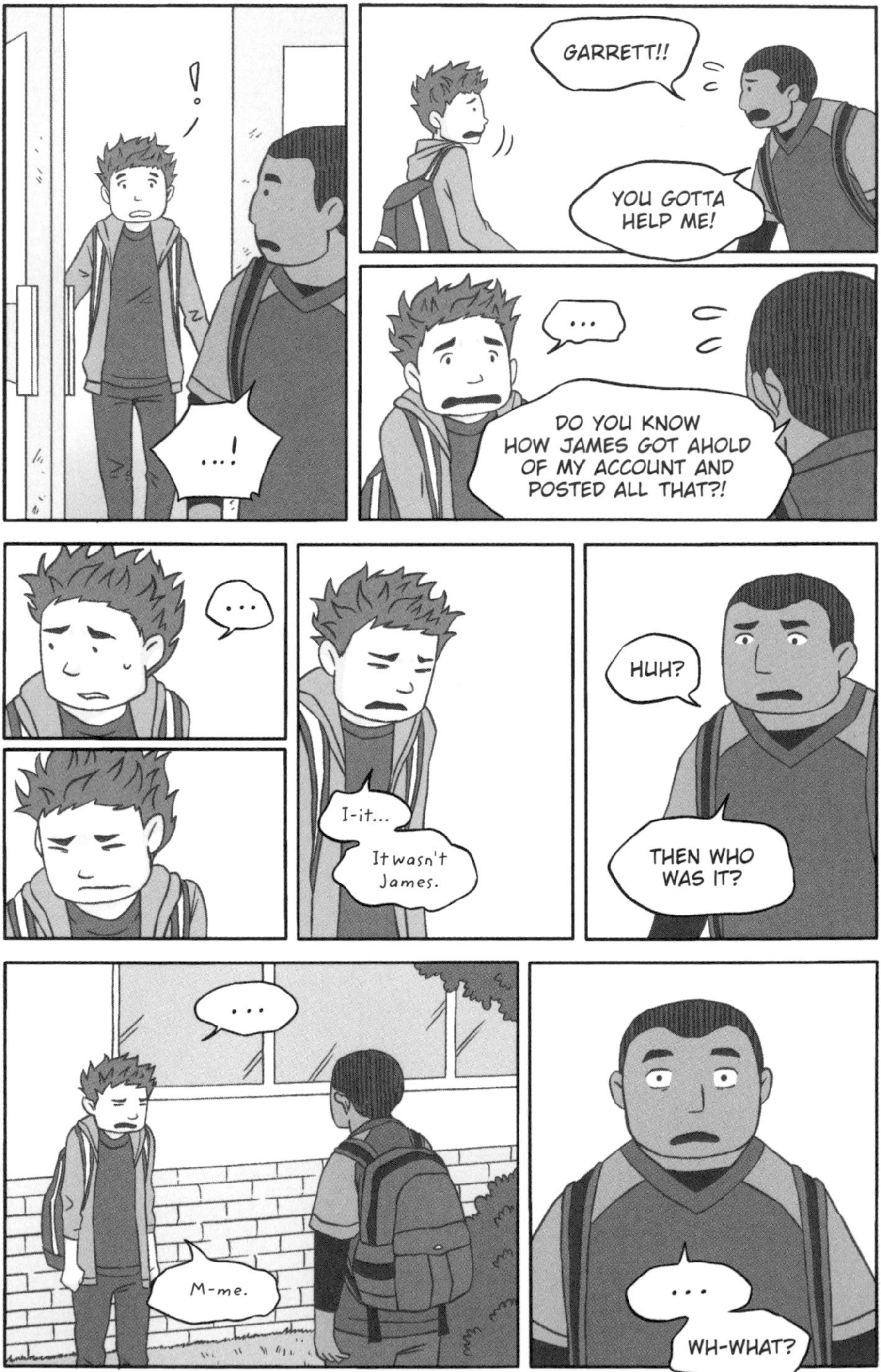
!
...!
GARRETT!!
YOU GOTTA HELP ME!
...
DO YOU KNOW HOW JAMES GOT AHOLD OF MY ACCOUNT AND POSTED ALL THAT?!
...
I-it...
It wasn't James.
HUH?
THEN WHO WAS IT?
...
M-me.
...
WH-WHAT?

CHAPTER 10

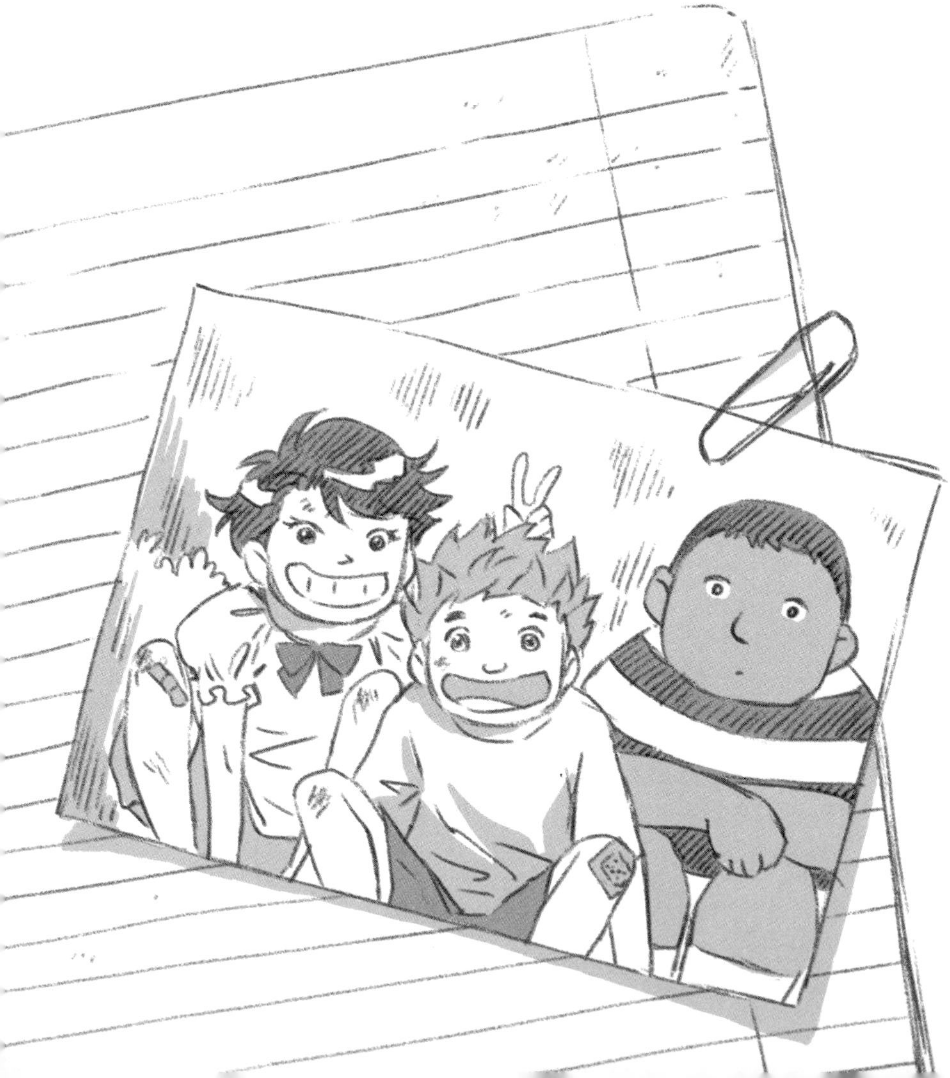

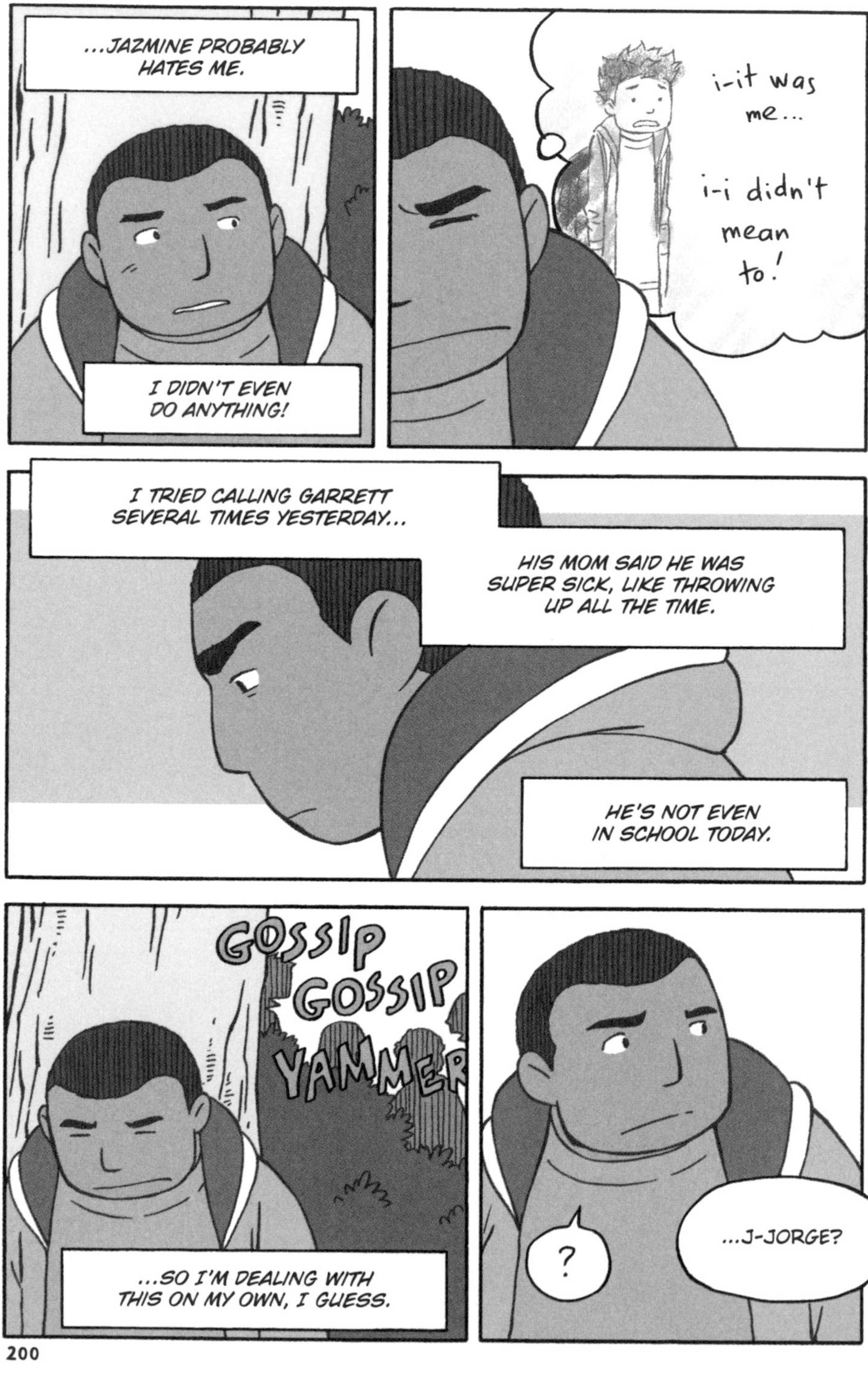
...JAZMINE PROBABLY HATES ME.
I DIDN'T EVEN DO ANYTHING!
i-it was me...
i-i didn't mean to!
I TRIED CALLING GARRETT SEVERAL TIMES YESTERDAY...
HIS MOM SAID HE WAS SUPER SICK, LIKE THROWING UP ALL THE TIME.
HE'S NOT EVEN IN SCHOOL TODAY.
GOSSIP
GOSSIP
YAMMER
...SO I'M DEALING WITH THIS ON MY OWN, I GUESS.
?
...J-JORGE?

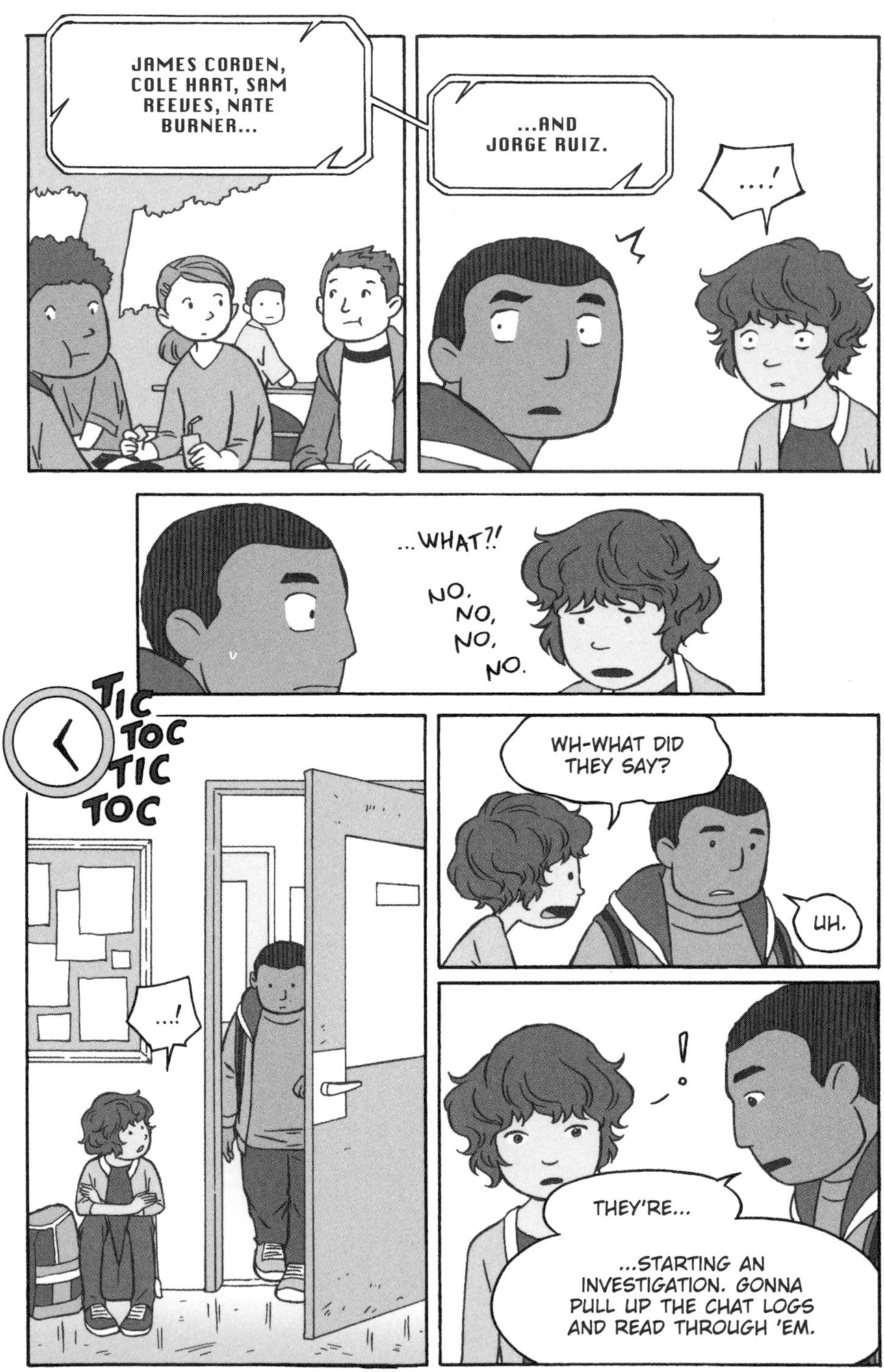

JAMES CORDEN, COLE HART, SAM REEVES, NATE BURNER...
...AND JORGE RUIZ.
....!
...WHAT?!
NO, NO, NO, NO.
TIC TOC TIC TOC
....!
WH-WHAT DID THEY SAY?
UH.
!
THEY'RE...
...STARTING AN INVESTIGATION. GONNA PULL UP THE CHAT LOGS AND READ THROUGH 'EM.

CHAPTER 11

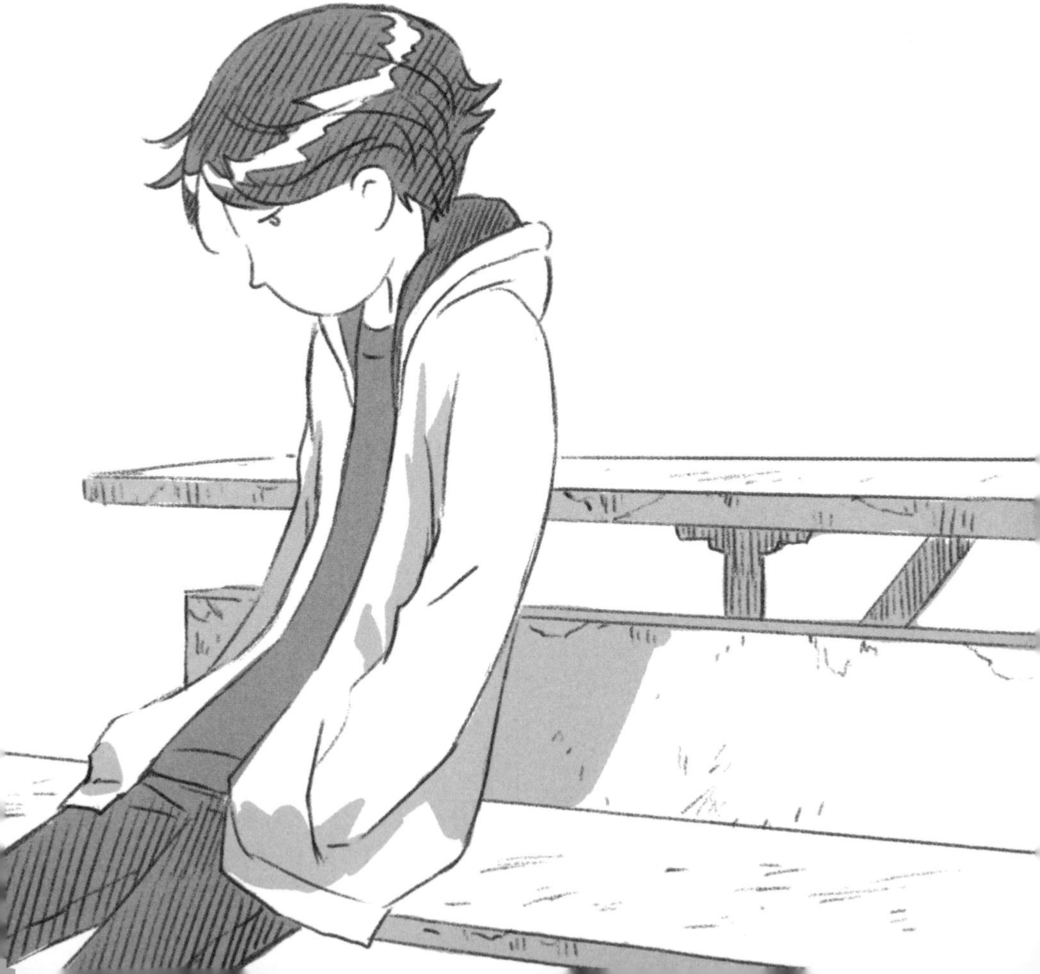

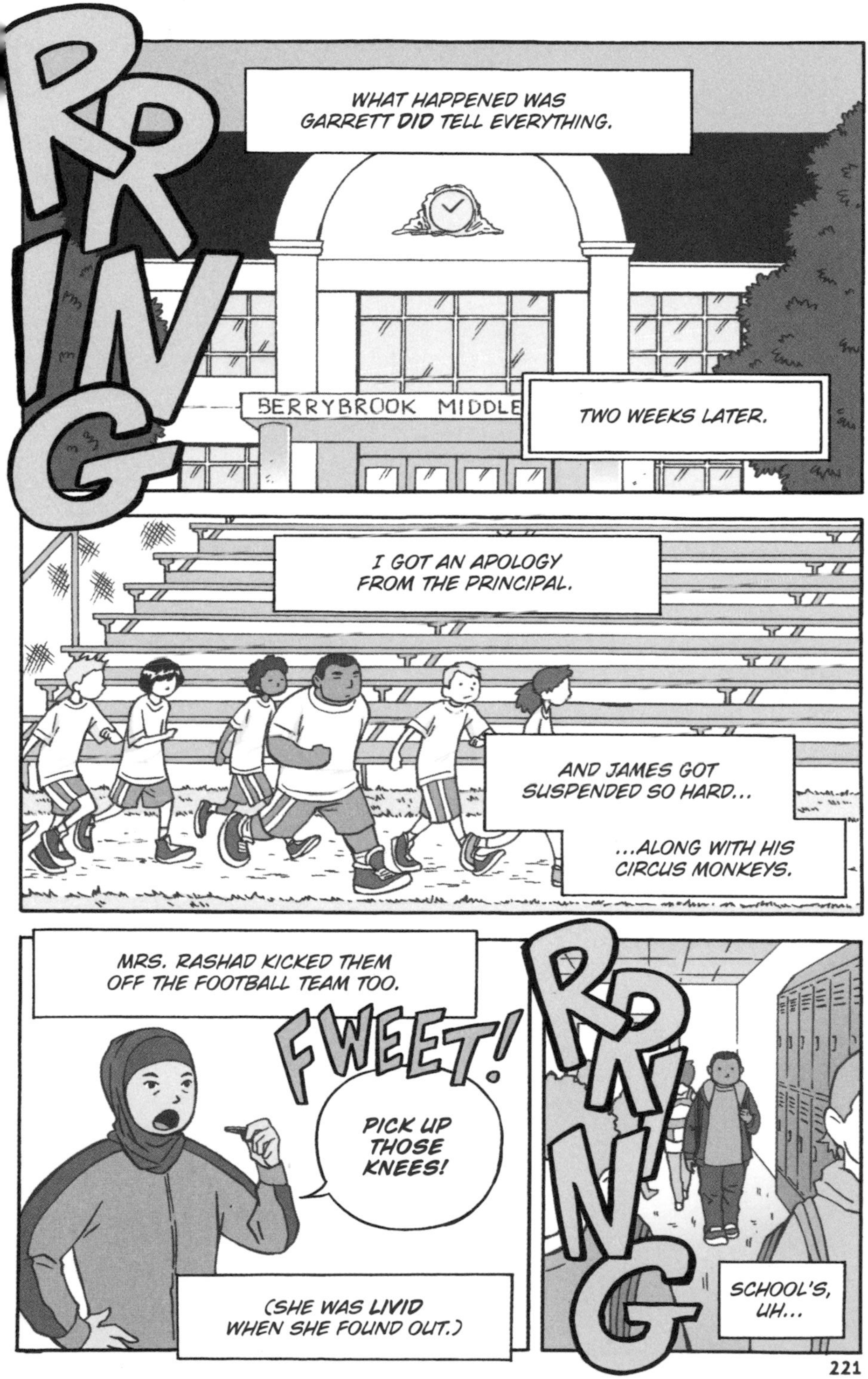
RRRING
WHAT HAPPENED WAS GARRETT DID TELL EVERYTHING.
BERRYBROOK MIDDLE
TWO WEEKS LATER.
I GOT AN APOLOGY FROM THE PRINCIPAL.
AND JAMES GOT SUSPENDED SO HARD...
...ALONG WITH HIS CIRCUS MONKEYS.
MRS. RASHAD KICKED THEM OFF THE FOOTBALL TEAM TOO.
FWEET!
PICK UP THOSE KNEES!
(SHE WAS LIVID WHEN SHE FOUND OUT.)
RRRING
SCHOOL'S, UH...

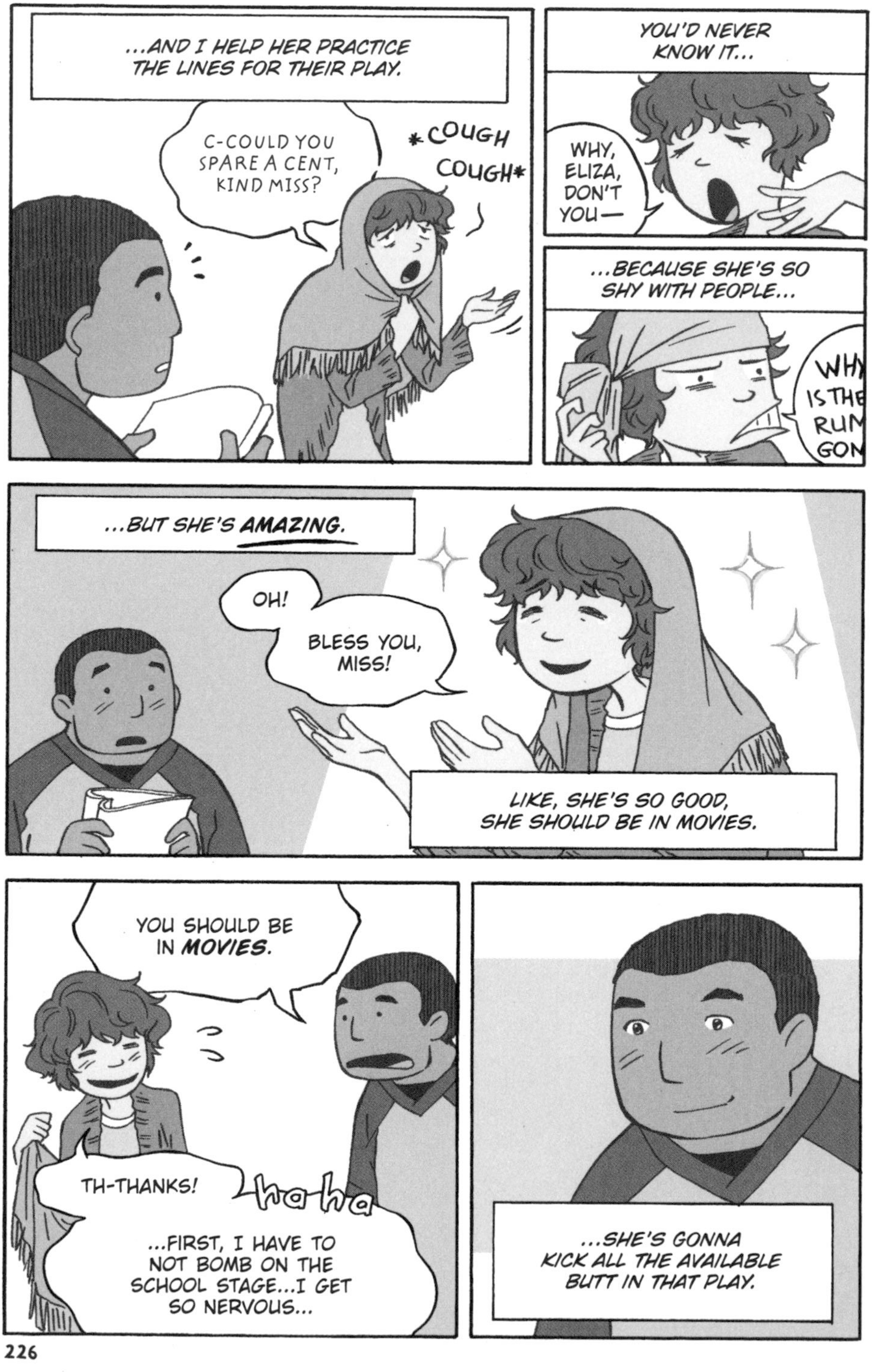
...AND I HELP HER PRACTICE THE LINES FOR THEIR PLAY.
C-COULD YOU SPARE A CENT, KIND MISS?
COUGH COUGH
YOU'D NEVER KNOW IT...
WHY, ELIZA, DON'T YOU—
...BECAUSE SHE'S SO SHY WITH PEOPLE...
WHY IS THE RUM GON
...BUT SHE'S AMAZING.
OH!
BLESS YOU, MISS!
LIKE, SHE'S SO GOOD, SHE SHOULD BE IN MOVIES.
YOU SHOULD BE IN MOVIES.
TH-THANKS!
ha ha
...FIRST, I HAVE TO NOT BOMB ON THE SCHOOL STAGE...I GET SO NERVOUS...
...SHE'S GONNA KICK ALL THE AVAILABLE BUTT IN THAT PLAY.

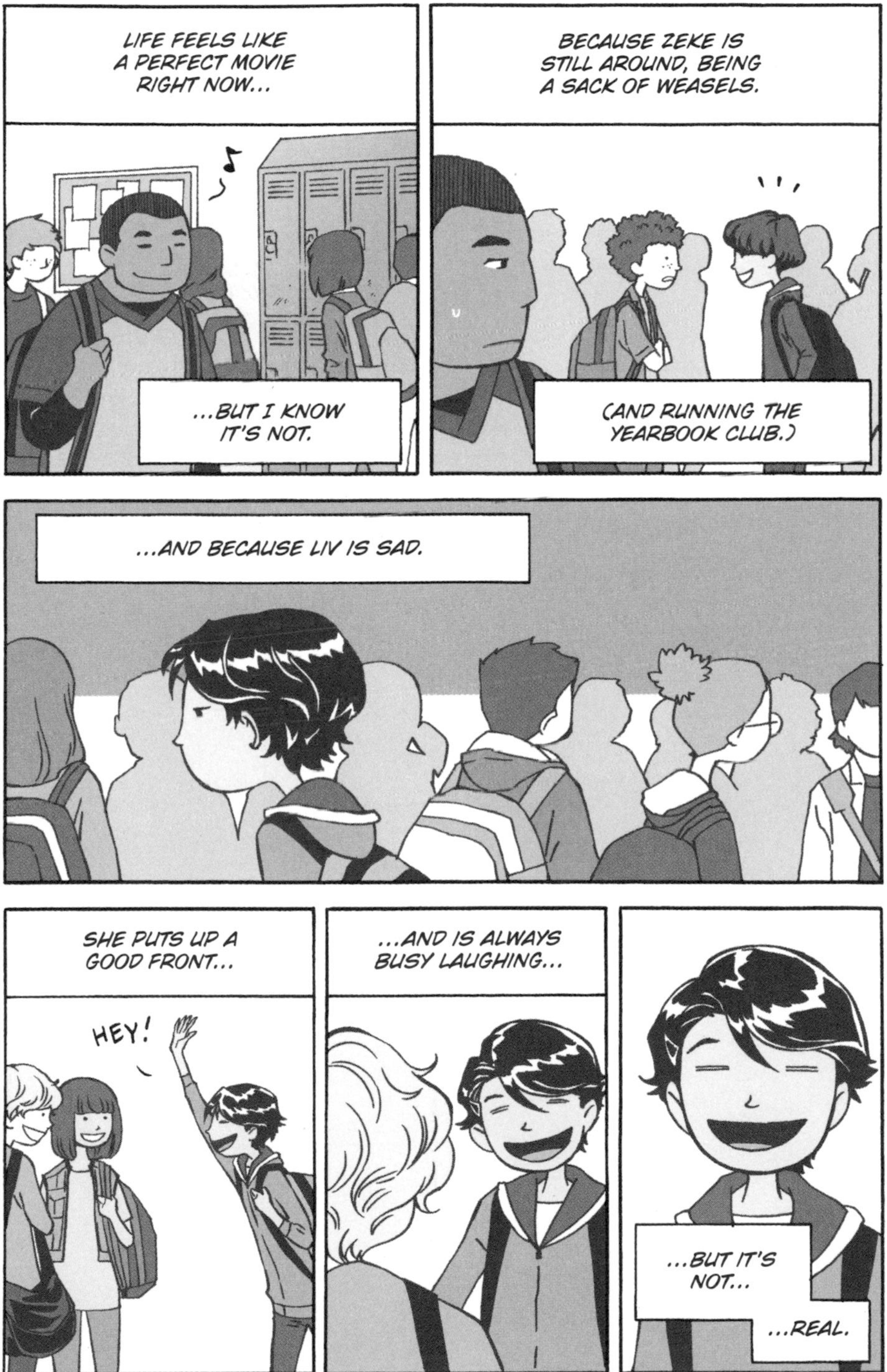
LIFE FEELS LIKE A PERFECT MOVIE RIGHT NOW...
...BUT I KNOW IT'S NOT.
BECAUSE ZEKE IS STILL AROUND, BEING A SACK OF WEASELS.
(AND RUNNING THE YEARBOOK CLUB.)
...AND BECAUSE LIV IS SAD.
SHE PUTS UP A GOOD FRONT...
HEY!
...AND IS ALWAYS BUSY LAUGHING...
...BUT IT'S NOT...
...REAL.

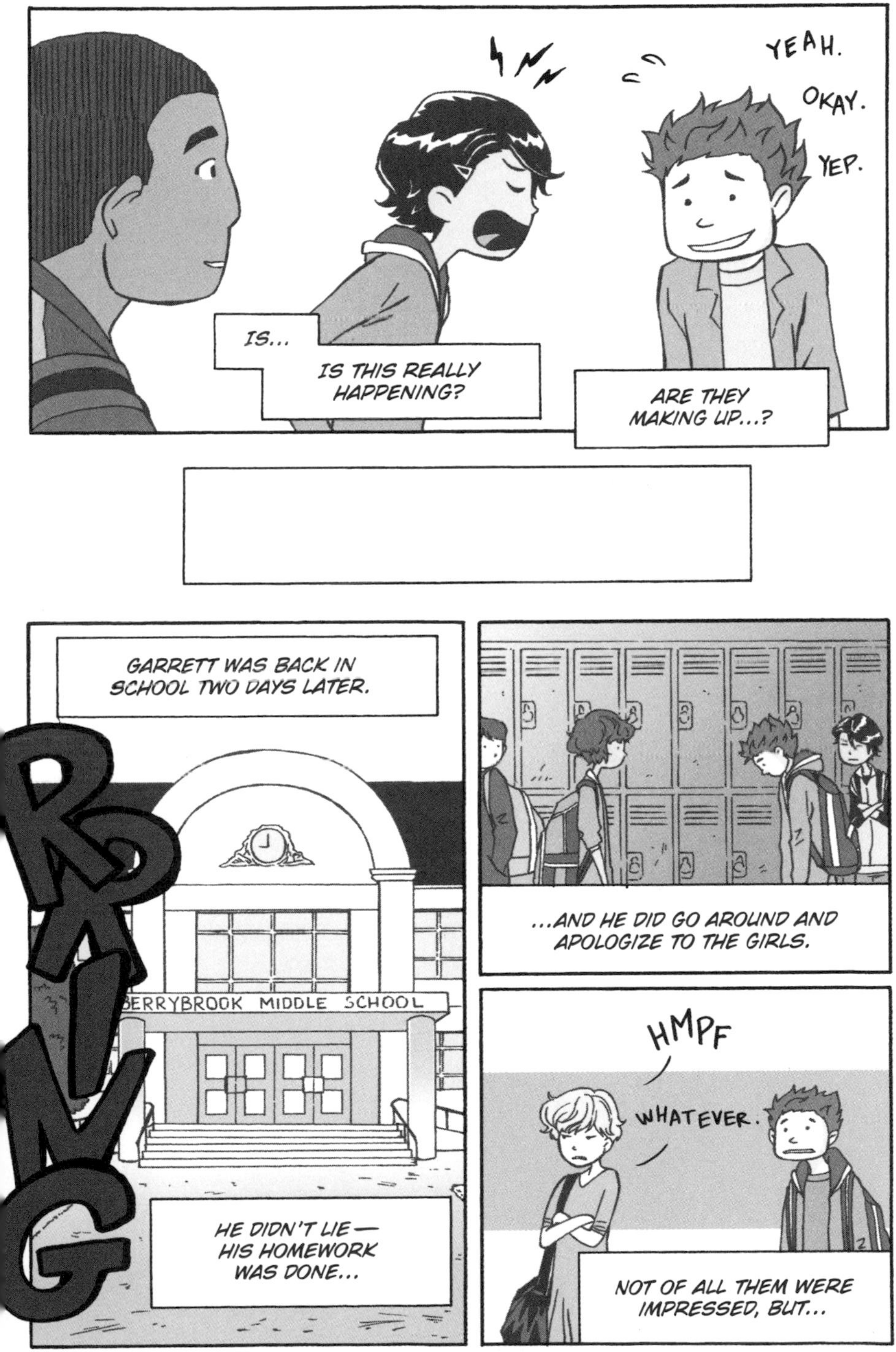
YEAH.
OKAY.
YEP.
IS...
IS THIS REALLY HAPPENING?
ARE THEY MAKING UP...?
GARRETT WAS BACK IN SCHOOL TWO DAYS LATER.
RRING
BERRYBROOK MIDDLE SCHOOL
HE DIDN'T LIE— HIS HOMEWORK WAS DONE...
...AND HE DID GO AROUND AND APOLOGIZE TO THE GIRLS.
HMPF
WHATEVER.
NOT OF ALL THEM WERE IMPRESSED, BUT...

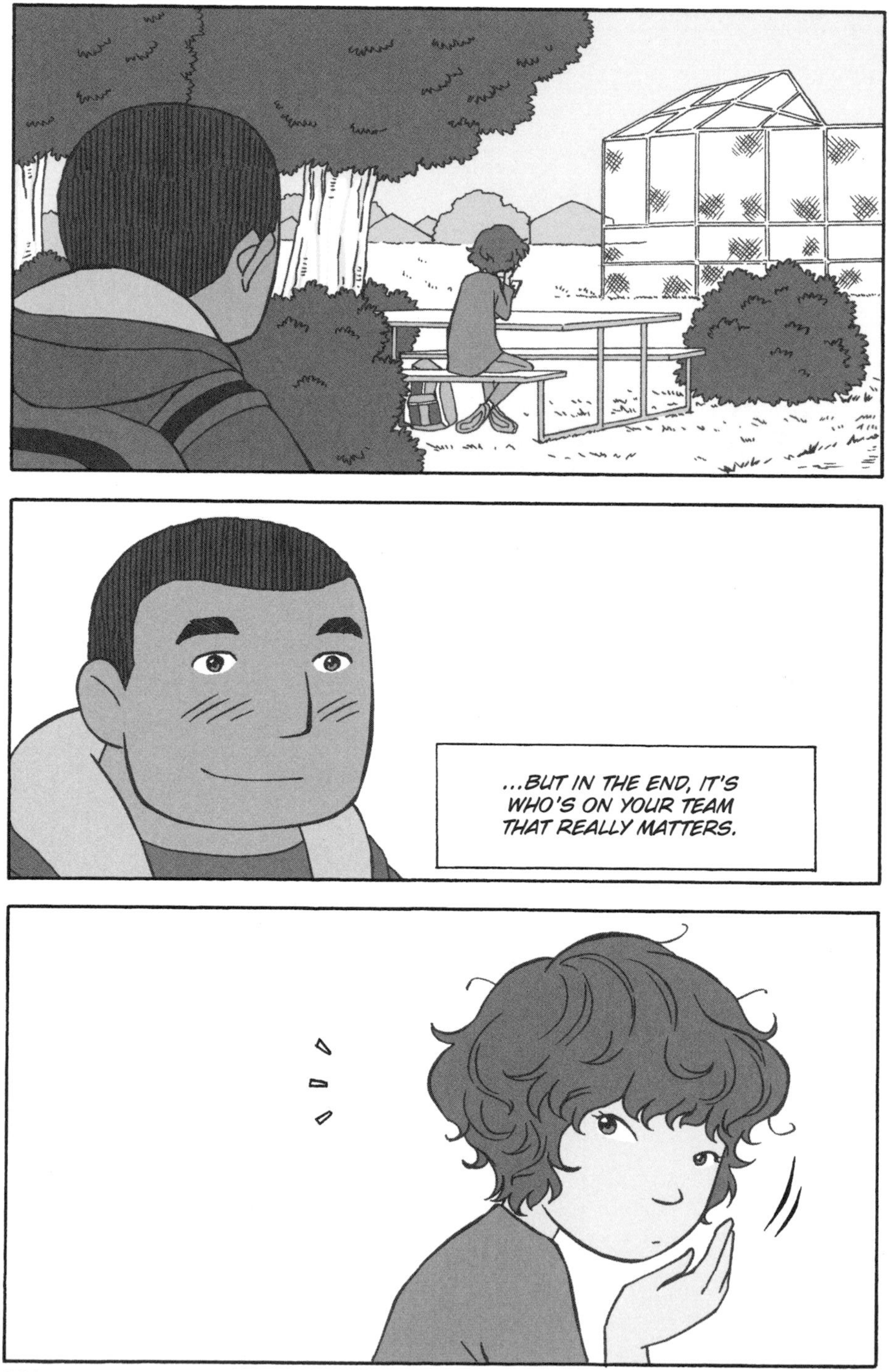
...BUT IN THE END, IT'S WHO'S ON YOUR TEAM THAT REALLY MATTERS.

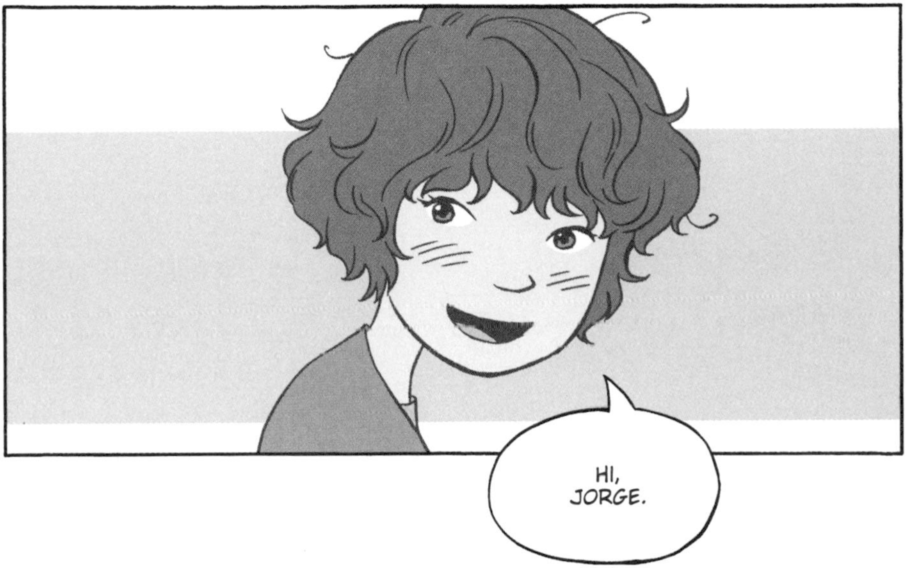
HI, JORGE.

THE END

... Hello, there! WE MEET AGAIN!

(...or we meet for the first time, in which case HI, I have made other books that you can read.)

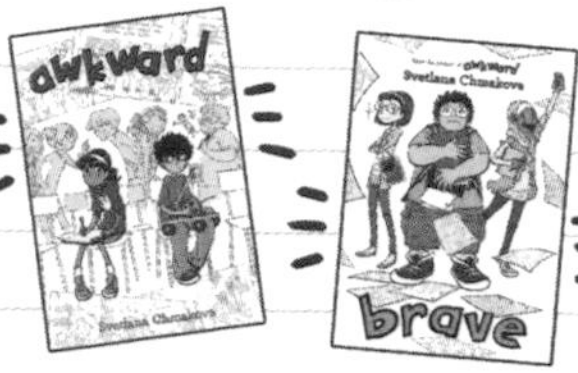
awkward
brave

crush was a book I've been SO excited to write. I don't know about you, but I had such huge crushes on people in middle school. All of them secret, because unlike Jorge, I was too shy to ask my crush out. So I just admired them from afar... Until I found out that my crush was actually kind of a mean and jerky person. Which is when I stopped crushing on them and started silently judging them from afar. Needless to say, my love life in middle school did not work out as well as Jorge's... OH WELL.

It takes a lot of work to make a graphic novel, and I try to always start with rough character designs so that I always have some reference to look to, when I am drawing the actual comic pages.
Sometimes characters change a lot once I start drawing them in the comic! And sometimes they stay the same. Either way, it's REALLY helpful to go through this design process before diving into the sequential art.

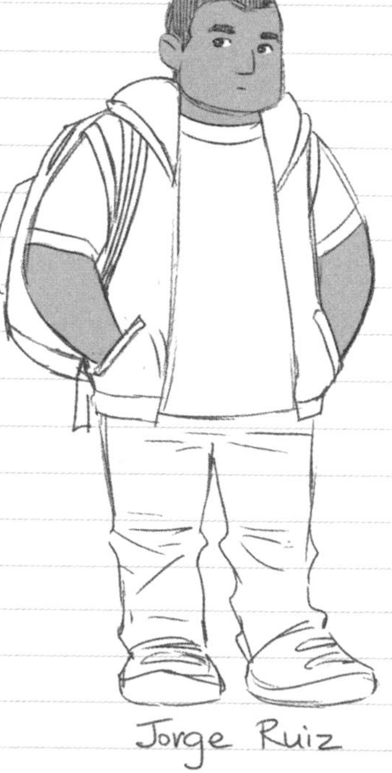

Jorge Ruiz

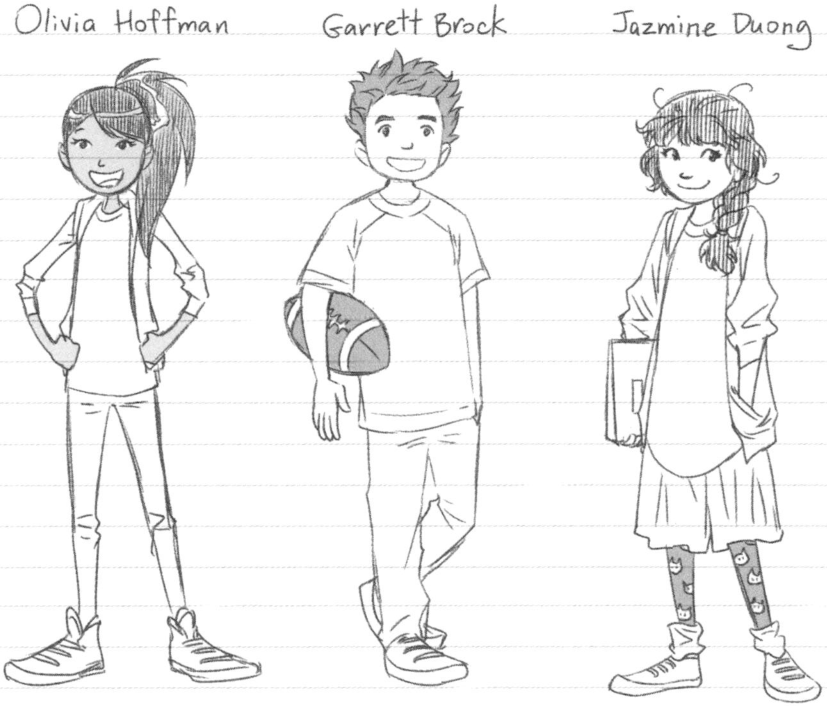
Olivia Hoffman
Garrett Brock
Jazmine Duong

BACKPACKS

... never thought I'd need a cheat sheet for backpacks, and yet here it is. So Many Backpacks! I couldn't remember who had which design, so having this model sheet really helped during the page-drawing stage.

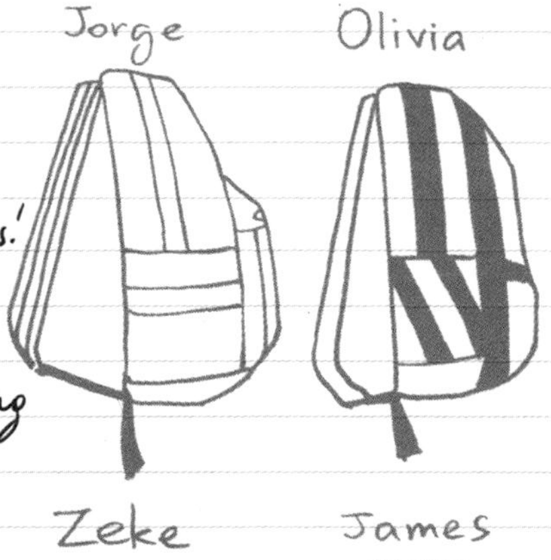
Jorge
Olivia

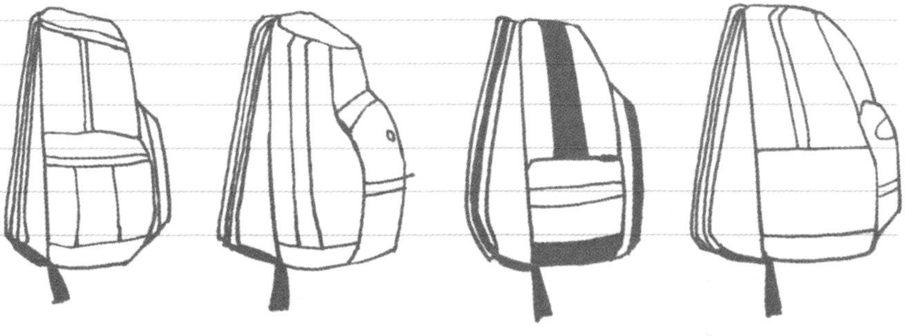
Jazmine
Garrett
Zeke
James

THE EVOLUTION OF A PANEL:

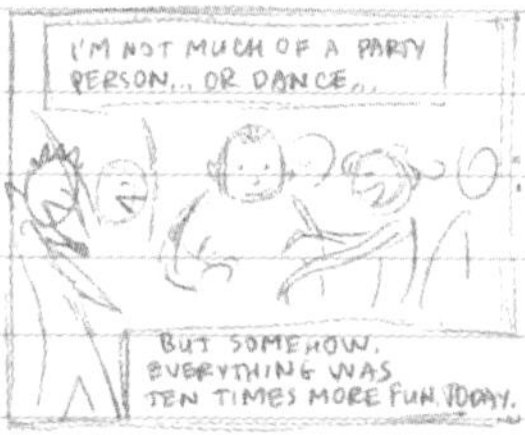

I'M NOT MUCH OF A PARTY PERSON... OR DANCE...
BUT SOMEHOW, EVERYTHING WAS TEN TIMES MORE FUN TODAY.

A book panel ALWAYS starts as a tiny rough sketch first. Once my editor and I are sure that the panel works, I draw the pencils (a larger, tighter version of the panel), which I then print out in non-photo blue for inking!

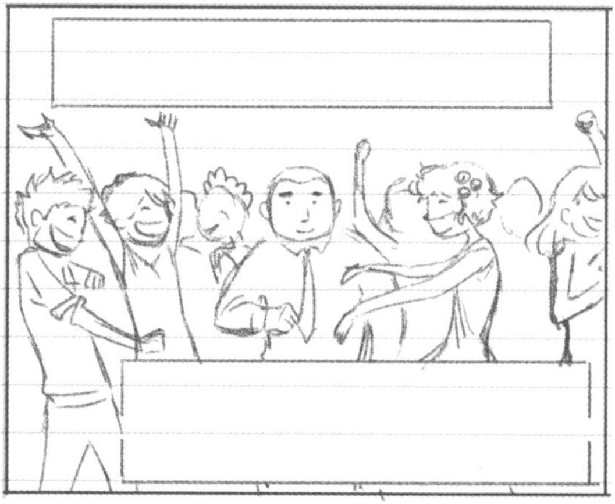

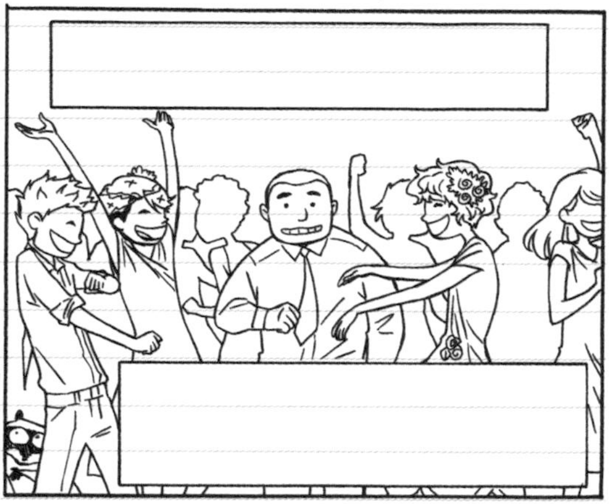

(During the inking stage, I sometimes change and add things — like Jorge's smile and Mr. Raccoon, here.)

Once the panel is inked, it is colored digitally, to make it ready for print. Ta-dah! Now I just have to do this 1,200 more times and I will have a book!

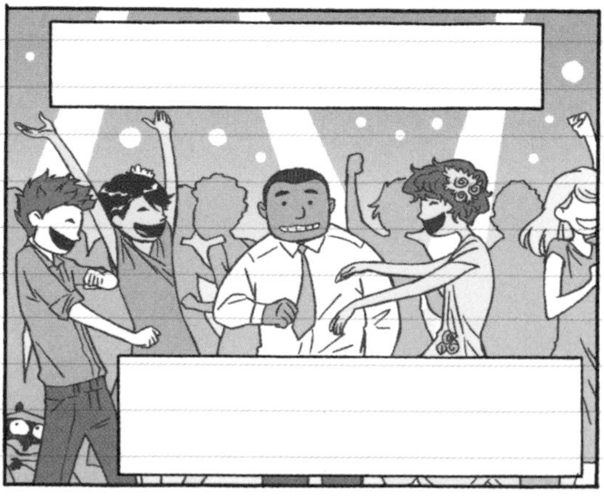

(... comics are a lot of work...)